# When the Hunter Cries

## Charles R. Wade

The Nautilus Publishing Company

OXFORD, MISSISSIPPI

For information contact Nautilus Publishing, 426 South Lamar Blvd., Suite 16, Oxford, M[S] 38655.

*This is a work of fiction. All names, characters, places and incidents are products of the author's imagination.*

ISBN: 978-1-936946-44-0

The Nautilus Publishing Company
426 South Lamar Blvd., Suite 16
Oxford, Mississippi 38655
Tel: 662-513-0159
www.nautiluspublishing.com
www.RevenantChronicles.com


First Edition

Front cover design and illustration by Silviya Yordanova. Front cover photos by Nathan Latil[.]

Library of Congress Cataloging-in-Publication Data has been applied for.


10   9   8   7   6   5   4   3   2   1

*To Dad*

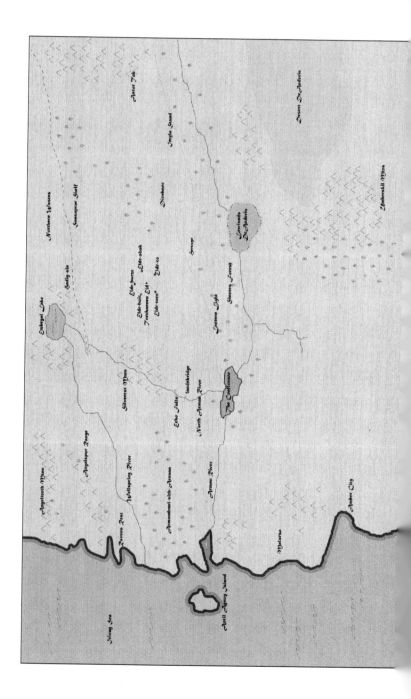

*F*our long days have now passed since the gray wanderer first came to me, though I now know him to be more than just a frail old man. For reasons yet unknown to me, I was chosen to take The Name and assume the throne of the new Way; nevertheless, there were no witnesses to my coronation save for my cowled benefactor. There was no music other than the wail of the lonely wind hissing through these lifeless spires. There was no grand ball, just a menagerie of shadows dancing beyond the flickering candles which surrounded us as we turned pages...brittle, yellow pages whose words were likely never intended for the eyes of a mere man. Yesterday evening, the Book of Black Hope lay open before me and, with encouragement and instruction from my new mentor, I did utter phrases laced with somber words that likely unleashed tainted waves of power upon the lands which I once considered my home...power that might well prove to be a plague and a pestilence for which providence has no contingency. He has since left, and I now sit alone in a sprawling city of ghosts; a city whose mighty towers were raised in the span of a few heartbeats by the inestimable might of the demon armorer, Morana Goll. History will ultimately remember this place as Valenesti's Bane, but I must choose for it another moniker; one that renders a hint or two of benevolence. I suspect that this will be but the first of many deceptions yet to come. And I must make my decision before this day fades, for tomorrow, I fear, swoops all too deadly near. Alas, I suppose it is only fitting that my new throne sits within the shadows of this grim domain, for it is a place ultimately born of desperation...a citadel that sprang from the bitter loins of bereavement. The gods which I betrayed have turned their backs on me, and other forces now direct my fate. The Spell of Black Hope has been cast, and events have been set into motion for which I hope those same gods may one day forgive me...if they themselves manage to survive. Tonight, I find myself praying not to the gods...but for them. Irony abounds while chaos surrounds.

Private Journal of Herodimae
Wintermonth 9
Birthyear of the Way

# PROLOGUE

The black wings of winter hovered over the cobbled streets of Hadig-vie. Those dark wings flapped frantically in the near-night, and even though they beat with vigor, their efforts barely kept the dire raven aloft. The harbinger of Eldimorah's cruelest season had been directed to fly especially low this day, shielding the Northern Wastes from the kiss of the daystar's faint but untainted light. That monstrous raven molded from the clay of gray and murky storm clouds finally settled, perching on the rim of the southern horizon; and beneath the shadows of its vast black wings, a dizzying storm began to rage.

Cold winds hissed; pellets of ice showered the isolated city and bounced off its cobbled streets. Even its hardiest inhabitants hunched their shoulders, drew hoods over their heads, and raced toward the nearest alleys and alcoves. They all sought shelter from this newest assault from their foes up in Haeven; they all sought protection—all but one. This one had learned many months ago that the concept of shelter was a cruel illusion proffered by even crueler gods. It was a flimsy fantasy and nothing more.

He walked alone. He should have been chilled to the bone, but he did not feel the first hint of cold…at least not in any way that truly mattered. Left alone in this foreign and vicious void, this world swallowed by sorrow and awash in gray, he recognized that he could actually *feel* very little as of late; and in these dreary days defined by numbness, even fleeting glimpses of what he once *felt* lasted just long enough to rip the scabs from recent wounds. For reasons known only to the gods that steered his fate, he had been buffeted by the winds of mourning, and the foul force of their gale had left him…damaged. Those winds whose howls were laced with treacherous whispers had turned his dreams of a love-rich life into a vortex of shattered dreams and flying debris, and that debris had bruised him well beyond the point of healing…of caring. It had altogether decimated his desire for even simple sentience.

For nearly two years, Valenesti had felt like little more than a lowly pawn in some stellar game of chess. Pathetic though he may have been, he had unknowingly been assigned a pivotal role that he must soon assume, one that would likely catch even the most vigilant of the gods completely unawares.

Except for the lingering ache that he hoped to briefly alleviate once he was seated inside the tavern that stood just ahead, he was in effect numb all the way from his skin to his soul. It wasn't so long ago that those hot winds of grief had first hissed past him, abrading him with the coarse agony of memories, fond memories though they were. They had left his thin skin scarred and scalded. A battlefield marred with boils, it now thirsted for the comparably soothing sting of this gray day's less malevolent storm, a more natural storm, whose raw and indiscriminate wrath made him feel less like the sole bastard son of fate. It suggested to him that he was not the lone target of Haeven's ire.

Sheets of freezing rain were beginning to glaze the cobblestones over which he trudged, and sleet was collecting in the folds of his tunic, but the nip of the ice presented no challenge to his contentment...his serenity...his comfort. He had known none of these for over two years. This icy assault might as well have been the anxious caress of a lover or a mother's warm embrace. Alas, providence had deprived him of both of these as well.

His poor tunic had certainly seen its better days, as had he. The threadbare garment was far too light and flimsy for these harsher seasons, even when he gave enough of a damn to keep it somewhat dry. But today, it was soaked from his stumbling hike through the cold rain, and the tattered material clung to him like a layer of blotchy, wrinkled skin. Skin it might as well have been, for he had worn it continuously for the last twenty some-odd months, and its blemished condition stood testament to much of the distress he himself had endured during that span of time when only the memories of his lost angel's breath kept his spark alive.

Yes, he had suffered through quite a bit, but he was able to remember virtually none of it. Such had been his plan...if a plan it could even be called. He remembered not what color his garment had been back in those brighter days, but it had more than likely been spotless and fresh. Back then, before all true color vanished beneath a sea of gloom, its wearer had possessed a measure of pride...a sense of hope. But then the baptism of stains began.

After he clomped up the three creaky steps, he heard the incensed sleet casting itself against the tin awning that stretched overhead, and on some buried level of awareness—one that barely mattered any more—he recognized that he had reached what others might call *shelter* and that the ice was no longer stinging his face. For the briefest of moments, he paused to look down at the street, which was rapidly turning white. The sleet was hypnotizing. For the briefest of moments, he felt something that might have passed for peace at one point in his past; but then he saw her gaunt face staring up at him. It was the face he now treasured and the face he used to dread seeing every time he entered her room during those last grim days when the reaper was striding so steadfastly toward the front door of his home...their home. He wiped yet another tear from the corner of his eye...a hot tear chilled by a few pellets of melting sleet. His hands were trembling; his heart was racing. He knew he had to get inside, and quickly.

Just as his unsteady hand reached for the door handle, an exiting patron barreled out of the tavern and shoved the shaky, bereaved wreck aside. Valenesti slipped on the glazed planks and went down on one knee. He knew better than to expect a hand up; he expected only spiteful laughter, and his assumption proved accurate. The rude brute leaving this rundown dump probably figured that pushing a smaller drunk around was an easy way to make a show for the cackling, painted whore clinging to his own left arm.

No matter. It certainly was not the first time the widower had been treated unkindly in this colony of outcasts. A rude push from another asshole meant nothing to him, especially now that he was so close to this, his last remaining source of solace. It was yet another nameless, smoky tavern. An apothecary for the anguished...a pharmacy for the faithless. Dozens of these ramshackle taverns were tucked along Hadig-vie's alleyways...reeking little rooms posing as palaces devoid of pain. Inside each and every one of these pits that doled out poison, dozens of patrons incapable of mercy mingled about, desperately seeking one merciful soul that might show them some pity or at the very least offer them a kind word. *Spirits always bleed where Irony abounds*. Valenesti silently recited the old proverb. He knew it to be true. Still he stepped through the door.

As he reached up with one shivering hand to brush the errant strands of wet hair out of his eyes, he felt all the pellets of sleet that had settled in the tangles of his greasy mop. A moment spent standing before the wide chimney might have provided comfort and gratification to anyone else who had slogged through this winter storm as he had just done. His situation was quite different, though; he stumbled right past the tables nearest to the hearth where a warm blaze crackled and danced. That lusty fire, recently stoked and roaring, offered the only illumination in the place aside from a few scattered candles and the meager gray light that clawed its way through the months of filth that had collected on the windowpanes of the little pub.

His tired eyes were immediately drawn to a shallow nook that was obscured by an alluring curtain of cold shadows. Yes, he had identified his ordained table as soon as he threw the door open and stepped out of the storm. Tucked away in the corner farthest from the front door, the table he spotted would certainly offer him the least warmth but the most seclusion. *Spirits always bleed where Irony abounds.*

"The least fucking light! Keep me forever in the shadows and subject me only to the least fucking light!" he croaked to himself to affirm his most precious priority.

The second he spotted it, he knew that the wobbly little table easily met all of his criteria, and there certainly seemed to be fewer of those standards by the day…fewer in number and far less exacting.

Perhaps it was the subtle urging of fate that ushered him to that dim corner. Or perhaps the shadows enveloping that isolated little alcove beckoned him simply because they epitomized his own deliberate retreat from the light. Whatever the case, it was not a difficult decision to make; not whatsoever. Whether it be a table in some shithole tavern or an empty crate in a filthy alleyway, identifying minor havens that offered anonymity and seclusion had become nascent reflex…a reflex instilled and then nurtured by months of abject despair.

*Spirits always bleed where Irony abounds.* Back in his more lucid days he probably would have appreciated the irony of some poor soul struggling to survive just long enough to kill himself. What a beautiful, paradoxical trade-off! And life was indeed a tradeoff. So was death for that matter. Valenesti had discovered as much, thanks to his recent and excessively bitter lessons regarding love and loss.

Love and loss—twin tails of a wicked whip wielded by the hands of gods that dealt jarring lashes for the sole purpose of watching a valiant soul bleed...just to have an outlet for their gory avarice.

"Divinity in motion..." he whispered as he drummed his fingers and waited for his server to arrive.

Valenesti bore a network of those wheals and seeping lash marks. They had been part of his horrific education, and those cruel lessons had cost him so much, though they had taught him virtually nothing. They had taken such a heavy toll and that toll was still being exacted. Those lessons had not made him the least bit wiser, but he was certainly more bitter from having learned them.

He was slowly drowning in the unforgiving and roiling waters of mourning, and his spirit exuded the stench of despondency. Those foul vapors spread outward and upward just like the detestable smell rising from a city gutter running high with raw sewage. His black mood surrounded him, swirling and spinning like a plague of flies, a swarm of sour spirits that held even the most well-intentioned strangers at bay, though he encountered damned few strangers that fell into that precise category.

This amorphous shell of lamentation was currently his only source of warmth, if warmth it could be called. At least it offered him a nominal level of protection against something that annoyed him far more than winter's sharp bite ever could. The shell was his most effective insulation against intrusive and unsolicited conversation. Now more than ever before, he abhorred the senseless small talk initiated by strangers about which he couldn't give less of a damn; he only wanted strong ale and lots of it. His plan was set; it was a plan to which he had adhered hundreds of times before—only the names of the saloons had changed. Glued to this rickety spindle chair, here he would sit and drink until he was either invited to leave or tossed into the icy street. Here he would sit and drink, a dark shadow of a man tucked within the darker shadows of another musty tavern.

Outside, the storm showed no signs of abating. Fat drops of cold rain blended with pellets of sleet pecked fiercely at the panes of the window right behind his table. Damn the Haevens for the incessant blows they continued to deliver to a spirit that was already gasping for breath! He had known no peace for nearly two years thanks to their unremitting assault. Tonight...again...he sat slumped forward with his head resting in his hands. A tear or two rolled down his palms and across his trembling wrists. The day was growing late, and the tavern was beginning to hum with the chatter of all the assholes who sought to spoil his coveted solitude.

"Damn! Another new arrival," he muttered to himself every time he saw the front door swing open. As the patrons drifted in, they shook the water and ice from their cloaks before hanging them close to the fireplace to dry. Inclement weather was always an easy opening topic where those simple fools were concerned, and today was going to be no exception. Every customer at the bar…interlopers all, as far as he was concerned…was discussing the rotten weather, all commenting on how happy they were to be inside on a bleak afternoon like this. The fingers woven through his hair clenched into tight fists.

"A goddamn roof and four walls…" he grumbled. That particular image did not make him feel the least bit *happy*. No heavy wool cloak, no shelter made of mere wood and brick could make him *happy*…ever again. He had forgotten the relevance of the word long ago and did not really wish to be reminded of that distressing fact. It maddened him to no end that those around him let the caustic word pepper their sentences so frequently…so casually…as though it carried no more meaning than the name of an ingredient in some fucking biscuit recipe or the name of their family's short-haired bitch of a dog that likely lay shivering under the front porch on an afternoon as foul as this one.

*Happy* held no meaning for him…not since the funeral on that sunny autumn morning when her shriveled body had been laid to rest. On that same morning, two twin souls fled from their mortal prisons. Though his body maintained a pulse, though it continued to suck in air, it was no longer any more alive than the inanimate husk he had dressed in that white burial gown. *Happy*? It sickened him that these idiots could so readily embrace that cunning word's empty promises and fall prey to the illusion of its inherent lies.

*Happy*. Just hearing the damned word spoken nearly made him retch. He found the sound of those two syllables strung together offensively hollow. More so in just the last few weeks, he caught himself actually loathing…actually wishing harm upon all those clueless bitches and bastards who dared voice the word while he was within earshot. But it seemed that recently the gods were garnering more and more pleasure out of surrounding him with packs of dolts intent on repeating the word like annoying mynah birds possessing a one word vocabulary. It was as if all the shallow fools who regarded themselves as being *happy* spat the vile word toward him like a malison, and hearing its septic song never failed to sting him like stout whiskey rushing into an open wound.

*Screw them all,* he thought. Then he realized that he had voiced his last sentiment for all to hear. It didn't really matter though, for no one was listening to him anyway. No one in this smoke-filled room was even listening to themselves. Damn them all! He rolled his head to stretch out the tightening muscles in his neck. The buzz of meaningless conversation was giving him a headache even before the ale had a chance to do so.

"Piss on them," he growled, making no attempt to mute his sentiments this time. Let them slap each other on the back and cheer each other on for dreamt up deeds and petty little domestic victories. Let them go ahead and congratulate each other on how *happy* they are. He simply did not care.

Let the winter winds blow, and let the sleet barrage the brittle glass behind him until it shattered into a thousand prickly needles and crystal shards. He did not care! Let the gods themselves reach through the ruined panes and tap him on the shoulder. Let them yank his oily hair like he was some street whore down on all-fours earning eight coppers for her night's work. They would get no response from him...not a glance, not a shrug, not a whimper. He did not care, though if he ever identified specifically which of those gods had been the pitiless architect of his sorrow he would offer that god a mug of warm piss to thank him or her for all the suffering he had endured. Then he would impolitely invite that particular deity to just go fuck itself.

At long last his first mug arrived, and the serving girl sprinted away from his table without saying a word. With his shoulders forced forward by the twin burdens of sorrow and apathy, poor Valenesti sat there staring at the blanket of foam floating atop the rich brown ale in his mug. The effervescent border of the foam head might as well have been the shoreline of an island unexpectedly spotted by a drowning man, a man who had just seconds ago decided to quit battling the waves...a man who had finally accepted that he was fated to go down in the churning swells of a vengeful sea.

He stared at the contents of the worn mug through two tortured, bloodshot eyes sporting dark bags and surrounded by deep wrinkles.

Those wrinkles may not have appeared quite so deep had he occasionally bothered to scrub away some of the callous streets' grime. His surrender to the insidious blanket of filth...his choice to largely forego personal hygiene...had left his face resembling the antique scrollwork on an old dresser.

A strange blend of indifference and self-loathing made him hesitate as he reached for the mug with his two grubby hands...hands plagued by tremors that were becoming ever more noticeable as the days of his volitional sentence of self-abuse dragged by. On some level he hated himself for the drink he was about to take. On another level he hated himself for the last one he had taken. He had accepted long ago that each swallow was just another step in a climb up a mountain with no obtainable summit, another stroke in a struggle to swim across a river far too violent and deep...another step down the walls of a dark canyon whose floor symbolized the bottom of a well...the well into which were cast the desperate wishes of bereaved spirits and the empty hopes of hearts left behind.

Every swig symbolized another step toward the dark gates of oblivion—another pointless step driven by the illusory promise offered by some inner fire, some whispered lie suggesting that deliverance from this profound spiritual suffering could be found at the bottom of the next mug. Yes, the descent into perdition had begun eight seasons ago...a gradual but inevitable descent into murky blackness, a sinister stain used to paint that special corner of Hel reserved for the truly lonely...reserved for the half-souls who had been forced by mourning to forget the wholesome taste of an angel's kiss.

By now he fully recognized the pattern, the trap that he insisted on tripping every day of his pitiable life. Even so, he acknowledged that he was doomed to perpetuate the cycle that had defined his wretched existence for much of the last two years. Every miserable day and every damnable night, he tried to use the bitter ale to drown memories that were even less palatable. Some had proven to be unremittingly buoyant though, and they refused to stay beneath the surface of the violent swells driven by winds of rage and resentment.

He slammed the mug down on the table like a grand gavel. If only he indeed wielded the power of some celestial judge. But alas he did not. Suds sloshed over the rim of the mug and ran down his knuckles. Damn it all, if he couldn't drown the memories by pushing them under, then he would pull them under instead, kicking and flailing until the outcome of this battle of wills was decided in the shadowy depths. If he was not destined to remain afloat, then at least he could cast himself wholly into those violent waters, breathe deep their salty essence, and pray that they would waste no time in either suffocating him or dashing him against the sharp crags of the veiled shore, marking the end of his suffering in this otherwise boundless ocean lachrymose.

Each round of brew taunted him with the promise of precious oblivion, a glimpse into some alluring black void where the flawless face of her ghost would not be staring back at him; each mug teased him with the possibility of having the horror of his darker memories erased. On occasion, when luck took his hand and when he was driven by just the right fusion of desperation and determination, the cool brew actually delivered on its promise and he was allowed to plummet into wonderful nothingness for a few precious hours...a few hours during which he could retreat behind that cherished pall of oblivion. But his reprieve was always short-lived; he would inevitably come to in one of the filthy alleys of Hadig-vie that had become both his home and his Hel.

With cold stone stinging his cheek, he would press his tremor-plagued palms against his throbbing temples. He would kick away the hungry rats that cautiously sniffed at his stench and wander back to one of the few taverns from which he had yet to be banned. He would try to ignore the predictable looks of pity and disgust carved into the features of whichever serving girl had drawn the short straw, and then he would begin the wretched process all over again.

With each passing day the routine was becoming more noble than pathetic, at least in his own tired, deluded mind. He was rapidly beginning to regard the whole scenario as a battle...a mission...a valiant crusade against the purveyors of the reprehensible injustice that had left him so broken and torn. Yes, he would continue the gallant fight, all the while hoping that he would quickly succumb to his grievous wounds. Today might be the day, then again it might not. He did not know exactly when the day would arrive, but until it did he was intent on pickling himself, spending his time and his few remaining coppers on his ongoing quest to somehow soothe the crippling pain of loss and escape this soul-shattering vacuum into which he had been thrust. After all, he had nothing better to do. He had no other dream to chase.

Some of the foam from his first round clung to his crusted beard as he slammed the mug down and signaled for the girl to bring him another ale. Although she raced through the dimly lit tavern like a frightened doe running from the scent of a hunter, that next round simply couldn't arrive quickly enough. His patience had become yet another victim of the hopeless battle he waged against the tide of loneliness.

His grip on the wooden mug triggered one of those damned memories that tended to attack when his guard was sufficiently dropped. It reminded him of the way he gripped the weathered handle of his shovel on the day he had buried his sweet Elise. He remembered leaning on that shovel for support after his legs lost both the will and the stamina to hold him erect even a second longer. He remembered casting the clay-caked tool aside and collapsing to his knees beside the mound of gray dirt and jagged stones that he had somehow managed to excavate between bouts of sobbing...between spells of screaming his anguish toward the unjust gods who hid behind the cloud-spotted sky.

The serving girl set his next mug on the table as though it was somehow burning her fingers, but before she could withdraw her hand Valenesti grabbed her wrist like a viper striking a rat. She recoiled, flinching at his grimy touch. Her reeking patron didn't utter a word. He just held up two fingers to indicate that she might as well double his next order and save herself the burden of making another trip to his table...the table tucked so far back in the forbidding shadows. When he released his grip, she nodded her understanding and backed away, wiping her hands nervously on her stained apron. As she sped back to the kitchen, she continued to scrub away at her wrist, laboring to scour away all the imagined filth as well as a few grubby stains that were a little more tangible.

♦♦♦

More unbidden images from that fucking day rushed at him as he hurriedly raised the next mug to his cracked and quivering lips. He recalled leaning against her headstone and sobbing until his ribs ached and his lungs burned...until his soul splintered beneath the strangely oppressive weight of the azure winter sky. Once or twice during his blackest of days, his stomach churned and he heaved; but nothing would come up except for a fetid cocktail of foam and bitter bile which singed his clenched throat much like the flood of tears that burned his eyes—a confused child's eyes that frantically pleaded with Haeven for mercy and solace. But Haeven was no longer listening.

He remembered a few of the tiniest details from that day, despite his deepest and most desperate need to forget them. As he massaged his temples, he recalled how dusk arrived and then gave way to darkest night. He had observed with absolute detachment that day and night looked much the same when viewed through an undulating veil of tears, that odious curtain of cascading misery. How many days he languished there beside her grave...atop the cold, stony mound that now separated him from his lost heart...he still did not know. He did not know. He did not care. It was no longer important. It never had been.

Valenesti stayed at her grave long after everyone else left. Leaving her out there cold and alone was never an option. It rained once... perhaps twice...perhaps forever. He only remembered that raindrops tasted like tears without the salt...without all the pain. After that initial but brutal storm of mourning passed, he awoke cradled in the cold arms of numbness, which perhaps shielded him from the most vicious cuts of sorrow's keen sword, but this new torpor could never be mistaken for peace. Beckoned by a voice that may well have been his own, he struggled to stand, leaning against Elise's new headstone...one that he himself began to carve in those dark days when she lay inside the house struggling for each breath; when he could no longer deny the inevitability of what he would be forced to face when her spirit at last took its leave and escaped the sick and brittle shell that his beautiful wife had so rapidly become. So rapidly and ever so unfairly.

He had erected the stone just one day before she breathed her last, and now he relied on its stolid solidity to steady himself on two faltering feet that had essentially forgotten how to follow even his simplest commands. Beyond that moment, all but a few details had been washed away by torrents of whiskey and ale...and by a visceral drive to disconnect from the horror and sorrow associated with Elise's valiant struggle against the black tide of ultimate shadow.

♦♦♦

Valenesti pushed his empty mug away and waited for his third and fourth to arrive, all the while cursing the frustrating tolerance he had developed for the stout brew's coveted effects. With his fingers laced together so that they would not tremble, he breathed...he waited. In no time at all, a delicate hand set two more full mugs in front of him. He focused on softening his mien when he glanced up to acknowledge the serving girl, assuming that she was the same girl he had so profoundly distressed earlier that evening. In addition to salving her fear and assuring her that he would cause her no further alarm, he simply wanted to convey his appreciation for her attentiveness and somehow separate himself from the other patrons in the seedy tavern that were constantly pinching, grabbing, swatting, and cussing the browbeaten servers. He just wanted to allay a few of her qualms and make some kind of amends for inappropriately grabbing her wrist earlier.

"Gods!" He mouthed the word, but he made no sound. Valenesti suddenly found it quite impossible to swallow, or even draw a decent breath. There had apparently been a recent change of shifts, for this was certainly not the same...lady. It was now his turn to flinch and withdraw. For the first time in a long while, his tired and bloodshot eyes registered a spark of promise, a hint of something besides grief and misery. Surprise. Even hope, perhaps?

The beautiful face that stared down at him like some haloed angel sent to comfort a dying child so closely resembled...Elise's! It was not his lost love looking down at him, of course, but the arresting resemblance made his weary and wounded heart leap into his throat. Only a few tears had he shed since the day he stumbled away from her grave,—and even those had been shed as errant strays—but he knew that a flood of unspent tears yet remained, just waiting for a chance to make their escape...and the moment of opportunity had just arrived. For the first time in two years he felt the old familiar sting, and branching lines of sweet heat coursed their way down his cheeks, following the network of dirty crevices all the way to his jawline, where the globules hung suspended like a row of brown, rotting teeth.

"I didn't mean to startle you, honey," she sang, and in her eyes he thought he could discern something that at least could pass as genuine concern. She was looking directly into his eyes and was perfectly comfortable holding his gaze. In her divine sky-blue eyes he detected an abundance of...humanity. Of course, there were unmistakable traces of pity in her penetrating gaze. It mattered not one bit to him by now. He had come to expect as much from just about everyone who even bothered to acknowledge his presence, but there was no judgment, no rudimentary disgust paired with this pure pity; and that novel degree of unconditional...acceptance...made him even more uncomfortable, because it quickly eroded the shield of seclusion he had endeavored so ardently to construct just so he could cower behind it.

"I'm sorry," he croaked. His own voice now sounded foreign to him. It had grown pathetically hoarse with disuse. "It's just that you remind me of...someone...someone very special." Valenesti reached up with a shaky hand to wipe away some of those blasted, murky tears as well as the beads of sweat that threatened to run down his brow and into his pained eyes.

"Dang, honey! She must have really hurt you," the girl said, then blushed as she realized how callous and critical her thoughtless observation must have sounded.

The young lady's kind heart howled and skipped a beat as soon as it recognized that her mouth and brain had experienced such a severe disconnect. She immediately felt horrible about it. Her reflexive response hadn't even come close to expressing the degree of empathy she felt upon catching her first glimpse of this poor bastard...this ruined shell of a man propping himself up at her assigned table. She closed her eyes for a second or two and bit her tongue to prevent it from misrepresenting her thoughts yet again.

Recognizing her embarrassment as evidence of a fundamentally gentle soul, Valenesti made a dismissive gesture with one quivering hand. Still he couldn't help but close his eyes and gently shake his head to suggest just how very inaccurate this poor girl's presumption had been. In an attempt to alleviate some of her unwarranted guilt, he tried to twist his lips into a soothing smile but found that he had simply forgotten how.

"No. She didn't hurt me, sweetie. But...losing her sure did. I surrendered all when I kissed her cold lips that last time. Letting go... letting go is hard when it's forever, dear. Never forget that. Harder than..." he choked on the words as his mind struggled to craft a suitable metaphor, but none existed. He couldn't continue, so he did the only thing he had been able to do for months. With trembling hands, he reached for his precious ale and raised it to his mouth, spilling part of it down the front of his soiled and shabby tunic in the process.

"I'm so very sorry..." she all but sobbed, and one glimpse into those azure eyes told him that she truly meant it. She took a deep, steadying breath before speaking again, "...for your loss, and for sounding like a complete ass just now. Tell you what, honey..." she continued as she leaned down, resting her palms on her thighs and exposing her ample cleavage in a way that would have definitely intrigued him at one point, back when the objects of his lust were... uncomplicated. Back when they were molded from simple flesh and not from the obsession to wrap his arms around the wispy remains of some wraith cloaked in a veil of distant memories.

"I'm gonna go get you another round and that one'll be on me. That's only fair, since most of this one is on you," she joked, and patted the wet patch on his tunic. "I'm Mallory, by the way," she added with a playful, winsome wink. With that, she spun about with the grace of a practiced dancer and headed for the crowded bar.

By then, he could barely breathe. She had touched him! She had actually, intentionally reached out to pat him on his chest...a tantalizing hint of affection, even if it was an awkward attempt at empathy...an indication that his presence had elicited a response other than utter disdain. Valenesti reached up and rested his unsteady hand over his racing heart, precisely where her touch had ignited a fire... precisely where the memories triggered by her entrancing face had pierced him.

Thanks to the twisted nails of fate he had been denied the luxury of physical contact for over two years, aside from the numerous times he had been bounced out of the city's sleaziest taverns... aside from the prick that had shoved him away so boorishly just an hour or so earlier. He tried his best not to stare at Mallory as she went about her other business, but he saw so much of his dear Elise reflected in her flawless features and even in the grace of her fluid movements.

It was almost like watching his late wife's ghost flit across the room, dancing from one table to the next, twirling and smiling as if it was all indeed just a dance. And perhaps it was. Maybe life amounted to nothing more than one long fucking dance, and his partner just had to leave that dance early. Maybe his role now was just to lean against the wall and watch everyone else move to music that he could no longer hear. His heart ached, and his eyes burned; he knew that he had to find something else on which to focus if he was to maintain what little trace of sanity his liquor-addled mind still possessed. He prayed for such a diversion, and this desperate wish was almost immediately granted.

Two short and somewhat dour men took the table next to his own, and they were making little effort to prevent him from hearing their conversation. They obviously assumed—and correctly so—that the grimy and unkempt man sitting alone and spilling ale on himself was just another shiftless drunk with no interest in anything besides who would pay for his next drink. Still, they were careful to speak in hushed tones lest others possessing more ambition listen in; but months spent in the taverns of Hadig-vie had taught Valenesti to become a skilled eavesdropper. He listened intently to their plans, even though he had no real interest in them…at first. He just needed a temporary distraction from the dangerous domains to which his thoughts dragged him each time he chanced a glance in Mallory's direction.

"I thought we settled this before we left Herezye, you old bastard," the younger of the men hissed at his partner. "We're not just talkin' about some simple trinket here…"

Valenesti lost his focus when Mallory returned to his table to deliver the round that she had promised him. As soon as he looked up into those vast hypnotic eyes, he committed to a decision that he had been wrestling with for a long time. He knew in that moment that he simply had to be reunited with Elise, one way or another. He didn't think he could wait even one more day. He felt he could not last…he was not that strong; this burden he could not bear. At first, he thought that he could handle it all, but he was wrong. He was in pain; he was defeated. The booze would eventually kill him. Of that, he had no doubt. Two years of intense self-abuse had certainly carried him closer to his grim goal, but his body had quite amazingly proven to be too resilient for his own satisfaction.

There were quicker ways to get to the other side of the cursed chasm that separated him from Elise, the beacon of his spirit and the governess of his wounded heart. Especially on this side of the city, locating a length of rope would present no challenge whatsoever. And that was all he would need—a rope and a good sturdy beam. One of the livery stables perhaps? More likely than not, his suspended corpse would be discovered by some greenhorn stable boy who would be scarred for life by the image of a blue and bloated man dangling at the end of a rope like some perverse Yule tree ornament. That damaged boy would eventually take the inevitable step into an even more warped adulthood, but by that point he would be intrigued more than ever before by the secret of the hanged man...the smile on his lips.

"We're talking about the staff of Morana Goll, for fuck's sake. Not some silly pendant that's gonna wind up hangin' from some fat bitch-of-a-socialite's neck!"

"Will you keep your damned voice down?! We've come too far to screw ourselves in the ass by broadcasting our plans to the whole cunting bar. Take a breath, count to ten, and then shut the fu..."

"You didn't leave the map back in the room!? Please tell me you didn't..."

"Of course not," the older of the two men assured his skittish cohort through gritted teeth. He patted the lapel of his tunic. "It's tucked away right here, and here it'll stay, damn it all. It's good and waxed, so the rain won't bother it none. Of course it won't do us a damn bit of good 'til we get outside the wall and actually manage to find the well."

"I know. I've seen the map, remember? And while we're on that topic, what'll we do if we happen to lose our way in those damned tunnels? They wind on for—"

"Precisely why we're going to take our time and mark our trail well. Precisely why we're taking plenty of coal markers. Precisely why we're going in well-provisioned. I ain't taking any chances on this venture, dammit. Quit worrying! Getting that blasted stick is all that stands between where I am now and living a life of fine whiskey and whores...whores what have at least most of their teeth!"

"Thought you liked 'em with no teeth, Cyril," the younger turd joked, poking the other man in the ribs yet again. His earlier irritation quickly vanished at the mention of women with little money and no inhibitions.

"Shit, with my share of the coin we're gonna fetch from fencing that stupid relic, I'll hire me a team of whores what can keep their teeth in or put 'em in a cup at the bedside, depending on my particular mood at the moment! And every time I let my seed slip, I'm gonna raise two finger shots to our deceased benefactor, Morana Goll."

*Morana Goll! Dogs and gods!* Valenesti came near to choking on his first swallow of the fresh ale. He hadn't heard that name, nor had he heard any mention of the staff of resurrection, in decades. His grandmother had likely read him the fable at least a hundred times back when he was just a pup, and he had always accepted it as just that—a fable.

Desperation, the residue of smoldering hope, caressed whatever faith remained in his wounded soul and towed his dearest wishes toward a horizon where the ghosts of the departed milled about like herds of lost sheep.

*Gods, what if such a staff really existed?* These two ruffians seemed convinced enough of the possibility, but that hardly sufficed as proof. Still, the mere implications were dizzying…intoxicating, in fact. Valenesti froze and fought to keep his gaze directed at his mug as he concentrated on tuning out the rest of the noise in the bar as well as a new and foreign sound: the rhythmic hiss of his own heartbeat in his ears. One hand gripped the handle of his mug and the other held tightly to one of his chair's loose spindles. As he downed another quick sip of ale, he resolved to focus on his eavesdropping efforts with renewed zeal.

*Morana Goll!* Before Elise's arduous bout with the wasting disease, Valenesti had been a mere uneducated wheelwright and farmer, but one need not have been a scholar to know the legend of the staff. Of course, he was perhaps more familiar with its lore than most. His grandmother had been obsessed by the extraordinary tale regarding the bewitched rod that could ostensibly reanimate a loved one who had passed beyond the final veil.

As his stout, shuddering grip threatened to shatter the spindle of his chair, he took a deep breath and fought back another wave of tears, suddenly realizing that this new flood of emotion was born not of grief but of hope…hope and more. These were tears of inspiration; or maybe desperation, inspiration's more reserved cousin. The distinction between the two was vague at times, according to most; but as of late, Valenesti had been granted very little opportunity to experience the former.

Desperation be damned, a viable means of being reunited with Elise may have just fortuitously presented itself…a means that didn't involve his malodorous, unbathed corpse swinging from some creaking ceiling joist in a filthy livery stable. Perhaps his demise would not involve improvised nooses, rough sisal, and the aroma of fresh horseshit after all. That idea provided some degree of…consolation. His self-pity was temporarily forgotten, and the rusty remnants of his will began to shake off the effects of their extended hibernation.

"Word has it the old farm hasn't been occupied in a couple of years. Don't know if you could really call it a farm, considering there ain't hardly any growing season up here atop this blasted shelf at the edge of the world," the older hooligan grumbled before throwing back a long gulp of his brew.

"Ain't nothing but rocks anyways...rocks and a few weeds," the younger thief interjected as his eyes cast about the tavern like a hare watching for a hawk.

"Exactly," the duo's obvious leader agreed with a slap on his own knee. "Even so, I guess a few of these idiots decided to pretty much fuck the safety of the city walls and do their own thing out there among the boulders, weeds, and shadows. Anyway, seems the fella's old lady kicked the bucket some two years past, and he completely lost his balls and his mind...off somewhere tryin' to drink his ass to death from what I was able to learn from that little urchin just before I knifed him in the ribs."

"You knifed a boy?!"

The older man paused long enough to release a loud belch. "Squeaky little eunuch seemed content enough living in the gutters and alleyways, so I figured he wouldn't mind dyin' in them as well. But, back to the farmer...with that poor fucker's wife dead and him all drunk and absent, we shouldn't have to worry about too many visitors showin' up when we tie off our ropes and rappel down into that well."

"I got me an idea, Cyril...maybe we oughta dig her up and thank her properly for dying and making things so easy for us," the younger thug joked as he jabbed his bony elbow into his partner's ribs. "As cold as it stays up here, she might still be in pretty good shape, if you catch my drift. Two years ain't too long if you're frozen, I hear tell."

"Your brain isn't right, boy! You listen to me, and listen to me close. Our little association is done once we're out of those tunnels, I'm telling you now. I don't wanna stay around you long enough to catch whatever it is that plagues your thinking. We ain't gonna dig her up," the older ruffian asserted as a disturbed frown settled across his face. After another swig though, Cyril's frown abruptly turned into a sly grin. "Shit, with all the tunnels running under that property, he might've dropped her right into one of 'em without even knowing it. Hel, we might trip over her bones on the way in. Guess we could tie an oily rag to one end of her thigh bone and use it for a torch." Both men snorted as they laughed and slapped each other on the back. "Now that'd be a tribute!"

At the next table, its sole occupant was gripping his chair so hard his hands were trembling and his knuckles were white with exertion. Almost all traces of Valenesti's extended alcoholic haze had lifted like a fog burned away by the morning sun. He took a breath and he could taste the air for the first time in months. The pipe smoke, the spilled ale, the remnants of vomit that the proprietor's mop hadn't quite managed to scrub away—he tasted it all, and the flavor was magnificent! Though he had done his best and his worst to keep it at bay, clarity's hammer returned and descended on him with a loud peal that echoed through his bruised soul. All of a sudden, he was the nail and the thorn.

There was no more confusion, no more apathy. There was only rage, and plenty of it. It needed no direction, for its targets had just been determined. As of this moment, it only needed release. These two louts were talking about his home, as impossible as the prospects sounded. The description was just too exact. His home…the seat of all his fond memories…the little patch of rock and clay where he had last seen the retreating shadow of his soul mate. What was worse, they were mocking his beloved Elise and the horrendous suffering that she had endured. They were mocking the depth of his grief and the integrity of his sorrow. This Cyril and his demented ward would soon pay for that affront with their lives, he avowed. He would execute them right beside the well; first the young one, then the other. There was a direct correlation between age and accountability.

That order seemed fitting somehow. And they would not die immediately; Valenesti wanted them to know the identity of their slayer. No pleas or apologies on their part would stay his hand, for he wasn't seeking atonement at this point. He simply wanted *his* face to be the harbinger of suffering for once and not the passive canvas for its angry brush strokes as it recklessly splattered streaks of red and black across the horizon of another gray tomorrow. Red and black…the hues of shattered hope. The two thieves would be granted no mercy, for there was not one grain of mercy left in his heart.

Thoroughly unaware of the fate that awaited them this stormy winter evening, the two men downed yet another round, paid their tab, then headed for the door…without leaving so much as a single copper as tip for Mallory. It was a minor detail that didn't go unnoticed by Valenesti, for throughout the evening he had seen both of them, on several occasions, slap her on her behind and then chide her for her annoyance.

"Yet more sins for which they must be...censured," he muttered as the hot, invisible arms of reprisal reached toward him, piercing the very shadows he once cherished so. These two bastards had avoided the garrote of retribution for far too long, and that injustice was soon to be remedied. Valenesti pledged this to himself as a wolfish smile tugged at the corners of his chapped and bleeding lips.

He motioned to Mallory with a sense of urgency he had not felt in at least two years. Using both hands, he shoved the mugs—one full, one partially empty—to the other side of the table and silently congratulated himself on the symbolic gesture. As she sauntered toward his table, he regarded once more the perfect lines of her face. Finally, he managed a smile that was no longer completely eclipsed by sadness. It was a meager smirk tinged with hope...elusive hope. It was just a hint of a smile, but it was cathartic on so many levels, and Mallory certainly couldn't help but notice the transition.

Though seduction was probably the furthest thing from her mind right then, she effortlessly struck a pose that could not have been any more seductive. She tilted her head to the side and crossed her arms, grinning with playful curiosity over the dramatic change in her patron's demeanor...the stern conviction that now defined his bearing.

"I've gotta say that you're looking better, soldier," she observed in a mischievous but thoroughly pleased tone as she shifted so that her hands rested on her perfectly-sculpted hips. She simultaneously cast a playful wink in his direction that made his pounding heart pound even faster. "Now, I know for a fact that the ale in this place is just a notch or two above cold horse piss—no offense to horses— so we can't credit the brew, now can we? So...did someone sneak in and bring you some good news when I wasn't looking? Answer me, champ! I need hope too from time to time."

"In a way, yes. Yes, indeed!" Valenesti all but shouted as he emptied his pockets of all the coppers he had managed to beg...and purloin...over the last few days. He even found two silvers in his stash that had somehow escaped his notice. Every coin in his possession he placed in a neat pile on the table, then backed away from the money as if it was an angry adder. He felt a peculiar blend of pleasure and liberation as he regarded the stunned expression on Mallory's face...the face of the sweet warm goddess that had unknowingly yanked him back from the edge of the abyss into which he had come so close to casting himself.

"I can't...I just..." she stammered, hesitant to take what was apparently the whole of this poor man's savings.

"I insist, Mallory. You saved my life tonight, love. What's more, you made it... worth saving. I could never thank you enough for that. If the winds of fate are at my back, I'll return very soon and explain. And I'm going to bring a guest with me that I want you to meet. The two of you have so...so much in common." Valenesti brushed a final dirty tear from his cheek and then rushed toward the door to catch up with the two ruffians before they disappeared into the night and the black shadows of the storm.

"You can't go out into this tempest without some kind of wrap!" Mallory called after him as he stepped into the freezing rain. He heard her, and he appreciated her concern, but he felt a profound warmth that he had not felt in a long time, so he let the door swing until the latch caught with a distinctive click, and he reveled in that toll of finality. It represented not just the closing of a door, but the closing of a dark chapter that he had already relegated to distant memory. Tonight, a page had been turned and a new chapter opened.

A fire now burned within...the fire of promise and possibilities. Squinting against the onslaught of pelting rain and sleet, he caught sight of two forms staggering along the sidewalk to his left. His hands were much steadier now. He was no longer plagued by tremors, for peace and promise had returned. His right one seized the pommel of the rusted dagger that had somehow managed to stay tucked behind his belt through all his recent misadventures. He took his first breath as a man freed from the shackles of grief, guilt, regret, and self-pity. The air was brisk...sharp. It was invigorating and fresh! Cold winds assailed him and his flimsy but precious tunic did little to turn them. For the first time in a long time, he actually felt the cold, but he was too busy celebrating to shiver. At long last he could savor the bittersweet bite of winter, but soon he would wrap himself in a heavy cloak, one taken from his designated prey...the first spoils of victory.

A mix of water and ice ran down his face, but he barely blinked. Gone were all remnants of pity and forfeit. Valenesti now wore the mask of a hunter, the mien of a determined and merciless predator. Elise was waiting; she was beckoning him with an insistent wave of one delicate hand. Her embrace would be denied him only until these two ruffians from Herezye lay eviscerated out in the howling wastes with their faces frozen and twisted, conveying the confusion and horror they experienced once they realized that fate was not their moll. It was its own beast with its own will; it did not always answer to the whims and wishes of the gods. It rarely showed any regard for the wishes of selfish men. Fate did not always reward well-laid plans. No, fate was merely an uncomplicated beast whose nature was defined by capricious cruelty and betrayal.

The two would-be thieves were vermin. Violent evisceration was simply their destiny, and Valenesti considered it *his* destiny to usher them toward that demise with extreme prejudice…and liberating delight. He would plunge his rusty blade into their bellies until his lust was sated, though that might take a while. With each thrust, he would feel the jar of his shovel striking the unyielding, rocky soil as he dug Elise's grave that fall afternoon. With each ragged cut, he would feel the delightful if imagined warmth as he drove himself into her moist and receptive loins. The thugs' death cries would sound like Elise's moans of pleasure in his ear…their dying gasps, her hot breath on his neck as he took her on the floor beside the fireplace which had remained so cold and so dark as eight slow seasons spun by.

Yes, he had some death to deal this night, but in so doing he would reclaim his own life, the very life that he had just minutes ago contemplated ending out of resignation and hopelessness. No more! Elise was buried out beyond the walls…out in the Northern Wastes. The beggar, the worthless drunk he had let himself become was now buried here in the muddy streets of Hadig-vie, in front of this sorry little tavern that had turned out to be the site of his salvation. He moved his blade to his other hand and rolled his head once more to stretch the ropy muscles in his neck. Without another moment's hesitation, Valenesti stepped into the full fury of the driving winter storm and in so doing, he unwittingly stepped into the darker pages of Eldimorah's history.

◆◆◆

Much like a riled bee, the morning mists delivered a jarring sting, and the mornings would only be growing colder from here on, for it was getting late in the year and he knew as well as any that the Ulverkraag Mountains were notorious for their harsh, unforgiving winters. Herodimae stirred and absently swatted at the annoying droplets as they lightly settled on his stubbly cheek to filch his warmth and ruin his sleep…sleep that had become his last real refuge. His mind was not yet willing to relinquish the beguiling fruit bearing the drug of dreams. It fought valiantly to shelter him from the inevitability of dour lucidity.

Damn them…but the mists settled so softly. His muddled mind embraced the illusion that the wicked water was being delicately applied by the bristles of a soft brush…a brush wielded by a loving hand that had forgotten how to love. The strokes were slow and deliberate. They were anything but violent; however, the intent behind them was innately harsh. His precious sleep had been interrupted, not by noise nor by the beckoning—if subdued—light of the daystar, but by the utter absence of legitimate warmth.

If only there was a fire nearby to challenge and chase off this greedy chill, then the ghosts that guided him through the maze of his own mind could return to their assigned task and he could once more kneel before the altar of the incubus. His addled inner self whispered to him through the heavy haze of slumber, reminding him that such a fire had indeed burned brightly. It had burned nearby and not so long ago.

No matter. He wriggled and scooted toward the foot of his bedroll, cocooning himself within its coarse but warm folds. One of his hands reflexively drew the bivouac bag over his head, creating a shelter against the unfriendly gray of this dreary morning. The prospect of facing the penetrating chill made him even more reluctant than usual to arise and tackle the tedious tasks of what would surely prove to be yet another fruitless day. Once more, he fell asleep as he settled into the silent storm of dreams.

Visions of low clouds, biting mists, and dense fog receded as sleep wrapped her gentle tendrils about his semi-conscious mind and began to draw it back to the shelter of her delectable embrace. That lithe temptress promised escape from the foul weather and the cold, hard ground. Using colors mixed on her unearthly palette, she painted a much more desirable alternative to this misty morning. It was, of course, another fragile masterpiece…one whose shades, somber though they were, still evoked the promise of asylum. It ensured respite to a soul that had grown weary from rejection and derision.

And Herodimae had endured his share of both for the better part of the last three months as he traveled the entire length of the Ulverkraag Mountain range seeking converts to his religion by proselytizing with a voice utterly devoid of conviction. His waking dreams had been denied—every last one. Thankfully, the deeper dreams found in slumber always trumped resentment...and another had just commenced.

◆◆◆

In this new reality, he was sitting peacefully on a stump decimated by several seasons of rot. All around him was a dense forest that bled torrents of dismal gray; every tree within sight had been stripped nearly leafless and bare by winter's gnarled hand. Even now and once again, he was surrounded by swirling mists, but the embrace of sister serenity combined with the coarse comfort of his long hooded cloak protected him from any whisper of distress. Another voice now demanded his attention, however; speaking only in silent pleas, it told him that he needed to make ready to depart. He was ready to leave, but before this next journey commenced, he felt compelled to sit beside a fire to warm his boots. Indeed, a pathetic little fire crackled at his feet, and its cherished smoke caressed his nostrils like the perfume and lingering musk of a recent lover. Its scent was pungent...divine. At first, he thought he was alone. But then he looked down.

He was perched beside a supine man wrapped from head to toe in thick blankets. Only the fellow's face was visible, and it was a familiar face.

The silent observer realized that he was watching himself sleeping, but that wrinkle did not strike him as odd...not in the least, in fact. He finally knew the breath of peace; he felt like a new father who had just rocked a cranky newborn to sleep. He was knowingly blessed. All was well. All that was about to unfold was just as it should be.

A deep roar off in the distance sounded like thunder...at first. Like a charging cavalry, the tumult rushed toward him until he could feel its vibrations through the soles of his boots as well as through the damp and spongy stump on which he rested. Shaken from their tentative perches by the seism that disrupted the crypt-like peace, the most stubborn of autumn's leaves and even a few loose limbs at last released their grip and rained down on him.

During all this commotion, his sleeping double never stirred, even when its head lolled to the side as its earthen pillow was wracked with ferocious vibrations. Then the waxing roar climaxed in a sharp explosion and the earth beneath them lurched. The viewer watched his slumbering twin bounce off the ground like a green apple in the bottom of a wagon that had just rattled across a deep rut. Coals from the little fire scattered everywhere, and the blankets tucked about his clone like some weird wool burial shroud began to smolder...then burn. Suddenly, the observer felt the searing heat blistering his own skin, but his innocence was the first real victim of this new inferno. He was stricken by the urge to utter an apology, a promise of fealty to someone standing within the surrounding mists. As the smell of smoldering wool reached his nostrils, he vowed to sell his soul to Hel for company.

♦♦♦

Herodimae came awake for the second time that morning, and as he lay there he could have sworn that he still felt faint tremors beneath his bedroll. They subsided and he readily dismissed them as remnants from his last dream. Sleep beckoned once more.

Using the back of his wrist, he mopped a stream of drool from his cheek. He had just begun to drift back into the theater of dreams, yielding to the delightful and abrasive warmth of his woolen blankets when the meanderings of his semi-conscious mind were disrupted by a hoarse voice that shredded the serenity of the moment and yanked his attention back to the real world...the world of piss pains, pungent wood smoke, and suffocating dampness.

"Yo, Herodimae! Snake oil peddler and noble protector of virgins, one and all!"

The sound of his own name tore through the wispy web of welcome illusion...a shout against the silence...causing him to come awake with a start, although whether his name had been screamed or merely whispered he could not tell.

Acrid and oppressive, the thick smell of a starved and dying fire greeted his nostrils and the overwhelming gray of the sunless dawn poured into his eyes...waves of raw umber every bit as irresistible as the waters of a flood-swollen river. For a moment, he wondered if he was in the midst of yet another dream as he stared into the surrounding forest. A thick, lazy fog occluded the trunks of the towering giants at the perimeter of the camp, but the tips of their branches and boughs jutted out from the haze, pointing at Herodimae like crooked brown fingers...accusatory fingers.

"Fuck me while I fiddle, but you priest-types are a jumpy sort, now are you not? You've been mumbling some *kind* of nonsense, I'll tell ya...and thrashing about like a snagged fish dropped into the weeds. What's the matter, cleric? Having yourself a nightmare? Maybe dreamin' that somebody else was takin' care of your old lady's private needs while you was gone? Oh, I forgot...you guys don't..." Spence made an obscene gesture with his fingers to finish his sentence and then broke into a grin that exposed two rows of crooked, tobacco-stained teeth. "I'll never figure that one out...why you so-called holy types use that thing for pissin' through and nothing more, I mean."

By now, Herodimae should have grown used to this fool's vulgarity; the gods knew that he had been its target enough times over the last few weeks. Still, he felt the burn of blushing cheeks even as he pulled the blankets up to keep the cold mists off his bare and hairless chest.

"We paid you to guide us through the Eastland, you heathen...not to offer your opinions or your worthless dream interpretations, thank you very much," the young priest shot back as he rubbed his eyes with the heel of his left hand. "Where's Brolki, you dolt? I'd much rather talk to the farmer than to his mule."

"Oh, that one. Sweet Hel, he's probably out sniffing the wind or taking a dump, knowing him. Actually, he's likely doing both at the same time," Spence grinned in lingering amusement as he raised the worn leather ale flask to his lips. He was not the least bit shaken by the reprimand he had just received. "Them Dwarves, now... they're a strange group. Between you and me, I think they just like the smell of ass!"

"I can think of no other reason why he would insist on keeping the likes of you around. There is a special place in Hel reserved just for you, scout. I am sure of it," Herodimae hissed as he leaned back on his elbows and yawned, not bothering to cover his mouth with his hand. After all, any show of etiquette would be wasted around this one; he had determined as much weeks ago.

At this point, there were very few incentives preventing him from falling back into the warmth offered by his bedroll. He ached to go back to sleep and retreat from his unsavory company and the sobering reality of his own seemingly hopeless plight. He yawned yet again and tried to orient himself, but that task would have been difficult enough even on a clear and sunny day.

The ensemble had pitched camp in a tiny clearing on the western bank of a broad stream that they had come upon last evening, well past dark and after two moons had already climbed high in the sky. It was one of the tiny tributaries of the East Arman, according to Brolki, their taciturn Dwarven guide. Saddle-weary all, the members of the company had still unanimously voted to chance a night crossing before making camp for the evening. The hour had been late and perhaps they felt that the creek represented just one more rudimentary obstacle that stood between themselves and the homes to which they were ever so anxious to return.

At any rate, Herodimae couldn't help but notice that the gloomy clearing looked far different now than it had the night before when it was bathed in the orange light of a crackling fire. It had looked far more inviting last night somehow, with fatigue dogging their every step and with the mistress of slumber beckoning them all with her slender, seductive finger. But now clouds had moved in, the fire had died and all the liberating dreams had retreated beyond the veil.

Herodimae shivered...partly due to the cold. The mists and eerie half-light of early morn in the Ulverkraags were far more ominous than the more familiar shadows of darkest night, he quickly decided.

He inhaled deeply and then let it out with deliberate impassivity, his breath condensing into steam as it mingled and merged with the crisp morning air. Unwelcome, wispy arms snaked out from the chilly stillness to caress his torso as the protective layers of blankets peeled away from his bare chest and settled in his lap.

"Yes, your highness, you are most probably right," Spence joked as he leaned forward in a mock bow. "Leave it to a priest-type to know how many rooms there are in Hel and just who they happen to be reserved for. Just rape me with a razor! For a moment there, I let myself forget that you little boys have all the answers. I forgot that them fancy collars make ya'll way smarter than me," the scout laughed and snorted. He was thoroughly enjoying this exchange; he was virtually slavering from the opportunity to further torment this moody young cleric that had rapidly become his favorite mark.

"A razor? Really? If only you spent more time bathing and less of it running your filthy mouth or conjuring up offensive colloquialisms, we might be able to see well enough to find our way out of here. I don't know if we're surrounded by fog or by the fumes boiling off your nasty, unwashed…body," Herodimae shot back. "And it isn't my collar that makes me smarter than you, by the way. For instance, that rock over there isn't wearing a collar."

Spence only shrugged, giggling like an old codger who had just won a game of checkers. He made no other reply. As far as he was concerned, his body odor was a badge of honor. From Herodimae's perspective, it was a badge of dishonor that was being worn with honor. With a thin stream of brown juice rolling out of the corner of his mouth, the scout leaned forward and threw some brush and stripped cedar bark onto the bed of dying embers, rekindling the fire for preparation of the morning meal. He then took a long swig from his precious aleskin and farted loudly as he did so.

"Gods! Is there no end to your crudeness?" an exasperated Herodimae asked as he scrunched his nose and fanned the air in front of his face with his hand, but to no avail. There was no breeze stirring this morning, certainly none strong enough to dissipate this tainted air…air bearing a tart odor which resembled a combination of clabbered milk and rotten lettuce. Damn Brolki for his stubborn insistence on bringing this bastard along.

"No, your highness; don't think so. Even I have yet to determine those exact limits, but you can rest assured that I am currently conducting exhaustive research in that area," another especially wet fart, "even as we speak." Spence cackled once more at his own crude wit and slapped his left knee four times…he would not go to five. Soon after, his tone became marginally more serious. Marginally.

"Enough of that, though. Might wanna get up and get your perfume-soaked panties packed away. Did your highness's latest volley of dreams suggest that we will likely encounter some…dampness during our travels today?" the half-drunken guide asked sarcastically as one hand swept back toward the deep gray wall of clouds that rose skyward from the western horizon.

Yet another mock bow. How that damned little habit had come to infuriate the green priest. Following the dictates of the very religion that he had so ardently tried to share with the outlanders, Herodimae had truly endeavored to find in the scout some redeeming value. He had accepted the futility of those attempts no later than their third night on the trail. Spence was a vile son of a bitch if there ever was one.

Herodimae considered himself a patient and tolerant man, but he had very nearly reached the end of his rope where this uncouth bastard was concerned, and he could barely wait to see the walls of Eldr-ro appear on the horizon. Once he caught sight of those crenellated battlements, he planned on kicking his pale steed in the flanks and speeding away from Spence and the others without so much as a *farewell* or a *fuck off*.

"I may be celibate, but I am not blind," an irate Herodimae hissed as he fished beneath the warm blankets for his trousers and shirt. The damp tinder finally sputtered into flame, drawing his attention to the fact that the fire had all but died while he and the others slept. Spence had probably fallen asleep during the last watch, allowing the fire to go unattended…again.

*The damned idiot!* Just because they were all one day closer to Eldr-ro did not mean that there was no danger lurking about. These were still the Ulverkraags, after all…"the beasts to the east," home to a host of predators that would not hesitate to make a quick meal out of any man stunned by the spell of slumber.

"Now wake the others, you heathen. I am ready to put this damned journey *and* our regrettable association behind me," Herodimae added as he pushed himself to his feet and turned his back to Spence out of modesty, hoping to don his heavy riding shirt and his cloak before the scout had a chance to phrase a comment. He failed.

"No need to turn away, cleric. You're not my type. I like my women more top-heavy than you, though I have to say that I've bedded a few that showed more knuckles in their knickers than you're obviously toting around."

"Glad to hear it," Herodimae mumbled through clenched teeth. "I'll go tend to the horses, since I'm fairly sure that you have not bothered to do so. After all, taking care of our animals would cut into your precious drinking time, now wouldn't it?"

"They're tough, lad…they can handle a little neglect now and then, I'll wager blood and stone. Believe it or not, I was neglected at one point…and look how I turned out! Magnificent, eh?" Another wink. Another storm of stifling flatulence. Another extended display of all those poor teeth turning brown with rot.

"I have to relieve myself."

"Relieve? Now don't go sneakin' off behind the wagon to rub

out the easy one, priest. I know how quick you celibate types are to fuck a fist when no one is around to keep a close eye on ya, especially in the morning hours when things are pointed more outward than downward," Spence slurred with a mischievous wink; a wink intended to stoke the fires of fury. It succeeded brilliantly.

"Heathen!" a scowling Herodimae repeated the insult as he spun about to see to the party's mounts.

♦♦♦

"Guilty as charged," Spence rejoined, slapping his knee yet again. He straightened from his bow and stumbled forward a step as his addled brain fought to recalibrate with his legs. After he paused to regain his balance, the puckish smile on his face widened ever more slightly. Another flood of brown spittle trickled down to drip from his chin.

The scout thoroughly enjoyed his last exchange with Herodimae; the other three upstarts were too easily intimidated, damn them. When he dug at them, they bowed their heads and scurried away from him like three scolded puppies. Cowards all, those three were. Shit! If he slit their throats in their sleep, he would likely be doing them a grand favor. That Herodimae, on the other hand, was annoyed *by* him, but he was not afraid *of* him. Spence knew that he could go so far as to spit in the faces of those other eunuchs and elicit little more than flinches, grimaces, and a trio of sheepish frowns. They would silently wipe away the spittle, regurgitate some inane verse drawn from their treasured scripture, and then carry on about their foolish business of saving that which ultimately could never be saved.

They were weak. They were too quick to forgive. Spence could sense, however, that this Herodimae character had more spunk and fire woven through the fabric of his soul. He was like a coiled, agitated adder...fun to toy with, and fun to poke at with a long stick, but you didn't want to find yourself suddenly within striking distance. You certainly didn't want to corner it.

Another draw from his trusty aleskin, and he stumbled over to rouse his three more passive charges. Indeed, he was already rubbing his palms together in anticipation of the perverse pleasure he would get from awakening the three other priestlings by applying the tip of his boot to their ribs in a not-so-gentle fashion, a tactic he decided to forego with the capricious cleric he had chosen to rouse first. Besides, carefully chosen words clearly bothered Herodimae far more than a firm nudge in the ribs ever could.

♦♦♦

Herodimae, as much as he detested Spence, had to work very hard to suppress his own villainous smile when he heard the groans and grumblings of his three puny associates as they were kicked awake and torn away from their dreams by the uncouth guide. Though he had taken the same vows as his colleagues, he did not remember swearing at any point to sacrifice his dignity. Truth be told, Herodimae respected his three cohorts even less than Spence did. He harbored an abiding lack of admiration for those milksops. His feelings toward them consistently bordered on disgust, but at times those sentiments crossed over into the dark territory of outright hatred. He took a deep breath, exhaled it, and fought to embrace more angelic thoughts.

"They are guilty of their sins, just as I am guilty of my own," Herodimae recited without any real conviction whatsoever as he slapped a leaf—dead and damp with morning dew—between his hands and rubbed the cool water across his cheeks and forehead.

After he relieved himself and made his way to the rear of the wagon, Herodimae turned up the collar of his coat to stave off the tide of damnable chill. With the last button on the front of his jacket fastened, he proceeded to tend to the horses and soon set his attention to the tasks at hand. He leaned forward and dragged the burlap bag onto the tailgate of the wagon. As scrawny as Herodimae was, he had no problem pulling the sack toward him; it was growing far too light and far too rapidly. This, the last bag of horse feed, was already almost half empty. The muscles at the base of the young priest's neck began to throb due to his frustration.

Their provisions were dwindling quickly. The group's inability to so much as barter with the frugal and cautious inhabitants in the remote settlements was just another indication of just how futile and unpleasant this whole damnable endeavor had been. None of the members of the expedition had anything to offer in trade for even a few bags of oats and grains. Pathetic! Herodimae and his three… peers…had brought only their message, and it had proven to be a most undesirable currency. All their bartering attempts had failed.

And then, of course, there was their failure to win even a single convert. The people inhabiting this wilderness were stern, their attention focused on survival. They had little time and even less desire to listen to the recondite doctrines of a strange new faith. Their old faith revolved around no deity. Their old faith...which amounted to little more than unwavering confidence in their own capabilities to survive...had seen them this far. It was defined by strong principles put into practice, and the settlers felt that it would be foolish at least and suicidal at most to abandon those convictions after they had steered and sustained the hearty pioneers through so many trials.

For reasons known only to them, the pilgrims had made their exodus from the safety of the Five Cities long ago. Since then, they had witnessed death, drought, animal attacks and brutal winters. They had lost friends and buried loved ones in the rocky Ulverkraags. In a sense, loss had become their constant companion. Some of the more jaded settlers even viewed loss as a fateful friend, for it had been the one invariable presence throughout all their hardships.

Indeed, what use had these noble, hardened souls for some new religious paradigm? Less than a week into the doomed mission trip, Herodimae himself had begun to doubt the relevance of the very message that he had—just days earlier—so enthusiastically volunteered to spread. Soon after arriving at the first settlement on their list, he had secretly been forced to admit to himself that he had virtually nothing of worth to offer these hardy folks, and he could see his own germinating doubt mirrored in the faces of the colonists, even the young ones...young ones that could not be called children, for life in the Ulverkraags had effectively truncated that cherished time of innocence and wonder that the citizens back to the east would call childhood.

As Herodimae patted his white roan, he willed his shoulders to relax and he allowed himself the luxury of an exasperated chuckle; after all, this whole enterprise was almost comical in retrospect. Skittish of even their own shadows, the four unsullied upstarts who rode into the villagers' midst promising a route to salvation were so soft and pale...so skinny and weak. They knew so little about toil...about legitimate sacrifice. The flimsy faith that they promoted and the unfamiliar gods that they worshipped might provide an adequate aegis of illusion for some. That fragile fantasy might be sufficient to steer the city-dwellers back west through one of their leisurely weeks, a week spent tucked safely behind high city walls. But it offered damn little assurance to men and women who had to sweat and sometimes bleed for every scrap of food that crossed their tables.

The four green priests and their guides spent the last three months amid such people, having visited over a dozen settlements in all. Each day delivered more rejection than the day before, and the whole experience left the well-intentioned men emotionally drained and quite thoroughly discouraged. All except for Spence, of course, who took great pleasure in pointing out the boys' unequivocal failure to win converts.

"Damn!" Herodimae barked to the mists when he tore half of a fingernail off while tying a knot in the rough burlap sack. While he gnawed off the rough edges of the remaining nail, he momentarily shifted his attention to some commotion back in the nearby camp. Not surprisingly, Spence was once again berating one of the younger priests, probably over something as trivial as an overturned cup of coffee.

As he continued to chew on the ragged edge of his wounded nail, Herodimae entertained a daydream: he fantasized about that verbal confrontation escalating into a full-scale knife fight from which none of the opponents would emerge.

"Damn them all," he muttered as his attention returned to the burlap bag in the back of the wagon. He endeavored to tune out the irrelevant quarreling on the southern side of the clearing. Herodimae put his hungry ears to work, making sure to turn his focus toward the hushed songs of late autumn. He let his ears sift through the subtle noises of the forest morning like a finicky dog might sniff through a pile of steaming table scraps, searching for just the right gravy-smothered morsel. Even dreary mornings like this one were defined by their own characteristic songs, and he busied his mind picking out all the different notes in the tune that floated toward him from out in the ghostly mists.

The brook they had crossed the night before burbled as the clear mountain water born of melted snow meandered over and around stones worn smooth by decades spent subjected to the steady current's influence. Nearby, a lone raven was complaining in a hoarse screech…perhaps about the lack of visibility. And drops of gathered mist were steadily falling from the few brave brown leaves that still managed to suspend themselves above the spongy forest floor. Most of the lazy drops landed on the thick blanket of loam and leaves that had already surrendered to the brownest season. Some of them, however, tapped a simple but steady rhythm on the slick and rotting husk of a fallen log that lay some six or seven paces from where Herodi-mae stood. That rhythm, steady as a thoroughbred's heartbeat at first, became obviously and ominously slower...and slower.

For a moment, he pondered the possibility that he had suc-cumbed to a sudden fever. And that would not have surprised him in the least considering all the consecutive nights that he and the others had spent on the cold ground. The air around him abruptly grew un-comfortably warm, and Herodimae wanted nothing more than to un-fasten the buttons on his jacket, but he was now so incredibly weak. He discovered that he could not even will himself to lift his hand to his collar.

A sheen of clammy sweat promptly burst out on his forehead as his soul screamed in silent warning. It was a warning that he was un-able to heed; instead, Herodimae surrendered to the thoroughly un-settling numbness that washed over him as though he was merely an insignificant pebble on the shore of some restless sea. His peripheral vision faded to black and he was sure that he was about to faint. Everything seemed to slow to quarter speed just in the time it took for his eyes to blink shut.

When his ponderous eyelids finally managed to slide back open, the dreary but natural gray light had taken on a strange lavender hue and his entire sense of awareness had become incongruent with what he formerly knew to be...real. Just seconds ago, the churning gray clouds had been speeding across the sky, racing each other to the north and east. Now they hovered in the air directly over the young priest's head and were moving no faster than the thin hand on a timepiece.

They were caught in a slow swirl, a grim spiral from which Herodimae thought he could hear volleys of girlish laughter blended with and balanced by a sickening barrage of women screaming...an incongruous cacophony that issued from this tornado of souls. The screams were wrong...all wrong. But they were wrong for all the right reasons; he knew instinctively that the dissonant chorus her-alded some grand transition. The choir concealed behind the swirling shadows was singing to him and only to him. That much he could sense, yet he paid the exordium no mind. He was now a passive ob-server...a worm writhing on frozen ground.

He could feel and hear the swish of his own heartbeat as loudly and every bit as distinctly as the hammer strikes of a determined blacksmith; but whereas that hammer would surely leave a lasting mark on its glowing target, the noise emanating from his racing heart left no such impression. It did not faze him. The exaggerated throbbing of his heart was vaguely interesting, but beyond that, it simply was. He was now a passive observer...a flower stung by early frost.

Moving with the sluggishness of a hare succumbing to a viper's paralyzing venom, one of the horses tethered to the wagon turned its head back toward the east and whinnied her approval of the morning meal, meager though it had been. And the beast's uncanny avowal was in no way attenuated by the mists and dense forest...not to the slightest degree. If anything, it was amplified, and the unsettling bray echoed in an interminable song that drifted skyward to meld with the chorus of screams issuing from the vortex of clouds overhead. Those echoes, punctuated by the hammering of his own heartbeat, reverberated and finally began to diminish as a light rain began to fall.

The raucous noises from the camp rapidly faded to memory, and they were soon replaced entirely by the rush and vivid whisper of a new wind descending on him from the plains directly to the northwest...a welcome wind that chased away the stale air which had threatened to suffocate him just moments ago. Wearing their tan shades of Earlywinter woe, the sparse blades of sage grass that dotted the clearing whipped and spun under the strange wind's influence. The bare limbs of the surrounding giants waved ever so rhythmically...ever so hypnotically. All the while, the dense mists hiding in the shadows of the bare trees continued to hover like white wraiths, stubborn and utterly undisturbed by the breeze.

For the second time in what felt like a mountain's eternity, Herodimae's heavy eyelids fell shut and then somehow struggled valiantly to slide back open, defying gravity's newfound might. He could now hear the wet sound they made and it reminded him of hunting boots buried and stuck in greedy black mud. His confused mind labored to piece together this new puzzle presented by his roguish senses. It labored to process and rationalize what his eyes beheld in that next instant.

*Was that old man there a minute ago?* His fading sense of reason whispered its inquiry from across this new abyss into which his sanity was threatening to topple. But there was no denying the fact that an old beggar dressed in rags stood just within the perimeter of jagged and shifting shadows created by the network of intertwined limbs which formed the forest ceiling. *This is all wrong*, the strained but distorted voice of reason tried to scream as the spiraling clouds continued to wail overhead. *He shouldn't be there. He shouldn't be anywhere. He should not be. He does not belong!*

Then all was silent. There were no more interruptions from that annoying inner voice. Herodimae lifted his own eyes to meet those of the stranger, and as their gazes locked the young cleric felt the last remnants of his will and resolve wither. He felt them drift away on the strange new breeze that had come from nowhere. The old man's eyes conveyed such an intriguing mix of wisdom and rage. Such beauty...such utter and consummate beauty...such evil beauty!

The face itself was wrinkled and worn like old saddle leather, but the eyes...the eyes were placid and penetrating—pits of power that Herodimae knew he should not see, but he also knew that he was not meant to turn away from them. They beckoned him to let go and submit to the forces that drew him forward and downward into this mystical spiral stirred by sanity gone astray and gravity gone mad.

And Herodimae did begin to fall. His mind lost all purchase, and he could feel an immense void open up at his feet, as though the very earth that he remembered suddenly ceased to be. It melted away. Without offering so much as a groan of notice, it had lost its substance and become a garden of tears that could no longer support even the mass of his slight, gangly form; stone and soil had just this instant parted to reveal a ravenous well. Buried ever so subtly behind the hiss of the winds that rushed by in a futile attempt to arrest his fall, he could hear the gods shouting down at him, warning him that he was becoming something he should not be.

Still, with every passing second he picked up speed, descending faster and even faster into a pit whose hidden depths he feared not in the least. He did not fear the fall...he did not fear striking the floor of this beguiling well. All the while his other senses, subdued though they were, assured him that he yet remained standing beside the wagon. His was a static body hosting a feeble soul and a frozen will. Though he could make out no discernable words, he knew that his tired heart was now singing. Ordinarily, blind panic might have been an appropriate response, but nothing about this encounter was ordinary. A niggling voice urged him to pray, but Herodimae was suddenly more certain than ever that no one would be listening.

The disoriented cleric could not pull his attention away from those godly eyes...those ungodly eyes. Their image remained set directly in front of him, even as he plummeted down the great well that had, over the eons, likely darkened scores of stars and swallowed armies of angels. With nothing but a relaxed and confident glance, those ancient eyes conquered and ultimately captured the core of his drowning soul, beckoning with a silent voice that obliterated every last one of Herodimae's feeble convictions.

*So lovely*, was the only thought—the only pitiful phrase—that the remnants of his shattered mind could manage to piece together. Oh, to spend the rest of eternity simply falling into this marvelous black void, staring into those fathomless eyes all the while...that would be reward enough for the twenty-something years of misery and sacrifice that had defined his pitiful life to this point. That would be more than enough of a reward, indeed.

But then the stranger spoke, and Herodimae's loins finally released their pent up burden. His vows of celibacy were now a muffled memory drowned in the sudden rapture of slick, spilled seed.

"Relax, child. Know peace and embrace your fate. Kiss it on the cheek, and perhaps it will offer you a taste of its ebony lips before long."

Yes, the stranger spoke, and the divine harmonics in that voice wove a net which offered safety and protection from whatever fate awaited Herodimae at the end of the long fall. Laden with sick love and dripping with stark divinity, the breath behind the voice slowed his descent and gave Herodimae's flagging mind another point of focus, one besides the seething omnipotence that resided in those churning, crystalline eyes.

He wanted to retch as he was forced to witness his own pathetic vulnerability. He rapidly realized that despite nearly three decades of memories and a smattering of stubble on his pink cheeks, he was ultimately no more mature than an unswaddled infant, shivering and alone...crying. He was just that—an infant longing to be wrapped in a warm blanket and cradled in the secure comfort of his mother's arms, crying for a solitary but simple caress, a caress that had been denied him until this singular moment.

His twenty-eight years, his memories, his education, his oath... it all accounted for naught, he now knew. Those signposts and accomplishments were just weak wisps of smoke caught in a stout breeze.

46

*So insignificant am I.* With his ears and with his faltering spirit, the priest-child reached out and wrapped the newcomer's voice around himself as if the old man's words were precious threads woven through the fabric of that warm blanket. That voice's tones were so soothing, so reassuring. Fatherly. Motherly. Sinister. A whisper inside a roar.

"The less I see, the more it decays," the stranger continued as his lean hand gracefully swept across the horizon behind him...the horizon where the daystar should have been dumping at least a fraction of its ample light. "Sickness abounds, my dear Herodimae. Words have been spoken, but those words have yet to be heeded. This world is begging to be purged, my friend. Can you not smell the need? Have you not witnessed the taint long enough? You have stayed in the saddle of this doleful mare for nearly thirty winters now...this mare, whereupon you trick and train and tire."

The cleric was reeling. His left hand snaked out and he managed somehow to grasp the spokes of the right rear wagon wheel for stability.

*Oh Gods, but what splendor that tranquil voice promulgated. What mattered the message when it was carried on the notes of such a beautiful aria? Could it not be accepted as truth by simple virtue of the cherished voice that delivered it?* Herodimae willed his eyes to close once more so that his sense of hearing might be heightened, for that musical voice demanded to be utterly savored. The words demanded to be parsed, relived, and remembered...devoured like moist roast at a banquet. In that moment, it became imperative to hear the rest of the message, even at the cost of his soul.

"Think, my child. Think about the plight of the pathetic beings that you strive to...*save*. To your credit, you have tried to empathize with their dire and pitiful state. Still, you will never truly taste the bitterness that bleeds from their calloused, collective spirit. I have! Their hope...it so quickly dives into the churning waves of desperation, does it not? Clueless! Clueless they are. Hapless characters on a stage that they long ago insisted on designing for themselves. How sad—how sadly ironic. They are doomed to repeat the same inconsequential script until their curtain falls. When that curtain is drawn, all is done. A generation is buried, but then the next generation steps forth. And it is already doomed to repeat the same script."

"The very thing that these blind ones need is the very thing they refuse to accept. *The truth.* Ah, but then you show up to apply your... faith, like some slimy salve. Your faith..." the oldster spat the words like he had taken a sip of clabbered milk. "You yourself cling to it like a drowning man hugging a log. Child, you have devoted your life to it, and you pray daily that the heathens learn to love or at least accept you for the so-called truth that you offer them. But the echoes of your prayers die quickly. They become muted by a gag woven from the fabric of ignorance. They seem to fall on deafened ears, do they not? Yes. Yesss..."

"I know you, son. I know your heart. I know it better than anyone else alive, I assure you. You gather your doubts around you like some bitch rounding up her pups. You nurse them, you lick them and you collectively refer to them as *faith*." The wind picked up and the cacophony of screams overhead suddenly rose in pitch.

"The weak will go to great lengths to avoid doubt, Herodimae. Just when was your last conversion? A week ago? A month ago? What is a *conversion* worth to you, Herodimae? Why does the prospect put you on your knees? Would you get down on your knees to survive?" The old man shifted his stance, but he did so without moving. "When you curl up beside the crackling fire each night, what is it that you hope for? I alone know the answer to that last question, priest." The musical voice fell quiet then, and the scalding silence rushed into the cleric's ears, burning and blistering its way through the labyrinthine turns in his mind. It left his soul writhing with an abject sense of lack. Hunger and panic made his heart beat even faster. Just one more syllable of that wondrous melody...one more word to complete the spell.

Then that word came, and it rushed onward with force that could have so easily dwarfed a loud clap of thunder. The old man's cracked lips moved, but the sound that issued forth did not reach Herodimae for three, perhaps four, seconds. In fact, the stranger's lips had closed and were already morphing into a baleful but fatherly smile long before the storm that carried that single word crashed into the unsuspecting cleric. But when it did reach him, it hit with the fierce force of a tempest. When the word arrived, it knocked the priest back a step or two, as though some giant's fist had punched him in his chest, knocking the breath out of him.

"*Power.*"

So forceful was the stranger's delayed but awesome whisper,

Herodimae's shoulder-length hair and the tail of his cloak whipped back like cobwebs caught in a stout winter draft. A deluge of damp, fallen leaves flew past his face, stinging his cheeks. The fetor of autumn's rot filled his nostrils, but soon it was replaced by the sweet aroma of newly picked irises. It took only a second for the potent wave to pass...only a second for shock to turn to satiation and then to surrender.

"Power to make your wishes come to pass, dear Herodimae. Power to convince these other fools that *your* way is the *only* way that can lead them to Truhaeven." Another pause ensued that dragged on for eons. "Can you even perceive such a future? One in which your values and beliefs are adopted and embraced by all? One in which your will is absolute law? Or is the one that you picture a bit more...bleak? Is your lone pass at life going to be spent battling your caged desire? Will you buckle it back with the restraints of laws that you, in fact, do not even accept as the truth? Can you buckle back what has begun, Herodimae? What *does* define your future, priest?" the voice asked, though now it was tinged with angst and acrimony. "Martyrdom? Is it yet another nameless martyr that you seek to become? Another dead worm whose name is doomed to disappear in the faded pages of a history that never was. If so...if so, then you are no less pathetic than the rest!"

That reprimand stung. It injured him every bit as profoundly as a rusty knife thrust between his ribs. In that moment, he was a helpless child that had just been beaten and left on the streets to starve. *Don't be angry with me. Don't take away the beauty*, his mind pleaded to the visitor, but his physical voice had abandoned him and was refusing to set the desperate plea to song.

Almost at once, the voice of the elder stranger softened. Gone were all the disconcerting tones of disapproval. All that remained was the familiar symphony that made Herodimae ache to surrender his soul, music that promised the soft embrace of acceptance that had been denied him for far too long. Unconditional acceptance. He had never been granted as much by his parents...his instructors...his colleagues.

"You are destined for greater things, son. Much greater things. I can see it, and I have seen much, let me assure you." The visitor allowed an ominous chuckle to escape from between his chapped lips. "Ally yourself with me and the world will no longer laugh. There will be no more doors slammed in your face, no more embarrassment, no more rejection. Think of it, my friend. You have always thought of destiny as a river without banks, a force without a face. Why not give it a face now...today? Why not let it be mine?" The voice took another interminable pause. "Why not let it be yours? Why not dare to follow me so much higher?"

If temptation was the stranger's intent, then he had surely succeeded, for young Herodimae was presently host to a flaccid will. He decided to heed the old man's words and pledge loyalty to him even before the last words of the appeal echoed into that damnable silence spawned by the hovering fog.

"Tell...tell me what I must do," the callow priest managed to whisper, his voice hoarse and uneven—cracking as if he was in the blasted midst of puberty once again. He felt nothing but embarrassment at having broken the beautiful silence with such a pathetic noise...such an inadequate squeak bereft of any melody.

The old man's expression, though it had been kind enough to start with, immediately softened even further upon hearing the fledgling priest's words...words dripping with determinate surrender. For the first time since his arrival, the old man turned his head away from where Herodimae stood planted like some inanimate, wilted fern. After studying the western horizon for a few protracted moments, the stranger turned back to the baffled cleric, pinning the boy once again with that mesmerizing gaze that either Haeven or Hel could claim as their own. Unbidden tears stung the corners of Herodimae's eyes. The stranger let forth a long sigh just as a cooler, more soothing wind picked up and whistled through the branches overhead.

"Oh, my son, it is so very easy," the oldster offered in fatherly tones that were painlessly patronizing. "An old axiom exists. It is one which is frequently used among my own...kind. It asserts that the surest way to achieve a goal is to systematically remove any obstacles that separate you from that goal, starting with the most minor ones. Simple enough, yes?" Then another damned pause that threatened to stifle the priest with sour silence.

"So, *what* are your obstacles, Herodimae? *Who* are they? Can you readily identify them? What keeps you rooted in place...chained to rejection and mediocrity? As I see it, there are only two things that stand between you and the life—the destiny—you dream of in the private moments just before your mind cowardly retreats into that silent bitch's realm of dreams. The first one is your fear of surrender to a much higher calling, which you seem to have just mastered. My deepest congratulations on that achievement, by the way. The second obstacle, however, may prove to be much more of a challenge to overcome."

The visitor shifted his stance all of a sudden, and Herodimae realized on some plane of consciousness that this was the first time that the old man's legs had moved since he appeared at the perimeter of the clearing those many moments — or had it been months — ago. Even his tone of voice transitioned to one laced with barely-contained eagerness. Hunger. Lust! Additionally, a blend of strange inflections and accents now melded together to weave a separate, newer spell...one even more hypnotic, more powerful than the initial one, though Herodimae would not have thought that possible. The wrinkled face twisted as its beguiling lips labored to spit out the strange words, syllable by mesmerizing syllable.

"Fear of conquest now stands in your way, my young friend. Those who claim to be your colleagues are destroying your dreams and your future by drawing you deeper and deeper into the quagmire of mediocrity that they so readily welcome and embrace. They are slowly drowning your visions, your aspirations, in the morass of ignorance and complacency that they strive to navigate just so they can justify their miserable reasons for being. Is that what you want, priest?" Once again the enchanting voice changed in both timbre and tempo. Once again the words were delivered with a tone suffused with reprimand and sprinkled with displeasure.

"Just look at the fools with whom you ally yourself. Given their way, they would choose to die as martyrs just for the sake of martyrdom. They live as beggars just so they can boast of their poverty as if it were a virtue! And," the old man chuckled, "they espouse celibacy because deprivation is supposed to somehow keep their souls *pure*. *Pure*? Heed my words: no soul is pure! Though they hold some tainted vision of Haeven in their sights, those three are bound for Hel; but before they reach the frosty iron gates, they are destined to go nowhere, Herodimae. Nowhere! And they are intent on dragging you with them. No one back in what you call *civilization* and certainly no one out in this dire wilderness accepts their beliefs, but that does not bother your brethren...not in the least. Why not, priest? Why do they not share your sense of frustration?"

*They are not my allies! They never were!* Herodimae wanted to cry, but his throat was clamped shut…and it was so damned dry.

Shaking his head reprovingly, the old man turned and began to glide toward the trees and shadows with the grace and ease of a snake slithering toward the shelter of a thick patch of brush.

"Wait!" Herodimae beckoned desperately in that damned raspy voice. It was the only word he could force himself to utter, but it was all that the old man needed to hear. The stranger stopped and looked over his right shoulder at the priest, waiting for him to continue; but by this point, Herodimae was too confused and enchanted to effectively put his comparatively irrelevant thoughts to words. When the old man sensed that no more words were forthcoming, he continued to prompt the young officer of the old church.

"You have the potential to do great things with your life, my dear Herodimae. But you are going to have to accept some changes, and no changes can occur unless you shed your self-imposed limitations and cast them aside like a soiled garment. Snakes shed their skin with the seasons, do they not?" The old man stared at his feet for a moment, then he lifted his gaze, and an impish grin was spread across his wrinkled face. "You had a dream early this morning, did you not? One in which the earth trembled, perhaps? Yes?"

Though he still could not speak, Herodimae leaned forward on the spokes and nodded vigorously. How could the old man have possibly known? Then again, how could he not know?

"It was not a dream, lad. You see, a very old magic was summoned last night. It was finally loosed and thanks to that magic, Mother Eldimorah gave birth to a magnificent new city…a city complete with a gilded throne, albeit a vacant one…empty so far, at least. It could well be that this very morning, your new destiny sprang from her bleeding womb. Someone must assume that throne, and soon. Mayhap it will be you. Mayhap it will be some other who bows more deeply before the altar of catharsis. Finish your business here, boy. Finish it and fly westward. I will find you when—if—I receive word that you have laid down your silly cross and left your reservations behind." With that, the mysterious stranger faded into the shroud of mist and disappeared from sight.

Herodimae felt his knees give way, and he fell hard to the ground beside the wagon. The morning sounds returned to normal… somewhat. He could once again hear the bustling and the grumbling coming from the camp behind him and off to his left. The fledgling priest rolled himself into a seated position and leaned his back against the wooden spokes of the wagon's rear wheel. His head was swimming and he could feel his heart striving to maintain a steady rhythm behind a shirt that was now saturated with cool perspiration. The old man's final words still echoed in his mind, and their mesmeric spell still snagged his darting thoughts like minnows caught in a tight net.

A rare and precious tear ran from the corner of his left eye as he turned and pulled himself up the side of the wagon so that he could study the center of the clearing where his companions were tying their bedrolls and breaking camp. By all indications, they hadn't witnessed a thing; they were completely oblivious to all that had just transpired on the north side of the clearing.

The old man had come to *him*...he had come for *him*. Another tear streamed down his cheek, and he felt prompted to stare at his right hand where a tiny, brown vial of liquid had mysteriously appeared. Herodimae looked to the gray skies and noted that the clouds once more followed a linear trek toward the northeast. He took a deep breath and wiped more dew across his forehead as he endeavored to steady himself. The dark wall of clouds eclipsing the western horizon, the harbinger of the approaching storm, was stealing ever closer. He would soon be riding through that storm...alone. With his left hand, he reached up and patted the flank of the horse nearest him. Ironically, it happened to be Spence's poor mount, a dappled mare that had suffered more than her share of neglect and abuse.

"Don't despair, my friend," he whispered, "you'll be free soon enough. There will be no more bit and bridle...no more beatings for you, m'lady." His hand shoved the brown vial into the pocket of his cloak. Herodimae rolled his neck as he stepped from behind the wagon and strode steadfastly toward the camp where his former comrades milled about like pigeons in a park. He had a special contribution to make to the morning meal, though he would not be partaking.

"Soon, we will both be free."

# 1

Squinting against the brisk and buffeting currents of winter's tantalizing breath, Quinn paused for a moment at the foot of the sanctuary steps and allowed his eyes some time to accommodate to the scant light which struggled to stab through winter's iron pall. Apparently intended more for ornamentation than actual utility, the meager oil lamps lining his route home were placed too high above the street and too far away from each other to be truly useful aside from fundamentally marking the boundaries of the wide street...his path toward home.

Perhaps the pitiful light that they cast did indeed drive away the blacker shadows which teased and chased each other around the bases of the lampposts, but the dim glow was just barely sufficient to prevent any unwitting pedestrians—had there been any about this dismal evening—from marching right into the steel poles and knocking themselves senseless. Tonight however, a thick blanket of fallen snow reflected a measure of the weak light back toward the cloud-laden night sky, highlighting in a pale blue gleam aspects of the avenue that would normally be veiled in inky shadow.

Shivering against the onslaught of tonight's bone-chilling breeze, Quinn pulled the stiff collar of his outer shirt snugly around his neck and started toward home. He dropped the butt of his smoke into the snow, and its glowing tip was immediately extinguished with a soft hiss. Hopefully the wind would wash away any remnants of smoke that clung to his wool coat, lest his mother climb atop another of her innumerable soapboxes. He certainly could not abide a sermon tonight...not tonight. There would be enough of that inane bullshit tomorrow morning, though it would not be furnished by Miriam. Instead, it would be delivered by Father Sigmund, that bloated bastard—that wheezing excuse for a priest.

Even though it was Saturday night, the street was deserted. Its new mantle of snow lay pristine and relatively undisturbed. He would walk alone this evening, the sole voyager across a white and placid sea, and that consideration did not unnerve him in the least. Far from it. Quinn allowed himself the luxury of a smile as another sturdy puff of winter's breath tossed his unruly bangs across his eyes.

Tonight, while the timid and the weak huddled around their little glowing stoves to stay warm, the empty lane would belong to him and him alone. If freezing his own ass off was the price he must pay for a moment of treasured solitude, then he would stand in the biting wind until he was too cold to even blink. Isolation would be his remuneration...a blessing granted him for his day's labor, though he hardly believed in blessings any more. If they indeed existed, then he was more than certain that they were not bestowed by the deities exalted by the Church of the New Way.

Whatever its sweet origin—from whatever quarter it sprang—isolation was now his insulation. It shielded his last intact nerve, the last delicate nerve that had not been savagely frayed by rude intrusion and by the ingrained ignorance exhibited by Eldr-shok's mindless citizens with whom he was so frequently required to share the streets.

He pulled his hands from his pockets just long enough to wrap his arms across his chest, symbolically embracing the privacy afforded him by tonight's rare and biting chill, for it virtually guaranteed that he would have to spend none of his precious energy reserves nodding, smiling and performing all the other absurd little obligatory gestures he was required to execute whenever etiquette demanded that he don the brittle veneer of courtesy.

Tonight, Quinn just did not think he could pull off the ruse without finally snapping—without yanking his blade from its sheath and slitting some blameless and unwitting oaf's throat—because tonight his mood was blacker than the underside of a bat's wing and his threshold for irritation was just about level with the soles of his boots. Before either of those boots had an opportunity to leave one more mark in the snow, his frown deepened even further. He remembered all.

"Shitty Saturndays...!" he shook his head and mumbled to himself as he crammed his hands back into his coat pockets. More so over the last month, he had come to thoroughly detest his once-cherished Saturnday nights simply due to the anticipation of the assault his intelligence would have to endure the following morning. But tonight was even worse than most, for this had been his designated week to help clean the blasted sanctuary of the very church that he had grown to abhor.

Not long after his sixteenth birthday, Saturnday nights came to represent a few filched hours of adventure...debauchery. Foam-capped mugs and a host of willing strumpets provided adequate distraction for a couple of years, but with the arrival of early adulthood, Quinn found that life in the city quickly lost most of its former wonder. Eldr-shok used to be like a lady—a mysterious enchantress that beckoned him to explore all of her secrets. And he had done quite an adequate job of doing so over the years. So much so, in fact, that familiarity and repetition had erased all of her intrigue.

Now, beset as he was by his latest nemesis *boredom*, he found that the city herself guarded very few secrets that he cared to explore. She no longer possessed the mystique of some new lover whose hot kiss was a chrysalis. Now she more closely resembled the floor of a large cage...one that relied on shadows cast by high walls instead of steel bars to keep him penned in and to prevent him from straying... from growing.

As the night wind stung his watering eyes, he began to formulate his rather un-ambitious plan for the remainder of the evening. The gods above had squatted and taken a collective shit on his one free day, but perhaps something resembling fun could still be salvaged from the later hours. Of course, he would have to wait for his mother to go to bed first. But damn it all, the second that Miriam's bedroom door clicked shut he was going to raid her wine cabinet like a lucky tin-pan ravaging the town's most requested whore. Gaining access to the rack would prove to be no challenge whatsoever, not after he procured the little key she had tried in vain to keep hidden from her son.

His frown turned into an impish smirk. It had taken him no time at all to locate that key, for by now he knew just how her thoughts spun. Some months ago, he discovered it in the left pocket of her kitchen apron, and he made sure to replace it each time he raided her stash. And Quinn was always very judicious in his pilfering. He knew better than to leave an empty bottle in her rack, of course. But tonight, he might be inclined to leave a stronger clue—one that clearly represented his disdain for the duties assigned him this wintry day.

Yes, polishing off half a bottle or so would ironically be his reward for polishing all those damned pews, and it would at least par-

tially numb the dread that always preceded those cursed services on
Sunaday mornings.

As his boots crunched through the snow, he silently wondered
if his aversion would metastasize even further. He wondered if his
precious Friday nights would become the next casualties of his un-
easiness and loathing. Shit! How he hated those redundant services.
He figured that he hated them every bit as much as his mother seemed
to love them...and he loved her. She was all that he had. He could
never hurt her, but his patience regarding all this Church idiocy was
growing thinner by the hour.

"I'll get a glimpse of Haeven tomorrow, but it won't be granted
by Sigmund, that pig," Quinn assured himself through chattering
teeth. His shoulders relaxed and his grimace softened as he pondered
the irony: his single favorite event of the week occurred on his least
favorite day. Church services be damned, he would still get to see
Catherine and dive into her shimmering eyes, but only for a few precious seconds...a few precious seconds that would have to last him
for an entire week, thanks to her damned Aunt Burdagette's decision
to pull Catherine out of Quinn's class and hire a private tutor so that
her niece would not be *forced to mingle with all those unsavory types*.

"Good old Auntie Burdagette," Quinn mumbled while he pulled
the hood of his cloak forward. As he watched his breath dissipate on
the wind, he gave himself permission for the hundredth time to throttle that old biddy with a boot string if pointing ever came to pissing.
If her snobbish insistence became the only obstacle to Quinn's dearest wish—to spend the rest of his life making her niece feel like a
princess—then he would all too eagerly steal into the old lady's room
in the middle of the night, place a pillow over her smug and snoring
sneer, and fight to suppress his own howls of delight as he felt her
sour spirit leave her pruny shell of a body so that it could speed its
way toward the hungry maw of Hel.

"Good old Auntie Burdagette," he repeated in a low chuckle.
"There is just no way that those two leaves sprouted from the same
tree." As he strode down the white lane, he shook his head just as he
did every time he saw Catherine and her withered aunt standing side
by side. *The goddess and the goat*.

The *goat* clearly loathed him, but Quinn was infinitely more intimidated by the *goddess*. A single wink from her could make his
heart stop...then another wink would compel it to start beating yet

again. Her delicate hands definitely held the reins to his soul. Somehow, the sting of cold winter wind abated as he imagined her walking beside him tonight with her arm wrapped around his like some hungry vine and with her head leaning against his shoulder as they crunched through the snow together…together as they headed toward home.

Tomorrow, he would stand paralyzed and mute like some witless statue as she appraised him with those scheming opal orbs which had conquered his will well over a year ago. Tomorrow, she would greet him on the sanctuary steps and repeat the seductive little ritual upon which Quinn relied to sustain his sanity…his pathetic hopes.

*Worthless church services be damned!* Quinn almost forgot to breathe as his spirit splashed around in the pool of blissful prospects. Not two weeks agone, dear Aunt Burdagette succumbed to a fever and Catherine attended the services unaccompanied. That wondrous day, she took a seat just to the left of Quinn. Shortly after the congregation was seated for the so-called message, she wove her fingers through his and held his hand for the remainder of the service. He did not wash his hand for two days after that, not until every trace of her beguiling perfume had faded from his calloused palm. For two days, he kept his nose buried in the creases of his left hand.

*Tomorrow, I'm just going to ask her what fragrance she wears and then by damn I'm going to buy two bottles of that spirit-shattering fragrance. I'll give one to her as a present; the other, I'll keep for my own periodic…needs.*

In the near darkness, he tripped over one of the uneven joints in the sidewalk and very nearly went down on his knees. His gloveless hands, already numb from the cold, plunged into the deep drift as they arrested his fall. In seconds, they were aching from the effects of their submersion in the wet snow. Quinn did his best to fling away the wintry slush before cramming both hands back into the deep pockets of his coat.

"Fucking retarded councilmen!" he yelled into the darkness as he spun completely around so as not to ignore any of the surrounding shadows. Then he looked up at the laughable little lamp that swung above his head and he felt obligated to repeat his curse, though clearly no one was around to hear him…not as far as he knew. Sensation was finally returning to his fingers, but his wounded toes were throbbing, and the pain in his foot did little to improve his mood.

After kicking his injured toes away from the end of his boot, he trudged on but he made sure to lift his feet a little further off the ground as he strode from one pale sphere of dim light to the next. His temper cooled and his pace slowed as he allowed himself to once again become lost in non-thought, hypnotized by the rhythmic crunch produced by each of his deliberate steps.

Quinn didn't hear a thing as she stepped out of the inky blackness and into the dim gray glow beneath one of the street lights off to his left. At first, he thought that the dark shape was just his own shadow tracking him, but ordinary shadows could not be cast without light, and there was precious little of that this evening. Still, he dismissed the dark form's approach…until he heard the volley of nervous giggling. Though he did not draw it completely from its worn sheath, he grabbed the hilt of his knife and dropped into a defensive crouch out of instinct; but a quick assessment of this stooped newcomer clearly indicated that the old hag certainly posed no threat to him…not any physical threat, at least.

"A bit jumpy are we, Master Tabor?" she snickered in a coarse whisper. She reached up with her left hand to brush away an errant stream of spittle that dripped off her cadaverous chin. The old lady was dressed in motley rags that were likely quite gaudy when viewed beneath the daystar's full light, but in this manner of darkness she appeared to be wrapped in some soiled quilt, a patchwork of all the darker shades of gray. A tattered scarf held her long, white hair back and away from her eyes…eyes that seemed every bit as colorless as her oily locks.

*A fortune teller! Damn it!* Miriam always warned him to steer clear of these wicked women. *Wenches sent straight up from Hel*, he remembered her saying on more than one occasion regarding the strange women that claimed divination and clairvoyance among their other questionable talents. *Sent straight from Hel to steal your money and to confuse your gods-fearing mind.*

"…and to make you nearly soil yourself," Quinn muttered while he waited for his breath to return.

"What was that, Master Tabor?" she cackled "You didn't actually soil…?"

"Do I know you, ma'am? You seem to have me at a bit of a disadvantage," Quinn replied, doing his best to keep his voice from wavering. Her unblinking stare reminded him of a cat readying itself to pounce on a mouse. The skin on the back of his neck tingled, and his heart simply refused to quit hammering away at his ribs.

"*Disadvantage*. Such a strange word, is it not?" she asked as her eyes stared upward and to her right, directly at the first of El-dimorah's rising moons. She did not move or speak for a few seconds, then those eyes slowly lowered to meet Quinn's gaze and her noxious grin grew even wider. "Stranger still that you, of all people, should use it. Irony is a cruel master. It beats its steed so that none of its appointments are missed. Irony always arrives in time. I have observed as much. And *Irony* abounds, does it not, Master Tabor? Yes?"

A single violent cough forced her to stumble forward a step. "No, you do not know me. Truth be told, no one really knows me, laddie. I suppose a few know my name, but that is all. They do not know who I am...*what* I am. No person of any station in this city would so much as piss on me if my robe was in flames. After all, no one wants to be even loosely associated with a crazy old woman," she spat with some impediment resembling a wet lisp. "Just as well. Insane I may well be, young one. But still...still, I see what others do not. So either they are correct, and I *am* truly insane...or perhaps my mind is every bit as sound as brick and mortar, and it is they who are truly blind," she managed to blurt out before a spell of unnerving giggling made her frail old shoulders shake as though she was an untrained rider sitting the saddle of a prancing horse.

That stifled snicker suddenly evolved into full-scale laughter that sent a shiver up Quinn's spine. Her head tilted back and even the dim excuse for light revealed that she sported but a single tooth up front, and it was well on its way to rotting out like its neighbors apparently had done some time ago. The night air once again surrendered to silence, and she dropped into a low crouch as though she had just been punched in her gut. Her earlier amusement disappeared in less than an instant, like the slamming of a door caught by a gust of wind. Her demeanor sobered, and there was genuine trepidation in her eyes... eyes that nervously scanned the surrounding shadows like those of a grazing rabbit watching for any signs of a wolf on the hunt.

Quinn began to bleed sweat despite the cold night air that assailed him. At the moment, he wanted nothing more than to put distance between himself and this hag. As he started to back away, the oddly-dressed woman's hand shot out and grabbed his left arm just above his wrist. Although her arthritic hand was gnarled and eerily skeletal, her grip was firm and amazingly so…so much so that it gave him little choice but to stand where he was, at least until his nerves settled sufficiently for his addled mind to formulate a better plan.

Those gray eyes squinted as they slowly slithered in so that she could more easily study his frowning face…so that she could look even deeper into his soul and study the secrets that resided there. His discomfort, already rather overwhelming, only ballooned under that silent but intense scrutiny. When at last her rigid grip on his arm relaxed to a degree, he shifted to march right around her, but before he could manage to take a single step, her hoarse voice broke the silence. His fear ebbed as his curiosity intensified. His fear ebbed…but barely so.

"No, you do not know me, but I know *you*, Quinn Tabor," she hissed, thrusting a twisted forefinger toward his chest as though she sought to stab him and pin him to the spot with some crooked dagger fashioned from a bony fossil. He flinched and leaned away from the perceived attack. "I know who you are, but more importantly, I know what you are to become. You have been named *Chosen* by the same Church you so despise; and though you have never been told as much, the tainted blood of Valenesti runs in your veins. If ever there was a combination ordained, better suited for the birth of chaos…" she trailed off in a whisper as her head bowed. Then, in a booming wail that was actually two disparate voices screaming in dissonant unison—one a piercing shriek, the other a low, primitive roar—she threw her head back and shouted into the silence, "…better suited for the rape and ruin of angels!"

The disturbing echoes died quickly, thanks in part to the muffling effects of the newly fallen snow. Quinn's earlier fear returned in a suffocating rush; he could taste it on his tongue now. His breathing was suddenly shallow and rapid. Every instinct ordered him to flee, but his muscles simply would not obey his commands in that chilling moment. That voice had not been of this realm. It was a frightened scream from a little girl who had just torn her hand open on a rusty nail, and the low but vicious snarl of a mother bear protecting her cub…in eerie harmony. The old hag's shoulders rolled forward and she coughed up a bolus of phlegm, then resumed her more human giggle. Her downcast eyes were almost apologetic, as if the outburst had been unplanned…as if it had caught her completely unawares as well. She shook her head and patted his arm, but the gesture was anything but comforting.

"I have to be on my way, old woman. I have no coin on me, so go pester some other. Perhaps the next citizen you startle the shit out of will fork over enough coppers to allow you to procure a bottle that you can nurse through this cold night. I have no idea what you are talking about...and you probably don't either, for that matter. My mother says that you people are only good at one thing, and that is making a profit off of others' fears." Hearing his own voice bolstered his own confidence, but not by a whole lot.

"Oh, that's what she says, does she? That's what she says, Master Tabor?" the aging woman cackled as she covered her mouth with the back of her hand, but not before Quinn caught another glimpse of the lone tooth.

"She does. Now, if you will excuse me..." Quinn tried to step around the beldam, but she suddenly shifted to her left, demonstrating a level of nimbleness that belied her advancing years. Once again she blocked his progress, and once more Quinn's hand shot to the hilt of his dagger, a gesture that did not go unnoticed by the hag this time. However she never broke eye contact with Quinn, and if she felt any intimidation from his restrained threat, she certainly did not show it. Her grin spread even wider, in fact...a grin that was just a black gash lined by thin lips and bare gums.

"You'll not be needing that blade, boy. Not tonight...not against me. No. I mean you no harm, I assure you. That blade there," she nodded toward his belt, "will take two lives before the month is out, you should know. Mark my words. And it shall not be my blood that it spills. Though in all honesty, I'd much rather be skewered by the blade you now carry than by the one which you will soon be given."

"Oh? Really? And just who is going to give me this new blade that you so clearly see in my future? This one *is* getting a bit worn, now that you mention it," Quinn quipped.

"Your father. Shortly, he will present you with a new and very special blade...a very special blade indeed. Yes. Furthermore, he will warn you to keep it close like a lover and show it to no one. Remember what I say! Have you heard me, Quinn?"

After taking a breath and allowing himself to finally relax just a bit, Quinn threw his hands up and chuckled. "Well, old woman, that tells me all I need to know about your abilities. It tells me all I need to know about your authenticity...your lack of it, rather. If you're any kind of adept seer, then I'm a pregnant pooch lugging around a pair of fuzzy balls! My father won't be giving me any gifts any time soon, because he…"

"…has been dead for near to ten years," she finished the sentence for him even as she futilely tried to bite one of her filthy yellow nails with her lone tooth and a smooth gum. "Yes, I know. I know."

Try as he might, Quinn just could not disguise his alarm. He stood and stared at the old woman while his chapped lips contorted and quivered. For several seconds, neither of them spoke; all Quinn could hear was the sharp rasp of his own breathing, and each breath came out in a cloud that scattered before the brisk breeze.

Had he not been so stunned by her last words, perhaps he would have noticed that no such mists formed when she exhaled…and there were none when she spoke. Had he been paying closer attention, had he been studying anything other than her ashen eyes, he would have seen that the snow around her feet was smooth and utterly undis-turbed. "You were only ten or so, I believe…were you not, Quinn?" she asked in a man's voice, a bass voice that in no way resembled her original one. It was the voice of Tomas Tabor. Quinn stumbled back a step and blinked against a flood of searing tears.

"Damn you! How dare you use his voice?" Quinn rasped as he battled to regain his composure. "Alright then, can you tell me how he died?" Quinn swallowed with some effort, but he stood his ground. Her shifting intonations were seven steps beyond unsettling. Still, he was determined to interrogate her until she was revealed as a fraud.

"I know how you *think* that he died. You were told that Tomas passed because of a taint…the dreaded wasting sickness, yes? You and your mother were both led to believe that. Well, you were both misled, I'm sorry to say. It was poison, lad. Poison!"

"Now I know that you're loony. I was in the fucking room, hag! I was only ten, but I remember standing there while the healers ex-amined him and said…"

"The healers that were sent by the Church? Oh, please! Oh, please, Quinn! Of course they told you…" the crone shook her head and wrung her crippled hands in obvious frustration. "Those so-called healers were agents of the very ones that ordered him poisoned, boy!" She shuffled just a step or two toward him and continued in a con-spiratorial whisper. Once again, her eyes scanned the shadows. "The

Church ordered your father poisoned, Quinn Tabor…and he knew the truth. Yes. He died knowing the truth, all to protect you and your mother."

"Care and caution lad, those be your bestest friends from now on. Them others that you count among your friends may not be there for you when things start to fall apart." The soothsayer took yet another tentative step toward him, stopping when their noses were just a couple of links apart. He was almost overwhelmed by her fetid, freezing breath as she continued her rant in a dramatic whisper. "And fall apart they will, sooner than later, I fear. Sooner than later."

Her hand settled ever so gently on his forearm, so gently that he could barely feel the pressure on his cloak's sleeve. But then he felt the cold serpent summoned by her unspoken spell cling to his arm and slither toward his chest—a searing hot spiral that climbed the bones of his arm like a vine wrapping around a porous stone column. The second that it reached his shoulder, it took a sharp turn and sped straight toward the heart, a stygian arrow fletched with raven feathers arcing toward its unsuspecting target. Quinn felt an instant of crushing pain in his chest and his vision—already challenged by the dim light—grew blurrier still. He battled a brief attack of nausea, but the sickening sensations finally receded and his vision returned to normal in an instant. It all transpired so quickly, he had been granted no chance to flinch or even blink.

"What did you just do to me?" Quinn wheezed after he leaned forward to rest his hands on his knees. Only then did he notice that his knees were quivering, certainly more from fear than cold. "What did you just do to me, you…you bitch?!" he demanded. There was more force behind his voice this time.

"I just gave you a little gift. One that I fear you will find very useful before long. It is the gift of…well, I guess we could call it *Cruelty*. Every human heart possesses it, Quinn; every spirit harbors its seed. A measure of it at least. We just thought that you might need to have yours…*supplemented* if you are to come through all of this alive. Hear me. Hear us. You will likely not be intact, but you will—at the very least—survive. This little gift, it will help you become what you cannot otherwise be. We have done you no harm, I assure you. We wish you no harm…far from it, in fact."

"*We*? Did you just say *we*? You are most likely talking about yourself and all the other voices floating around in that bat shit brain.

But don't you ever touch me again! I'm warning you..." Quinn backed away a step and tightened his fingers around the hilt of his knife yet again.

"Ah, that...there are no other voices, Quinn. Just one. You only need know that there are others who want very much for you to succeed in your endeavors. If you fail, then victory will go to the enemy, and the consequences of that victory shall be dire. The spoils of that victory shall be *considerable*, you see." She lowered her head and stared at the undisturbed snow at her feet. Whether it was a melting snowflake or just a trick of the faint light, it appeared as if a single tear formed on her left cheek as she bowed.

"I still say that you have lost your mind, old bat." Quinn's voice was now little more than a harsh whisper; it lacked most of its earlier ire, and he continued to rub his chest where fate had buried her latest arrow.

"You do not know me, Quinn Tabor. But I fear the day is quickly approaching when you will remember me...my words, at least. Soon, you will discover just who and what you really are. Be aware that you may well be dissatisfied by what you learn. Every man is ultimately plagued by certain...philosophical considerations, let us say. Matters that taunt them in the solitary hours when they are left alone with their own thoughts and their own somber memories."

"All mortals try to make peace with ourselves at some point, Quinn Tabor. We go to great lengths to justify our darker deeds. When all is said and done, we are all but gnats swarming around a rotten melon. Yet, it is still in our nature to strive for absolution and climb the ladder to a Truhaeven that, alas," she paused and shook her head, "does not even exist. We try—sometimes at the expense of our own sanity—to reconcile all the niggling disparities and vague little distinctions which assail our conscience. Distinctions, Quinn...distinctions between true life and true death, in your case. Yes. Yes. That will no doubt define your impending battle. I wish it could be different, but fate owes me no favors. It owes favors to no one!"

She bowed her head again and became perfectly still. For a moment, Quinn thought the crazy old crone had lapsed into some kind of trance. Perhaps she had simply fallen asleep. Perhaps this would be a good time to slip past her? Suddenly she snapped her head up and pointed at him with that same distorted finger. However, the fires of a fierce new determination now burned in those eerie, albino eyes.

"*Those* distinctions will be your devils, boy, and they are going to haunt you like they have haunted no other. In the dark days that lie ahead you will revel in the rapture of taking lives, though you now think yourself incapable of such a black deed. You will become a slayer. You will rend flesh and spill blood, all in the name of simple vengeance. And you will, out of sheer desperation...and sorrow... endeavor to restore life that is not really life—anything but, I'm afraid. Yes. I fear it is your destiny to propagate the curse visited upon your kinsman, dear old Valenesti. Dear old Valenesti..." she repeated, and her wet bottom lip now stuck out as if she was just a pouting toddler.

That last nerve that Quinn had so hoped to shield was now ruined, and his patience had worn thinner than a beggar's boot sock. He was suddenly aware that his cloak was too thin as well. The night had become colder than its snow.

"I don't have time for any more of your foolishness, hag! Be gone. Be gone! I am freezing, and you are clearly nuttier than a squirrel's spring turd," Quinn shouted. He sprinted around the old woman, taking his chances on the uneven cobblestones as he raced down the poorly lit street toward the safety and comfort of home.

"Enjoy your trip next month, laddie!" she shouted in that inhuman rumble beneath a shriek. He had no idea what trip she was referring to, but at the moment his only point of focus was to put a door and a stout bolt between himself and his wrinkled, toothless tormentor. Hearing that abominable voice a second time put extra spring in his legs as he raced along the poorly lit lane. Its echoes chased him like a pack of hungry wolves. For a few terrifying seconds, it sounded like they were gaining on him, but then they fell behind...they fell silent. Luckily, Quinn navigated the dim and icy street without losing his balance even once. After he figured he had placed sufficient distance between himself and the loony old hag, he allowed himself to slow his pace to a brisk walk and took advantage of that slower gait to catch his breath.

"What the holy fuck was that all about?" he wheezed to himself as he started to climb the familiar stairs to the apartment that he and his mother had shared ever since his dad passed away. Fatigue prompted Quinn to drag his right hand along the worn railing. He applied just enough pressure to coax a coiled, concealed splinter to reach out and slither beneath his skin. The sting was immediate; the pure pain was impossible to ignore.

"Gods! Damn this night!" he cursed in a mumble, for the bleeding finger was already crammed into his mouth. Soon, however, the coppery taste of fresh blood would be washed away by the burgundy vintage of paradise, he assured himself. Hopefully, his mother was already asleep and he would be allowed to forego all the unimportant chatter in which he really hated to engage, especially after spending his Saturnday cleaning that damned church sanctuary.

Aside from that, his encounter with the smelly old self-proclaimed seer had rattled him a bit...far more than a bit, he had to admit to himself after he finally locked the door behind him. His hand was shaking so badly he could hear his keys tinkling together on their ring.

One component of his prior plans for the rest of the evening had changed, to be sure. Only half a bottle of wine? Nope. Not quite. He now had more on his mind than could possibly be drowned by a single carafe; that would hardly suffice. He meant to down the whole damn bottle and bury the empty at the bottom of their trash. If need be, he would uncork yet another. He was determined to throw back as many glasses of his mother's cheap vintage as necessary until the old hag's words no longer resounded in his head. Even as he strode into the kitchen to retrieve the key from her apron, he feared that more than wine would be required to smother the echoes of the old woman's final shriek.

◆◆◆

The next few weeks passed by steadily but slowly, like a river whose lazy eddies and tranquil currents represented time staggering forward like some sluggish drunk. It crawled. It did pass, but at a rate that was agonizingly slow...far too slow to be mistaken for progress, and the numbing pace was driving Quinn up the proverbial wall. To make matters worse, his encounter with the old crone beneath the streetlamp was a memory that he just could not erase, although he could attribute much of her convoluted ramblings to the likelihood that her upstairs room had too many corners and too few candles. Still there was no denying that she had known things about him that no stranger should have known, and the ominous tones that colored her cryptic discourse haunted him.

Whatever her motivations might have been, she had seen fit to offer him her version of a warning, and portions of it were bellowed in that chilling, distorted roar. Memories of that unearthly wail still made him shiver, even when he was inside his home, safely seated beside the warm stove and protected by a chained and bolted door. Certainly, the little drama that had unfolded beneath the streetlamp that night left ragged scars all across the formerly lustrous surface of that illusion that he used to call *security*. Lately though, Quinn noticed that security recoiling like a wounded animal, leaving him to stand alone in this new arena of apprehension. He was now more aware than ever that anxiety's sentries tended to advance whenever the illusion of haven retreated.

And more anxiety was all that he needed right now, for boredom and restlessness had already established themselves as his new nemeses. Boredom and restlessness…twin beasts with sharp teeth and thick, enduring hides. Quinn felt stuck and stifled, a wagon whose wheels were caught in ruts brimming with thick mire; a gagged man aching to shout his frustration to the unsympathetic sky. Every chime that emanated from the clock on the mantle teasingly remind him of how very stagnant the world around him had become. He felt like some dimwitted quarry whose ankles had been caught in a cleverly concealed snare. Hoisted into the cold but cloying air, he had been relegated to an inverted view of a world which had ceased to spin. He was a wanderer seeking shelter from his insipid days; a whistling kettle left to boil; a chained beast begging for release.

As he waved the flag of regretful surrender, Quinn retreated into a shell of serene silence. He closed his ears and opened his eyes; he temporarily handed them the reins of his awareness. He allowed his eyes to become the sole authors of his private journal.

They turned his otherwise bland experiences into noiseless and perfect images caught in time. Quinn saw everything, but he chose to hear nothing. A flag flapping in the wind, an eagle riding the morning thermals, two new lovers sneaking a kiss in the park. Each silent and discreet slice of an instant became a memory, but they were destined to become his memories and no one else's. Those memories—vivid and precious though they were—might as well be pieces of art hanging in a black gallery, a shuttered and forgotten museum bereft of light.

All the while, he walked alone. He pragmatically recognized that each of his desires was doomed to become nothing more than a daydream, and all the while, he lamentably acknowledged that every wish he voiced was ultimately only a sad soliloquy. Surrounded by a sea of people, he found himself utterly alone.

◆◆◆

To make matters even worse, today was Sunaday. Ah, yes. Another Sunaday morning and Quinn sat still as frozen stone, even while his gut was writhing like a beheaded adder. Not a muscle moved, for he was well past the point of even nervous agitation. Twiddling his thumbs, drumming his fingers on the hard seat of the pew—none of those tricks worked anymore. He sat still, certainly not out of any manner of reverence for the Way, but as an indication of sheer detachment. As always, daydreams were his salvation. He invoked them to step in and deftly slay the seconds as he served his weekly sentence in this vast hall that might as well be a tiny prison cell.

And he would be required to repeat the same absurd routine next week unless he was lucky enough to succumb to a fever next Saturday night. There was always that hope. Perhaps if he let one of Eldrshok's homeless beggars sneeze in his face...perhaps if he then doused himself with water and ran through the snow wearing nothing but his boots...?

Quinn closed his eyes for a moment. Before he allowed himself to open them again, he promised himself that he would not so much as glance at the pulpit today; in truth, he didn't think he could stomach the sight. Quite absently, he peered down at his hands as they rested on his knees. He tried to tune out every chorus from the choir, every cough from the congregation, every last nuance of today's silly mass which was in no tiny way any different from last week's. For lack of anything else to ponder, he focused on his fingertips. And then he watched them, at least without any initial reaction, as they started to turn...purple?!

"Shit!" he thought as he flinched, banging his heels against the base of his pew. Then he froze, wondering if he had actually shouted out loud. No one around him so much as stirred or glanced at him, so he assumed that his reaction had gone unnoticed by the entranced members of the congregation seated all around him. Purple? He blinked hard and looked once more at his fingers. Though its advance was barely perceptible, the discoloration had already reached his second knuckle and was continuing to creep ever so steadily toward his wrists.

Reason returned and alarm eventually receded after a quick assessment of his situation revealed the cause of his consternation… the etiology of his imagined affliction. Quinn had neglected to notice the new stained glass windows which had been installed just this past week. The bright rays of late morning were filtering through one of the new images adorning the southern wall of the sanctuary. It was the image of a regal angel with wings spread wide, an angel with angular features—one whose eyes were twin wells of brilliant lavender.

Outside the sanctuary, the clouds parted briefly as the daystar climbed toward its noon loft. Its brilliant winter light passed through all the prisms of purple, projecting the angel's focused gaze by way of two distinct beams of lavender light which swept across the sanctuary; and Quinn just happened to be seated in their path…precisely where those beams converged.

He stared into those eyes every bit as intently as he had been staring at his hands just a few seconds earlier. The handsome angel's strange eyes—devoid of anything even resembling a pupil—provided a welcome new distraction.

Time. If it had been crawling by before, its passage ceased entirely as he lost himself in those lavender prisms. They called to him in a chorus of silent cries. Quinn felt something stirring and squirming in his chest. He closed his eyes and the angel's face disappeared, but it was quickly replaced with the wrinkled countenance of the old seer. Not only did he see her face, he felt her gaunt hand resting on his arm…once more, he felt the serpent's coils hugging his heart. For an instant everything went black. When light at last returned, Quinn discovered that the taint of timidity no longer colored his vision. When light returned, he was once again staring at the windows…at the image of the grinning angel.

♦♦♦

Nothing had been necessarily wrong with the old windows as far as Quinn could tell, and the gods only knew that he had studied every pane hundreds of times over throughout the years. They hadn't appeared to be broken or chipped at all, but according to today's bulletin, Lord Invadrael had nevertheless insisted on the conversion, claiming that the new images were more congruent with the teachings of the New Way…more symbolic, or some such horseshit.

Following Lord Herodimae's recent passing, Invadrael had stepped forward to take the Name. Replacing the sanctuary windows was probably some stupid means of flexing his newly inherited muscle and pissing away some of the massive budget that was now part of his demesne. Quinn thought it a waste of time and resources. Then again, he had come to expect little from the Church apart from waste, repetition, and misplaced priorities.

With only one exception, the priests and other officers of the Church were a brotherhood of buffoons and nothing more. Why in Hel's name could the hundreds of adults now seated around him not just as easily see through the deception?

His curiosity was unquenchable and—by his own estimation— his mind had always been dynamic. Admittedly, it had always been restless as well. Whether these were attributes or flaws of character, they were nevertheless factors that made it increasingly difficult to sit still and endure the ridiculous repetition involved in these weekly...rallies.

Quinn wanted to spit. Instead, he swallowed...and the taste was unexpectedly bitter. He allowed himself a stifled yawn and stretched the stiff muscles in his neck. He harbored no desire to make a noise, yet someone inside of him continued to scream.

◆◆◆

*When will these godsdamned prayers ever end?* The hard pew was quickly making his rear end go numb, so he shifted his position to give a different area of his ass a turn to contend with the polished and unyielding wood. *Godsdamned prayers...what a tasty contradiction*, Quinn thought to himself as a smirk morphed into a yawn. Well before his mouth closed, he was congratulating himself on his private little sojourn to the indistinct borders of blasphemy.

While he sat in silence, he acknowledged that—ever since his fateful encounter with the hag—he had begun to fully embrace rebellion and the invigorating redemption that it boded. From his budding perspective, it was not some elusive concept as much as it was a bottle of elixir that sat before him, just waiting to be downed in a single gulp. It represented a heady tonic formulated just to fortify his emergent individuality.

Loneliness had begun to make him feel prematurely old, but regardless of how old his soul was beginning to feel, he reminded himself that he was most definitely a young man, damn it all. Rebellion. He needed to drink from its cask and quickly so. He so looked forward to treating himself to a long and satisfying draft, for it alone could slake the caustic thirst that threatened to quiet Quinn's true voice...the voice that was endeavoring to have its shouts heard above his self-imposed shell of silence.

Delicious rebellion...the proud herald of dissatisfaction...the trumpeter whose assigned tasks included announcing the inevitable retreat of innocence. Shadowed at times by its ally *resentment*, its arrival wasn't always necessarily uncomplicated, but it *was* always necessary—vital, even. Quinn intuitively knew that it was no less essential to his survival than the blood being pumped through his heart. At the moment, he wished that some of that blood would trickle down to offer some aid to his numb butt.

Sitting here bathed in lavender light and viewing all that surrounded him through a lens of renewed cynicism, he acknowledged that he had finally been ushered to the crossroads. He had just this second reached an inevitable decision. Rebellion was a cloak that he must fully don...today! Today, he must shrug off the last vestiges of adolescence's flimsy mantle. Of that, Quinn was certain, though he was certain of little else. In the course of just a few short weeks, he had grown into that cloak and he immediately liked the fit and feel of it. Yes, he would don it and wear it proudly, but it would more closely resemble armor...armor against ignorance! And *clarity* would fuel the fire that would temper his sword.

He straightened in his seat. Quinn smirked at the clever turn his internal dialogue had taken. Armor against ignorance. Yes! Armor. Perfect. While those around him regurgitated yet another tired verse pledging their undying service to their precious Church and its silly Way, Quinn was quietly phrasing a pledge of his own. Sitting amid a sea of acquiescent converts, he made a pact with himself that he would never outgrow his new armor, nor would he cast it aside for any cause constructed by submissive and unimaginative minds.

"No one will ever convince me that I cannot be...me," Quinn whispered. He could sense that Miriam cast a glance his way, but her attention quickly returned to the pulpit where Father Sigmund stood, grunting like he was battling to keep his bowels from emptying.

♦♦♦

The lavender "plague" had passed, and Quinn's fingers were now laced together, his hands resting casually in his lap. He had quite reflexively followed his subconscious prompts to mimic the others in the sanctuary. But whereas the others pressed their palms together as they sought some kind of peace through prayer to a host of imaginary gods, Quinn took the opportunity to seal his clandestine pact with an improvised handshake with himself.

Every plate of the armor was in place at last and its thick cuirass hugged him like a second skin. But unlike physical armor, this new mail of his was not a burden whatsoever. Indeed, he felt like he had just dropped a burden beside his special path, a path whose direction would be determined only by time. He knew not where it might lead; he only knew that it was a hidden road that could lead either to nowhere or everywhere. Everywhere and nowhere...twin destinations ultimately distinguished from one another only by a few discrete degrees of youthful perception.

As the service progressed, Quinn scanned the sanctuary and the members of its pitiable congregation. Everyone was clad in their little Sunaday uniforms. All of them were staring at the dais with the same blank expression pinned to each of their pasty faces. It was as if they were wholly mesmerized by some new play...some grand production that they had not, in fact, seen a hundred times over. Quinn caught himself shaking his head in bemusement. No one would likely notice his gesture, and he found he didn't give a whittler's damn if they did.

He kept his focus trained on his own pledge. *Individuality*. That was the well from which he would have to draw if he was to continue on the path that simple wisdom had been kind enough to carve for him...a path that was now so clear and unmistakable; one that bisected the maze of tangles and traps through which all these hypnotized neophytes wandered. As long as wisdom did not forsake him, Quinn knew that he would never fall into the same quagmire, the same spiritless swamp to which his *brethren* had so completely succumbed.

His new armor would protect him, but in turn he would have to protect it. It would need periodic polishing, of course. For that task he would use an amalgam of vigor and angst. They would be the perfect agents to remove any signs of tarnish induced by the corrosive effects of complacency. Vigor and angst...he would need both in his battle to avoid the fate that had befallen the vast majority of the fools seated around him.

Quinn squirmed in his unyielding seat, partly to punish a different pressure point on his rear, but he primarily wriggled with newfound excitement regarding his impending liberation from this cursed place...his final liberation, in fact. He would not return next week.

Already, he was readying for a battle of sorts. He imagined himself buckling on his helmet as his noble mount danced nervously beneath him. In unrelenting black waves, the screaming enemy was even now charging across a field which would soon be soaked with their own blood, not his. Fate was even now whispering in his ear that he was destined to emerge as victor. He would be the recipient of a few nicks and scratches, but no mortal wounds.

Defiance would be the tint used to dye his flag…antipathy would be the theme of his fierce battle cry. And his antipathy felt especially gratifying when it was directed at those fools up on the podium. Those fools robed in silk and cloaked in condescension. Those obese clowns who silently bowed and nodded to each other like shepherds changing shifts. The priests fancied themselves as guardians of secrets which only they shared, silly secrets of their own conjuring, secrets perpetuated for the sole purpose of wielding power over the mindless masses.

Yet again, Quinn wanted to spit in disgust as he watched the choreographed little production up on the stage. It was a circus of pomp and pointless ceremony…a glorified puppet show and nothing more. Hel, ungainly puppets on strings deserved far more respect than did these bloated jesters. Puppets on strings warranted far more credibility. Puppets were not born with a will, therefore they could not be blamed for surrendering it. Puppets were carved from wood, a noble and natural substrate. These robed dolts, on the other hand, were fashioned from layers of fat covered by pink, pampered skin.

He wanted to bolt toward the sanctuary doors; he did not belong here, and that fact had never been more evident. Still…here he sat glued to this blasted pew, sitting beside his mother who cherished the unexceptional services in a way he would probably never understand…and he didn't want to understand, damn it all! That was the crux of his dilemma: he dearly loved someone who was staunchly devoted to something that he detested. He wanted to grab her by her thin shoulders and gently shake some sense into her skull, not that she lacked any sense on the other six days of the week. That's what was so confounding, so frustrating. Why would anyone with her intelligence nuzzle her way into the herd just so she could follow the other sheep through the fallow fields of spiritual stupor?

Every week, he clinged to the hope that Miriam would come to her senses and see the services for the meaningless carnivals that they were. The gods knew that he would not intentionally hurt her for the world, so he had genuinely tried to keep his growing disdain for the Church masked, but it was no longer possible for him to maintain the deception. Damn! How had he let his love for Miriam lead him so far down this dead end road? He respected her and he could only hope that she would respect the decision he had made just minutes ago. Never again would he bow or kneel in this musty chapel!

He took a deep breath to calm himself. He realized that he had managed to work himself into a lather over a situation that he likely could not change. Not today, at least. He reminded himself that he would be on his way home in just a few more minutes. Once there, he would don his regular clothes and pitch his stupid suit into the corner one last time. Perhaps he would even go so far as to chunk it into their trash. Or maybe he would cast it out his bedroom window. He needed it no longer, for he now wore armor.

With a smirk playing at the corner of his mouth, Quinn said a silent prayer of his own. He prayed for a quick end to this blasted service, even if the more merciful gods saw fit to let the walls and roof of the sanctuary collapse as means to that end. He wanted to leave this place behind for good, and he would almost rather dig his way free through its rubble than leave through its doors.

Up in the pulpit, Sigmund's latest invocation dragged on. It always seemed as if each of his prayers lasted long enough for a mare to give birth to its foal, though Quinn knew that in reality it was usually just a matter of two or three minutes. As the bloated one bleated on about how the Church's "loving children" must strive to exhibit pity and patience for all the poor souls who had yet to accept the Way, Quinn's head remained bowed but only slightly so. That was where his conformity ended. It ended here...now. His eyes remained open...more open than ever.

At last, just before his impatience became almost too strong to bear, the pipe organ began to bellow the majestic notes of the benediction, signaling to Quinn that the end of the torment was at hand. He shot to his feet and arched his back as he guiltlessly surrendered to the urge to actually massage the feeling back into his rump. Miriam nudged him in the ribs to demand his attention.

"Now, wasn't that a lovely service, dear heart?" she asked in a voice that was peppered with more than just a dash of displeasure. She noticed that he had kept his eyes open during the last of the damned prayers. Her question was a trap, but he felt no compunctions about springing it.

"Oh, definitely. Every bit as lovely as last week's…and the one from the week before…" he answered. His reply had been ambiguous enough, but his tone had not. Who was he kidding? He had reached the point where his passive aggression was becoming far less passive.

Miriam somehow managed to simultaneously squint and arch an eyebrow at her son. His glib words had hit their mark and had not slipped past her. Even better!

*Shit,* he thought to himself as he held Miriam's gaze for a few seconds, *why do you—all of you—feel obligated to go through the motions every single week? What are you trying to prove? What exactly are you supposed to be learning from all this kneeling, chanting, and singing? Why are you intent on taking "sheep lessons"? Why can you not just…?*

"Quinn," the deep voice tolled from right behind him, "you *boys* did a marvelous job yesterday, I must say."

"Excellent. Thank you for noticing," Quinn replied as his eyes rolled toward the ceiling of the cathedral…again. Unfortunately, he recognized the voice before he even turned around. It was old man Brailer, Devon Brailer's dad. Devon had been one of the four other young men *recruited* to help clean the sanctuary yesterday. As the youngest of the boys, Devon's inexperience made him an easy mark for his older chums and their conspiracies. After a rigged round of drawing straws, Quinn had somehow wound up with the relatively easy assignment of polishing the pews, while Devon won the dubious honor of sweeping the floors. Sweeping in and of itself was not so bad; but the coarse grouting between the tiles in the sanctuary made the chore incredibly enervating. Quinn had learned as much from past experience—an experience he would never repeat.

"These pews are so slick, I almost slid out of mine twice during the service," old man Brailer joked, but there was not the first glimmer of humor in his…eyes.

"Yessir, me too…at least twice. Actually I lost count around…" Quinn quipped, drawing a quick elbow in the ribs from Miriam. "Thank you sir, we worked real hard," he quickly added as he rubbed his side, but the bruising blow did little to dispel his impish grin or his sarcastic tone.

"That you did, my *boy.* And might I say that the floors look es-

pecially tidy," Mr. Brailer rasped as he winked at Quinn with his right
eye. It was Sunaday, but his left eye was already looking toward
Tuesday. Ever since Quinn had known the man, Brailer had never
been able to put both eyes on the same target. He could watch the
daystar rise and set without ever turning his head. At any rate, he
smiled weakly as he gave young Master Tabor a knowing look. His
divergent eyes narrowed in a squint that silently shouted disapproval...one that guaranteed eventual retribution in some form or
fashion.

"Yessir, Devon did a right good job with them, he did," Quinn
stammered as he half-heartedly sought to exonerate himself from the
rigged drawing of the straws. He didn't fear any reprimand that this
old fart could dish out, he just wanted the conversation to end so that
he could get home and shed his blasted suit once and for all. "Why,
he practically swept the whole cathedral himself by the time me and
the others had completed our own sentences, I mean *chores*. Of
course, we pitched in to help him as soon as we could, you understand," Quinn tacked on with a grin that was definitely not intended
to convey anything resembling sincerity.

"Why yes, he did mention something about you four helping
him...there at the *very* end. I'm sure you all were quite anxious to be
gone from here after a full day of labor, weren't you lad? Or is it still
even considered an honor to serve the Way by preparing this blessed
sanctuary for Sunaday services? I'm curious. Which is it, Master
Quinn? Honor or labor? Hmm?" This conversation was rapidly turning into an inquisition, Quinn thought to himself as he nodded his
head, but he wasn't about to back down from this bug-eyed bastard.
His black steed whinnied and reared; his new armor pinched the skin
stretched across his chest.

"Oh, I'd definitely have to say *labor*," Quinn answered without
any hesitation at all. The old prick wasn't the least bit intimidating,
and a swift kick in his ball bag would quickly put him in his place.
For a second...maybe ten...Quinn fancied himself as the one delegated to deliver that attitude-altering blow. The visual must have
prompted his smirk to spread like a puddle of fresh piss, because
Brailer's frown suddenly deepened and his eyes moved even further
apart than normal.

"Hmmph! Chosen the path of disrespect, now have you? Considering your upbringing, or lack of it, I guess I shouldn't be too sur-

prised. I'll be sure and pray for you," he tacked on as one eye labored to meet Miriam's stunned gaze.

"While we're on the topic of upbringing," Quinn growled, "should Devon manage to become anything beside a pompous, wall-eyed faggot, then I'm gonna lose two silvers. You see, there is a pool among those of us whose parents aren't bloated, entitled fu…"

"Well, maybe next time, you *boys* should leave the straws in the brooms. You can sweep the floors a lot faster that way," the old geezer commented as he turned toward the doors at the back of the chapel. "A blessed day to you and to…yours, Miss Miriam. Best of luck turning that one around so that he can face the light of the Way," he whispered in an exasperated wheeze before disappearing into the crowd filing up the aisle.

*There isn't going to be a next time!* Quinn came close to shouting at the retreating bastard's back. *I've spent my last Saturnday tidying up this spiritual slop jar that you call a sanctuary. Fucker!*

"And just what the devil was he talking about, Quinn? What did you boys do to poor Devon?" Miriam hissed as she grabbed his elbow. Her manicured nails dug into his skin even through the sleeves of his jacket and shirt. This was perhaps not the time for a reprimand, but she was perfectly capable of conveying her displeasure to Quinn without cuing in anyone else; she did so with a smile that was anything but. It was the detached grin of a cat toying with a mouse. Her lips smiled but her eyes did not.

"Devil? Really, Mother. Let us remember where we are, after all," he sang in sweet tones that dripped with sarcasm. He even lay one hand across his heart melodramatically, feigning shock that he was clearly incapable of feeling. He knew where her buttons were, and over the years he had learned just how to push them. "As a devout student of the Way, you know full well that no Church member worth her weight in salt would dare invoke a devil while standing in the middle of Eldr-shok's sacred sanctuary. Let's see," he continued as he stared at the ceiling, tapping his chin with a lone finger, "does that not count as blasphemy according to the Way? I don't recall the precise book and chapter, but…"

Miriam knew her son was being a smartass, but she nevertheless blushed and looked around anxiously, praying that none of the other churchgoers had heard her oath. As it turned out though, she had nothing to worry about. Almost everyone had already abandoned their seats; by now, they were all far too occupied with their retreat from the crowded cathedral to have heard her conversation with Quinn. When the route cleared, mother and son stepped out into the aisle and made their own way toward the bank of doors at the back of the sanctuary. Still sporting the fake smile expressly for the benefit of the other members, she leaned toward Quinn's ear.

"You didn't answer my question, dear heart," she pointed out just as they reached the rear of the line at the southernmost doors. She spoke through clenched teeth. Miriam nodded politely to one of the acolytes holding the doors open as she stepped through the portal; but then their progress halted. Too many thoughtless idiots had stopped to visit with each other in the broad alcove that sheltered the exits, so Quinn and Miriam had to push their way through all the clustered pods of inconsiderate pricks. Miriam was polite, as always, and begged pardon as she wove between the giggling gossipmongers. Quinn, on the other hand, wasn't bound by quite the same code of etiquette. He used his elbow more than once to remind a fellow attendee that they were blocking the doors…that they should be more thoughtful and just migrate back to their pathetic little pockets of bogus domestic bliss.

"We didn't do anything to him. The luck of the draw just wasn't with him yesterday." Had he even been trying, Quinn couldn't have held back his mischievous smile as he glanced at Miriam. "Why would that even matter to you? I have to ask. Mom, that bug-eyed bastard just maligned your integrity and parenting skills to your face. Besides, you've always said that Anna Brailer is the biggest bit…"

"That's not exactly the point, Quinn…dearest," she said loudly, interrupting him just in time. Her grip on his arm tightened…her nails came near to drawing blood.

"I know! The *point* is that nothing that I could do to Devon is going to make your social life any less dismal. I'm not trying to be mean, either," Quinn asserted, but she knew that much already. "You're just envious because you've never been granted an opportunity to make sure that Anna Brailer drew the short straw. That's it! Am I right?" His beguiling smirk returned, and virtually all traces of annoyance fled from Miriam's face. Annoyance fled and coy feistiness readily rushed in to replace it.

"Score one for my crafty little rascal," she muttered as she snaked her arm affectionately through his when they finally broke free from the crowd. They stepped into the unobstructed cold and started down the stairs. It was certainly a petty victory, and a vicarious one at that; still, she drew some comfort from the notion of Anna's face turning red as a beet after finding out why her son was so late getting home the previous evening…after discovering whose son was likely to blame, at least in part.

"And Anna Brailer is a bitch among bitches," Miriam whispered to her son after casting about to make sure that no one could hear her. With a stifled chuckle, she squeezed Quinn's forearm in silent appreciation for his wiliness. "From whom did you learn to be so devious, I have to wonder?" she whispered to him.

"I learned it back when I was an orphan on the streets, stealing radishes, picking pockets, and pleasuring warped old men for three coppers per…round."

"Gods! What a mouth! You're a true smartass, but you already know that."

"Yup. I rehearse in front of the mirror every morning. Think all that practice is paying off so far, do you?" Quinn quipped. Miriam squeezed his arm again and he felt his new armor turning the cold wind. His spirit soared on the cool breeze and it felt every bit as untouchable as an eagle riding the updrafts.

That was until Quinn once again caught sight of old man Brailer and his heifer of a wife—Miriam's tormentor—at the foot of the sanctuary steps. They were waiting on an opportunity to cross the busy street, but the old crank surely didn't have to turn his head in order to look both ways. The snooty couple waddled across the street and made it to the other side without being run down by a speeding wagon.

"Damn it all!" Quinn cursed under his breath.

♦♦♦

Offering his rigid arm as a second handrail, Quinn helped Miriam descend the icy steps. All the while, he kept his gaze pinned to Anna Brailer's upturned nose and her three jiggling chins as she wobbled down the sidewalk on the opposite side of the thoroughfare. Once again, he felt the serpent writhing in his chest. His victory had been petty and vicarious as well. He had bested her son with a harmless little deception. So what? Truth be told, Quinn held no real grudge against Devon; but he had certainly been looking for the easy way out last night. After all, it had been his second day of service in little more than a month, which meant that yet another weekend had been turned into two consecutive days of steaming dog shit.

Quinn actually liked Devon, but he wanted nothing more than an opportunity to drop a strong purgative into Anna Brailer's soup bowl right before she embarked on a long carriage ride through the treeless countryside. That would suffice as partial payback for the way she had treated Miriam over the years. *Partial* payback.

*Poor Miriam*, Quinn thought as he and his mother neared the bottom step. After her husband Tomas's tragic death well over nine years ago, the Church members had been supportive and sympathetic—initially, at least. But as time dragged on—as days turned to months, then months to years—the other ladies in the Church had seemingly gone out of their way to make her feel excluded. And it had clearly not been just an innocent oversight. To Quinn, it became obvious that this coven of crotchety and bitter bitches was conspiring to wring even more tears from the young widow's eyes.

Quinn could never quite put his finger on it, but it always seemed as though the other ladies' conversations took on a syrupy, condescending tone whenever Miriam drew near. For the last several years, she had been conspicuously overlooked whenever the other ladies of the Church sent out invitations to their little parties and receptions, most of which were hosted by that bloated cow, Anna Brailer.

On a few of those occasions, when Miriam's spiritual defenses were low and her sensitivities high, she had succumbed to the wounds and cried on her son's shoulder—the only shoulder she had left—until his tunic was soaked; and the wholly undeserved hurt that assailed her always brought bile to the back of his throat. Her suffering vexed Quinn to the point that he wanted to crash one of the petty parties, jump up on the table, and kick all those dainty daisy arrangements and pearl napkin rings aside. Then he would just take a long, satisfying leak in their crystal punch bowl. Smiling like a cherub, he would stand there for as long as it took him to drain his pipes, all the while mimicking some perverted garden fountain. If any piss or punch happened to splash onto the Brailer bitch's dress...or face... then all the better. After all, if pissing in the face of one's enemy didn't define victory, then what possibly could?

◆◆◆

*Who needed them? Fuck that cow and her wall-eyed chaperone!* Quinn silently shouted to himself as he turned his gaze northward and resolved to put all that business out of his mind. Church was behind him for good, and the promise of reprieve pulled the corners of his mouth back toward his ears even as he and his mother slipped and skidded along the icy sidewalk. They shuffled home arm-in-arm with the chill wind nipping at their noses and cheeks.

Usually, it was Quinn who outpaced Miriam, but today she was virtually dragging him along by his arm as she fought for footing on the packed snow. She was in a hurry to get back to the apartment because she was expecting a special guest for lunch. Damn it all, she had food to cook and final preparations to make. Quinn tried to match her pace. True, he was dying to shed his suit for the last time, but he was equally eager to greet their guest at the door for this visitor was perhaps the only man in all the Five Cities that the angst-ridden youngster actually considered a genuine friend.

Yes, the wind was cold. No, Quinn's suit wasn't nearly thick enough to turn that wind. But he reminded himself that beneath that flimsy blue suit he wore a new layer of shiny, stout armor. That single image warmed him like a down-filled quilt; it warmed him to the point that the chill wind whistling past was utterly forgotten.

♦♦♦

Suction from the stout wind pulled the apartment door shut with a loud bang, but well before its echoes died in the small den, Quinn was off to his room to change out of his best clothes and into something far more comfortable. In addition to all the foul memories associated with them, his Sunaday clothes had a bothersome tendency to bind him in the most delicate of places, especially when he sat down...or when he spent a little too much time picturing Catherine Brinna's curvaceous frame after all her clothing had been tossed aside. Tossed aside for him! That day might never arrive, but if it ever did, he was going to throw everything he had at that poor girl. Twice if he managed to survive that first fevered campaign.

He kept his Sunaday *best* on just long enough for a quick self-assessment in his mirror. How he hated this stupid suit...everything but the tie. The precious tie, he would never part with. He squeezed the fine crimson silk between his fingers and lifted it to his nose in hopes of catching even a hint of her perfume...any trace that she had left behind this morning. In what had become a weekly tradition, a delicious Sunaday ceremony, Catherine insisted on slinking up to him under the pretense of straightening his tie.

In fact, Quinn had resorted to purposely shoving his trinity knot to one side as soon as the damnable sanctuary hove into sight. He then knew that at least a moment's bliss was just a few paces away… bliss that would largely negate the anguish associated with the rest of the morning's draining services. With her head tilted to the side, she always spent just a few seconds pulling the sloppy knot left, then right. For the next step in the dance, she pressed imaginary wrinkles out of the fabric with the palm of her hand before offering him two playful pats on his chest. Exactly two pats, every time. Then her gaze would lift to meet Quinn's own. The fires of mischief danced in her emerald eyes each and every time she surveyed the damage she had wrought on her hopelessly helpless prey.

"We've gotta keep you straight, soldier. Gotta keep you ready for inspection. Never know when the brass might show up, now do we?" she always purred as she shot him a tantalizing wink. But then Catherine's Aunt Burdagette would unfailingly clear her throat to summon her niece away from this young man that the old bag, for whatever reason, considered beneath her family's notice.

"That's one repetitious ceremony I will certainly miss," Quinn murmured to his reflected image as he buried his hungry nose in the tie once more. "Yes indeedy, Cousin Petey. I'll just have to find a way to see my angel when *Aunt Turdnugget* isn't around." He shook his head to clear his thoughts; he had to block Catherine out of his mind if only for a minute. Nearly every time he pictured her face, time stopped and he felt his heart skip a few beats. It felt as though stout drawstrings were being pulled that stole his breath and stalled his pulse; even now, he felt faint. He leaned forward on his dresser until the spell passed, then he turned his attention back to the mirror. He simply had to get out of the suit; this snake had to shed its skin.

"Not bad," he joked to himself as he reached up with his comb to re-establish the part in his dark brown hair, which the stout wind had utterly wrecked. Quinn ran the back of his hand across his cheeks to check the progress of the coarse stubble that had managed to peek out since he last shaved his face. "Not bad, but not good enough." Then his shoulders slumped forward. "Not good enough to win that sweet angel's heart. She's looking for a man, after all…not a boy."

♦♦♦

Wearing only a long-sleeved undershirt, Quinn stood before his closet, hopping from one bare foot to the other to spare his soles from prolonged contact with the chilly floorboards. He rubbed his hands together as he scanned the rack for his thickest wool shirt and his favorite pair of canvas pants...the ones with holes nearly worn in the knees...the ones with tales to tell and history hanging from every frayed thread.

When he had at last donned some warmer clothing, he got a running start and skidded playfully across the smooth floor in his socked feet as he headed for the kitchen to help Miriam with the meal. Or maybe he would just hang around the doorway and harass her. He still had a few seconds to mull over his options before he would have to commit to a final decision, but right now he was leaning toward benevolent harassment.

However, one glance at Miriam's fretful, sweat-beaded face persuaded him to pitch in and do whatever he could to help.

◆ ◆ ◆

They had almost finished setting the table when there was a knock at the door...a distinguishable knock that they had heard scores of times over the last ten years. Quinn, still shoeless, got another running start and skated across the waxed floor to unlock the door and let their guest inside. Smiling as usual, Obadiah had his hands tucked in his armpits as he hurried into the warm den. At last, he slapped the snow off his gloves and stuffed them into the front pocket of his coat.

"Good afternoon, my friends. I see you have the table set, but I have a proposal..." As soon as he uttered that last word, he and Miriam shared an uncomfortable glance...one that did not go unnoticed by Quinn. "I think we are ignoring a great opportunity for a picnic today. It would be a shame to stay indoors and not take advantage of this lovely autumn breeze. We can go to the park, brush the snow aside and..."

"Go on with you, Obadiah. My lands, if we could only bag everything that comes out of your mouth, I think the three of us would enjoy the profits from a thriving fertilizer business," Miriam called through the kitchen door as she pulled off her thick oven mitts and slapped them on the countertop.

"Why m'lady, I am not kidding in the least. Shall we pack a basket and go to the woods so that I may prove my point? As you know by now, I will go to almost any lengths to prove a point—even freeze half to death. Small price to pay to be proven right, if you ask me."

"We didn't ask you; but I doubt that any of us would come close to freezing, you old fart," Quinn stated as he took the parson's coat and hung it on one of the pegs in the wall, "what with all your hot air to keep us warm and toasty. Hel, it'd be like having a picnic beside a blacksmith's forge."

Miriam broke out in laughter upon hearing Quinn's innocent but accurate dig. With a phony scowl painted on his face, the cleric lunged forward and faked a quick punch to the lad's midsection. The two picked at one another all the time; that fake punch had become their version of a gentleman's handshake, a special ritual shared by two special friends. Even so, Quinn's reflexes betrayed his wishes; he flinched, as always.

The contrived scowl disappeared in half a heartbeat. Obadiah reached out and mussed Quinn's recently combed hair into an unruly mop, then the guest plopped down on the settee and crossed one leg over the other. The old couch's frame complained with a faint squeak as he leaned back, tugging his belt down a bit in order to make himself more comfortable. Obadiah wasn't obese by any means, but he had developed an isolated paunch some time during his middle years that detracted from his otherwise slender frame. Quinn noted that his older buddy, in profile, looked like a starving man trying to sneak a stolen melon from market by shoving it under his shirt.

And that was not the only trick that the spinning of seasons had played on the clergyman, either. His thick hair—once jet black—was now streaked with hints of white, and his shoulders were rolled forward further than they had likely been back when he was closer to Quinn's age. They were rapidly morphing into the stooped shoulders of a scholar, or perhaps the shoulders of a man who simply bore a few too many burdens.

The two men sat and exchanged small talk for a minute or two while Miriam wrapped things up in the kitchen. That was until she apparently discovered a thin patch on one of her oven mitts. Both fellows struggled to stifle a laugh when they heard her shout the first half of an expletive and toss the pan onto the countertop. Thankfully, a moment or two passed before she appeared in the doorway…time enough for her sophomoric guests to straighten up and wipe away the tears of suppressed mirth.

When she finally slapped the doorframe with her bare palm and called them in for lunch, they leapt out of their seats and raced each other toward the stifling warmth flooding the kitchen. Laughing like brothers, they shoved each other playfully out of the way when they reached the narrow doorway. The speed and agility of youth offered Quinn a distinct edge in this competition; by pivoting and squirming past his opponent, he squeezed through the portal just ahead of the cleric. In this competition, Quinn had triumphed, but Obadiah never minded losing a low-stakes round to the only son he would ever know.

♦♦♦

Miriam had clearly outdone herself this time. A huge glazed ham sat on a pewter platter in the middle of the table. Two of her special casseroles were flanking it, and both were bleeding lazy wisps of steam. There was even more grub on the stove: iron pots stuffed with steamed carrots and mashed potatoes. Nearby sat a tray of steaming rolls that were shedding drops of melted butter much as a canvas awning might shed a light but steady drizzle.

"You two go ahead and grab a plate. Dig in," she directed when it became obvious that the two men were just going to stand there and gawk at the steaming fare until ordered to do otherwise. As it turned out, they did not need much prompting to dig in; they did so eagerly and then hurried to their usual places at the table. Both held their plates by their edges to keep from burning their fingers.

For more than half an hour they talked, ate, and laughed like the family that they had essentially become. At last, Miriam stood to begin clearing the dishes. Though she kept insisting that her two gentlemen keep their seats, Obadiah winked at Quinn as he slid his chair back and started to stand. Quinn, understanding the old signal, hopped to his feet and prepared to pitch in with the clean-up duties. This had, after all, become an after dinner rite over the years.

"No! Not this time you don't. Now, you two have a seat. Sit! I mean it! I have a special surprise for you. A couple of surprises, actually," Miriam said with an odd gleam in her eyes as she ushered the two fellows back to their respective places around the table. Quinn and the cleric consulted each other by way of a brief glance. No words were spoken…they cast their votes in silence. They approved and adopted the motion to heed their hostess's wishes. They thought it prudent not to argue the matter, for they shared a hunch that one of Miriam's locally famous desserts was soon to grace the table. Neither of them were to be disappointed, for she reached into the icebox and retrieved one of the most elaborately decorated web cakes they had ever laid eyes on. The fabulous web cake—named for the intricate patterns of chocolate drizzled over the underlying layer of rich, white frosting—was a rare treat indeed, due mostly to the obscene price of the amaretto rum that the recipe called for.

The purest of those rums often brought eight or ten silvers for a mere half-pint bottle. Quinn knew that his mother had to stretch her coins to keep the two of them housed and fed. She rarely splurged, but he also knew that frugality was unceremoniously booted out the window when she had either a reason to celebrate or some incredible news to share...or both, of course. Obadiah had been a guest in the house often enough to be aware as well that something unusual was in the works.

Adding yet another dimension to the deepening mystery, Miriam reached into the cupboard and produced a bottle of Redscape wine. Quinn rolled his eyes to the ceiling. If she and Obadiah were going to share the bottle, Quinn knew that it would certainly not be an even split. Obadiah would get one glass, maybe two if he downed his first quickly enough. The rest, Miriam would quickly soak up; and it wouldn't be long until she showed her ass, figuratively speaking.

Miriam did not drink often, thankfully, since she simply could not handle it well...at all. Quinn's concern, however, quickly turned to optimism when he realized that she was carrying three glasses instead of the two that he was initially expecting.

"My gods! This must be a special occasion, indeed," Obadiah uttered while he hungrily eyed the web cake. "Is someone getting married? Did...did Quinn here knock some girly up? Is it the one you've been pining after for a few months now? What is her name... Catherine something?"

"No, you horrible man! I see the collar around your neck does little to filter what comes out of your mouth. Maybe it needs to be tightened a notch or two; and mayhap I am the best one for the job!" Miriam wiped her forehead with the corner of her apron; she was close to blushing. Quinn however, was already well beyond that point. "It's nothing quite like that, of course. Ahem. At least it better not be," she tacked on and sent a bogus frown Quinn's way. "But I do have an important announcement to make," she stated proudly as she poured the wine, shoving one of the glasses to her son, who was flushed but also alight with anticipation.

*Damn, what a day!* Drinking with his mother's endorsement was unprecedented. It was…not going to be nearly as enjoyable as sneaking it behind her back, he quickly decided. He had quaffed wine on more than a couple of occasions, but never when Miriam had been anywhere nearby. In most of those instances, she had been in the next room, snoring and succumbing to the spell cast by sleep's hungry shadow. But now…now she was actually handing him a glass of her finest stash. Her secret stash.

The two men sat there as patiently as they could manage, waiting for her to issue her revelation. At last, after smoothing her apron and giving her son a proud but playful smirk, she cleared her throat and took what was intended to be a steadying breath.

"Quinn and I have been *Chosen* by the Church to go to the Citadel at Tarchannen Eid this year for the Festival," she announced. She was so excited by then her voice was breaking. "We have both been *Chosen!*" She was tensed and poised to jump up and down in glee, hoping that her men would leap out of their chairs to join her. It became immediately obvious that she had grossly miscalculated the fervor with which they would respond to her news. Neither Quinn nor Obadiah moved a muscle at first; when the initial waves of paralysis passed, they both hastily raised their wine glasses to their lips.

## 2

**S**ilence reigned for several protracted seconds. Only the periodic ping of the cooling oven's walls disrupted the hush that brusquely stifled all gaiety. Time ceased to pass...the air in the kitchen ceased to stir altogether. Waves of static smoke hovered all around, threatening to choke Miriam and her two guests. She could have probably heard a sewing needle bouncing across the slick tile floor in the moments following her proclamation—hardly the response that she had been anticipating. Neither her son nor the clergyman uttered a word; both were struck speechless, though for entirely different reasons.

Of course, both of them knew that every year five citizens from each of the Five Cities of Eldr were appointed by the Church to travel to the fabled Citadel for nearly a full week of celebration and sanctioned carousal. Becoming a *Chosen*—being picked from the entire populace of the city—was viewed as an extreme honor by the followers of the Way.

Rows of knots erupted all along the crests of Quinn's shoulder muscles. Each drawn and throbbing bundle now shouted, warning him to strain all that his ears had just heard through a fine filter of suspicion. He was stunned stupid. On no level did his mother's announcement seem plausible. The echoes of her last words were swiftly muted by a dense haze of doubt. It seemed to him as though her news was just some cryptic message he had received while in the throes of a fever dream.

Though it had been delivered just seconds ago, nothing about her announcement seemed vivid. It did not feel real...not nearly as real as the memory of the toothless old seer cackling and pointing at him with her crooked, arthritic finger...not as real as the echoes of that inhuman voice that roared at him as he had sped away in near panic that night just a few weeks past. *Enjoy your trip next month, laddie!*

He shook his head in an effort to forget his encounter with the old hag and to process the other implications of the news with which his mother had just ambushed him. *Chosen*. Him? And his mother as well!? For months—if not years—he had made it a personal priority to distance himself from the doctrines and ways of the Church that he so loathed, but he did, after all, live in one of the Five Cities of Eldr. Quite unavoidably, he had been obliged to witness the annual furor that surrounded the *Choosing*. A reluctant observer he may have been in those years past, but he had gleaned enough familiarity with the ritual to recognize that it was indeed rare for two members of the same family to be named *Chosen*, especially in the same year. Hel, he wasn't even sure that it ever happened in the same generation.

Quinn raked his hair back from his eyes with his left hand as his right one lifted the glass of zesty burgundy to his lips once more. He took a long sip of wine as he pondered that lone detail. If Miriam noticed how easily he chugged the alcohol, she didn't comment on it; the pout she was wearing told Quinn that she was wholeheartedly focused on other matters at the moment.

When he lowered the glass, yet another mischievous smirk was pasted on his lips.

That smirk was now the sneer of a ruthless hunter...the mask of a pragmatic schemer. A schemer whose wheels were suddenly set spinning by the promise of potential conquest. Just this very morning, he had vowed to himself to no longer mask his growing disdain for the Church and its ridiculous Way. Just this minute, though, he decided that wearing his cynicism on his sleeve might not serve his best interests...not while all this *Chosen* business was transpiring, at least. He had just now been handed a huge hammer, the means to mold his new fate, and he intended to attack his latest project every bit as eagerly as a master sculptor might approach a mound of moist, gray clay...with wringing hands, wide eyes, and sweaty pits.

This was all going to work in his favor, by the gods! The fruits of his new station would be part of his reward...part of his revenge against the very robed idiots who had apparently pulled his name out of some velvet hat that likely bore a sweat-soaked band. When Quinn returned from Tarchannen Eid, he would be somebody. Hel, he was somebody now! Soon, everyone he encountered would know his name. The men who had always snubbed him would now be obligated to tip their hats to him and call him *sir*. And the girls...the *girl*...Catherine! He reckoned he would now be several steps closer to winning her heart and possibly her hand upon his return.

Master Tabor wiped his mouth with the back of his hand. Screw the folded cloth napkin. All of a sudden, he felt his heart beating with an alien, primitive pulse. He reveled in the unfamiliar but luscious sensation for a few seconds, but it promptly dissipated when he set his wine glass down on the table and cast a quick glance toward Obadiah's side of the table.

Like stinging drops of wind-driven rain, the sweat rolling down the parson's kind face neatly washed away Quinn's heady daydreams and ushered his thoughts away from any involving liquor, lust...and even love. Obadiah's mind was occupied—his wrinkled brow indicated as much. Nestled just below his sweaty brow was a grim glower. It was a deep scowl spawned from the bowels of blatant misgiving, though he was intrepidly coaxing his thin lips to turn up at the corners. But those thin lips were twitching—quivering with the effort of faking what he hoped might pass as genuine delight.

The unconvincing smile was pasted on his face strictly for Miriam's benefit; of that, Quinn was sure. The parson was struggling to appear supportive and happy for the two who had become like family to him, but he had never sported a face any less suited for the poker table. It was as if Obadiah smelled thick smoke, yet he was relying on his shallow smile to convince his two hosts that there was no fire raging nearby.

"What's the matter, Obadiah? Surely you won't miss us that much. It's only for a week, after all. We've been apart for longer stretches than that before...much longer in fact, yes?" Quinn probed as he took another long draught of the piquant burgundy wine, the yield of the vaunted Redscape Vineyards. But he kept his eyes pinned to the parson's face all the while. Something was bothering the cleric, and profoundly so. Quinn was now on a mission; he was mining for more information. He was digging for a reaction—an explanation—and his wily smirk was no less subtle than the priest's forced frown.

"What's that? Oh no, lad. It's nothing like that. It's just that, for the life of me, I can't remember the last time two were *Chosen* from...under the same roof." It was now Obadiah's turn to throw back more of the pricey wine. Then he offered his host and hostess another of his strained smiles, though Quinn did not buy it for a second. One glance at Miriam's glower told him that his mother was

equally skeptical, for they both knew Obadiah far too well to be
fooled even for a minute by any of his thinly veiled bullshit.

"My, my. What a day! This is indeed an honor for you both, I
must say," the parson added, slapping his knee weakly for emphasis,
but it only emphasized what he did not feel. Enthusiasm. He was trying his best to sound more supportive, but thanks to the presage in
his eyes and the deep wrinkles of worry surrounding them, he failed
miserably in his attempts. His hollow congratulations struck Quinn
as distant…formal…two and a half steps beyond hollow.

◆◆◆

Miriam instantly picked up on her old friend's unwonted lack of
enthusiasm as well, but she made no effort whatsoever to mask her
dejection. All light vanished from a face that had been a shining beacon just a few seconds ago. She was visibly crestfallen, and she
crossed her arms over her chest as her glossy lips twisted into a
puerile pout. Miriam had tried so hard to make this day special, a
memorable celebration of what most would consider the bestowal of
a genuine honor, one conferred upon only a select few. Above all,
she had expected the two most important men in her life to share at
least a measure of her joy. She fully anticipated that they would mirror some small fraction of her enthusiasm.

She assumed that Obadiah — as a member of the clergy — would
leap from his seat after hearing the news, grab both her hands and
sling her around the kitchen in a mad celebration dance. She thought
that he, of all people, would rejoice. For days, she had pictured him
knocking his chair over as he shouted his delight toward the kitchen
ceiling. Of all people, Obadiah should have been ecstatic…but the
bastard had rendered little more than an insincere, obligatory excuse-
for-a-smile in response to her surprise news. Not only was he unim-
pressed, he seemed absolutely troubled by the revelation.

*How quickly celebration can turn to contradiction*, Miriam
lamented while her eyes cut left then right as she assessed the disparate reactions of her guests. Quinn, who was usually the cool and
reserved one — especially in matters relating to the Church and the
Way — was currently demonstrating far more zeal for the upcoming
trip than was the enigmatic parson.

"My lady, if you don't mind my asking, when…just exactly
when did you hear of your *Choosing*?" Obadiah inquired after he
cleared his throat. The strained smile was still pasted across his face.

Even more stray beads of sweat now dotted his forehead, which threatened to converge and then cascade into his already troubled eyes. The kitchen was warm, no doubt, but it had been so ever since the three had taken their seats about the table...and he had not begun to sweat until Miriam delivered her news.

Sniffing back a tear or two of disappointment, Miriam smoothed her apron and tried her best to maintain her festive spirit, but she found the task increasingly difficult in the face of her old friend's odd comportment. "Well I don't see why such a thing would possibly matter, but if you must know, a messenger of the Church brought a letter...*the* letter by. I suppose it was four days ago," she replied as she yanked the document out of her apron pocket, almost ripping it in half in the process. With a disgusted grunt, she chucked it across the table.

Though his hands were now trembling like dried leaves in winter winds, Obadiah reverently unfolded the wrinkled parchment and read it silently. He read it twice — at least twice. His furrowed forehead dumped out even more sweat, as if he was trying to decipher some arcane riddle...one on which a loved one's life depended.

"Is something wrong, Obadiah?" All ten of Miriam's fingers were woven through her long, curly locks. They were tugging against the delicate roots like starving farmers trying to harvest potatoes and onions from a sunbaked field. "Silly question...of course it is. I should say *what* is wrong?" she asked finally, her new tone now utterly devoid of its earlier glee. She sat down heavily and, despite the unexplained somber turn the conversation had taken, started carving the web cake. She flung a large wedge toward each of the three plates and took damned little care to keep those wedges intact.

♦♦♦

"What's that? Oh, nothing at all...my dear. It all seems in order. It's just that..."

"Quit addressing me like I'm some witless orphan!" Miriam screamed and slammed her palm against the top of her table...*her* table.

"No need to raise your voice to me, my dear. It's just that I happened to catch a glimpse of the list of the *Chosen* not three weeks back, and..."

"And...?" Miriam pressed. Her voice was tainted by impatience and...venom.

"And neither of your names were on it then. Something must have happened with the two whose places you…"

"So what you are saying is that Quinn and I are merely runners-up and we're going just because the Church's first choices have rashes or runny noses or…"

"…or the screaming shits?" Quinn offered, but the older two ignored him.

"No. No! Not at all. The Cardinals always put a great deal of thought into the annual *Choosing*. It isn't as though the names are drawn out of some hat."

Quinn coughed and nearly choked on his Redscape, but neither Miriam nor Obadiah seemed to notice.

"They likely changed their minds at the last minute for…for whatever reason. I won't lie and say that I pretend to know what those reasons may have been." He struggled to relax his smile a bit more, but he would have had more success sawing down a red oak with the dried bones of a bream. "All that doesn't matter. I'm just being silly. My sincere congratulations to you both. Really." Again, Quinn was not convinced, and one glance at the troubled expression on his mother's face told him that she was now well beyond the point of simple skepticism as well…Miriam was thoroughly pissed at the turn her special evening had taken.

"Personally, I don't think your *congratulations* are any more sincere than that weak-ass smile you're fighting so hard to maintain," Miriam shot back in a huff. Her teeth were clenched. She was taking no measures to conceal or sugarcoat her thoughts. "Just never mind. Fuck it!" she spat before tossing back the rest of the wine in her glass.

Quinn did choke on his Redscape this time, and he could feel the alcohol burning his nostrils. Not once in all his life had he heard his mother let loose with so much as a *darn*, and now she had rolled a petard across the table. And with a cleric in the room to boot!

After Miriam issued her bitter little exclamation, neither man could muster the balls to break the silence…not right away. The conversation lapsed into tense silence as they dove into the rich web cake, not so much out of hunger, but rather out of a need to retreat from awkwardness. Each of them opted for a second helping, but Miriam served only one of those second slices—her own. When the plates sported nothing but stray crumbs and a smattering of icing, the three adults shifted in their squeaky chairs.

Two pairs of eyes remained cast downward, but Quinn's alert gaze studied the faces of his mother and his unofficial stepfather. There was certainly some complex chemistry floating around in the room this evening. Not half an hour ago, the older couple's faces had surrendered to frowns, and those frowns were spawned from different springs—one from exasperation, one from foreboding.

♦ ♦ ♦

Worn wooden spindles creaked as the chairs' three occupants finally leaned back and drew in deep breaths, then allowed those breaths to escape in a chorus of long sighs that conveyed satiation but certainly not satisfaction.

"I must say, that was an incredible meal, Miriam," Obadiah wheezed in an attempt to both break the tense silence and close the previous topic of conversation. "I sincerely thank you for inviting me." The other two glanced at the cleric and both mother and son noted that the parson's bearing had relaxed a bit, but only a bit. His eyes and lips were no longer quite so engaged in their earlier conflict, and the sheen of nervous sweat had—for the most part—evaporated from his forehead. Of course, the three glasses of potent wine had probably helped to a large extent. Nevertheless, Miriam accepted his latest reference to sincerity as an apology…of sorts.

"It sure was, Mom. Dang! I don't think I'll even be able to bend over and take my boots off tonight."

Obadiah couldn't resist the opening. "Well I for one hope you can't, son. We wouldn't want to ruin a perfectly good meal with the smell that would come boiling off those rancid feet of yours. There's probably a garden growing in those boots by now, but for the life of me I can't figure out exactly what crop you chose to plant this season, lad. Onions maybe? Garlic?" Obadiah leaned forward in his chair and snapped his fingers. "It must be garlic!"

With all her will, Miriam fought the urge to laugh. She was committed to sustaining the tension that had suddenly become her most effective weapon in this evening's battle against invalidation. It was her desire to continue swinging the sword of displeasure just to defend her position atop this pile of broken hope. She bit her lip as she fought the urge to laugh, but she quickly succumbed when she saw Quinn's cheeks turn the color of ripe beets. For the first time since Miriam had made her announcement, she and the parson who had become her partner in so many ways shared a bout of candid laughter, and the oppressive feeling in the room lifted. It lifted only to a degree, but the deepest shadows of resentment retreated, gathering and hurriedly consulting each other before fleeing through the frosted panes of the kitchen window.

After the remnants of the mutilated web cake had been packed and put back into the ice box, the three retired to the den. Though the living room stove was creaking and groaning from the inferno which it struggled to contain, the den was still considerably cooler than the kitchen had been, partly because of the steady draft that slithered through the cracks surrounding the apartment's lone door. Obadiah threw a couple of additional chunks of seasoned oak into the stove that sat on the hearth. He adjusted the damper and then joined Quinn on the narrow settee. The cleric smacked his friend on the knee.

"I have a carpenter friend who can make that door fit its frame more snuggly, Quinn. While you two are away, I'm going to have him come and take a look at it, if that's...?"

"Don't bother yourself," Miriam chimed in. She had once again returned to her defensive position. "It's been that way for years. You two...turds...need to learn when to just leave well enough alone. You get more animated about some stupid draft around a door than..." Her face shed some of its inherent beauty as its features twisted in disgust; she waved her hand and launched from her chair. She made a pass by the wine cabinet and retrieved another bottle of burgundy, though it did not bear the distinguished Redscape label. She refilled everyone's glasses and then took a seat in her sliding rocker next to the stove. Obadiah dabbed at a patch of the vintage that Miriam had spilled down the front of his vestment. She offered no apology.

"Quit being an ass, Mother," Quinn blurted out. "Obadiah is just trying to help. You and I both know that time does a piss poor job of healing hearts. What makes you think that it can fix a door?"

"You two do what you think is best," she replied with a shrug and a toss of her hair. With a single gulp, half of the wine in her glass disappeared.

◆◆◆

A few more moments passed in uncomfortable silence as Miriam studied the two men seated across from her. They were both hypnotized by the flames dancing behind the window of the stove. Their expressions were eerily similar, but she knew in her heart that their thoughts were running down different trails. She still had no idea what factors were responsible for driving away Obadiah's consistently jovial mood and ushering in this alien wave of...brooding.

Of course, as far as Quinn was concerned, Miriam's motherly insights allowed her to fill in a few blanks. She immediately suspected that the font of her son's enthusiasm for the upcoming journey was perhaps more primal than spiritual. She could tell by the swirling fires of yearning in his mesmerized eyes that devotion to the Way was not presently a consideration. His thoughts were consumed by the goddess who held the deed to his helpless heart, and wholly so. One glance at his face told her that the mistress of his five moons sported long brunette hair, two fathomless green eyes and a musky, tantalizing ruoska between her legs. His poor soul had no way out... no means of escape. He had fallen; he was thoroughly entranced by the mystique of this delectable maiden that fit so neatly into the mold that defined his ideals of perfection. Sucked into the swirling vortex of that complex spell, Quinn had become yet another pitiful victim of that sweet but fleeting illusion called love. As Miriam stared into his distant eyes, she felt a moment of empathy...and envy.

◆◆◆

Miriam was hesitant to breach the subject again, but she finally surrendered to the effects of the wine and the insistent call of curiosity. Her eyes were growing heavy and she felt the need to dive into a sea of dreamless sleep, but she knew that it would be denied her until she learned more about the parson's earlier lack of fervor. After pouring herself a refill, she once more plopped down in her rocker.

"Are you at least coming to see us off next weekend, Obadiah? Will you be at the service?" she asked almost timidly, like a child asking for a raise in allowance. The storm had passed; there was no more thunder. All hints of ire had vanished from her voice.

The parson strived once more to smile as he answered, but he never allowed his troubled eyes to wander away from the flames that flickered behind the window fronting the stove. He took a deep breath and swished the wine in his glass. "Of course I will. I will do my best, that is. As a matter of fact, I might even ask Cardinal Voss if I can join you in the field, at least for part of the week."

"That would be wonderful!" Quinn and Miriam shouted, almost in unison. Miriam had finally opted to sheathe her sword. Aside from a few short excursions into the plains, neither of them had really ever ventured outside the city gates, much less to the Citadel at Tarchannen Eid! Why, no one was even allowed to pass through the Forest unless they were summoned or sent by the Church. The prospect of visiting the spiritual center of the Church was exciting and daunting at the same time. Quinn, of course, was more excited by the promise of adventure and the imagined spoils that awaited him on his return than by the obtuse religious aspects of the trip to the Citadel. But Miriam's heart was beating in perfect time to the rhythm of the Way.

"Now you two don't go and get your hopes up. I have to go wherever I am sent, of course. In fact, I have to leave early in the morning for Eldr-ro. At any rate, I can't promise anything, but I will certainly see what I can do...see what I can see," Obadiah continued as he drained the last drops of the cheaper wine from his glass. "I haven't had any proper rest in some time, come to think of it. I do grow tired. Very tired, in fact," the parson emphasized as his hand wiped away what might well have been an errant tear. "It would likely do me a world of good to visit the grounds surrounding the Citadel for a while...let my guard down, as it were, and yield to peaceful sleep 'til dawn's new day."

"In all the time I have known you, I've never considered you to be the type to keep your guard up, mister. Don't take me wrong, Obadiah," Miriam explained in a tone that had grown considerably sweeter over the last half hour, "but you always seem so...at ease with everything." A token sip from her glass. "Ahem, except maybe this evening," she muttered under her breath as she shot a subdued, waggish grin his way. It was enough of a smile to let the parson know that he was at least partially forgiven. "I can't imagine you feeling as though you have to maintain any kind of...guard."

"Well my dear lady, we are all beset by our own pesky little demons, now aren't we?" he shot back, offering only a cynical wink as he rose to fetch a refill from the new wine bottle sitting on the kitchen counter. Quinn and Miriam exchanged puzzled glances. For the second time that evening, Quinn was reminded of his encounter with the old hag a few weeks ago. *Those distinctions will be your devils, boy; and they are going to haunt you like they have haunted no other.*

After downing that last glass of the burgundy elixir, Obadiah pulled on his heavy coat and hugged his hostess. The embrace lasted longer than any other that Quinn could remember ever witnessing. Forgoing the fake punch, the parson simply shook Quinn's hand as he opened the front door, letting a cold blast of Earlywinter air rush into the den. "You two take care of yourselves. Take special care. I'll talk to Cardinal Voss and get back to you toward the middle of the week, hopefully." With that, he descended the squeaky stairs and disappeared into the hungry shadows enveloping the street below.

As Quinn watched his dear friend fade into blackness, he felt a shiver run up his arms, and some innate voice suggested that this latest chill could not be entirely attributed to the blast of night air which spilled through the doorway. Obadiah was gone. Gone! Tainted by just a kiss of benevolent tension, tonight's farewell seemed so much like a...goodbye. Maybe it was just his imagination; maybe it was just the abruptness with which the inky winter night swallowed the stooped parson. Whatever the reason, it felt wrong watching his friend march into the darkness this frigid night. Quinn's gut churned as he locked the door behind him. When he pulled the key from the lock to hang it on its designated hook, he noticed that his hand was trembling.

♦♦♦

Miriam raced into the kitchen to begin cleaning up, but Quinn stood with his back against the closed door for a bit. A full stomach was not the reason for his sudden bout of queasiness; there was some other factor at play...one that he could not identify. It sprang from concern for the special man who had just disappeared into the starving shadows.

Obadiah came to their home every five or six Sunadays. True, he was a clergyman in the Church. Even so, Quinn had always liked the man. He loved him, in fact. He wasn't at all like the other Church officials. Obadiah was not only mellow, but he possessed an actual sense of humor; he had so little in common with that troupe of stern fools and uncharismatic clowns that were considered his brethren.

"*Brethren!* What a fucking joke," Quinn muttered as he raked his fingers through his hair to usher his bangs away from his eyes once again.

"What was that, hon?" Miriam called from the kitchen.

"Nothing. Just thinking out loud," he called back as his eyes rolled to the ceiling.

Obadiah wasn't really involved in the Church's dealings within the Five Cities. Unlike Father Sigmund's cushy post as head of the Eldr-shok diocese, Obadiah's duties took him to the smaller settlements out on the plains and into the mountains east of Eldr-shok, the Ulverkraag Mountains. The notorious Ulverkraags...the stage upon which nature rehearsed her many acts of unbridled brutality. Even so, that was the harsh frontier frequented by Obadiah, the domain of desolation where he served those in need not by proselytizing and spreading false hope, but by actually getting his hands dirty—even bloody on occasion.

Quinn had heard the rumors. He knew from confirmed accounts that if a roof needed patching, Obadiah was right there near the top rung of a ladder swinging his hammer, even if deadly lightning was streaking through the turbulent skies. If a barn burned somewhere out in the villages of the Ulverkraags, Obadiah was there to help raise the walls of a new one whether it was by daylight or torchlight. If someone caught ill, Obadiah would sit up with the patient all night long, nursing them and even cleaning them so that the other family members could get some rare, cherished rest.

This special cleric, this unique man, had never lost sight of what Quinn considered to be a church's true purpose. Obadiah had never gotten so caught up in all the rituals and politics that he forgot the people's fundamental need for unity and a sense of collective purpose...their need for simple comfort and compassion when that erratic bitch called *fate* directed her ill winds their way.

One question continued to plague Quinn, largely because he was perceptive enough to recognize the obvious contradiction: what could possibly account for Obadiah's allegiance to an organization that appeared to stand for everything he was not? Try as he might, Quinn just could not reconcile his old friend's affiliation with the Church of the Way, an institution of utter fools, and a menagerie of self-important and fraudulent charlatans.

As he nursed the remaining wine in the bottom of his glass, Quinn's thoughts logically turned to ones involving his late dad. Tomas Tabor had made his untimely exit from Eldimorah when his boy was most in need of a father. Tomas was someone who embodied and exemplified self-reliance, responsibility and determination, someone who could imbue those qualities to his son simply by setting the proper example...just by being honest and authentic.

Alas, the fates had seen fit to let the curtain fall on Tomas's performance before his whole story could be told, but they had seen fit to fortuitously introduce a new character around the same time...a character bearing—ironically—the collar of a cleric. Of course, Miriam had witnessed the bond evolve between her son and Obadiah, and she had done so from the perspectives of both mother and widow, which possibly explained why the parson was invited to be a guest in their home so frequently. Possibly.

An especially violent gust of wind outside the window produced a harsh whistle, and Quinn caught himself hoping once again that their guest would safely find his way back to the warmth of his own home. With that wish whispered in what might even pass for a prayer, the teen drained his glass and sat back to watch the hypnotic fire.

♦♦♦

"You had better throw some more blocks in the stove, dearest," Miriam instructed her son as she bustled about the kitchen. Her voice had regained more of its characteristic musical lilt. Ordinarily, she would have been content to just leave the dishes alone until morning, but she bore an abundance of nervous energy tonight that demanded to be expended. She knew that mindless motion would be the most effective means of buckling back the tide of doubt that began to rise the very second she shared her news earlier that afternoon...the very second she had peered into Obadiah's stunned and apprehensive eyes.

Yes, she simply had to keep moving at this point, lest she split open like an overly ripened melon that had been inadvertently kicked by the toe of the farmer's boot. She was struggling with the trifecta of emotions that plagued so many torn and troubled hearts...disappointment and frustration scampering around beneath the inevitable shadow of their big brother, resentment.

Logic and love were doing their level best to intervene on Miriam's behalf and buffer the effects of this new squall of trepidation. They were feverishly spinning a dizzying web of perspectives and possibilities that might pardon the two most important men in her life from all but ruining this afternoon with their restraint...with their confounding lack of anything resembling spiritual fire. Their lack of animation had neatly attenuated her own excitement regarding this afternoon that she thought would be so very special, that had been the focus of so much planning and preparation on her part... this afternoon that had ultimately elicited slightly more sanguinity than a funeral wake on a rainy autumn day.

Deep in her heart, she knew that their tepid responses to her news were in no way intended to hurt her feelings, so simple spite was immediately eliminated from the list of their possible motivations. In her estimation, that left only hesitation, suspicion, and fear. *Damn.* Obviously, none of those options comforted her in the least. Still, at least one of those probabilities likely accounted for Obadiah's odd behavior upon hearing the news about his adopted family being named among this season's *Chosen.*

Miriam withdrew her hands from the dishwater and pressed her pale, wrinkled fingers against her throbbing temples. White suds ran down her jaws, but she made no effort to wipe them away. Why had her news rattled Obadiah so profoundly? She could ponder little else as she scrubbed the last few dishes and placed them in the rack to drain.

♦♦♦

In the next room, Quinn was busy with his assigned chore: stoking the fire in the stove to a low, comforting roar. He closed the damper to throttle it back to a slow smoldering burn, one that would allow the fire to last through the cold night. His eyes had grown heavy and he was more than a little drunk, though he would never admit as much to Miriam. The Redscape certainly packed more of a punch than the cheaper vintages that he was used to pilfering, which normally filled his mother's locked cabinet. The fine wine had set his boat to rocking; it had dulled his senses and he felt the sudden and compelling need to be horizontal.

"I think I'm going to turn in, Mom. I'll see you in the morning."

Miriam stepped around the corner, wiping her shriveled hands on a dish towel. Quinn could definitely tell that she had been struggling to fight back a tear or two. "Not before you give me a goodnight kiss, you don't," she said playfully.

"Aw, Mom. Don't you know how old I am?" he groaned as he sauntered over and gave her a cursory peck on the cheek.

"To the day, dear heart," she sniffed as she pressed her palm to her cheek. "That's more like it, now. Sweet dreams...but don't go too far with Catherine tonight. Save it until you two are properly married. You hear me? You put a ring on her finger before you move on to other...concerns. I don't want a bastard grandson running around, not even in a dream!" Miriam teased her son, and it was now her turn to wear a smirk as she watched his cheeks blush bright red. She had learned how to push a few buttons along the way as well.

"Now don't you start..." Quinn began, but he couldn't honestly

deny that he enjoyed entertaining the possibilities of that dream actually coming to fruition. He had spent very little time near babies in
his day, and he wasn't at all sure what having one around actually
entailed. The conception part, though…ye, gods! Aside from that,
just the thought of starting a family with the angel of his dreams, the
prospect of slipping a ring onto her delicate finger, made his heart
skip at least two beats.

Those heartening images made every muscle in his body tense.
He had to will his right hand to relax before he accidentally snapped
the stem off his wine glass.

"So, do you need me to stay and help?" he asked, hoping silently
but desperately that Miriam would say no.

"Nah. I've got it all under control. I'm done in the kitchen.
Maybe I'll stay up for a bit and finish my wine. You go get your
rest…unless…"

"Unless…?" he prompted. He fought a valiant fight to stifle another yawn. He could sense that she needed something…someone.
It was clear to him that she did not want to be left alone during these,
the loneliest hours. The gods knew that he understood that feeling.
He had paddled that canoe too many times not to be able to sympa-
thize with her reluctance to tackle those violent but unbearably quiet
rapids.

"Well, I had something else special planned for tonight, but it
can wait…I suppose. You go on to bed. We can do this some other
time."

"What is it? You can't tease me like that and then expect me to
just go to bed!"

Miriam's eyes lit up. She tapped her chin thoughtfully and then
gently ushered her son away from the kitchen door. She was animated
once more, just as she had been right before she dragged the web
cake out of the ice box. "You go sit on the couch, then. I have a special present for you, but you might need another glass of wine. I know
I'm gonna need one for this…maybe two…or five."

"Nah, I'm good on the wine, I think. What could you possibly
have in mind? I don't think you would ever be able to top this afternoon's little…*revelation* shall we call it?"

"Oh, don't be so sure," Miriam whispered, and her voice was
near to breaking. A tear was already forming in the corner of her right
eye, and Quinn realized in that moment that curiosity and concern

both had powerful sobering effects. "Just go have a seat, you rascal. And quit asking so many darned questions. I have a present that I've been saving for you. It's from someone you know...used to know."

He took a deep breath to calm nerves that had rapidly shaken off the shackles of drowsiness. Curiosity threatened to get the best of him as he sat there on the settee, listening to his mother rummage around in her kitchen cabinets. At one point, he heard a spice bottle hit the floor and shatter. He thought that he heard Miriam utter a low curse as she paused to sweep up the mess.

"If that was the lorespice, I'm going to just shit my pants and slit my wrists right here and now," he promised himself through clenched teeth. Though it had been over two years past, he still remembered the quest on which he had been sent to locate that little bottle. He had spent the better part of that summer day running along the city streets, zipping from market to market as he attempted to find a merchant that carried Miriam's brand. It had been a maddening chore and one that he did not care to repeat...ever.

She appeared just a moment later carrying a present wrapped in simple brown sack cloth. A long green ribbon bisected the gift and its ends were tied in a carefully crafted bow. She took a seat and nestled against her son, so close that he could feel her legs trembling. Ever so reverently, she placed the mysterious present in his lap.

"What in...?" he stammered, utterly confused and almost afraid to touch it.

"It was...it *is* a gift from your father, Quinn. On his deathbed, he made me promise him that I would give this to you on your twentieth birthday, when you were a man." Miriam dabbed at her tears with the corner of the apron that she even now donned...even at this late hour.

"But that's not until...that's not for a few..." Quinn trailed off.

"I know. I know, but your birthday is just an arbitrary date though it is certainly a special one. You're already a man, love. I've seen the signs for some time, and now...now you have been *Chosen*! You are a man, and you are more than ready to receive this gift and whatever secrets it may hold. It is just as your father left it, I assure you. I was never even tempted to so much as shake it. To do so would be tantamount to spitting on the memory of a man that was my life— a man that gave me a very special present one time...some nineteen years ago," she concluded as she patted his knee and bit her lower lip to keep it from quivering so.

"I…I don't know what to say," Quinn whispered. His own voice was now threatening to break. Tears streamed unbidden down his cheeks as he ran his fingers reverently around the loops of faded green ribbon.

"You don't have to say anything to me, dear Quinn. I'm simply keeping a promise I made to my love before he…breathed his last. Whatever you eventually decide to say, you can say it to him. How about that? Whether they are spoken or silent, send your words up to the wind, and he'll be able to hear you; of that I am certain. I've conducted my share of conversations with him in the same manner, I assure you."

Sniffing back another troublesome tear, Quinn rolled his neck. He began to gently untie the bow and noted that dust had collected on it…some ten years' worth of dust, he figured. With great care, he opened one end of the sack cloth and tipped it so that the box could slide out with ease. Scrawled across the top of the box in faded ink was a single word. That word was written in his father's unmistakable handwriting.

*Quinn.*

Upon seeing that familiar script, a lump formed in his throat that prevented him from swallowing. For a moment, it disrupted the rhythm of his heartbeat. He hesitated and glanced at Miriam just long enough to confirm that there were indeed four watering eyes in the room and not just two. She was holding her breath, and he realized that he was doing the same. Willing himself to exhale, he lifted the lid off the box and stared at the contents: a huge leather-bound book with yet another green ribbon wrapped around its middle, a ribbon that was not quite wide enough to obscure the broad leather band and lock that was intended to keep the old tome's contents protected from prying eyes. Quinn lifted the massive manuscript out of its box and placed it on his lap. Apparently, that was Miriam's cue to press a tiny key into the palm of his hand, and she did not release her grip for several seconds…several seconds pregnant with meaning. He choked and his shoulders began to shake with silent sobs. For a minute or two, he and his mother sat side by side, weeping. They wept in silence. They wept separately…together…in silence.

"I don't know what's inside, obviously, but I think I need to be alone when I find out if you don't mind. I'll share it with you later, of course…" Quinn finally managed to sniff; then he had to take a moment to gather his composition, for he could sense that his voice was about to abandon him again. "Goodnight, Mom. And thank you. I realize that sounds incredibly insufficient, but…"

"Goodnight, dear. It sounds just fine, trust me. It couldn't sound any more perfect," she managed to whimper through the shower of tears that she no longer bothered to suppress or wipe away. "Sweet dreams, again—and with no conditions this time. You and Catherine do whatever you can while you're both still young," she half-joked through another suppressed sob. "Tomorrow isn't promised to any of us, after all. If you have any love in your heart, spend it on someone today. Don't wait, hon. Don't you dare wait! I've seen it in your face whenever I mention her name, Quinn. There is a special bond between you two. There's a fire there. The coals glow bright red because they are stoked by the breath of your soul. Light a candle if you know. Light a candle before any foul winds set in. You would rather take an arrow in your chest than see her take a tiny thorn in her hand. You would beg for more pain just so she would suffer less of it. That is love if I have ever seen it…and I have. I have, Quinn. When you feel that way about someone, you better tell them. Tell them now, and damn the consequences! Damn the odds, for those odds are imaginary. They are illusions spawned by your own insecurity, and you have nothing to feel insecure about. She is yours; all you have to do is step forth, claim her and smother her with all the love in your soul. Do you hear me, dear heart?"

"Where the Hel did all of that come from? Will you stop it, already? She's just…never mind. Good night." He pecked her on the cheek a second time and rose to retreat to his room before he broke down completely in front of Miriam. She might not consider him so much of a man if she witnessed him bawling like a newborn. Between receiving a present from his late father and having Miriam so succinctly and so poetically express his feelings for Catherine, he felt himself being shoved out into a storm where tears threatened to spill down like warm rain.

"You sure you don't want to reconsider that glass of Redscape, hon?"

"I think that bottle got drained well before Obadiah hit the door," Quinn managed to croak. Standing in the shadows of the hallway, he mustered just enough courage to turn his head and peer into his mother's watering eyes.

"Oh, there's another one on the counter. I went ahead and bought two. After all, I had to get something to replace that bottle of cheap shit that you polished off a few weeks back," she said in a sly grin that was devoid of any hint of censure. "Remind me later to ask you just exactly what happened that night, will you?"

"Now that you mention it, I think I might need a small bracer for this one," Quinn conceded as he patted the box beneath his arm. He took a slight detour to the kitchen counter where he waited for his mother to uncork the fresh bottle and fill his glass. She did not spill a drop, even though her hands were trembling with emotion. His were trembling because she had just reminded him of his encounter with the old hag; that, and he presently held a mysterious book under his arm that was left for him by his father, now ten years gone. She poured what he judged to be about six fingers of the fine vintage, reminding him of a grim toast that he had once heard in a tavern when he had tried—unsuccessfully so—to convince the owner that he was old enough to buy a mug of cold ale.

*Two fingers for love, and two for fear*
*Two fingers for the grave that slithers too quickly near*

♦♦♦

He closed the door to his room and sat down heavily on the side of his bed. The mysterious present was once again resting in his lap. One of those worthless street lamps just outside his single window had apparently blown out or had run out of oil. The scant light that usually filtered in through the gauzy drapes had disappeared altogether, prompting Quinn to turn the wick up on the oil lamp that stood on the bookcase beside his bed.

Ten years' worth of memories assailed him as he stared at the worn leather binding that had protected the enclosed pages for several decades more, judging by the tight network of scrapes and abrasions on the tome's brittle spine. Ten years of fond memories, and there should have been ten more…ten more, at the very least.

But, alas, the poor fellow had died of the dreaded wasting sickness when Quinn was just a child. Still, he remembered certain things about Tomas, the extraordinary man who sired him. A handful of vivid images had been permanently carved into the craggy stone, the

hardy medium reserved exclusively for preserving a young boy's infallible memories—banks of images captured in bright shades of innocence and unblemished by the taint of judgment and cynicism.
Quinn stood for a second, just long enough to catch a glimpse of himself in his dresser's mirror. For a precious but fleeting moment, he
could have sworn that he saw a hazy reflection of that man…Tomas
Tabor…standing behind him. Healthy and hale once again, he was
smiling and standing bathed in the glorious light of an early morning
sun.

Quinn plopped back down onto his bed and hugged the book to
his chest. He allowed himself another silent but very necessary sob.

His father had been a voracious reader. Once Tomas Tabor dove
into a book, nothing could pry him away from it save for a loving
but slightly aggravated appeal from Miriam. No, he did not just read
his books…he devoured them, reveling in the silent yet inescapable
spells that they cast. He was enchanted by their feel and their musty
aroma, the unmistakable whisper of a turning page, and the subtle
flickering that resulted when that turning page fanned the lone candle,
the tiny wax torch that served as the sole source of light during those
late night sessions of absorption and intellectual rapture. Curious almost to a fault, Tomas Tabor feared no topics, but he especially loved
history and the science of numbers. Even more, he loved his wife
and young son.

Another avalanche of sweet memories swept over Quinn as that
darned lump in his throat returned, more swollen than before. Tomas
had been a kind and patient father; distant and aloof at times, but in
a manner that was thoroughly benevolent and easily excused, for he
bore that sacred yet silent burden shared by all thinking men…the
onus of wisdom.

Determination, imagination and the untarnished recollections of
a grieving child all represented threads that Quinn frequently gathered and spun into a web of fragile fabric, a thin and gauzy veil
through which he could occasionally catch a glimpse of his father's
ethereal ghost. Those threads were wispy and weak, indeed. Though
he had repeatedly poured his soul into the effort, he simply could not
weave them into a more pleasurable new world for himself and his
mom…two individuals living under the same roof that suffered from
dissimilar varieties of loneliness. And dissimilar though they may
have been, they were equally profound. He and Miriam both felt the

bites of seclusion's long fangs. True, Quinn had seen his dad only through the eyes of a child. Even so, he felt robbed…bitter.

Every time the matter crossed his mind, Quinn's hands reflexively curled into tight fists as he wrestled with the actual meaning behind his unwarranted loss, if there actually was any real meaning. After all, what supposedly benevolent gods would take such a man away from those who depended on him, and wholly so? What gods would end such a fine man's life in such a foul manner? What sadistic deities had devised and unleashed on their subjects this foul disease that let an outstanding father and husband starve to death in front of his family, shriveling into an emaciated husk that—toward the end— begged to be put out of its misery and was none too picky about the means?

And then, as if Quinn's grief and innocent confusion had not been enough with which to contend, that pimple-faced upstart of a priest delegated to officiate at the funeral had delivered such a sterile, uncannily canned message that made no mention whatsoever of who Quinn's dad had really been. What was worse, the brat of a priest possessed the gall to declare how Tomas Tabor had been such an outstanding servant of the Way. That collar-wearing teat baby had used the deceased man's sepulcher as a podium from which he could promote more of the Church's fucking propaganda.

*Shit*, Quinn thought as he sat there caressing the old tome with two quivering hands, *Dad wouldn't have pissed in that upstart priest's ear if his brain had been on fire and smoke had been pouring from both nostrils. He only walked past the sanctuary when he was on the way to the library, and even then he crossed the street just to put more distance between himself and that nest of sodomistic rats.*

Aside from the bitter memories of his father's battle with the scourge, Quinn had also inherited his dad's modest library, a number of volumes covering everything from the history of Eldimorah to alchemy and the discipline of complex numbers. But why had this book been special enough to hold aside for all these years? He set the wine glass back on his nightstand; his nerves were as steady as they would likely ever be.

"One way to find out, I suppose," Quinn muttered to himself as he commanded his trembling hand to insert the tiny key into the lock. A quarter of a turn and the taut leather band snapped open, but Quinn thought it necessary to have a generous gulp of Redscape before he dared open the front cover. The fragile spine crackled as the book was opened for the first time in at least a decade. A plain envelope with the first hints of yellow kissing its borders slid down the front page and came to rest against Quinn's stomach. Nothing was written on the envelope, but Quinn logically assumed that he was the intended recipient. As much as he hated to break what may well have been his father's last wax seal, he promptly opened the letter and unfolded the page, eager to devour its contents.

> *Dearest Quinn, my only son and heir. You are no doubt reading this with mixed emotions. Please know that I am battling an overabundance of conflicting sentiments as I lay here writing these words. Today, for better or worse, I bestow upon you some secrets regarding your heritage that you will likely find unsavory. Nevertheless, they are the truth and the truth is more important than your sensibilities at this point, I fear. This tome that you now hold is very special, as you might surmise. It contains chapters pertaining to Eldimorah's rich history, mythology, and religious lore that have been unedited by the Church and the pit of vipers that now govern it. No malady killed me, lad. 'Twas poison administered by the Church. They sought certain answers that I was unwilling to surrender, for your sake and for your mother's. Our friend Obadiah knows some of what has transpired, but do not fault him, for he was complicit in my attempts to turn the Church's attention elsewhere. If he still lives, he is your ally, perhaps your only ally. This book has not been censored and filtered by the architects of the "Way". I want you to read Chapter 9 and read it very carefully. It chronicles the last ignoble deeds of Valenesti. You need to know the unabridged version of his tale, son. Read the whole chapter…every word. Then read my note at the end and heed it. Take care of my Miriam, lad. Know that I am watching over the two of you and will do whatever I can from wherever I am, but I'm guessing that your resolve will trump the wishes of a mere ghost. I loved you and still do, my dearest Quinn. Farewell.*

Though the wind whistled by his window, he did not hear the first note of its furious song. As he sat on the edge of his bed, Quinn only heard his father whisper a word in one ear…and in the other, he heard the old hag shouting the same word. *Poison? Poison!* A sudden bout of silent sobbing made his shoulders shake like two bucking stallions, but he was finally able to take a deep breath and steady his nerves. Brushing away the latest flood of tears with the palm of his left hand, Quinn recruited his right hand to reach for the glass that he quickly realized had been grossly under-filled. Six fingers would not be nearly enough for the secrets that would be unearthed this frigid night.

He took a relatively conservative gulp of the Redscape, set the glass back on his nightstand and slid off his bed to sit on the floor. He pulled the top blanket from the bed and draped it about his shoulders to stave off the chill that pervaded the room now that his closed door prevented the already-meager heat from slithering in from the hallway. With fingers that quivered with anticipation, he flipped the brittle pages…he turned to Chapter 9. He handled the old tome with all the respect that it somehow demanded with its mute authority and its musty scent. It smelled old but at the same time it smelled…important. The pages were starting to turn just the least bit yellow, but the book was in remarkably good condition considering its obvious age. The tears abated for a moment as he started to read, but they would soon return, and when they did they would fall like heavy spring rains.

◆◆◆

As he turned the last page to finish the chronicles of Valenesti and his quest for the staff of Morana Goll, another envelope fell into Quinn's lap. Released from their pink prisons by the poignancy of the grim tale he had just tried to digest, hot drops were once again rolling freely down his cheeks; but he took care to see that none of them landed on the pages of this, the most recent addition to his inherited library…the most recent and certainly the most precious one.

"Gods!" Quinn gasped to himself as he let his head fall back and bounce against the seam of his down-filled mattress. He rationed himself another sip of the wine as he struggled to absorb the significance of the convoluted tale that he had just read. The envelope would have to wait for another moment or two while he processed the account of Valenesti's tragic descent into madness.

◆◆◆

Poor Valenesti had been a simple and unassuming wheelwright

with simple intentions. He wanted only to live and to love. Not until after his sanity fled into the flitting shadows of bereavement did he ever imagine himself capable of altering the entire history of El-dimorah. But despondency and mourning had driven him to seek a remedy for at least one aspect of history that had left him so very alone and so very resentful. Just as he neared the zenith of happiness and contentment, he lost his beloved Elise, the only light in a world that he soon discovered could be extremely dark.

She had been taken from him, ripped away, torn from his embrace so cruelly by a terrible withering disease, similar perhaps to the foul malady that had allegedly ushered Quinn's father into darkness. After Valenesti buried his wife, he spent most of his remaining time withering away as well...withering away in the filthy taverns of Hadig-vie. There, he watched his weeks march by. There, he passed his days pickling himself and attempting in vain to purge the profound blight—the crippling pain—of loss. Loss. An ace tucked up the sleeve of that sadistic dealer, Destiny. Loss. The cruelest card that Fate could ever play.

Quite unfortunately, the pubs became Valenesti's new element... his new habitat. Very early on, he learned that any who chose to listen with disciplined focus—any who managed to adeptly parse all the clamor of the diverse conversations—could become privy to all sorts of rumors and myths floating around in the congested bars...floating around ever so recklessly along with the cloying smoke and sour, shit-scented air. One dark night, fate seated Valenesti close to two cloaked men who had just arrived from Herezye, the settlement of thieves and assassins situated deep within Sinners Forest, hundreds of leagues to the southeast of Hadig-vie.

In hushed tones, the two discussed their own plot to recover and appropriate the legendary Staff of Morana Goll. Months spent in the taverns had taught Valenesti to become quite the skilled eavesdropper; he listened intently to their plans, mainly because he was familiar with the staff's purported attributes. According to legend, it possessed the capacity to restore life. It could read the will and wishes of its bearer and then engage its inherent power to reach beyond the veil of death to reincarnate one—but only one—fallen soul before its magic was spent.

Upon hearing of their plan, his alcoholic haze began to lift. The wheels driving his will began to turn again. If the staff even existed...if it could be found...these two ruffians planned to whisk it away and sell it to the highest bidder for gold that they would quickly squander on liquor and diseased whores. As an heir of bitter mourning, Valenesti entertained other designs for its awesome power...designs that he deemed far nobler. He planned to unearth The Staff of Morana Goll and call forth its power, summoning it to return his lost love to him...his beloved Elise. The ghost that danced at the fringes of his dreams, the face that haunted his bittersweet memories, would finally be replaced by flesh! Flesh that he had felt once, so long ago. Flesh whose floral aroma he had once inhaled like a tantalizing spring breeze. Flesh he had licked and tasted when the fires on the hearth burned low and when the flames of passion burned high.

Valenesti, as the appalling story unfolded, brutally stabbed the two men after they left the tavern that night. He butchered them and stole the map, which he was sure would lead him straight to the gates of his own Haeven. For two long years he had sought only to dig his own grave using a pewter mug instead of a shovel, but now he had become an impenitent murderer, and would soon become much, much more. Driven by desperation and single-minded focus that history might one day judge as madness, he returned to the farm that had been the cradle of his short-lived joy. Climbing down the wall of a well from which he had drawn hundreds of buckets of clear water, he descended into the network of tunnels that, unbeknownst to all but a handful of the staunchest historians, formed a dizzying and tortuous web through the very bedrock of Hadig-vie.

Even with the aid of the precious map for which he had committed his first mortal sins, he lost his way countless times and was forced to backtrack to reference points that he adroitly marked on the blood-stained parchment. Never losing patience and certainly never losing heart, he searched through most of that month for the staff before finally locating it in the broad catacombs secreted beneath the very heart of Hadig-vie.

The fragments of his broken heart hammered with renewed anticipation as he stepped into the chamber where the staff had been lain reverentially on a stone dais, a cold and crude altar swathed in violet velvet that had somehow retained its faultless sheen...a dustless drape that had somehow escaped the insidious rot and ravages of time. The pitiful little pack containing his remaining few provisions dropped to the stone floor with a clatter, and he took a wavering step toward the coveted relic that had driven him to kill yet persuaded him to live.

But then something stirred in the shadows and he froze in mid-stride. Valenesti saw the flaming eyes first...orange slits leering at him from deep shadows that became more shallow with every step that the wicked angel took toward the single column of light—light stretching from floor to ceiling near the center of the cavernous chamber. A lone, shimmering ray of lavender radiance shot upward from the dais on which the staff of resurrection rested.

One minor detail that the map's maker failed to mention involved the presence of the staff's pitiless guardian, the estranged angel, Azrael. Azrael—bastard of Haeven and outcast from Hel. A single glimpse into the swirling infernos that were Azrael's eyes conveyed to Valenesti without any ambiguity precisely how the angel planned to end the bereaved drunkard's pitiful life. Within and behind the orange flames dancing in those baleful wells, Valenesti saw flashes of nauseating images...glimpses into the black non-soul that had been deemed too foul to enter even Hel's gates. He was allowed a glance at Azrael's blood-soaked blueprints...horrific plans regarding not only Valenesti's gruesome and impending doom, but also designs to personally punish all the unsuspecting citizens of the city that sprawled overhead. Through his own bloodshot eyes, he read the will and peered into the soul of an angel that had been turned. An angel that had renounced its ties with Haeven. In doing so, it had become a true demon and more.

♦♦♦

Since the night of his cursed conception—when brother and sister had lain together in a fevered but forbidden embrace—this foul angel had been destined to become a vessel of chaos, a beast utterly engaged in the eruption of indiscriminate wrath. The price of his perverted heritage was a profound, disturbing sickness of mind. Through a protracted series of black deeds and bloody betrayals, he had earned his ignoble rank in Haeven's already convoluted hierarchy. He was arguably more cruel and less trustworthy than any of his feathery-winged brethren.

And all those considerations had earned him his present post... his present sentence. But now, fate had finally sent a wink his way— a wink in the form of a pretty little plaything with a wasted frame, fading pulse, and bloodshot eyes. As the stranded angel strode forward from the post he had assumed for decades on end, Azrael thought at first that he would leisurely torture this pathetic little wayfarer. In due course, he would likely slaughter this worm of a man, his first visitor in decades aside from the occasional sewer rat.

Like a starving kitten attacking a saucer of milk, the angel would lick the streams of crimson spilling from the wounds that he inflicted while driven by the unquenchable lust for human suffering. He would lose himself in evil rapture, caress his calloused loins to the rhythm and the intonations of this dying man's primal screams. Every precise cut, every calculated slice would represent but another graceless step in a grand dance macabre. Azrael would revel in the ruthless deeds just to slake his angelic lust for cruelty…sick hunger which had only intensified during the agonizing years of his sentence…one that he deemed entirely unjust.

♦♦♦

In the instant that the mad angel stepped fully into the halo of lavender light surrounding the staff's dais, Azrael's stiff wings stretched to full span, quivered and then retracted like a child's hands withdrawing from a hot stove. He took a menacing first step toward the spot where Valenesti stood, but the despondent man made no move to flee, so ready was he for an end to his emotional misery.

Valenesti had come seeking redemption, but if he was to be denied that, then he would accept darkness in its stead even if it involved enduring a brief stint of exquisite torture…even if it involved a choreographed series of cuts and punctures, an iniquitous art of which angels were purported to possess an innate mastery. He would see Elise either way, after all.

He may bleed a bit during the transition, but he would not plead for mercy. He would not plead at all, by damn! As the reddened eyes of one mourning man engaged those of Haeven's foulest angel, so too did their thoughts. Their minds merged yet again for one ugly but magnificent instant, and Valenesti became a witness to the deep wells of horror's harshest components. His spirit, however, was already seven steps beyond numb. He was not afraid of any fate that might await him, not in the least, for fear had years ago abandoned its throne to sorrow and pity. And to apathy, utter and complete.

♦♦♦

Azrael's eyes narrowed into thin slits of orange fire. This winged one became a slave to heady anticipation, and his eunuchoid loins throbbed with impotent lust. Initially, he was astounded that this fool-ish little interloper was making no effort whatsoever to scurry away in fear, but ultimately it would not matter...ultimately, neither of them would see Haeven. Azrael tilted his head and leered at his new pet, one whose screams would soon echo from the cold cavern walls for a time and temporarily break the monotony of the merciless angel's lengthy exile. But then an alternate plan quickly began to take form in Azrael's scheming mind, one that would promptly deliver him from these catacombs, ending the expulsion decreed by those bickering idiots up in Haeven.

Once he attained his freedom, he would not be limited to only one victim. Oh, no. Oh, gods no! The world above was literally crawling with potential targets, fodder just waiting to be hurled into the black void of his lust. It was a void that could never be filled... not until the last man was slain...not until that man's children were torn apart like so many bloody little rags...not until his expectant wife had spent her last precious breath screaming her anguish and horror toward the Haevens, pleading for the gods to — at the very least — spare the life of her unborn child.

At that point, like a starving wolf whose instincts to survive sur-passed any other urges, Azrael would finally dine on fresh blood. He would revel in her terror and pleasure himself as he studied her dis-torted and tear-stained visage. He would likely achieve some sick manner of spiritual climax as he beheld the revulsion and betrayal that defined her twisted death mask. With one hand, he would brush the sweaty hair out of her dead eyes...perfect patches of canvas for the strokes of his cruel brush...perfect media for the stain of disbelief. No gods would heed her last shriek, he knew. And it would not be because they could not hear her. It would be because they simply did not care. With his other hand, he would calmly finger the rim of her cooling womb.

Yes, Azrael must achieve freedom above all else, even at the ex-pense of a single, fleeting moment of gory rapture. He must delay gratification. This stoic intruder — this wasted little man — might sur-vive for a while longer, but Azrael had an entire harvest of souls to reap and bodies to ruin. He yearned to swing his scythe and cackle beneath the gray winter clouds as he gathered his blood-drenched crops.

The demented angel's plan was now set. He would willingly surrender the dormant staff to Valenesti, for Azrael alone knew precisely the extent of devastation that would follow and he would finally be able to end the exile through which he had suffered, tucked away so far below this city that had obviously been doomed from the beginning. Ultimately, it was revenge against his Haevenly brethren that he sought; and the removal of the staff would thwart their carefully laid plans, at least for a time. Valenesti dropped to his knees as Azrael severed their psychic ties. *Fuck them all*, the fallen one decided as he relaxed his stance and put his hands behind his back, endeavoring to appear as unthreatening as a deranged angel possibly could.

♦♦♦

As Valenesti rose and cautiously approached the platform, Azrael unexpectedly stood down, giggling and grinning, an animated statue of a disturbed and truly twisted seraph...one who had eons ago elected to step through the gilded archway separating discretion from heartless lunacy. No mortal man untouched by the wily fingers of insanity could have so much as held Azrael's gaze for very long, but mad Valenesti had done that and more—he had, for a few sickening seconds, stared into the bottomless depths of the evil one's warped essence. He had already survived two years of torture far more intense than what this malicious whore of Haeven could possibly dish out. He had not feared death since the day it had seized Elise and enveloped her in its abrasive, ebony cloak. How often had he fantasized...how often had he ached for the chance to sprint toward the reaper and impale himself on the curved blade of that legendary scythe...how often had he hoped for the chance to die by the same blade that had already cost him his life?

By now, he was ready to become anything except what he was. He fully expected to fall victim to treachery, but—in truth—he did not care if the angel ended him right then and there. He met Azrael's vulturine gaze once more. Valenesti perceived no overt threat in the angel's blazing orange eyes, for he only saw them through the boiling mists of his own madness. He returned Azrael's conniving glare without so much as flinching.

"Don't stop at the staff. Why not take the blade as well, little man? It too was crafted by Morana Goll. Who knows? Someone in your lineage might find a use for it when they inevitably experience the same kind of soul-shattering loss that even now impels you. The staff and blade are twins, after all; and no twins should be separated, now should they? No. That would be…sad," Azrael tacked on in a little girl's voice. He even stuck his bottom lip out in a mock pout. It lasted for only a second. Then his face morphed back into the mien of an incensed demon.

"Take them. Take them and be gone, worm! I will not hinder your retreat, though a hasty retreat it must be else you will be buried beneath the wreckage of the city above, for it is doomed to collapse into these very chambers once you seize your prize. You do not have wings like mine, now do you, little man? No. Mine will deliver me from ruin. Mine will deliver me from all that remains. You, I fear, must rely only on your weak little human legs. My role here is finished, at last…my *penance* done. There are tender throats to be slit in Haeven…throats all pale and pasty…stale yet tasty," Azrael snickered. His dark wings shuddered once more. "Destiny—that devious whore—summons me finally to stand beside her throne, and I find myself anxious…compelled to heed her clarion call. It summons you as well, I suppose. But it does not call you to Haeven. No. Certainly not Haeven. And after tonight, worm," Azrael paused to chuckle, "Hel will have little to do with you either, I'll wager. Guilt from the destruction of Hadig-vie shall be the price you pay for disturbing the staff. Remorse for the death of thousands shall be the toll you pay for exhuming Goll's staff from its own velvety tomb. And yet you do not even care. I can see as much in your tired eyes."

Valenesti had not noticed it before, but now he clearly beheld the curved silver blade lying beside the legendary staff. It, like its sister talisman, was adorned with a single brilliant lavender gem, this one set in its gleaming pommel, just beneath the sterling cross guard. The dark angel's last portentous words had made no more of an impression on him than a swallow's song on a spring morning. He stumbled forward toward the source of his only remaining hope.

In the precise instant the tortured and lonely wheelwright extricated the archaic artifacts from their resting places, the very bedrock on which Hadig-vie sat started to quake and crumble. Convinced that the deafening din was caused at least in part by his lovely Elise extricating herself from her cold grave, Valenesti hurried from the chamber where the mad angel continued to cackle as he slowly flapped his black wings, warming the muscles in preparation for his overdue exodus from these cold caverns.

◆◆◆

Valenesti raced through the tortuous tunnels, following the urgent whispers that hissed at him from the shadows, relying more on his foggy memory and the unraveling remnants of his instinct than the scribbled notes on his worn and bloodied map. Somehow, Fate steered him through the maze, though history would have to decide whether Fate had intervened on behalf of Haeven or Hel.

By the grim grace of providence, he at long last climbed out of the tunnels and into the relative safety of the brutal and wind-scoured plains. Though the gravity of the close call did not even register in his diseased mind, Valenesti barely managed to escape the catacombs with his life. He was intent on one thing and one thing only — reaching the stand of swaying pines where he had buried his love and his light two years prior; and it was toward that very spot that he sprinted despite the inky darkness. It was toward that spot that he sprinted despite the sharp boulders and the uneven, throbbing terrain. He stumbled and fell numerous times, but he hardly noticed the sensation of slick warm blood trickling down from both knees...from both palms.

When he reached the outskirts of his old farm, he looked over his shoulder just in time to see the magnificent city crashing down, collapsing into a mountain of rubble that the historians would later name Hadig-sin, to curse the place for the mass tomb that it had become...a tomb for the thousands of people who had been caught unawares by the violent earthquake that sent them spiraling into the vortex of nevermore.

He stood there supported by wounded, wobbly knees. He was wholly spellbound by the swift collapse of Eldimorah's loneliest city and by the plumes of dust that boiled skyward to obscure this winter night's stars. Those choking stars...damn them! He finally saw them for what they truly represented: tiny crystals trapped under ice, their light rapidly fading. Damn them, but they reminded him of cold, condemnatory eyes that belonged to a gallery of jurors. Their light was fading...thankfully.

On that crisp but caustic night Valenesti laughed, then cried, then laughed yet again. His bruised spirit was now a well of contradictory squeals offering an unintelligible, babbling testimony to his inveterate plunge into the ravenous mouth of madness. The earth beneath his feet continued to complain by way of intermittent shudders that were violent enough to throw him off balance, so he widened his stance to keep from falling on his face. All the while, he leaned on the staff of Morana Goll for support…the staff, his newest and most precious treasure.

He wept. Hot tears poured from his eyes and soaked into the thirsty fabric of his shredded soul. They coursed down his dirty cheeks, across the backs of his hands. Sizzling like spit on hot coals, they trickled down the length of the varnished staff and disappeared into the dusty, parched ground. As he wailed and watched the destruction wrought by the power he had so selfishly unleashed, Elise's gaunt corpse limped out of the shadows behind him. She limped to his side and took his shaking hand in her own, a wasted husk of a hand, cold and caked with the grime of a winter grave.

Valenesti did not as much as flinch at her touch, but he did battle for breath as he turned to face this barely recognizable newcomer that he immediately…recognized. Faded shreds of his wife's burial gown hung from this creature's emaciated torso. It was a torso that no longer housed a heart, and that absence of spirit told him all he really needed to know. Once more, his hopes had been eclipsed by the grins of malicious gods. Alas, he had been deceived by the hollow promise of some foolish legend. Remnants of that damned burial gown and a few stubborn strands of painfully familiar dark hair that hung from her rotten scalp provided the only evidence that this… shell…used to be his Elise. Her eye sockets were now dark voids, and the brittle gray skin clinging to her gaunt face split like a dry leaf as she tried to force a frivolous smile. The stench of decay prompted him to retch, but the underlying fragrance of her favorite perfume — the fragrance with which he had embalmed her — made him want to ravage her on the spot. Lust and disgust wrestled one another as he stood there weeping and leaning against the staff. More tears fell.

A shell of a woman long dead smiled, and the shell of a dying man wailed, both beneath the same dim sky. One stood, the other kneeled as thousands of released souls and a lone winged form rose through the roiling clouds of ruin's rust.

◆◆◆

Hours after the earth ceased shuddering, hours after the last violent tremor had passed, Valenesti felt…led to scramble through the rubble of the vast wreckage that he had wrought. For every jagged stone over which he stepped, a dead and disfigured face stared up at him with wide, lifeless eyes. All were caked in a sick sandy glaze… the settled dust of devastation. Only a few craggy sections of the city walls stood now. All but the sturdiest of structures that had been enclosed by those walls had been brought down by the Sansaprar Shelf's grand convulsions. Still, the shadows cast by those few towers of twisted stone were all that distinguished east from west on this eerily quiet morning. Using those shattered remains of the walls as his sole points of reference, he picked his way through the maze of debris. Suppressing his sobs, he wove his way to the street where that last tiny tavern had stood...the tavern in which his destiny had changed...the tavern in which he had been betrayed by the gods for at least the second time in his miserable life.

As he tripped over the end of a timber, he went down again. Many of the fresh scabs on his knees and palms were re-opened. His chin even struck the rubble and he felt his teeth pierce his tongue. He tasted blood, but he felt not the first inkling of pain. The pain came only when he caught sight of a limp hand protruding from beneath a jagged slab of stone that lay just ahead. His flagging spirit screamed to him that he should recognize that pale and gentle hand, and he immediately began to weep yet again. He wept in remembrance of a cold and distant light.

The first time he had seen that hand, it was delivering a mug of ale to him as he sat alone at his little table on that wintry and fateful night. It had patted him on his chest and sparked a critical fire in so doing. Later that night, those precious fingers had held forth a warm wrap as his last living goddess rushed toward the door...a wrap that he could have used to turn away the worst of the storm. Like some blind fool who chose to deny the warm kiss of fate, he had allowed the door to close behind him, cutting him off from what may have well been his second chance at true happiness. Yes, a door had certainly closed behind him that evening as he stepped into the ultimate storm and away from the beaming light surrounding the second angel that had been sent to save him from himself. Pacing the hallway like a blind man, he had stumbled away from the glow of yet another divine halo.

By now, blood was freely rolling down his chin. With amazing ease, he pushed aside that fucking, jagged slab of masonry; staring back at him were Mallory's angelic eyes. They were still utterly perfect, even though they were now glued open in death. But even in death, her unanimated smile was beguiling and seductive. Her flawless face, though bloodied and bruised, was still far more beautiful...

infinitely more natural, than the grotesque mask worn by the grim shadow of Elise that even now stood unsteadily behind him as he leaned forward, bracing his hands on the cold rubble.

Behind him, that rotting and farcical excuse for subsistence studied him with the blank, vacuous face of some distorted porcelain doll. She watched him with innocent curiosity, as if the sobs that shook his shoulders and the wails of anguish that rocked his soul were no more demoralizing than a butterfly that had just lighted on the back of her hand. Elise's body was just that...a corpse without a spirit... just a babe in a black abyss.

Valenesti collapsed beside the spot where Mallory had died and ever so lovingly brushed some of those amazing, long locks away from the face that he should have never left behind. His knees bled freely as he rocked back and forth screaming his torment to the unsympathetic morning skies, though their azure depths were still occluded by the hovering dust of devastation. Daylight began to fade as he kissed her palm and pressed the back of her cold hand against his damp cheek, all the while wishing that hot tears could accomplish what the spent powers of Morana Goll refused to. He wrapped Mallory's dead fingers around the staff and doused them with the bitter rain from his soul, praying that the ancient magic would perhaps allow him a second chance at redemption. But its power had indeed—apparently—been spent, and its only yield had been a putrid husk donning a few scraps of a white burial gown.

He continued to rock and his abraded knees continued to leach crimson into the dust coating the jagged rubble. There he kneeled, there he vomited, and there he wept until the daystar finally relinquished the cold sky to the twin quarter moons that stared down at him like the squinted eyes of some cosmic judge passing sentence for all the horrendous crimes he had committed in the course of just two days. Morning arrived; by then, his tears were mostly spent. He pushed himself to his feet and lovingly wrapped Mallory's head in his old tunic. The fabric that had served as his second skin for so long would now shelter the face that had stolen his heart. It only seemed fitting. He stumbled through the wreckage until he reached the city's western gate. Then he left Hadig-vie behind forever.

Within just a fortnight of Hadig-vie's destruction, all things living and all things green had forsaken the rocky wilds atop the Sansaprar Shelf. Hadig-vie and even the relatively unforgiving farmlands surrounding its mighty walls had once represented a haven in a harsh and barren wilderness; a refuge whose vitality and very spirit had been intrinsically linked to the presence of the mighty staff that Valenesti now used as a simple walking cane. Now, bereft of that magic's presence, Hadig-vie had fallen and the collective voice of its former citizens had been forever silenced, relegated to the hiss of winter winds that raced across this vast expanse of jagged boulders.

With Hadig-vie reduced to mounds of ghost-infested rubble, the sterility of the Northern Wastes was now complete and unspoiled. In the span of a single night, the bustling city that once floated alone in a sea of stone had instead become the seat of restless serenity. Its ruins had sprung from the womb of a dead world, the stillborn progeny of a vengeful angel's improvised strategem married to the desperate aspirations of a man decimated by mourning and heartache. Its streets were now desolate graveyards of memories, stony and barren, silent but for those mournful northern winds that never had to take a breath as they continued to sing their lonely song.

And that song haunted Valenesti day and night. Each time the daystar retreated, he would lay awake, nestled among the cold rocks. Those rocks, however, were far warmer than the mute and rotting likeness of his Elise who insisted on resting her balding head on his shoulder. It was during those moments that the spiteful wind truly began to sing, and he listened to every verse, every chorus. He had no choice. In the language shared by broken hearts and failing minds, the winds sang to him, regaling him with tales of towers torn and dreams turned to dust...tales of quiet desperation and atonement. And then there were the incessant echoes of children's laughter silenced now and forever by tons of jagged rubble. Those vengeful winds shrieked as they brushed his raw, tear-stained cheeks. He heard their icy breath whisper in his ear, reminding him that an era of innocence had ended. It had ended violently, and he alone was to blame.

Valenesti, tormented by the horrific consequences of his deed, wandered the wastes aimlessly for days using the cursed staff of Morana Goll like a blind man might use a cane to navigate a dipping and diving forest path. He and the macabre mannequin that had been his spouse turned south, though he did not really know why. At last, they reached the lip of the Northern Wastes, a sheer cliff wall that ran east and west for tens of hundreds of leagues, spanning the entire breadth of Eldimorah. The two specters made the laborious descent down the Sansaprar Shelf and spent the next stormy day recuperating in its hungry shadow.

Heavy rains turned gentle, then heavy again. Those determined drops hissed against the boulders and loose shale lining the base of the cliff, and their spray washed much of the clingy mud off of his mute companion's pocked skin. Elise tugged at the rotting remnants of her burial gown, and soon stood naked and colder even than the winter rains. The filthy waters gathered in a pool at her feet. The showers intensified, washing away layers of fouled earth which— had the gods been granted their way—should have served as her blanket for eternity.

From the shadows of the shallow outcropping, Valenesti watched her clumsy and uncoordinated movements as she tried to wipe away the stubborn grime. She endeavored to wash her wispy hair, but its roots had lost all purchase during her stint in the grave, a stint which spanned eight seasons. Clumps of matted hair fell free from her dead scalp, and she stared down at the locks with all the curiosity and wonder of a child studying a baby bird that had fallen from its nest. He watched every second of the surreal show, and as he did so his emotions swung like a pendulum…they swung between sick lust and sheer revulsion.

After she staggered in from the storm, after most of the grave's darker stains had been rinsed away, he aimed to at long last make love to the animated remains of his Elise. Enough time had passed. He would do so for the sake of forsaken memories; he would do so to satisfy insanity's unremitting insistence. It would certainly not be as he had once imagined. There would be no fireplace…and there would ultimately be no trace of Elise.

Steeling himself, he leaned in and chanced the kiss for which he had waited so long—the kiss for which thousands had died—but the taste and stench of rotting carcass made him disgorge. Nevertheless, he laid her down and sought to move on to other endeavors, stoking his desire and duping his senses with the traces of distant memories of passionate nights spent on the thick rug in front of their hearth where logs once crackled and cozy fires blazed.

Demanding that at least one dark debt be repaid, he pressed downward. He longed for her chill carcass to rub him raw. The moment he achieved full penetration, a long worm cloaked in sticky black loam slithered out of Elise's empty eye socket, tumbled down her cheek and began laboring to burrow into the stony soil to find another, more suitable winter home. That image paired with the revolting sensation of her cold, dry loins promptly spoiled his madness-inspired mood. He withdrew, leapt to his feet and fastened his trousers; the waters of insanity had suddenly grown too deep. No seed could he spill in this dead womb, for to do so would leave his soiled soul even more unclean.

Without any consideration for the storm that raged just beyond the outcropping that had sheltered them throughout the morning, he seized his staff, shouldered his small pack and headed out across the plains of Rayll. Day and night, he marched doggedly on, not stopping to eat, drink, sleep, or even defecate. All the while, the reanimated horror that was, in another age, his lovely Elise followed him like a limping but loyal dog...a dog that felt its master's pain but knew of no way to alleviate it. Lacking a will of its own, it simply followed and obeyed.

When at last his body was near exhaustion and when his spirit was completely broken, Valenesti collapsed in the tall grass blanketing the Plains of Rayll, weeping and wallowing in his own filth that his bowels had finally seen fit to discharge. No longer did he harbor any desire to put distance between himself and the immense guilt dogging him. No longer did he consider himself worthy of any fate short of Hel's deepest and darkest cellar. No longer was he even able to remember a time when he was not thoroughly insane. Love was dead. Love lay still. He was almost free.

Never again would he scream for life. He looked toward a raven, a black shape flying away in the dark. One lone glimpse of those dark wings and his lips twisted like blades of green grass tossed onto hot coals. Without a moment's hesitation, he broke the cursed staff over his knee and, in so doing, unleashed even more of the staff's latent power...a component of its power of which legend had made no mention. Valenesti's arms were struck momentarily numb and fell to hang lifelessly at his sides. Lavender lightning erupted from the faceted stone that dropped from the fractured staff, and that lightning blazed across the starry night sky.

His voice had failed him, although he did not know for sure when he had fallen mute. With some sick stranger's tears rolling down his cheeks, he mouthed a simple apology to the night sky and then drove one sharp stake through the dead heart of the abomination that had followed behind him like a lame and rancid shadow. Her balding head tilted to one side, more out of confusion than woe, perhaps: like a poor puppy who was unaware of why it was being punished. Aside from a stifled grunt, there was no scream for life. She remained utterly silent as she died for the second time. Without so much as a groan or a gurgle, all that remained of Elise fell in a filthy heap, tainting the pure grasses of the plains with the toxin of perversion, a soulless puppet ripped from the grave by an ancient magic that delivered far less than the fables had promised.

With lavender lightning still racing across the cloudless sky, he grasped the remaining stake with both hands and drove it deeply into the soft earth as he fell forward to await his own death and the descent to Hel that would surely follow...a trip to Hel that he had earned through his recent chain of dark deeds. He wanted so much to scream, but his voice had abandoned him, never to return in this life. So he did all that he could in that agonizing moment...he wept in silence. His last tears shed beneath the moons of Eldimorah were shed without as much as a whimper. With his cheek resting on the damp grass he could once again feel the fair earth beginning to quake and shiver beneath him. Was it the earth, or could it possibly be Mallory's fair hand trying to shake him awake from this brutal nightmare? Valenesti tasted salty tears from his eyes. He tasted coppery blood from the tongue that his teeth had recently pierced. No, Mallory was gone. She was not where she belonged, but she was where she was supposed to stay.

*Where had that raven disappeared to?* His eyes scanned the evening shadows as he searched for the harbinger of doom, and they bled both madness and fear. There had to be another explanation for these new tremors, he decided. Valenesti, suddenly convinced that the souls of his many victims back in Hadig-vie were thundering southward to seize him and exact their revenge, stopped weeping. If only that was the case. If only the casualties of his selfishness would rip his flesh apart, then perhaps his soul could begin to heal. Everything he ever wanted was suddenly so far away; he wasn't the least bit interested in redemption at this point. He could offer no apology and no explanation to the very voices that had directed his errant actions. He only longed for death, and he considered any suffering that preceded that death welcome and well-deserved.

After all, he was by now largely immune to true suffering; he had journeyed to its limits and could map every detail of its jagged boundaries. It simply held no command over him anymore. There was nothing left to fear behind this final door, for he had reached the very apex of human anguish. Perhaps some twisted semblance of peace was finally at hand. Perhaps he had endured enough grief to receive absolution...or to secure annihilation. Once the rumbling ceased—once he made his descent into Hel—he would hopefully find tranquility at last, despite the blisters and boils on the surface of his soul. Once he arrived in that dark realm, he would stake his claim. Peace he would claim as his own province, even as his flesh, subjected to the insatiable fires of the damned, charred to black crust.

But the rumbling did not cease; it escalated. It escalated, prompting him to open his tired eyes and lift his head. To his ultimate surprise, trees of every species began to burst forth from the ground. They made the wondrous transition from seedling to sapling to hardened adult in the span of just a few heartbeats. Firs, pines, and mighty oaks groaned and cracked as their green limbs sprang toward the winter stars, showering the surrounding plains with the moist loam that had hidden their tiny seeds only moments earlier.

When the eruptions finally ended, Valenesti found himself squatting in a broad meadow that was completely surrounded by the dark and swaying giants. The hardwoods sported full green foliage, despite the late season. They completely encircled him and the broad field in which he now sat. His weary and bloodshot eyes—mirrors of madness and disbelief—surveyed his new surroundings. The clearing probably measured two leagues or more in diameter; but compared to the boundless plains that had claimed every horizon just a few minutes past, the field almost seemed confining, cast as it was in moonless shadow by the huge trees that now encircled it.

Silence once again settled on the plains and the new forest which they hosted, but the silence was not fated to last for very long. Once again, the earth started to rumble. This time the roar was more violent and even deeper in pitch. As the sonic assault grew fiercer, Valenesti pressed his palms to his ears but to no avail. Vicious vibrations made his teeth hurt. He was being pummeled from every direction at once by invisible fists that seemed intent on breaking every one of his ribs, and they were already so very sore from his recent bouts of weeping. It seemed as though the vengeful air about him was morphing into a nest of agitated, invisible vipers striking and slamming his frail body

with the implacable anger of all the gods whose codes he had disparaged for the last two years. As the rumbling grew even more intense,
the earth under his chest and belly started to move, writhing and shaking…it was complaining in a low, groaning hum.

Fighting the lurch of living earth, he pushed himself up on all
fours and surveyed yet another inexplicable transformation, this one
occurring in the very center of the broad field. Everywhere he looked,
rounded domes of gold jutted from the ground. Like immense, gilded
mushrooms, the fantastic roofs shot skyward, pushed up into the
night sky by walls of white tapered stone. Astounded by the blooms
in this surreal garden, Valenesti watched in mute awe as the odd
structures rose steadily into the starry night sky. When the rumbling
finally ceased, a grand city stood in the middle of the new forest.
Tarchannen Eid had been born, delivered from a womb that had lain
silently and secretly beneath the gentle rolling hills of the Plains of
Rayll. A grand city that had sprouted from its own unique seeds…
pods of magic and mourning. It was a project that had called for no
architects other than the will of gods, and no masons aside from the
latent might of the sorcerer supreme, Morana Goll.

By now, Valenesti's nerves had utterly abandoned him. They had
followed his faltering sanity off a disturbingly steep cliff. Convulsions seized him, forcing him to fall back into the tall grass, every
muscle wracked by uncontrollable tremors. Once again, he bit
through his tongue and the coppery taste of his own blood registered
in his mind, but it caused him no real concern. There was no pain.
His head was resting on Elise's naked torso, but in yet another ironic
twist, the feel of her cool dead skin on his cheek comforted him until
the fit passed. At last, he sat up. Valenesti wept, then laughed, then
wept again as he surveyed the new creation. He scanned the city and
forest born of a truly strange marriage…a marriage between his own
anguish and the potent magic trapped within the shattered Staff of
his faceless tormentor, Morana Goll. Morana Goll, the reaper
wreathed in cold flames.

Back at the tavern on that stormy night, he had made the decision
to forego suicide and embark on this fateful journey largely due to
desperate faith in the fables. He made the choice to take a chance.
He came near to drowning that night. The only lifeline offered to him
was the possibility that the staff was indeed host to some inconceiv-
able and immense power to grant its bearer one precious chance to

cheat the grave and resurrect a lost loved one.

But now, in this moment, sitting in the night air and surrounded by the huge trees and the magnificent buildings and temples, he realized that the staff was capable of granting not just one wish, but two...one that taunted and another that taught. His wish to bring Elise back to him had ultimately been superseded by his sorrow over the destruction he had unwittingly visited upon Hadig-vie. Here he knelt wide open, surrendering to fate's grim sighs. He long ago laid down his armor, and he carried no sword at his side.

Valenesti's latest torrent of tears dried as he considered that twisted slant. Though he knew that he could never restore all the lives that had been lost due to his selfishness, he took solace in the realization that more people would someday come here to find shelter in this wondrous city created from the depths of his sorrow and perhaps from the labyrinth of his own muted imagination. Maybe not tomorrow, but one day soon, the many darkened windows that stared down at him like the eyes of unsympathetic accusers would shine with the light of life. And perhaps the laughter of children would echo through these empty streets.

He had witnessed...no, he had been a catalyst to...a rebirth. After a few unsuccessful attempts, he finally managed to stand, though he wobbled and wavered like a babe about to take its first solo steps. His coordination returned to a degree as he stumbled toward the broad arch of the magnificent city's eastern gate, all the while wiping the tears and the dirt away from his face with his soiled and tattered sleeve. Sustained only by stern resolve, the wheelwright followed the beckoning rush of cascading water and walked straight to the wondrous fountain near the city's heart. He paused there for a moment and let the mist from its cascading waters wash his face clean. Over the roar of those rushing waters, an insistent voice whispered in his ear. It summoned him. It directed him through the narrow alleys and along the broader cobbled streets. It was the voice of his fragmented spirit, the voice of this deserted city's oblivious architect.

Following that instinctual summons, he turned onto yet another quiet and dark street to his left. At long last, he stood before the tallest building in the city, a mighty tower that pointed like a rigid finger toward the placid roof of Eldimorah...toward the floor of Haeven itself. Valenesti mounted the steps and disappeared into the blackness that hung about the place this night like layers of thick velvet curtains.

More than an hour later, he emerged from that darkness and stepped out onto a balcony suspended hundreds of cubits above the vacant streets. At this height, a cool breeze pushed his long, greasy bangs back and away from the exhausted eyes that had beheld so much in the span of just a few days. When he was but a child, he had a fever and his mother brushed his hair back in much the same fashion, though she used warm fingers that still felt cool against his forehead. In this breeze, he could hear her calming voice promising that all would end well. It promised that he had just been the victim of a bad dream that would soon end...as soon as the new day dawned.

With that gentle and familiar voice from the past prompting him, he walked over to the parapet and once more drank in the unfathomable beauty of the symmetrical buildings that had sprouted within this amazing garden bounded by the high walls. Though he was now immune to disbelief, his heart still tried to sing as he regarded the sea of swaying trees that spread out to the margins of the four horizons beyond the city's bleached, white walls.

The air was noticeably cooler as he climbed atop the balcony's low parapet and battled to keep his balance. His legs were quivering with fatigue, rage, and confusion...with madness and surrender. Finally though, they calmed and allowed him to sway, matching the rhythm of the tall trees being tossed about in the breeze. That bracing breeze felt like a teasing taste of Haeven. It continued to blow across his clammy skin, calming him like the gentle breath of a lover. He smiled to himself as he surveyed his handiwork from this new vantage point. At last, after years of selfish indulgence and after one terrible day of destruction, he had been party to the creation of something pure...something beautiful. At last, something beautiful.

But his penance was not complete, not just yet. Valenesti, with at least some remnant of his elusive sanity finally returning to him, closed his tired eyes and allowed himself to fall forward, offering himself body and soul to the whimsical winds that had grown used to hissing unimpeded across the barren Plains of Rayll. As this fateful night drew to a close, they had abruptly been commanded to weave through a maze of towers, a network of new obstacles that had been erected from the blueprints of providence. The cool air turned cold as the velocity of his descent picked up. Early morning air whistled past, caressing his skin as the street below rushed up to meet him, but his spirit escaped its frail prison and soared away long before he was impaled on the sharp morning shadows cast by these strange new towers. Long before his emaciated body struck the unyielding stones. At last, he was free to be reunited with dear Elise...the true Elise, beautiful and unblemished. Wrapped in radiance, she would be waiting for him at the bottom of the fall.

# 3

$Q$uinn reverently closed the book and laid it ever so gently on top of the squat bookcase that doubled as his nightstand. After handily polishing off the rest of the Redscape in his glass, he climbed into bed and fell back against his fat, down-stuffed pillows. He pressed both thumbs against the bridge of his nose to arrest any wayward tears, but to no avail. A single rivulet snaked down the side of his face and the drops were eagerly soaked up by the thirsty pillow sham. That tear was soon followed by another, and he found himself fighting the need to sob yet again. *What an incredible story; what a horrific tale*! He thought to himself as he spread his arms wide for a quick stretch.

It was at that precise moment that the dizziness kicked in. It was then that he realized that his arms might as well have been crow's wings catching the thermals on an autumn morning. Sweat broke out on his forehead and the recently downed Redscape rose unnervingly close to the back of his throat. As much as he wanted to tear it open this instant, that second envelope would simply have to wait until morning. The bed below and the ceiling above were spinning in opposite directions, and closing his eyes didn't help matters much, nor did attempting to sit up on the edge of his mattress. Eventually, after sucking in a few deep breaths, his vertigo subsided. It was quickly — and thankfully — replaced by a cool, comforting wave of drowsiness.

By all indications, his mother had succumbed to the sedating effects of the wine as well, for he could hear Miriam's unladylike snoring echoing down the short hallway. Thankfully, the grating echoes didn't last very long, signifying to Quinn that she had turned up on her side. He would be safe until she rolled onto her back once again. By then — gods willing — he would be sawing away at his own stack of logs. Howling its lonesome lullaby, the winter wind abruptly picked up outside; like a frustrated hunter trying to gather up his dogs, it whistled around the corners and eaves of the two story apartment building. A few of the stronger gusts caused his window to rattle against its worn and weathered sill.

As the turmoil in his mind subsided, so too did the worst of his dizziness. This was going to be a wonderful night for sleeping, he decided as he pulled the blankets up to his chin. He did not even bother crawling beneath the smooth sheet. Quinn reached over and turned his lamp's wick way down, pulled the covers up over his ears and fell fast asleep.

That night, he dreamed of the Citadel nestled in the center of the forest deep. He dreamed that it was just as Valenesti had left it...just as the cursed one had viewed it from the lofty balcony on that fateful night several generations past. In Quinn's dream, the city was still Eldimorah's newest secret, it was still dark and uninhabited, except for two lone ghostly figures who walked hand-in-hand along the quiet streets. They were laughing, loving, and embracing the freedom known only to doves and ravens...and to those who had finally passed beyond the grand veil. In the dream, Quinn could hear the rushing waters of the tiered fountain that sang its song against a backdrop of reticence.

Reunited beneath a magnificent blaze that shamed even that offered by the daystar of Eldimorah on the clearest of days, Valenesti and Elise now had an eternity to spend with each other. After years of separation and hollow sorrow, the wheelwright had been granted his fondest desideratum: a silent, plush garden unspoiled by the choking coils of that foul snake, despair.

♦♦♦

When the faint but blatantly bitter glow of daybreak alerted Quinn that dawn had arrived, he pulled a pillow over his eyes and prayed for the gray taint to recede. His head was throbbing and the air in his room was far too stale, far too warm, even though the hallway door separating his cramped bedroom from the den stove had remained closed throughout the night. His mouth felt every bit as dry as a bale of November straw. All he could taste was bile mixed with hideous hints of Redscape wine mixed in. Had he not known better, he could have sworn that some bird on an all-grape diet had perched on his headboard and continuously shat in his mouth throughout the night. Wiping a streamer of cool drool from the corner of his mouth, Quinn rolled groggily out of bed and stumbled over to his window. It complained with a loud screech when he raised it just enough to let some fresh winter air rush in; it was bracing air that shocked his senses and brought him around as it filled his greedy lungs and stung his bare skin.

Though morning had broken, there were no sounds coming from the kitchen yet, he noticed. Miriam was undoubtedly taking advantage of the quiet, gray dawn and the silent song of falling snow by sleeping a little past her usual time. *That may be for the best*, Quinn quickly decided, for he had important business to take care of this day, matters that wooziness had required him to postpone until sunrise. His head was no longer swimming, but it *was* pounding; his thinking was perhaps no more clear than it had been last night. Still, certain affairs had been delayed long enough. On this gray morning, his curiosity pleaded for resolution.

The contents of that second envelope were beckoning him. That envelope contained a message meant for his eyes only…a message from his father, a message penned just days before its ailing author had taken those last wobbly steps through infinity's grim pall. That brittle, final letter had lingered in hibernation, huddling within the musty margins of its yellowed envelope for over ten years. But its sentence of confinement and secrecy ended today. It ended this minute, in fact. Its liberation could not wait a second longer, for Tomas had an urgent message to convey to his son.

Quinn did a rather graceless belly flop onto his bed and reached for the timeworn tome that represented some incongruous component of his delayed inheritance. After cramming a pillow under his chest and turning up his lamp to chase off some of the morning gloom, Quinn propped himself up on his elbows and eagerly turned the pages of the old book to where the second sealed envelope marked the conclusion of Valenesti's heart-wrenching tale.

It took all of three seconds for him to break his father's second wax seal and liberate the carefully folded pages from the envelope. Though it was graceless and quite erratic, the handwriting was unmistakably Tomas's. Quinn could feel his father's spirit sprouting wings and lifting off the brittle paper like victorious angels returning to Haeven after routing the ranks of their enemies. Still, it was clear to his orphaned son that the letter had been penned by a hopelessly unsteady hand that just barely allowed the letter's dying author to transfer his last and most urgent message from heart to quill to parchment. Those last hastily written words were legible, but barely so.

As Quinn began to devour their contents, his heart started to race yet again. It began to race...and ache.

*Now that you have read Valenesti's tale, Quinn, I must share a secret with you that will forever change your path, I'm afraid. Still, I cannot shield you from the truth, and it would be unjust for me to attempt to do so. Valenesti had a brother, lad. They were never especially close, nevertheless they were of the same blood. The tale that you just read was not some concocted fable rife with embellishment, the favored tool of most self-proclaimed historians. It was transcribed directly from a journal that Valenesti kept during the last days of his tormented life. We know not exactly when he commenced the log, but as close as we can tell, he started chronicling his last days during the time that he and the reanimated version of Elise were wandering the Northern Wastes, perhaps a day or two after the destruction of Hadig-vie. Though his sanity was quickly failing him, some voice...some instinct... led him to spill his soul for the sake of posterity. That same voice prompted him to bundle his journal and the Blade of Morana Goll together right before he stepped onto the parapet from which he took his plunge to the empty streets that awaited him below the dark city's highest balcony. Incredibly, he retained enough presence of mind to address that package to his brother, Harvenal, who lived hundreds of leagues away in Malorsa. The next mortal to arrive in Tarchannen Eid was Herodimae. He discovered the bundle on the balcony from which Valenesti leapt. Whether it was out of a sense of nobility, penitence, or just sheer naivety, Herodimae later recruited a courier to deliver the package to Harvenal. Had the first leader of our "beloved" new Church known what the package contained, he would have surely chosen a different course of action. The up and coming regime especially...Invadrael and his ilk...will stop at nothing to procure the blade. That is why they killed me, Quinn. They tried to get me to disclose its whereabouts, but I would not. I could not! I ultimately died to keep that secret, Quinn...I died to pass the secret on to you, and may the gods forgive me for handing you this burden. Harvenal had a son as well—Malachi. And Malachi was my great-great-grandfather, son. You are the direct descendent of poor Valenesti! As such, you are the rightful heir to the truth regarding his last days...and you are heir to the blade that Azrael spent decades guarding. As you probably know, I crafted your bed in my shop; and I knew that your mother, being the sentimental soul that she is, would never part with it. I gambled the fate of Eldimorah on that, in fact. Follow these directions closely, lad. Pull your bed away from the wall just a link, then kneel on the mattress so that your chest presses the large center finial back toward the wall. Reach out with your arms and pull the two corner finials back toward you. A compartment will open on the back side of the headboard in which you will discover the Blade of Morana Goll. Gods help you! I can offer you no advice other than to keep it close like a lover, lad...and show it to none other, not even to those whom you consider worthy of your trust. Alas, in the end, you will be able to trust no one. Carry it, guard it, and respect it. Fear it, but never ever use it on another's flesh! Promise me that much, son, though I may seem beyond the grim limits of hearing such a promise. Keep it from the Church of the New Way, lest Invadrael's corrupt designs for Eldimorah come to pass. My light is fading fast, Quinn. I figure that I have two more days at the most. Heed my words. Keep the knife away from the eyes of the Church, let no one else peruse the pages of the special tome that I have left you, for it quite boldly contradicts the teachings of that same Church...it offers some proof that their doctrines are founded on nothing but lies. You may keep my letters within the pages of the book or you may destroy them, whatever you think best. But show them to no one. Not even to your mother, Quinn. Her lack of complicity in all this business is all that keeps her alive. I love you both, son. I'm truly sorry for the burden that I have dropped on your shoulders ten years or so after my passing. Nevertheless, it is fate that dictates our roles, and not choice. We can improvise to a degree but when the curtain falls—and it will fall—we will ultimately be remembered for our portrayals of the roles set forth in scripts penned by the puppet masters, whoever the Hel they may be. Remember, lad...keep it close like a lover!*

At the bottom of this last page, Quinn noticed an unintentional and macabre post-script: an array of tiny specks were scattered along the lower margin of the aging and brittle parchment...a spray of co-agulated blood that had turned from red to black over time. Some of the memories of his father's last days were just too bitter to gracefully fade away. He remembered all the violent coughing spells and how they launched those grotesquely familiar trickles of crimson that coursed down his dad's pale and quaking chin. Quinn traced his fin-gers across the dried droplets of lifeblood and blinked back yet an-other budding tear—the first tear of this new day. Then he forced himself to swallow against the sudden need to vomit.

His father's last warning...a warning he had deemed important enough to repeat...echoed yet again in Quinn's mind. That warning triggered another unsettling memory, this one involving a toothless seer dressed in tattered rags whose unhandsome features were evident even in the pale light beneath the street lamp where he had encoun-tered her just a few weeks ago. *Keep it close like a lover*, they had both told him, his father and the old seer. Both offered the same warn-ing, but the warnings were issued more than a decade apart. How could she have possibly known? He rolled over onto his back and wrung his hair with two trembling hands. Cold air from the window drifted across his sweaty chest and the ensuing shiver provided more comfort than any of the thoughts spinning through his head.

In the span of a single disconcerting night, the world that he rec-ognized had been thoroughly razed and replaced with this new mad-dening maze of questions. And the only person who might offer any useful guidance was ten years dead. Quinn's teeth began to grind. He stared at the ceiling as if some of the answers that he so desperately needed might be carved into the stippled plaster. They were not, he finally decided. His ears began to ring; he needed something else on which to focus. Something...

"Shit!" he cursed his own predilection to distraction as the var-nished finial fastened to the center of his headboard loomed over him, leaning down and taunting him like a wraith assigned to deliver a cold kiss. It all but shouted and waved for his attention. The blade! The blade for which the Church had killed...the blade for which his father had died! Quinn scanned the letter one more time, then hopped to his knees and faced the headboard. After following Tomas's pre-cise instructions, he heard the little door on the rear of his headboard swing open and thump to a rest against the wall.

Quinn's heart raced ever faster as he contorted himself so that he could reach down between the wall and the massive, hand-crafted headboard. His fingers closed around a slender burlap package, and in a matter of seconds he was sitting on the edge of his bed, staring in dumbstruck awe at the unblemished silver Blade of Morana Goll—a blade for which no fables had been written, as far as he knew. Unlike its sister staff, this knife had been ignored by bards and historians.

"Not ignored, you idiot," Quinn chastised himself in a weak whisper, "they never even knew about its existence. Only Azrael and Valenesti could have known, and Valenesti told no one except..." he trailed off as he shifted his gaze to the old book containing Valenesti's unabridged journal. He shook his head as another wave of confusion and contradictions capsized his reasoning. "So how did the Church find out about the blade, and how did the old hag know about it?" Quinn continued to mutter to himself as he paced the cold floor wearing nothing but his baggy shorts. Goosebumps broke out on his exposed skin.

"The seer!" he hissed out loud and snapped his fingers as the grain of a plan began to develop in his mind. Although she spoke in incomprehensible riddles and was clearly touched in the head, she had just been redeemed—if only to a degree—by the revelations made in Tomas's letters...and of course by Quinn's special present, a present only recently received. Crazy as a rabid bat she may well be, but she had just earned a modicum of credibility with the eerie accuracy of her month-old prediction regarding his new blade. Quinn simply had to find her, though the odds of tracking down a nameless beggar in a city the size of Eldr-shok were slimmer than catching a feral cat during a lightning storm.

Next week at Festival, he fully intended to drill Obadiah regarding the inferences in Tomas's last letters. But until then, he would spend as much time as necessary tracking down the old seer who possessed pallid eyes as well as a command of a whole array of terrifying voices and inflections capable of making any soul shiver. Inspired by a renewed sense of urgency, Quinn danced across the room on one leg as he tried to pull his favorite pair of pants on. He finished dressing, snatched his heavy cloak, and slammed the window shut. He would be getting plenty of cool air soon enough.

♦♦♦

Three days dragged by, and each day Quinn did his best to cover a different quadrant of Eldr-shok, but his hunt was gallingly futile. The old hag, the toothless host to that intermittent roar that originated someplace behind Hel's cellar door, was simply nowhere to be found. It was now Thursiday; he and the other *Chosen* were to leave for the Citadel in just three short days. Damn!

Earlier this blustery morning, Miriam had handed him a long list of items she needed from some of Eldr-shok's markets, all of which were located in different districts of the sprawling city. Under other circumstances, Quinn would have dug his heels in, bitching and griping about all the seeping blisters that would likely sprout on his heels. Ordinarily, he would have balked and complained that she was just trying to run his legs off. But not this time. Not today. Impatience pecked at him like a buzzard snacking on an unfortunate dog. He was so blasted eager to find the haggard seer...! Today's expedition would provide an excellent opportunity to make a final, random sweep of the city; perhaps today he would chance upon the hag and pose to her a few of his burning questions.

His hopes began to fade, however, as the late afternoon shadows swallowed the teeming sidewalks like a dark gray tide advancing from the west. To make matters worse, the last item on the list was proving to be very elusive. His already thin patience waned every time another damned store clerk offered a theatrical frown and shook his head in petty apology. As luck would have it, of all the bottles that Miriam could have possibly dropped and broken last Sunaday evening, it had indeed been the vial containing her precious lorespice. On this bitterly cold afternoon, he had spent north of two long hours zipping from one shop to the next searching for a mere half ounce of the musky seasoning. Miriam had made it quite clear that not just any brand would do, otherwise he would have eagerly settled for a substitute and turned his ass toward home long ago.

But no, she just had to have the Green Turtle brand. The yield of this label, according to whichever picky bastard had authored the recipe she insisted on following, was grown in the rich soil of the southern Arman delta. The loamy soil in that area ostensibly lent a *subtle* tang to the earthy taste of the herb, but Quinn surmised that he surely would never be able to discern any difference...and he doubted that anyone else could unless they read the same recipe and then looked at the label on the bottle. When—after an exhausting search—he finally procured the elusive spice that Miriam needed for baking gods-knew-what, he scratched through this, the last item on his long list, and headed home. With an irritated sigh, he shoved open the door to the market.

As he exited the shop and turned left following the flow of the crowd on the sidewalk, he glanced ahead and froze in mid-step. His heart felt like it stopped beating altogether. Quinn had to remind himself to breathe, because he saw…her. The seer! She was just standing at the street corner, and she was staring directly at him with those steel gray eyes…eyes the color of old campfire ashes. In the light of day, fading though it was, she looked slightly less ominous…slightly.

Tightening his grip on the ties of his shopping bags, he tried to launch into a full sprint, but lost his footing on the icy walkway and almost went down. Never taking his eyes from his mark, he wove among the other pedestrians and collided with several of them in the process. Whenever some obese citizen crossed between him and his grubby target, he would lose sight of her for a moment; but she seemed to be waiting for him ever so patiently…expectantly almost. The hoary soothsayer paid no attention whatsoever to the bustling crowd as she stood there like a granite statue, a ragged isle of stillness amidst a swarming sea of commotion. The tide of evening shadows raced toward her…then engulfed her. A sad and considerably compassionate smile softened her weathered features as she monitored Quinn's approach. Otherwise, she never moved.

He was closing the distance rapidly and his heart raced, though it did so more from expectation than from exertion. Then, a portly man wearing some ridiculous, ankle-length fur jacket passed in front of her and she was suddenly gone. Quinn skidded to a halt near the spot where she had been standing just a moment before. He spun about scanning the sidewalks for even a glimpse of the gaudy rags and gray scarf, a flash of the oily white hair waving in the wind. Nothing! There was no sign of her or her garish attire anywhere. Shit! Had she shown herself to him just to taunt him, perhaps? That possibility hardly made sense, he quickly decided. Then again, damn little was making sense of late. Something slick slithered behind his ribs.

"Crazy old bitch!" Quinn grumbled in disgust. Frustration prompted him to tighten his fists around the drawstrings of his shopping bags until he felt the rough weave of sisal burning and abrading his palms. He was suddenly compelled by the need to hit something or someone; but his hands were full, so kicking would have to suffice. His booted foot struck the metal lamp post, and the impact produced only a muffled ring.

"Damn! Damn!" he grunted through clenched teeth.

"Ahem," the man standing next to him cleared his throat in haughty disapproval. Quinn looked up and spotted the priest's collar before he even bothered to look at the pudgy man's mole-covered face. At this point...especially at this point...Quinn didn't give a flying damn about some condescending priest's censure. He rolled his eyes, and just then a hatful of snow showered down on the cleric's head, a good portion of it settling between collar and skin. Quinn opened his soul to the marvels of providence and allowed an insolent smirk to play at the corners of his mouth.

"Fuck me running! Seems there might be a god or two floating about after all," Quinn chuckled as the priest swatted and brushed away the ice. In the process, a jar of pickles rolled out of the parson's haul and shattered on the frosty curb. Both men were fully aware that the kick had freed the snow from its tentative perch atop the arm of the streetlamp. Teen and cleric locked gazes, but the mole-marred priest saw a trace of the raw, unflinching fire swirling in Quinn's eyes and he promptly backed down like some rangy runt facing a bully. The holy man turned away, trembling.

"Don't worry about the pickles, friend. I'm sure you have access to your share of acolytes. That should suffice until you acquire another jar of...pickles. Oh. And by the way, the hag I was looking for...just so you know, she *is* a crazy old bitch," Quinn muttered flippantly as the two men stood side by side, waiting for a chance to safely cross the busy street. This day had been long enough. Too long, in fact. Quinn did not want to be run down by a wagon or carriage, though he secretly hoped that the son of a bitch standing next to him would get trampled into a pile of bloody, fat-marbled meat...a contorted mass of meat and skin tags wearing a meaningless collar around its broken neck.

◆◆◆

It was just past dark when Quinn stumbled through the front door of his home. One of the damned bags he was juggling fell to the floor as he tried to push the door shut with his hip. The brisk wind was no help. Miriam wiped her hands on her apron and hurried over to help her son round up the scattered items, some of which were rolling across the smooth floor. Despite all his fatigue and frustration, Quinn couldn't help but let a sly grin escape when he caught sight of all the flour she had managed to inadvertently smear on her face and neck. There were even a few stray globules of dough clinging to her dark bangs.

"There you are! I was beginning to get worried. Did you have any trouble?"

"Trouble? No, no trouble at all. I'm used to filling shopping lists two links long in a single snowy afternoon. It's a cinch," he jested as he dropped a heap of packages and bundles on the settee.

"Did you find the lorespice, dear? The Green Turtle? Please, please tell me you did. I hope you didn't break the bottle! I'm getting ready to start my baking and..." she rattled on as she stepped into the kitchen to start rummaging through the bag that Quinn had dropped.

"Yes. Yes I found your precious spice, but it took me over two hours to do so! I went to every fu...every bakery and grocer in the northern part of the city before I finally located that label you wanted. What are you going to do with that, anyway? I hope you can use it to turn lead into gold. That Green Turtle crap is expensive!" Quinn complained as he kicked off his wet boots and set them next to the stove in the den to dry. With a frustrated sigh, he pulled the precious spice from the lapel pocket of his coat and carried the bottle into the kitchen. He presented it to his mother with both hands as if it was a trophy. He had not chanced transporting it in a thin bag, so he had prudently tucked it into the padded pocket of his coat and buttoned it securely shut before hiking home.

"I'm making my special spice bread for the trip this weekend," she announced to Quinn with a shifty wink. A wet glob of batter was barely clinging to the end of her long wooden spoon. Its fall was averted by a quick swipe of her finger and she promptly popped the sample into her mouth to analyze it. "Needs just a tad more brown sugar," she muttered to herself before continuing the conversation with her son. "Everyone is supposed to bring something unique to the festival, and I thought a few loaves of my famous bread...well, locally famous...would certainly cover our admission to the festival grounds."

Her voice was blithe, bordering on melodious as she flitted about the kitchen like a bee in a flower garden; she was so excited about the upcoming journey, and her delight was practically contagious. Despite the smartass attitude that he displayed perhaps all too frequently, Quinn had to admit to himself that he was genuinely happy for his mother right now. His eyes suddenly felt dry. He saw a warm aura surrounding her. A glow. And he had no desire to do or say anything that might diminish its luster. Though he was anything but a follower of the Way, he could ignore his reservations regarding the Church's practices for the time being because he realized that he hadn't seen her this merry in years…many years…ten years. For a moment, he put all the business regarding Valenesti and the blade in the back of his mind, though getting those foul affairs *out* of his mind would be futile indeed.

Miriam darted about the kitchen rolling dough, stirring this and sifting that. She was beaming, giving off light that he was now somehow able to see. Out of the blue, Quinn recalled an adage that Obadiah had shared with him once not so long ago. "Lad, the illusion of happiness might well be only an illusion, but it will do quite nicely until real happiness rolls into town," the cleric had told Quinn. "They are twins after all." The parson offered that tidbit of wisdom along with an impish grin and his trademark wink—and of course the obligatory fake punch to his ward's gut. Quinn remembered those details, though he could not for the life of him remember the context of that specific conversation. Suddenly, the kitchen felt even warmer.

♦♦♦

"Well, that's all fine and dandy, but what are my chances of getting something to eat *before* this weekend?" he joked as he began to rummage through the pantry. "I'm starving. I haven't had time to fart in order to even make room for a snack."

"Such a mouth on you! Have I pointed that out lately? There is a whole pot of potato stew simmering on the stove, hon. It should be ready in just a few minutes. Why don't you go get cleaned up. I'm ready for a bite or two myself, but I'll not share my table with someone who is covered by half a fingerswidth of filth and street grime."

"I'm only covered in grime because…" Quinn started to protest, but before he could finish his sentence Miriam rushed over and gave him a quick peck on his forehead. He grimaced, but just because he could feel remnants of the sticky batter left by her smiling lips.

"I know, mister. Thank you for all that you did today. You're truly a lifesaver!"

That acknowledgment smothered the fire that was going to fuel his argument. Besides, he had already decided that a quick wash wasn't actually a bad idea. He felt the detestable filth of the city burrowing through his clothes and into his skin like an army of hungry mites. His fingers were sticky from all the nasty doorknobs he had turned, and both palms were clammy just because he had spent the day swimming through a churning sea of strangers. And now he had a patch of slimy batter on his face.

Balancing himself with outstretched arms he slid across the floor in his socked feet and disappeared down the hallway, unbuttoning his heavy shirt as he went. After he filled his basin with crystal water from its matching pitcher, he splashed the cool water over his face and hair. A quick glance at the mirror let him know that the water had indeed lightened his color by a few shades. Murky as rainwater in a hoof print, the cloudy basin water provided yet another indication that he had carried more home with him besides the items on Miriam's lengthy list.

When he toweled himself off, he donned a fresh shirt and stepped back into the kitchen where Miriam was meticulously setting the table. Quinn stopped just inside the door. He shrugged and rolled his eyes, though she presently had her back turned to him. Both napkins had to be folded just so, both spoons had to lie parallel to the napkins' edges. No matter the occasion, all of her preparations had to be perfect. Her spirits sometimes dipped, but her standards never dropped.

"And all for a simple bowl of soup..." Quinn mumbled to himself. "Gods!"

She sent a smile his way but never quit humming her tune as she ladled the steaming stew into two glazed yellow bowls.

"Well, now I recognize you," she blurted as she juggled the hot bowls from stove to table. The bowls rattled and rolled to rest as she blew her burned fingertips. Then she took her seat. "You're that young smart aleck who lives just down the hall from me...the one who snores like a drunk coal miner every night. I swear, your snoring nearly shakes the loose plaster off my walls and the tranquility out of my dreams."

"Oh, very funny," he responded dryly as he took his own seat at the table. "If I do snore, I probably inherited that tendency from my mother." Quinn combed his damp bangs back with his fingers. "By the way, any word from Obadiah yet?" he asked innocently enough, but he almost immediately regretted posing that innocuous question, because Miriam's face blanched, instantly losing a measure of its earlier glow.

She fell silent for a moment as she fought valiantly to maintain her serene smile; she cast her gaze downward while she folded the napkin in her lap just a bit too painstakingly. "No. No, I'm afraid not, dear. I surely thought we would have heard from him by now. Maybe he's planning on surprising us…?"

"Now, Mom…" Quinn groused and both his hands were suddenly rubbing his temples. He realized that his tone was annoyed, and he tried to temper it out of consideration for her obvious concern. "He wouldn't exactly be surprising us, now would he? I mean…he basically told us he was going to try to meet us there, after all." She was still staring at her lap, so he saw no reason to fight the impulse to let his eyes roll to the ceiling once more as he blew the first spoonful of steaming stew to cool it so that it wouldn't blister the roof of his mouth.

With increasing frequency, he found that rolling his eyes somehow relieved perceptual pressure. It was a simple, mechanical gesture that more frequently than not offended others, but on some level it served as a vital, cerebral belch. It was a trivial and reflexive twitch that kept the mares of psychotic joy from taking the bit in their teeth and sprinting across the rolling fields of indiscretion.

"I suppose you're right, hon. Still, he said he would try to let us know something by the middle of the week. Something, either way. It just isn't like him to forget his word. It isn't like him to forget. Period."

"Don't worry, now. You heard him say that Cardinal Voss was sending him to Eldr-ro this week. He has a full schedule, it sounds like. Maybe he's planning on just showing up at the forest gate this Sunaday with bag in hand. That's the most likely scenario, if you ask me. Or…maybe he has just been busy filling some long-ass list of things that he needs. Kind of like the one you gave me this morning, for instance. That must be it! At this moment, Obadiah's probably sitting in his bungalow and rubbing horse liniment on his aching calves and feet." Quinn paused long enough to shovel another spoonful of steaming potato stew into his maw. He didn't even bother to look at his mother's face; he didn't have to, for he knew that she was smiling again…smiling ever so genuinely at his little joke, though her underlying worry likely remained.

"Do you ever plan to quit being such a smarty-pants, Quinn? My money says that you probably won't."

"Your money says…? Oh, I thought you blew all your money on Redsape Wine and Green Turtle Lorespice. You mean to tell me that you have some coin left over that you're willing to wager on my…reform?"

"Well, I guess that's all the answer I need, now isn't it, dear heart?" Miriam shot back, and now it was her turn to roll her eyes.

"Gods! Hopefully it is. Then we can leave the matter behind us once and for all. All kidding aside, you're not the only one hoping that he can be there with us. But if he can't, he can't. We will have plenty of fun even without him as long as they're serving Redscape… or even some cheaper vintage."

Miriam reached across the corner of the table and mussed his hair playfully with her right hand, just as Obadiah would have likely done under similar circumstances. "I know we will, love. It's going to be great, I tell you. It isn't every day that a mother and her son are both *Chosen*, after all. I can hardly wait until we leave Sunaday!"

Quinn's lips twitched with the effort of a forced smile. He tried his best to share his mom's waxing enthusiasm. He really did, but something was preventing him from fully committing…something he couldn't quite account for. Though weeks had passed since that demoralizing encounter, the old fortune teller's words continued to echo throughout all his memories and musings. Why was it that a cold shiver shot up his spine every time his mother mentioned the upcoming trip to the Citadel and the fact that they had both been *Chosen*? Why couldn't he just relax for a moment and revel in his mother's joy over the honor that the Church had bestowed upon them? Of course, he personally didn't consider it any kind of honor. As far as he was concerned, it was a meaningless accolade, much like being named *most beautiful* by a panel of blind judges.

*Chosen*. No, he did not regard this preposterous title to be especially notable, but everyone else in town certainly did, and that was worth something. The distinction would be worth something to the one that his own heart had *Chosen*. Even as he clutched the spoon, he imagined Catherine's delicate hand gripping his. He pictured those perfect verdant eyes, those roiling tarns of contradiction, and now there was a new component mixed in with their distinctive magic... admiration. In a fleeting, fanciful image his love leaned in for a kiss; but when her lips parted, she sported a lone tooth!

Quinn flinched—enough to spill the contents of his spoon onto the table. A quick swipe of his napkin and the mess was no more. He dipped himself another spoonful of the steaming stew and hoped that Miriam did not notice how badly his hand was now shaking. A deep breath helped to steady it until his lips closed around the spoon. He did not—could not—blow across the soup to cool it. The scalding pain was immediate. It was jarring, and it was...quite welcome. Quinn relied on his tongue's agony to draw his mind away from this latest volley of vagaries. Clenching his fist around the spoon's handle, he quelled his reflexes and forced himself to swallow. Now the raging fire spread to his throat. The blisters left by the savory broth offered him a new point of focus. The liquid inferno indeed managed to burn away some of his doubts and his misgivings...for a while, at least.

Still, whenever he consciously let go of his mind's helm, its bow unfailingly turned back toward that night on the shadow-draped sidewalk where he confronted the wrinkled and reeking fortune teller. Her words planted a seed, and that seed had sprouted despite his best efforts to forget the odd encounter. Her cryptic message had upset him more than he initially realized. *The dark days that lie ahead,* she said. Recalling that lone phrase froze his soul and it made him shiver with cold, despite the piping hot stew he was eating and the suffocating warmth in the kitchen. *Of course,* he tried to tell himself, *the old hag probably used that very phrase to dupe most of her customers into shelling out more coin.* She made her living by preying off of fear and foreboding, after all.

Even so, the accuracy of her warnings and predictions had gone a long way in reinforcing the misgivings Quinn had harbored ever since observing Obadiah's strange behavior after hearing the news regarding this year's special list of *Chosen.* And then, of course, there was this afternoon's near encounter with her as the daystar was diving toward its nighttime home. Quinn promised himself that he would put his cleric friend to task over the matter the next time they were away from Miriam. Perhaps when the parson joined them at Tarchannen Eid the following week. *If* he joined them at all.

♦♦♦

Floating ever so silently, like a lost ghost weaving through the headstones in a graveyard surrounded by a wall of vines and iron fences, the snows moved in later that evening, blowing in from the north and west. Earlywinter was starting to show its true colors...white mostly, with only a few kisses of gray. When Miriam and Quinn awoke the next morning, a thick layer of the frosty powder blanketed the streets and rooftops. Except for the dim glow that illumined the gauzy brume that swirled through the deserted streets, the daystar was nowhere to be seen. The skies were a cheerless leaden gray and low clouds that barely cleared the city walls threatened to shed even more of their frozen feathers before the morning grew too much older. And just before midday, shed they did. Lazy flakes with no will of their own sped along circuitous paths, following the erratic but insistent commands of the shifting wind before they settled like fine white down atop the mounting drifts that, as the day wore on, grew deeper by at least half a link as best Quinn could tell.

Thankfully, Miriam had no more errands for him to run at this point. Her prodigious preparations were — by all indications — almost complete. All that remained on her once-lengthy list of chores was baking her spicebread loaves and packing her bag. The latter task would take no time at all since she owned too few clothes for packing to pose a true quandary. Since Quinn had burned enough eggs and spilled enough milk on previous occasions to demonstrate that he was of little use in the kitchen, Miriam was content to just let him lounge around the apartment for most of the day.

And he had absolutely no objections to the unambitious plans she had laid out for him. He took advantage of the opportunity to read Valenesti's tale again...and again. Doing so never became tiresome; indeed, the tale grew more poignant with every read. He would reach the last page then stare through the panes at the deluge of winter's white and winsome breath. How he longed...how he ached to let Miriam read the tale, but his father's grim and insistent warning barred him from doing so. *How ironic was it that he had been asked to shield his own mother from his grim legacy?* Quinn thought to himself as he debated the implications of letting her read Tomas's blood-spattered letters and the account of Valenesti's dismal last years, his descent into the deepest and most heartbreaking pits of despondency that could be imagined. He hoped that keeping her in the dark would not be listed among his life's regrets, but he reminded himself that nescience had kept her alive so far.

♦♦♦

Saturnday arrived and passed by in much the same manner, but by now the air that had been charged with silent anticipation had mutated into a shroud of edginess and disquietude. When Miriam and Quinn weren't pacing around the apartment like animals sharing the same tiny cage, the two passed their time pretending to rest. Otherwise, they busied themselves packing…then repacking…and playing cards. Most games began innocently enough, but as nerves eventually began to wear thin, some of the matches concluded with one player accusing the other of cheating by some means. A few tense moments of silence would pass, then the next hand would be dealt and all would be forgiven. Neither Quinn nor Miriam ever made mention that Obadiah had still not contacted them, but it remained one of many niggling details that Quinn just couldn't put out of his mind.

Sunaday morning finally came, a morning whose sky was providentially cloudless and azure. After a simple yet satisfying breakfast of eggs and toast, mother and son dragged their bags, tattered and moth-eaten though they were, to a spot just beside the front door. The last little stretch of the maddening wait had officially begun. In accordance with tradition, the Church was supposed to send a carriage to deliver each of the *Chosen* to the cathedral where they would attend the regular service before heading out to the rolling fields flanking the soaring walls of Tarchannen Eid.

Quinn plopped down on the well-worn settee, crossed his arms and endeavored to fight off the insistent spell of sleep. Though slumber had eluded him so proficiently throughout the previous evening, his eyelids now felt heavier than rain-soaked hunting pants. With bloodshot eyes he studied his two bags, taking yet another mental inventory of their contents. Valenesti's fateful story and the urgent tones lacing his father's letters buzzed around in his sleep-deprived mind like determined bees defending their hive…bees that were on a mission…bees that could not be simply swatted away.

Just an hour earlier—following a round of agonizing self-debate—he had returned the Blade of Morana Goll to its secret compartment on the rear of his bed's headboard, and he had locked the old tome before shelving it rather inconspicuously among the other volumes in his nightstand's shelves. Though logic suggested that he keep those two items as far away from the seat of the corrupt Church as possible, the faint but forceful voice and guide that he had over time learned to trust was now screaming its displeasure at his decision to leave the two precious artifacts behind, guarded by nothing but a flimsy door lock and the diaphanous illusion of concealment.

"I forgot something, Mom. I'll be back in a minute," Quinn stated as coolly as he could manage when he grabbed the smaller of his two bags and stumbled sleepily back to his room, pulling the door shut with care. After he manipulated the finials on his headboard with practiced precision, he pulled the burlap bundle containing the Blade of Morana Goll from its place of concealment and tucked it into the zippered pocket on the side of his bag. Then he pulled the old tome from its place among the other more mundane volumes and, after giving its leather cover a respectful pat, situated it securely behind the blade in the same compartment of his bag. Suddenly, he found that he could breathe more easily; he felt no remorse, no regret as he headed back to the front door to set his small but special bag beside its larger twin.

"You sure you got everything you need, hon?" his mother asked groggily as she sat up with a start. Quinn arched an eyebrow after pausing just long enough to assess the lines on her face. Miriam was apparently another victim of a restless Saturnday night. She had very nearly yielded to the allure of an unplanned nap while he was back in his room addressing matters to which she must remain absolutely oblivious, at all costs.

"Yup. Hope so," Quinn answered as casually as possible while he studied the new bulge straining against the seams on the side of his smaller duffel. "I sure hope so."

♦♦♦

Regardless of his abiding disrespect for the Church and the saucy attitude he had exhibited earlier in the week, there simply was no denying that his gut was now tied in knots. Insurgency's stout walls were suddenly beset by the burrowing minions of insecurity. Quinn was beginning to succumb to a new and almost venomous strain of impatience. The fabric under his arms was saturated with the sweat of apprehension, but his throat was as dry as a summer stump. His heart skipped at least two beats when he heard that unmistakable but unfamiliar racket — unfamiliar on their tiny side street, at least — of a carriage clattering to a halt in front of their lackluster building.

He and Miriam swallowed simultaneously, the pair exchanging anxious glances before hopping up like two school children bolting from their desks on the last day before summer break. They grabbed the handles of their worn and tattered bags and stood there beside the door, erect as two soldiers in formation, holding their breath and their luggage as they listened to their escort clomping up the stairs. The Church emissary halted on the landing just outside their front door... their only door.

Quinn's mouth remained drier than late autumn sage when the driver knocked on the front door exactly five times, for five was the sacred number of the Way and thereby the revered number of the Church. Finally he gathered himself and was able to swallow some of the sand coating his tongue. He cast a sideways glance in his mother's direction. Perhaps she was holding back a tear or two of excitement, or perhaps they were tears of trepidation. Whatever the case, Miriam's eyes were closed and she took a deep breath as if she were using her nose to assess the progress of some new sauce recipe. After exhaling in a long and satisfied sigh, she leaned forward and opened the door to invite their escort inside.

"Ah, excellent! A blessed day to you ma'am...and to you of course, my lad," the tall man added as he bowed to Quinn. The driver grabbed the two largest bags and stepped back through the open door. "You would be the Tabors, yes? Yes. I'm Corporal Andrews, but I ask that you simply call me Arlis," he requested with yet another slight bow. "Well first off, allow me to offer my congratulations, of course. Now, if you'll excuse me, I'll just throw these on board. I'll be right back to retrieve the rest. You two just hang tight...or hang loose. Whatever suits you best," he tacked on with a genial wink.

Before Quinn could politely ask Arlis to use care and not *throw* the bags anywhere, the driver was halfway down the stairs to the first landing.

His mother disappeared almost as quickly, leaving Quinn standing alone by the open door through which the bitter morning breeze surged. Much like a hummingbird zipping from flower to flower, Miriam dashed through the rooms of the apartment one last time, checking to make sure the windows were secure and everything else was set for the upcoming week. Apparently satisfied with her final inspection, she stepped back into the den where the proficient coach driver had already reappeared. The tall, almost gaunt man was wrapping the straps and the handles of the remaining bags around his lank fingers so that one more trip down the stairs would be sufficient. Quinn reached down to help him with the load, but the man *tut-tutted* him away, insisting that no honored guest of the Church was to lift a finger or bend a knee while Arlis Andrews was on the job.

Since his father's illness, Quinn had inherited—among other responsibilities—the role of designated pack mule, and for the last decade he had handled those duties without complaint...without *much* complaint, at least. But now, here was Arlis insisting that Quinn assume a new role. Mr. Andrews was all but demanding that the youngest of this year's *Chosen* shed the symbolic uniform of the servant and don the robe of the served. And Quinn wasn't about to argue with the proud coachman at this point. He promptly determined that he had no real issue with someone else being delegated to carry his luggage for him. In fact, he imagined that he could get rather used to the idea.

♦♦♦

Quinn and his mother followed Arlis out the door, and Miriam turned to make sure that the lock was fastened securely. She jiggled the worn knob at least half a dozen times; her son rolled his eyes skyward. *There's nothing in there worth stealing*, he chided her silently, *not anymore*.

As they descended the steps leading from their narrow landing, mother and son were met with a sight that prompted them to very quickly shrug off any lingering effects from their miserable, sleepless night. They were both suddenly confronted with a reminder of the abiding zeal with which the citizens of the Five Cities viewed this yearly rite. Even though a substantial blanket of the fine snow still covered the ground, and even though the morning breeze came armed with a piercing chill, people of all ages crowded the sidewalks and lined the narrow side street. Rubbing warmth back into their arms, they craned their necks just to catch a glimpse of their neighbors... the two *Chosen*. The daystar's bright rays clawed away at Quinn's dilated eyes, but his ears were caught up in the aural orgasm spawned by the roar of the crowd.

Entire families stood along the avenue, whistling, waving and wishing Miriam and Quinn all their best. A few of the admirers wiped tears away from their eyes, but whether those tears were educed by sentiment or by the cold wind, Quinn could not begin to guess, and he truly did not care…not as long as they were clapping and cheering for him.

♦♦♦

A lump rose in Miriam's throat as she surveyed the applauding crowd, and her eyes began to water as well. They had all come to see *her*…a lowly widow…and to wish her a happy, safe journey. For as many years as she could remember, hers had been just another face in that same shivering crowd, but this year the masses had thrown on their winter wraps and gathered for *her*. The very minute the Church's messenger delivered that precious and unexpected letter, she had been quite abruptly snatched from the swollen sea of anonymity. For almost two weeks she had dreamed of this day, but not until this very moment was she truly struck by the actual weight of her new role or the significance associated with this journey upon which she was about to embark. Rank upon rank of her new fans waved to her and she waved back, coyly shrugging her shoulders as she did so, for she was new to this game of adulation…new to the role of recipient, at least.

♦♦♦

Right by her side strode her son who was ardently scanning the crowd for Catherine Brinna's perfectly chiseled features. Quinn held his breath as he searched for any trace of those cascading brunette locks. They were unforgettable. They were so damned unmistakable…to *his* eyes. He was confident that he could — with ease — pick her out of a crowd of thousands. Those damned, divine locks. He could still remember their scent from last Sunaday — from every Sunaday. He knew in his soul that he was less likely to overlook them than a panic-stricken ship's captain was to miss the sweeping strobe of a lighthouse perched at the mouth of a safe harbor.

Perhaps she had made the effort to tromp through the deep drifts of snow just to watch him march from his modest apartment to the carriage like some bridled idiot. Perhaps she would be donning a hungry but sad smile that conveyed to him that all the feelings he harbored for her were, in fact, mutual. Perhaps she would push her way through the throng like a ship plowing through towering waves and throw her arms around his neck. Then again, perhaps the daystar would turn suddenly pink and plummet into a farm pond.

When the duo reached the bottom of the stairs, Quinn was so caught up in his hormone-driven whimsy he tripped over his own feet and nearly went down in the snow. With the reflexes of a trained acrobat, Arlis deftly dropped the bags in the shallow drift that had collected against the curb and spun about to catch his young charge in mid-fall.

"Fu…," Quinn began as he felt the blood rush to his cheeks, but he managed to arrest his tongue before he embarrassed himself and his mother prior to their journey even beginning. There would be ample time for causing embarrassment later, he surmised.

Without a word, Arlis retrieved the bags from the sidewalk and set them on a narrow platform that ran along the rear of the wagon. He pushed them snugly against the back of the carriage and drew a broad leather strap across them to fasten them in place. As an added measure, he wove a second strap through the frayed handles of each bag and anchored each end to the brass brackets supporting the shelf. Once he was satisfied that all the bags were secure, Arlis spun around and opened the door of his shiny rig, bowing slightly as Miriam and her humiliated son climbed aboard.

Still cursing his ill-timed clumsiness, Quinn took a seat in the plush coach and angrily shoved aside the thick velvet drapes so that he could get a better view of the citizens who crowded the icy sidewalks. After he cooled down and gathered his wits, he found himself caught up in their enthusiasm and waved back to his fans as the carriage rattled along the potholed side street. As a matter of course, he made a special effort to wave to the young ladies…and there were so damned many of them! Gods! They stared like gorgeous predators into the coach, each one hungry for a glimpse of the handsome young man who had been *Chosen*. If they were half as taken with him when he returned as they seemed to be this cold morning, he was going to enjoy the rest of his winter indeed…and his spring…and his summer…

"Catherine who?" he whispered when he caught sight of a buxom little blonde who wasn't wearing nearly enough clothes to stay very warm, especially on a nippy day like this. Quinn instinctively knew that she was more concerned with landing a man of station than she was with staying warm. Mentally, he awarded her additional points for her tactical skills, even though her body had already placed her neatly at the top of her class. She had to live nearby, he figured. "I have to make sure to look *her* up next week. She shouldn't be too hard to find. I'm gonna look her up and then lay her down," he muttered to himself, but he immediately recognized that oath as nothing more than a private, pathetic little lie that he conjured to bolster his denial of what could no longer be denied. This new girl might temporarily hold sway over his loins, but she definitely did not hold the deed to his heart.

"Catherine who?" he repeated in an attempt to deny the voice of his heart as he studied — as best he could — all the nubile ladies whose faces whizzed by the carriage window. A part of him wanted to somehow open that window and yell up to Arlis to pull the reins back just a might. But Quinn knew that he would be no more successful at slowing down this seductive show than he would be at speeding up the annoying Sunaday services. In at least two contexts, his force of will simply could not alter fate. Ah, well. Besides, he would only be entertaining a lie, for the elusive Miss Brinna had seized his heart and he would never be able to settle for any other.

"Catherine who?" he chuckled, chastising himself for his own helplessness as he shook his head and bit his lower lip. His eyes burned as he silently acknowledged for the thousandth time how hopelessly in love he was.

"What was that, hon?" Miriam asked over her shoulder. She was busy waving out the window on the opposite side of the coach and had been too distracted by the crowds to pay any attention to Quinn's muttered musings...thankfully.

"Nothing," Quinn replied as he casually used the lapel of his coat to dab away a tear or two, then closed his cloak over the growing bulge in his lap. "Nothing you need to concern yourself with, dear mother," he tacked on in a hoarse but impish whisper. When the carriage turned onto the main route, Arlis cracked the whip in the air just over his team once again, and the faces of all the young ladies began to speed by Quinn's window in a dizzying deluge. He began to get queasy. Rimmed with tears of sweet spiritual pain, his eyes struggled to follow the show, though it was a show that no longer held much appeal, for the vision of a lone winsome angel had taken center stage.

At last, he pulled himself away from the blur of faces whizzing by his frosted window and settled back in his seat. After he took a breath and closed his eyes for a minute, the nausea and disorientation subsided.

One problem yet remained. His brief glimpse of the nameless

blonde girl had established the bulge under his coat, and visions of sweet Catherine's pouting face had sustained it. Quinn thought it prudent to find a distraction before the coach door opened, so he set his mind to studying the rich interior of their carriage. The thickly padded seats were covered in a velvety, lavender fabric that latched onto his cloak, preventing him from sliding across the bench as the vehicle rounded all the sharp corners and turns. There was even a metal box, ingeniously mounted to the floorboards, filled with glowing coals to keep the special passengers comfortably warm as they were transported to the courtyard in front of the cathedral.

Quinn was beginning to feel like a king, and he liked the buzz that the illusion provided; so much so that he caught himself groaning with disappointment when Arlis finally set the brake and leaned back against the reins. Corporal Andrews brought his huffing team to a halt in front of the lofty cathedral that the young *Chosen* had grown to loathe so. He groaned in part because his parade past all those beauties had ended, but mostly because he knew that yet another Church service awaited him despite the ardent promises he had made to himself only a week past.

The coach jostled slightly as Arlis hopped down to pull open the sturdy door. When Quinn and his mother stepped down to the street, they saw that their carriage was the last of four to arrive. The other three *Chosen* stood together on the sidewalk behind a thick velvet rope that separated them from the horde of worshippers filing up the steps and through the bank of massive doors fronting the sanctuary.

"Ma'am. Sir. You can wait over there with the others if you will, please. Father Sigmund will join you in a minute and give you your directions for the rest of the service," Arlis whispered as he bowed to them again.

"Mr. Arlis, what about our bags? Should we not take them with us?" Quinn asked, trying his best to sound naïve; in truth, his palms were beginning to sweat. All of a sudden, he found himself utterly petrified by the prospect of being separated from his smaller duffel and its extraordinary contents...items which had ultimately cost Tomas Tabor his life. Quinn had just assumed, and mistakenly so, that he would retain possession of the book and the blade for the entirety of the trip.

"Certainly not. Oh, no my good sir. This is *your* day. I'll take them around back and load them onto the Citadel coach myself. I'll take good care of them, I assure you," the lanky driver offered with a wink as he bowed yet again. "No one else will put so much as a paw on them. Not on my watch, they won't!" Another quick bow. Damn! One part of Quinn was comforted by the driver's words. Another sincerely wished that Arlis would quit doing that. Nobody had ever bowed to him before and it made him more than a little nervous...more than a little self-conscious.

Yet, another more conceited and playful side of Quinn's spirit entertained the urge to push his imaginary crown to the side of his head and bark out terse orders to his new servant. "Bow a little further down next time, Andrews. I am your master, after all! Now, like a good dog, go fetch your most fetching daughter and bring her to me. Make double sure that she is thoroughly bathed and ready to please me! Oh, and bring a tray with you—a bottle of Redscape along with two glasses. You are dismissed."

"Quinn!" Miriam hissed, doing her best to draw her son out of what she had come to recognize as one of his *trances*. Once she had his attention, she jerked her head vigorously to the side to remind him of the instructions they had just received from the driver.

Taking special care not to lose traction on the slick sidewalk, mother and son waddled over to where the other three stood waiting. Quinn noted right off that none of the others looked to be especially at ease. But that came as no surprise to him, really. Hel, the other three *Chosen* were likely simple citizens just like he and Miriam were. Working folk, simple shits and inconspicuous faces in the crowd every other day of the week...every day except for today.

No, one glance told Quinn that the members of this group were not the least bit comfortable with all this flowery formality, all this absurd pageantry. At least they weren't comfortable being the focus of it all. Quinn figured that—just like himself—they were out of their element and in no way accustomed to being targets of adoration that they felt was purely circumstantial and fundamentally undeserved... especially the short, rotund man who stood slightly apart from the others, nervously chewing the nails of his left hand and glancing about like a skittish horse waiting for a chance to bolt.

If Miriam was at all intimidated by this new role in which she had been cast, she hid it well...far better than any of the rest. Outpacing her son by two strides or more, she politely smiled and nodded at the other three *Chosen* as she threw a leg over the velvet rope, not even bothering to step around the brass posts supporting it. The obese man's face twisted into an even more acrimonious scowl. The portly fellow tossed his head back and grunted his displeasure at Miriam's minor breach of etiquette, so Quinn felt obligated to promptly follow suit. He hopped over the token barrier like it was a low fence erected to keep rabbits out of a spring garden.

Quinn locked eyes with the fat fellow and was making ready to properly *introduce* himself to the snotty bastard, but before any such introductions could be made, Father Sigmund shuffled toward the rope and greeted them all with a stiff bow. Another bow? Gods! As a matter of course, Quinn rolled his eyes skyward, but at least he managed to keep his tongue in check, though that exercise in restraint made his jaws ache. He wondered, and not for the first time, if all these Church bastards had been conditioned to bow from the moment of birth. Had time at the teat been their reward for learning to bow at the waist?

"A blessed Sunaday to you all, my children," the priest rasped. His voice was gravely almost to the point of being…masculine. Almost. But he continually dabbed the tip of his nose with the corner of a lace-trimmed white handkerchief that could not have been any less manly. The vicar was fighting a winter cold, from all indications, and Sigmund seemed to be losing this particular battle. Quinn held his breath when the ailing priest walked by him, for he had been told by someone—perhaps it had been Obadiah—that sharing air with a sick person was one sure way to catch the illness they carried. Kissing them was another means of transmission, but Quinn had no intentions to lock lips with Father Sigmund. The blonde girl he had seen just a few minutes ago, however…

"And a blessed day to you, father," four of the five *Chosen* replied in unison. Quinn consciously fought the urge to roll his eyes yet again as he chimed in with the others, though he was rather late on his cue, and purposely so. Last Sunaday evening, he had promised himself that he would put forth his best effort to rein in his cynicism toward this whole *Chosen* business, if only for his mother's sake. Actually, he had sworn to just try and mask it somewhat effectively, not necessarily to rein it in. After what his father had posthumously revealed to him in those blood-peppered letters, Quinn acknowledged that his cynicism and his unequivocal resentment toward the Church would endure until his lungs no longer continued to suck in air. The seed of vengeance had been sewn, and Quinn was determined to see that seed sprout and grow until this silly church withered beneath the shade of reprisal's dense boughs.

"Well, this is indeed a special morning for the five of you...a special day for all of us, of course. Now," he began, but paused to stifle a sneeze by pressing a finger against the septum of his red nose. "Please excuse me. Anyway, when everyone else is inside and seated, I would ask that you follow me up the steps and then down the center aisle. Please walk in single file. The order does not matter in the least, I assure you. Oh yes, we do ask that you hold your hands behind your back as you march toward the pulpit. Once we reach the front of the sanctuary, you may take your seats on the front row. Front row, center aisle. The pew is reserved for you and it is cordoned off with white ribbon. Are there any questions so far?" he asked as he again dabbed his raw nose with the cloth. Four of the *Chosen* shook their heads from side to side. Quinn was too occupied watching the wind sweep loose flakes of snow from the roofs of the buildings across the street.

"Good. Very good. Now, as the service draws to a close, I'll ask you to stand in place while the rest of the congregation files past to congratulate you on your *Choosing*. Yes. It might take a while. It usually does, as you likely recall, for you were all part of that same procession last year, were you not?" Father Sigmund managed to ask with a shallow smile before he finally succumbed to the sneeze that had been taunting him like a mother bluejay diving at a rat snake. A viscous streamer now danced from the end of Father Sigmund's nose that reminded Quinn of someone taunting a kitten with a dangling string. "Excuse me, please." Then another pass with the handkerchief, and Quinn observed that the rag was now spotted with disgusting patches of yellow slime. "When everyone else has exited the sanctuary, we will all proceed to the back yard where the Citadel coach will be waiting."

Father Sigmund tapped his chin with one finger as he stared at the blue winter sky in contemplation. "Let me see. Am I forgetting anything?" he muttered to himself. "Oh yes, I did fail to mention one thing. Before you board the Citadel coach, we will have you all change into special Church garments. It's one of the customs set forth in the Way. Once you arrive at our glorious Citadel and get settled into your tents, you are free to don your other clothes." He dabbed his nose once more. "Now, are there any questions?"

Again, four of the five *Chosen* shook their heads. Quinn spat into the snow near the toe of his boot and watched as his warm saliva formed a miniature pit in the smooth white blanket. It all seemed simple enough, although none of them, especially Quinn, liked the idea of sitting on the front row during the service. His usual practice of making quick but disrespectful faces at the priests and acolytes would have to be forgone today...perhaps. He would make that decision when he was in the moment.

Blast! And there would be no quick escape during the opening notes of the benediction this week. No, this week he would be forced to stand down at the front of the sanctuary, shaking damn hands and kissing babies, kissing asses and shaking damn babies, whatever the shit would get him out of the limelight and out of that cunting cathedral in the shortest amount of time. Quinn silently wondered if any of the others would be counting the minutes until this blasted service ended. One look at the short, stocky man's sweaty face told him that at least one of the remaining four *Chosen* would be equally glad to scramble aboard the Citadel coach and leave the crowded sanctuary behind. The toad of a man had already chewed his fingernails down to the quick, and now he had taken to digging in his nose with the forefinger of his left hand.

"You should have left some blade on your shovel," Quinn taunted the squat fellow. "Don't plan on hitting the mother lode with that rounded stub, friend. You'll find that I am a wellspring of friendly advice before the week is out."

The portly man blushed and drew a breath to issue a reply, but before he could say a word they all felt the bass notes from the magnificent chapel organ vibrating the icy cobblestones beneath their feet. Father Sigmund spun about and launched himself up the steep steps as if he was once more a teenager, healthy and hale. Following along like obedient pups, the five *Chosen* hurried to match his brisk pace. Whichever taint it was that made thick sap pour from his nose had apparently not limited his ability to run up stairs like a mountain goat racing uphill to safety.

As they had been instructed, the five fell into single file and followed their priest down the wide, vacant aisle. Helen, the only other female *Chosen* aside from Miriam, moved the ribbon aside, since she was the first in line. Feeling more than a little self-conscious, Quinn took his place on the front pew that had been reserved exclusively for the five *Chosen*. He could feel the eyes of the entire congregation staring at him. He felt their eyes boring into the back of his skull, and he conceded to himself that he would be far more comfortable cowering under that front pew than sitting in it.

◆◆◆

Aside from sporting two blushed cheeks and being a little winded, Father Sigmund appeared to be holding up fairly well despite his infirmity. Before ascending the last five steps to the podium, the ailing priest paused to sneak a healthy slug of service wine from the silver chalice on the floor beside the pulpit as the organ's last majestic notes reverberated through the sanctuary and then faded into silence.

"A very blessed Sunaday to you, my children," he called in a voice quite noticeably stifled by head congestion.

"And a blessed day to you, father," the congregation of hundreds replied as one.

Quinn rolled his eyes and prayed for speedy deliverance from this foul place.

"My apologies for my faltering voice this glorious morning, my children. It seems as though the snowy breath of Earlywinter has caught my system somewhat off guard. But the gods of the Way will lend me strength as they always do, so that I can conduct this service...this most sacred of services, I might add. For today, we send our five friends and fellow congregation members to the magnificent Citadel in Tarchannen Eid to honor our Church and the glorious Way. They will travel westward to witness the grandeur of the city that was spawned from the grief of our poor forefather, Valenesti, after he fell victim to Hel's grand but grim deception." Father Sigmund swept his left arm down the front row, and a round of applause might have followed, but Quinn had already mentally removed himself from all these ridiculous proceedings. Much like all the other Sunadays, he fled to a place leagues away from Eldr-shok, but today he was driven away with an extra sense of urgency. Maybe he was driven, maybe he was drawn...but he certainly didn't have to be dragged.

◆◆◆

No, Quinn didn't hear another word Father Sigmund said. At the mere mention of the Citadel, his attention sprouted wide wings and sped back to the rich realm where daydreams and nightmares united. Lately, it had become a favored retreat for his restive mind and at times a staging area for all his latent suspicions. He fantasized for the thousandth time that week about the upcoming trek through the fabled forest surrounding Tarchannen Eid.

In his mind's wide but increasingly jaded eye, he could picture the towers and the cloud-crowned spires he had read about in his father's book...in *his* book. For the thousandth time that week, he dreamed of passing beneath the gargantuan trees that had sprung from the earth just a few generations past, towering evergreens and hardwoods freed from their loamy prison by Valenesti's grief and despair paired with the incomprehensible might of Morana Goll's unleashed magic. He was still battling to wrap his mind around the notion that Valenesti was his ancestor...his blood kin. Quinn could not yet fully accept that he and the unfortunate architect of Tarchannen Eid were separated by only six generations.

As his extraordinary imagination was recruited to weave its weekly spell, Quinn's ears turned inward and the remainder of the service—as far as he was concerned—carried on in perfect silence. He could no longer hear the priest's dispassionate verses nor could he hear the congregation's mechanical refrains. He instead surrendered his senses to the deep, resonant groans that the earth made as the sprawling Citadel sprouted from the ground and shot toward the starry sky on that fateful night. His ears heard Eldimorah's rumbles of protest, and his mind's eye looked on while Elise's eyeless corpse was tossed across the grassy plains like some pebble in a miner's tin pan.

Then the dream retreated, whisked away by a short blast of scorching air that rushed past Quinn's left ear. His reflexes prompted him to reach up and run his fingers across his stubbly cheek. The waft was warm and moist; an acrid hint of spoiled venison lingered in the air for a few seconds before dissipating. It had not been a draft, but a breath. A single breath. Quinn never moved his head, but he cut his eyes to verify that no one was at his left ear. Still, he could sense that he was the target of an intense stare that was not entirely benevolent. He felt his heart begin to race.

Swallowing to steady his nerves, he slowly turned his head toward the gaze that was beckoning him so insistently. It took less than two seconds to discover the identity of his silent tormentor. Quinn found himself once again staring directly into the lavender eyes of the archangel depicted in the new stained glass window. He simply could not look away this time. Indeed, he harbored no desire to. Those eyes drew him into their violet web and held him fast. As the seconds crept by, his apprehension was replaced with something far more unnerving—recognition. Quinn got the unsettling impression that he was staring not at some sparkling stained glass window, but into a mirror...a mirror whose silvering had been supplanted by ebony. The wings and handsome features slowly dimmed until Quinn saw only two lavender eyes captured on black canvas. Two familiar, slanted eyes...swirling, glimmering performers dancing on an otherwise darkened stage. They were two penetrating, crystalline prisms surrounded by the vile shadows of unrealized nightmares.

Quinn continued to stare into that pair of lavender eyes, and despite the opaque fields of ebony surrounding those sinister orbs, he sensed the morning sun rising behind them. For the second time in a week, twin beams of violet light sought him out and painted his skin purple for a fleeting moment. He felt singed by these new beams and somehow betrayed by his own vulnerability. They were only rays of colored light, yet his skin felt blistered. He yearned for a stout shield to cower behind...some charm or spell to protect him.

So deep was his trance and so vivid was the bewitching image, Quinn flinched and nearly jumped out of his seat when the organ exploded into the familiar benediction, his weekly cue to make a sprint for freedom. Purely out of instinct and association, his legs came damn near to hauling the rest of his body up the aisle and through the rear doors of the sanctuary.

The youngest of the group and certainly the maverick of this season's five *Chosen* took a few calming breaths and struggled to regain his bearings. Quinn's heart was finally slowing down to a manageable gallop, but he noticed that sweat from his armpits had soaked all the way through his suit jacket. He had no idea what had just transpired. He could think of no explanation for what he had just felt... what he had just seen.

"I don't know where the shit I was just now, but at least it wasn't here," he muttered to reassure himself, but he couldn't even hear his own words over the boom of the organ. "At least I wasn't here," he repeated, congratulating himself as he realized how far away from this foul place his mind had just strayed. He was shaken, but as disturbing as it may have been, his last diversion had served some purpose. It had taken him *away*. Never mind the sweat stains under his arms, this morning still counted as another Church service spent wal-lowing in inattention. It was rapidly becoming a habit, but he felt only an instinctive need to feed it, not fight it.

Now came the part of this week's prolonged ceremony that he had truly been dreading…greeting all the strangers who were sup-posedly his *brethren*. Scores of brainless bastards and witless bitches would soon be filing past. As a *Chosen*, his station demanded that he somehow cope with a ceaseless barrage of vacuous and insincere smiles. The organ music finally faded away. Cued by that pervasive silence, the procession of simpletons commenced.

*Just kill me now,* Quinn prayed to non-existent gods as he clasped the first outstretched hand…the first of hundreds.

Most of the men who shook his hand regarded him with undis-guised envy bordering on hostility. Many of them probably had daughters around his age, he decided. *You had better be worried, you aging bastard*, Quinn silently warned through an ambiguous smile while all the fathers of young daughters did their level best not to openly glare at him as they offered all flavors of disingenuous con-gratulations. On the other hand, most of the older ladies felt obligated to hug his neck as if he was their favorite grandson whom they were welcoming him back from war. Quinn quickly yielded to his need to mentally recoil from this parade of fools. In seamless transition, he retreated into another of his exclusive zones, one in which his mind was free to wander like a mare in a broad meadow. All the while his body and facial muscles performed their duties in a reflexive but im-pressively appropriate fashion.

That was until Catherine—the angelic governess of his soul, the focus of his every tender thought, and the target of his heady lust—suddenly stood before him, granting him a generous hint of the smile about which he fantasized at least once every waking minute. Though her green eyes had been beguiling enough before, they were now var-nished with a glossy sheen of mischief and wiliness. For the second time in the same morning, Quinn saw part of his soul reflected in someone else's eyes.

Then she reached forward and took his sweaty hand in hers. For the second time in the same day, Quinn was transported beyond these sturdy walls and away from the confines of this so-called sanctuary. The storms boiling in those emerald eyes sheared his soul away from the anchors of his resolve with tornadic force. He now saw all he needed to see…he knew all he needed to know. In that moment, he acknowledged that he had surrendered long ago, and all along he knew the reasons. He could never let her go.

She stepped toward him and kissed him lightly on the cheek, just as many of the other ladies had done that morning. The kiss itself was innocent enough, though it razed his will and knocked the pins from his knees. But then she leaned farther in and hugged his neck in such a manner that her marvelous moist lips brushed his left ear.

"Be sure and look me up when you get back, champ," she purred, and her hot breath was a divine wind that scorched everything in its guiltless path…and that wind set his flesh on fire. In that lone command, she whispered words of an enduring spell that was no less potent than any that could have been cast by the mightiest of mages. Miriam was standing just to his right, and Quinn was so very glad that Catherine had not chosen to whisper that prodigious spell into his right ear.

"I have something I need to tell you…something I need to *show* you. I'd show it to you now but we don't need an audience for what I have in mind. Besides, that handle of a horse whip is already about to break through your zipper." She pretended to make a misstep and bumped her crotch against his. The contact lasted only a split second, but it was nearly enough to make Quinn fire off a warning shot in the pants of the suit that he had grown to hate. All but the tie, of course. "Gods, how I hate zippers," she panted, and he thought his knees were indeed going to fail him. "Don't you agree? Don't you agree, love?"

Stunned. Mesmerized. Paralyzed. Bedazzled. Quinn fit snugly into all four categories at once. He simply was incapable of answering. Everything resembling congruent thought withered and shriveled in the blast of her hot breath. Try as he might, he could not will himself to phrase anything approaching an intelligible response to this onslaught of raw sensuality. His tongue had swollen and his brain had shrunk quite proportionally. Before she withdrew from that brief but miraculous embrace, she flicked his earlobe a few times with her wet tongue and he found himself now leaning on her just for support—just so that he would not fall forward.

No one else saw that advance, for her long hair obscured the entire exchange…the long locks that Quinn had so vividly pictured cascading down to brush his face on that magical night that was now all but inevitable. That night when she would insist on taking control and climb atop him; when she would straddle him like he was a mustang she was trying to break, and grind against him with a steady, unremitting rhythm that matched that of her beating heart.

It would perhaps be the only night that he would remember as an old man, but it would be enough of a reward to justify growing old. A night when two unchained lovers moaned beneath the winter moon…beneath the howling stars. It would be the night when the mantle of true manhood would be donned as the gauzy and delicate shell of shed innocence smoked and smoldered, brittle tinder for a blaze fanned by her hungry sighs.

She squeezed his hand once again, and he at least managed to squeeze back, but that was to be his only pitiful contribution to their exchange. She was in charge, of that there was no doubt. Hel, she always had been.

Then, the next impatient asshole in the long line of well-wishers cleared his throat to prompt Catherine to move on. When she withdrew so that Quinn could devour her features again, he noted that her perfect face had quickly transformed into the perfect picture of erotic mischief. She wore the predatory leer of a lewd temptress, a vile huntress armed with a veritable arsenal of weapons, not the least of which was the promise of rapture dancing in her eyes. Further down that list was the searing fire that resided in her flesh. Though it perhaps wasn't her most devastating weapon, it was formidable enough, by damn. It had just now proven to be more than sufficient to stun her prey with the assurance of ecstasy and the promise of protection from the frozen world outside.

Then, part of the wall came down. For whatever reason, she allowed him a glimpse of the fragile soul that huddled behind her own suit of armor. For a fraction of a moment, Quinn saw a little girl cowering in the corner of a dark room. In that flash of a second, contradiction reigned. He could no longer tell whether his spirit was drowning beneath the waves or soaring above the surf.

"Love ya, soldier. No kidding. I really do," she whispered with tears teasing the corners of both perfect eyes. She sent him a quick wink that promised him everything he had dreamed of. Her delicate fist delivered a playful punch to his left shoulder, then she spun away and sauntered up the aisle, falling into line with the rest of the retreating congregation. He watched her walking away, but his eyes could not decide whether to drink in her luscious hips or the long, brunette hair that spilled over her shoulder like an exquisite waterfall. With her last words echoing through his thoughts like the peal of a heavy bell, he faced a more profound dilemma. He could not decide whether to shout his joy at having heard her last words or scream his frustration over having to watch her leave.

Great green gods! Yes, when he returned from Tarchannen Eid he fully planned to offer a ring to that one. If it cost him all the skin on both his knees, he was going to ask for her hand as many times as it would take. She might eventually accept. She would likely decline. Love was a razor and he was willing to walk the keen edge of its silver blade. The list of events over which he had control was a short one indeed. That much he had learned even before his twentieth birthday.

Either way, he resolved to at the very least kiss her mouth like a dark red rose. He planned to kiss her mouth, but he was already imagining the gentle but eager pressure of her hands on his shoulders as she silently demanded him to kiss so much more. He could feel her thin fingers tugging at his hair as she offered him gentle instruction, gentle directions through territories that he had mapped in his mind numerous times, but they were territories that he had never actually explored. That blissful kiss would eventually end, but not until both parties had their fill. Then he would throw himself against her with the entire weight of his soul as she pleaded for her liege to…

Someone grabbed his hand just then, and Quinn flinched like a grazing deer struck in the shoulder by a hunter's arrow. It was the bastard that had cleared his throat, urging Catherine to move along. Upon catching a whiff of the newcomer's breath, Quinn immediately had to wonder if the man possibly had morsels of rotting carcass tucked between his crooked teeth. This balding and obese man with horrid breath offered his artificial congratulations, and they were accompanied by a shower of foul spittle.

Perhaps the arrival of the man with corrosive breath was a fortuitous development after all, for it allowed Quinn's *handle of a horse whip* to shrug off some of its…zeal. He quickly retreated back into his zone, but his daydreams were no longer mere unattainable fantasies. They were specific plans for savoring all the delights that had just been promised him by the goddess walking up the aisle behind him.

♦♦♦

As the last of the congregation shuffled up the wide aisles leading to the front of the chapel, the sanctuary grew increasingly quiet. When the last member exited through the wide doors, Father Sigmund signaled to one of his acolytes, ordering the portals shut and barred. The gangly acolyte rushed to do the priest's bidding, and soon Quinn heard the resounding booms as the massive oak doors slammed to, closing him in and cutting him off from his world. The discomfiting sound reverberated through the sanctuary, bouncing over the marble floors and around the long, varnished pews that he himself had polished so many times in months past.

There was a certain note of finality carried on those echoes that signified to him that it was too late to turn back. Things were, for better or for worse, about to change for him. Though he did not know the rules of this particular game, he was about to be dealt some cards...a hand to play. But fate, the ultimate tarot dealer, was keeping the cards close to its chest as always.

Clasping his hands together and offering a rather banal smile to the five *Chosen,* Father Sigmund addressed the small group once again. "My children, the time of your departure to our glorious Citadel draws nigh. If you would follow me please, we ask that you all change into the special travel cloaks that the Church has provided for you. As I mentioned earlier, once you arrive at the festival grounds you may change into your everyday attire." The aging and ailing priest dabbed his nose once more with the white cloth that was becoming less white and far filthier with every swipe. "I hope you all enjoy yourselves thoroughly this week," he added with absolutely no conviction in his voice as his gaze settled on Miriam for what seemed to Quinn to be an inordinate amount of time. Finally, the vicar spun about and motioned for everyone to follow him.

The five citizens fell into pace behind the rotund priest, filing through one of the smaller doors flanking the pulpit at the front of the sanctuary. Hardly a word was uttered as the six navigated a maze of hallways, turning left only to take an immediate right. Quinn fell behind the group several times as he paused to look at the unsettling works of art that dotted the walls of the dimly lit hallways. Most of the paintings depicted grisly scenes of battles between sword-wielding angels and foul demons armed with pikes and scepters. Ornate wall sconces, gilded and elegant to the point of gaudiness supported oil lamps whose flickering light was obviously intended to emphasize the disturbing artwork, but they did a piss poor job of exposing the buckled seams in the dark maroon carpet.

Not long into their march, Quinn tripped over one of those blasted seams and barely managed to suppress another of his trademark expletives. Before long, his eyes adjusted to the dimness, but his lungs continued to rebel against the heavy stale air that hung like curtains of dense cobwebs from the ceiling of this maze's tight confines. This air was so thick, Quinn figured it could have been stirred by nothing less than a wooden spoon. Traipsing behind the ailing Father Sigmund, the group made a hard left and the hallway they now entered was wider than the old one by at least a famn. The air in this new course seemed less eager to suffocate the five interlopers, but the rich ebony paneling and matching wainscoting that cloaked the walls and ceilings—not to mention the dark maroon carpet that covered the floor—still made the labyrinth seem every bit as dark as winter dusk.

# 4

At last, a thoroughly winded Father Sigmund called a halt between two unremarkable six-panel doors, one on either side of the wide hallway. Both were adorned with little more than a worn brass knob and three tarnished hinges. Yet again he dabbed his raw nose, which shone red even in the faint and flickering light.

"My friends, I will ask the two ladies to step into this room," he wheezed as he motioned to the door on everyone's right. "You gentlemen may change in this room. Your travel garments are on hangers. Please notice that your names have been embroidered into the inside of the lapels. Now if you will excuse me, I am to proceed to the courtyard, but one of my assistants will be waiting here for you when you get dressed. Goodbye, for now," he offered with a wet snort. Quinn grimaced as he heard the man swallow the thick snot.

The priest offered the group a shallow bow before he turned to hurry on down the gloomy hallway. Well before he was out of earshot, he blew his nose and he blew it hard…probably hard enough to rupture a few blood vessels. Quinn silently wondered if a lobe of the cleric's brain might have been shorn off and dumped into the crusty folds of that filthy yellow handkerchief.

"No one would even fucking notice," he muttered as his lips twisted into a cynical sneer.

After the priest turned the corner, Quinn and the other two men stepped into their assigned dressing room. They squinted and shielded their dilated eyes once they discovered that the Church had been a bit more generous with the oil lamps in here, thankfully. As promised, the three garments were hanging on a rod suspended above a padded dressing bench. None of them spoke a word as they started to undress. There was little to talk about at this point, and none of the three were inclined to engage in meaningless chatter.

The thin, bearded man with slumped shoulders was painfully shy, Quinn quickly decided. No, he was not just shy. He was haunted by at least three decades of humiliation and derision. This silent scarecrow possessing skittish eyes, a slow pulse, and even slower thoughts retreated to the far corner of the room; he turned his back to the other two men and began to unbutton his threadbare plaid shirt. Periodically, he would glance over his shoulder like a skittish squirrel. He was the only male *Chosen* who did not wear a suit, and the humiliation painted across his emaciated face offered Quinn evidence enough that the chap was acutely aware that poverty represented just one of his many banes. It was one, but it was not foremost on the list. He began to shed his flannel shirt, but he did so with hesitation born of some consideration that surpassed simple timidity.

At long last, his plaid shirt fell to the floor and he warily turned to face his two associates. Quinn immediately noticed that a network of jagged white scars marked and marred both the front and back of this poor bastard's torso. After spending a few seconds gawking at the web of old welts on the lanky man's upper body, Quinn lifted his gaze to meet that of his fellow *Chosen*. The pathetic fellow's eyes were more sad and distant than they had been all morning. Those eyes reflected fatigue and suspicion—but damned little intelligence. Dark bags hung beneath those dim spheres, and the pouches reminded Quinn of an old hound's long face. All of the man's movements were slow, but not necessarily deliberate. It seemed as though he could barely muster enough will or determination to perform even simple little tasks like tying his shoes or rising from the low bench.

Weariness and lassitude bled from the very air surrounding the dullard, as did waves of bitter, oniony body odor. Quinn felt less alive just from being in close proximity to this gangly mess of a man whom the gods had evidently designated as a target for their unsympathetic spite. On the day of his conception, all the gods had been frowning.

The short, nervous turd on the other hand was energetic enough—he was just downright unsociable. He was a nexus of contempt and cynicism, and he managed to convey as much, all without uttering a single syllable other than the occasional grunt. His haughty bearing fueled Quinn's initial desire to knock the shit out of this pig. Certainly, this bastard's range of facial expressions did not encompass much territory. His baseline sneer occasionally twisted into a downright hostile frown, but that was the extent of his repertory. That snooty leer was indication enough that this heel held himself in high esteem, and was equally indicative that no one else was likely to meet whatever distorted standards he had set for himself. He was in no way likeable, yet he seemed quite aware of that fact and was…curiously comfortable with it.

Quinn shrugged and reached up to grab the garment hanging just in front of him. He tore off the fragile parchment sheath, fully expecting to discover some sort of lacy suit or perhaps a silly uniform that would make him look like one of the ridiculous toy soldiers in the Church's annual Yule production. No such luck, but hope still remained, for the gossamer garment that Quinn pulled off its hanger had another man's name stitched into the lapel.

"We have yet to be formerly introduced, gentlemen," Quinn began, and his voice was dripping with syrupy sarcasm, "but which one of you is Mr. Tollis?" He readily acknowledged that he stood no chance of even chipping the outer stratum of ice that likely could never be entirely broken, and he readily admitted to himself that the thick ice was doing him a great service by insulating him from any further interaction with these two sons of bitches.

With a huff, the short man rudely snatched the flimsy robe from Quinn's hand and threw the garment that he had been holding onto the edge of the slick bench so that it promptly slid onto the floor. He regarded Quinn with undisguised suspicion bordering on disgust, as if the youngest of this year's *Chosen* was just some filthy street urchin who was keenly waiting for an opportunity to pilfer and then pocket some trinket that did not belong to him. Tollis deduced that the third garment obviously belonged to the tall simpleton. He snatched the remaining hanger off the rod and pitched the wad of fabric across the room. It hit the wretched one square in the chest, but the tall man's reflexes were too slow to prevent the package from falling to the floor.

"Keep your stink over there, Ament. Your first order of business after we arrive at the Citadel is to give yourself a good dousing and scrubbing. You hear me?"

*Screw you!* Quinn kept the thought to himself as he angrily tossed his sweat-soaked suit jacket to the side. He buried his nose in his silk tie before unraveling the knot, and the remnants of Catherine's exquisite perfume calmed him, but just barely to the point where he no longer seriously entertained the notion of using his knuckles to flatten this rude little fuck's nose.

"You stop look at me! You too, boy! You no friend of me! Scars for me to look at, not you," the one named Ament bellowed, but then he backed away and defensively crossed his arms in front of his face.

*Screw you both then!* Quinn thought to himself once again as he shook his head and focused on arranging his own thin wrap to cover as much bare skin as the paltry fabric allowed. Aside from the portly man's irksome wheezing, the three changed in complete silence. Whatever criteria the Church had followed while picking this season's *Chosen*, Quinn easily discerned that enthusiasm, devotion, and joviality had most certainly not been on the short list.

One glance over his shoulder told Quinn that the three men definitely had at least one thing in common, however: they all looked absolutely ridiculous dressed in the absurd robes their Church had been so *gracious* to provide. The impractical garments in fact more closely resembled dresses than robes. Made of some thin weave resembling cheap twill, the single layer of fabric was far too light for the late season. These useless housecoats would barely suffice for early autumn wraps, even with thick street clothes worn beneath them. The long blue travel robes fell below their knees, almost to their ankles, but still Quinn felt naked and exposed. Even though the dressing room was heated by a small coal stove, a cool draft spilling in from beneath the hallway door gave him goose bumps from his underpants to his ankles.

With their backs turned to one another, they finished cinching the waist belts as tightly as they could and gathered their other clothes into loose bundles. Donning their flimsy feminine robes, the three stepped back into the shadowy hallway where they were greeted by Father Sigmund's gaunt...assistant.

♦♦♦

Quinn did an awfully conspicuous double-take when he moved in close enough to scrutinize the bony young aide as best he could under this measly lamplight. So thin was this homely bastard, so very pale. His skin was a shade or two lighter than the bleached parchment used for the Church's bulletins. The acolyte's delicate hide was so white the sickly lad glowed like a firefly, even in the dim shadows that hovered about the dismal hallway. To make matters worse, the boy sported the single worst haircut Quinn had ever seen on anyone over the age of five. It looked as if a blind drunk with dull scissors had been set loose on the poor chap's head. A blind drunk in the saddle of a nervous horse.

"My name is Malloway, kind sirs," the boy greeted them in a lisp heavy enough to make Quinn's scalp tingle and his butt pucker.

*Gods,* Quinn thought, and he halfheartedly tried to suppress a disparaging grin. However, he didn't even try to disguise the rolling of his eyes this time around. Skinny, pale, shitty haircut, *and* a lisp? Quinn assumed that Catherine was likely being hounded by a bevy of drooling suitors, but he quickly decided that he wouldn't have to worry about her running off with this particular…boy…while he was at Tarchannen Eid. Shit! Which rigged deck were the gods dealing from when this kid was conceived?

"The ladies are not ready as of yet, it seems, but as soon as they…"

Just then, Miriam and the other woman stepped out of their dressing room. Quinn blinked twice to be sure that his eyes were not deceiving him in the faint orange light. Everyone was wearing pale blue travel cloaks…everyone except for Miriam, who was sporting a light gray cloak with crimson piping adorning the lapel, the cuffs and the hem.

"Umm, *Mister* Malloway, if I might bother you with a question?" Quinn asked after raising his hand like he was back in school, asking for permission to make a run to the outhouse for a quick sloppy shit to alleviate a stomach cramp. He immediately felt stupid for having done so, and he let his arm drop to his side as he warily eyed his mother's dissimilar garment.

"Of course. How may I be of assistance?" the acolyte lisped, and cocked his head to the side as if he was some curious white puppy… a starving puppy at that. As he did so, his eyes ran down and up Quinn's robed body like he was trying to decide what to have for lunch.

"Well *sir*, why is it that four of us are wearing royal blue except for my mo—Miss Miriam? Is there some significanth to the…differenth?"

Miriam closed her eyes and placed the slender fingers of one hand across them in embarrassment, even though she was no longer really shocked by anything Quinn said in public. She still remembered her son's exchange with Mr. Brailer last weekend.

Malloway's eyes, on the other hand, narrowed in undisguised malice. But Quinn noticed right away that the new fire behind this pale kid's glare was fueled by something other than insult. Disap-

pointment possibly? What might have been a blush born of rejection's rage temporarily turned the color of the acolyte's skin from the
white of new fallen snow to the ghoulish pink hue of a newborn rat.
Quinn knew that he had struck a nerve with this effeminate twerp by
openly poking fun at the little turd's sissyish impediment. *Mission
accomplished*, Quinn silently congratulated himself.

Still, the emasculate disciple did not entirely lose his composure.
He warped his delicate little lips into a derisive smile, though it was
clear to Quinn and the rest of the group that their new guide's eyes
held no measure of mirth whatsoever. "Why yes, young sir. You see,"
the emaciated acolyte continued to lisp in irksome and condescending
tones, ignoring the fact that Quinn was at least three years his senior,
"Miss Miriam has been designated to be…group spokesperson for
the next few days. Her special role will become more apparent very
soon. Your mother has been conscripted to a most distinctive position,
you see. You should be very proud for her." Malloway's fingers
began to quiver noticeably as he fidgeted with the ends of his purple
sash, and the previous kisses of color rapidly retreated from his face.
When they did so, it left him looking entirely unhealthy. Even more
so than when Quinn had initially stepped into the hallway.

♦ ♦ ♦

*This smug, homophobic prick will learn a bitter lesson in humil-
ity soon enough. Such a conceited little man. Utterly clueless. This
upstart has no idea just how devastated his soul will be before week's
end. His precious world will soon be laid to ruin*, Malloway reminded
himself, and a gratified smile contorted his pouty feminine lips. That
single consideration offered him comfort beyond measure as he stood
there facing the brash son of a bitch that had just mocked him in front
of the other four *Chosen*.

Yes, in less than six days, this arrogant *Chosen* asshole would
forfeit a tall pile of chips that he had not even placed on the table.
He would soon lose a bet that he had never dreamed of wagering.
The stakes were high and the deck was stacked against him on this
play. The dealer would take all, for this fucker's mother wore the lone
gray robe! Malloway's smile spread wider still, and his fifth ap-
pendage grew stiffer than a hickory sapling as he pictured Quinn
rolling around in the cold snow, shouting his raw grief to the godless
skies.

Malloway shook his head to clear those grim but gratifying

thoughts from his mind. Satisfied that the matter of the robes was temporarily settled...hoping that it was, at least...the sneering acolyte spun about and raced into the shadows, almost tripping over his own long feet as he did so.

"Follow me...pleathe," he called over his shoulder. He made no effort to mitigate his lisp as he locked eyes with Quinn.

♦♦♦

The five *Chosen* almost had to run in order to keep up with Malloway as he dashed through yet another sector of the dimly lit maze. At last, they caught up with him after he skidded to a halt before a massive door that rather patently marked the end of this section of winding hallway. Sweating and struggling for a proper breath, Tollis finally waddled up to join the rest of his party. Malloway's delicate hand grasped the brass knob and turned it. So perfectly balanced was the door that it swung open with barely a push from the anemic acolyte, and the hinges didn't complain with so much as a single squeak. Bright sunlight surging from a cloudless sky flooded into the hallway, virtually blinding the five *Chosen*, so accustomed had their eyes become to the near-darkness.

Squinting and shading their eyes with their hands, they stepped through the portal to be met with the cheers and applause of hundreds of well-wishers who had gathered in the courtyard to see their revered representatives off to the Citadel...the seat of the Way...Valenesti's bane.

Quinn could hardly hear the crowd's roar. His attention was immediately called to the vessel parked just a couple of rods away from the alcove in which he hesitated while his eyes adapted to this new light. Never one to be easily impressed by the Church's indulgences, even he couldn't help but marvel at the huge, ornately decorated coach that awaited the five of them at the far side of the crowded courtyard. Like a weathered oak, it dwarfed the assemblage that stood about clapping and waving to the *Chosen* as the five strode out of the shallow alcove and down the short flight of marble stairs. As impressive as the other coach may have seemed at the time, the one that had delivered Miriam and himself to this morning's service could not even begin to compare. Two of those tinier carriages could have easily fit into this magnificent vehicle and there would have been room to spare for part of a third. The outer shell was constructed entirely of dark cherry wood that had been varnished and buffed to a flawless glossy finish, and it was dressed out with rails, rungs, and hinges fashioned from bright untarnished brass. Decorative scrollwork cast from pure gold lined every contour and accented every corner, giving the vessel the appearance of a huge gilded spider web.

But it was ultimately the sight of the team that pranced before the carriage that took Quinn's breath. What beautiful beasts these were! Never had he seen horses so massive...so sleek...not in all his years spent behind the protection of Eldr-shok's walls. They were all solid black but for tufts of long white hair, which hung down from their knees, cascading over massive hooves that pounded the loose powdery snow into patches of densely packed ice the size of dinner plates. There were six horses in all, and all were huffing and prancing in place, each one as eager as a mother in her ninth month. They were eager for motion. The beasts longed for a chance to launch...for the moment when they would be prompted to lean against their burden. It was obvious that they had been bred for action and for executing the dynamics of the dance unique to their proud breed. It just was not in their blood to stand idle, held static and cruelly restrained by brake, bit and rein.

Parting in polite deference, the crowd made way for the five *Chosen*, and Quinn could see that a rich velvet carpet runner had been laid out for them, which led to the steps allowing access up into the grand coach. And up the five went. Quinn paused to give his mother an arm for support as she climbed the brass steps. Making sure to hold the front of his robe together, he climbed in after her and took his seat on the couch at the rear of the spectacular carriage. He found himself situated between Miriam and Tollis, the nervous and sour little man who had barely spoken a word...the toad of a man whose edematous knees were no longer concealed by the gauzy robe. They were puffy, pale, and blemished with a dense network of blue veins. How Quinn hungered to hyperextend those feeble joints with two well-placed kicks. That scenario warmed him in ways that his thin dress simply could not.

That short dash between church and carriage had been uncomfortably chilly. Winter's cold breath enthusiastically rushed under the hem of Quinn's flimsy new robe, causing his flesh to shiver...and shrink. *Handle of a horse whip, indeed*. He was glad that Catherine wasn't assessing his endowment right at the moment, although the notion of such an inspection did nullify the more profound effects of the cold. Irony abounded, he decided as another impish grin crossed his face. The grin disappeared when Tollis cleared his sinuses with a wet, obnoxious snort.

"Have you been locking lips with Father Sigmund lately, by any chance?" Quinn asked under his breath. He was leaning close to Tollis and pretending to peer out the window.

"What? What did you just ask me, you little…?"

"You must have misheard me. Just calm down, will you? I didn't ask anything, I was just making an observation. Don't get your knickers in a knot, Mr. Tollis. All is well."

"So, what exactly was your *observation*, you snotty youngster?" Tollis asked as he cleared his sinuses with another sick snort. Quinn didn't comment on the irony of that last statement, but doing so definitely crossed his mind.

"All I said was…*nice legs*. You're a sexy little bugger, but you know that already now don't you? I sure hope they let me room with you at Festival. I want you all to myself," Quinn finished with a wink and a crafty smile. The smile grew broader as he watched Tollis's face turn red with the twin plagues of rage and embarrassment.

◆◆◆

If the exterior of the coach was impressive, then the interior was nothing less than lavish. Royal purple velvet covered the padded seats, and thick curtains fashioned from the same material hung over the windows that comprised most of the vehicle's side walls. Plush carpeting coated the floor, and five fluffy footstools were even provided, as was a miniature bar that afforded water and an array of stronger refreshments for the five special passengers. A knee-high coal stove pinged as the metal expanded from the heat that drove away the worst of the winter chill. Quinn could barely smell any smoke at all, since the stove's steel flue was cleverly designed to vent all its exhaust to the outside.

The carriage jostled, though ever so slightly, as the two uniformed coachmen took their seats above the passenger cabin. With a shallow smile and a final nod to the five passengers, Father Sigmund closed the thick door, but not before staring at Miriam once again. He allowed his gaze to linger on her face…then on the crimson piping adorning her robe. His crusted eyes betrayed a contradictory mix of loathing and pity. Quinn couldn't help but take special notice of that flinty look, and another odd tingle ran up the back of his neck.

Without asking for permission or offering any apology, he leaned across Tollis' lap and pulled the curtain aside. A dozen or more ravens were making lazy circles above the church's lofty steeple. Their black wings stood out in contrast to the gray background...a new bank of snow clouds that had suddenly moved in from the north and west. The daystar was suddenly gone.

♦♦♦

The heavy carriage door was now closed, but that did little to drown out the escalating cheers of the crowd as the fiery horses leaned into their harnesses, propelling the five *Chosen* and the two coachmen through the gates and into the fabled forest that lay beyond the walls of the courtyard, the forest summoned from the plains on the night of Valenesti's ghastly death...the night of his ultimate liberation.

Still more than just a little overwhelmed by it all, four of the coach's curious passengers peered out from between the opaque violet curtains and into the dense forest that sped past the windows. Green cedar boughs as well as the leafless branches of hardwood trees whipped by, mere links from the spotless panes of glass. Tollis the Sour seemed far less impressed than the others by the spectacle. His serious little frown didn't soften a bit...not initially. Had the other four been paying any attention, they would have noticed that a measure of relief softened his toad-like features slightly as he leaned toward the small bar and poured himself a tall glass of amber liquid from one of the crystalline decanters. The contents of that first glass were dispatched with fervor, and Tollis was doing significant damage to his second glass by the time the other passengers were even properly settled in. The second round was soon followed by a third...

The remainder of the trip, a little less than three hours by Quinn's reckoning, passed in similar fashion. He did notice that the robust leaves glued to the limbs of the oak, hickory and sweet gum trees became denser and certainly greener as the coach raced toward its goal. It was as if the season had by some means changed from early winter to late spring just since the magnificent carriage had clattered through the forest gate behind the cathedral. By the time the gilded wagon at last broke free from beneath the canopy of trees and clattered into the vast clearing, Quinn had wholly surrendered his smugness to the spirits of sheer spectacle; he was now a willing victim of wonder. The apprehension that had plagued him earlier that morning was now a distant, diluted memory.

Tollis was clearly feeling very little pain at this point. The potent liquor's effects had done nothing to loosen the grumpy toad's lips, however. Although his grim frown had indeed grown shallower by a degree, it could never be mistaken for a smile. Miriam and the other lady, Helen, had tried to engage him in conversation as they all rattled and rolled along the forest road, but the ladies' attempts had not met with much success. An occasional, frustratingly ambiguous grunt was all the two ever managed to elicit.

"Is this it? Are we there yet? Where is the Citadel?" Quinn asked eagerly of his mother as he pressed his forehead against the cold panes and tugged at her sleeve like he was seven years old again.

"Now, how in Haeven's name should I know, mister? This is my first time to make this trip too, you know?" Miriam replied in mock exasperation. But her own face was aglow with thinly veiled excitement, and she was doing her level best to prevent her voice from faltering. Her forehead was pressed against the panes as well and her thin fingers clung to the drapes as if she was trying to wring dirty water out of a rag mop.

All five passengers were thrown toward the port side of the carriage as the drivers finally wheeled the wagon around to head due north. Tollis spilled most of his drink into Quinn's lap during that hard turn, but the youngest *Chosen* barely noticed the sting of the icy drink that drenched the front of his gauzy gown, for his attention was focused elsewhere. He fought to draw a legitimate breath, so astounded was he by the sight that hove into view through the window on Miriam's side of the carriage. The Citadel's high outer walls were still almost half a league off to the west, but the sheer scale of the legendary city exceeded even his wildest imaginings.

Pristine spires and spiked steeples, many times higher than any of those in Eldr-shok, stabbed into the cerulean Haevens. Had there been any clouds creeping across the sky this afternoon, Quinn was quite sure that the tallest of the spires would have pierced clean through the frail strakes of those billowy vessels. The sight was beyond astounding, but alas the coincidental tour ended before the five from Eldr-shok were granted anything more than a perfunctory glimpse of the immense walls and the indescribable towers enclosed therein. The team whinnied and the carriage skidded to a halt. Once again the massive coach lurched slightly as the two drivers hopped down from their stations.

Almost immediately, the round door on the right side of the coach swung open, and the two smiling drivers beckoned the guests to carefully exit the comfortable confines of the carriage. Miriam pulled the thin gray robe tightly around her slender frame, expecting a blast of earlywinter wind to tear through the cabin. However, as the five stepped out onto the grass, they found that the weather was astoundingly...spring-like!

"How the f—how can this possibly be?" Quinn asked of no one in particular. "Just this very morning back in Eldr-shok, my nut sack was shriveled enough to have comfortably fit into a raisin's skin, perhaps twice! But..."

Thoroughly addled by the multiple doses of strong bourbon, Tollis stumbled down the carriage steps but steadied himself once he caught hold of Quinn's left arm. The fat man still regarded those around him with that disapproving glare, but he was apparently not too proud to use Quinn's lean body as an improvised handrail.

"Dunno lad, but I'm not one to argue with it. Never been a big fan of freezing my arse off, I haven't. Shtill a little cool for my taste, though. Sheems like they could've done better," the man slurred. "And they are going to make us stay in tents, did they shay? Tents? Ye, gods! Are we *Chosen* of the Church or a pack of hunting dogs? There had better be blankets aplenty is all I can say. Lanterns and blankets, damn them. I'd rather spend my time behind those walls, not out here with..." This was the most that the foul little man had said all day, but Quinn suspected all along that the first full sentence springing from Tollis's fat little jowls would involve a complaint of some sort.

"Follow me please, my good people. We need to get you settled into your tents and then the celebration can begin in earnest," called a shirtless young man in baggy breeches, apparently one of their assigned hosts. "Oh, and of course, welcome to Tarchannen Eid," he added with a curt bow. "Welcome one and all! Yes."

*Another goddamned bow,* Quinn rolled his eyes even as he fell in line behind the escort, but his gaze was still riveted to the towering spires just on the other side of the high wall...spires that, at the very least, reached the ceiling of Eldimorah if not the forbidding floor of Haeven itself. Close to what Quinn had to assume was the center of Tarchannen Eid, one slender tower peeked over the gilded heads of every last one of its neighbors. The gripping account of Valenesti's tormenting last days spun stunning images in his thoughts at that instant, and a familiar shudder ran along his spine despite the unexplained, unseasonal balminess in the air.

Along the course of the short hike, their gracious attendant with the baggy pants introduced himself as Mason and proceeded to lead his five special guests along a path that had been worn fairly recently through the tan, knee-high grass. It funneled them toward the lofty white walls that ringed Tarchannen Eid, the seat of the Church of the Way. Beyond those enormous walls, slender spires clawed hungrily at the margins of a few errant clouds that had just now begun to lazily slither across the vibrant blue evening sky.

Just ahead, Quinn could make out a collection of squat tan tents that had been set up near the base of the magnificent city's eastern wall. There were a dozen or more of the canvas cottages in all. They were scattered among the shifting grasses in random fashion, but none of them had been erected very far from the broad wooden pavilion—the lone permanent structure in the compound. It was nestled snuggly against the base of the city's eastern wall, just to the south of the broad iron gate.

Today, the pavilion itself was festooned with hefty, spruce wreaths and white bows whose ribbon streamers flapped gently in the baffling spring-like breeze. Long tables were arrayed beneath the pavilion, and people milled about the steaming buffets in a manner that reminded Quinn of ants endeavoring to repair their mound after a harsh rain. On the south side of the shelter, a small stage complete with a podium had been erected and the steps leading up to it were perfectly aligned with the pitch of the pavilion's roof. The group's guide led them through the shelter and then back out beneath the deepening afternoon shadows. Scratching his jaw in deliberation, Mason stopped in front of one of the tents and thumbed through a deck of dog-eared cards he produced from his hip pocket.

"Umm...Mr. Tollis, Mr. Ament...you two gentlemen will be sharing this tent during your stay, if you please. Go on in and make yourselves at home. Your bags will be brought to you shortly, and then you may change into your everyday clothes if you wish. I suspect that you will." He held one of the flaps aside, inviting the two older men from Eldr-shok to go in and assess their new digs, modest though they were.

"Actually, I think the pudgy one is fond of wearing dresses," Quinn tittered.

Tollis shot his young tormentor a venomous glance as he ducked to enter his tent, but the only response he elicited was a wink and a blown kiss. Quinn suspected that his taunts might well contribute to whatever seizure or stroke would surely cause this turd's eventual decline into pants-shitting derangement ...and that image warmed his heart.

"Yes, well," Mason tried to retreat from the tension by shuffling through his cards. "You three will follow me, if you please." Mason nodded toward Quinn and the two ladies as he spun around. He wound through the maze of other tents before consulting his cards once more. "Ah, here we are...tent number six," the shirtless boy announced after halting in front of another nondescript canvas tent. "Tent number six it is for Miss Miriam and Miss Helen from Eldrshok. You two ladies will be lodging here during the festivities...if it suits you, of course."

Quinn tensed and started to protest, but caught himself before he began to sound like a nursing pup threatened with separation from its mother's pink teat. A fraction of his enthusiasm faded in that moment; he had naturally assumed that he and his mother would be housed together throughout this week-long party. Like a professional steward, Mason sensed his guest's apprehension and waved him to the adjacent tent with a sly smirk and an understanding wink.

"Master Quinn, I trust you will find this one suitable—tent seven. Your roommate has yet to arrive; he is with the Eldr-burze group, I do believe. But go on in and make yourself comfortable. Your things should be delivered any moment. Orientation isn't for a couple of hours. Your mother is just one tent over. Besides, I don't think you'll be left wonting for entertainment, judging from what I've heard about your new...roommate." At that, young Mason wiped the sweat from his forehead, bowed and then sped off toward the looming pavilion to tackle the next chore on what was quite likely a long list on this extraordinarily busy day.

Quinn stepped into his meager new abode and plopped down onto the cot closest to the south side of the pavilion...the one closest to the tent's front flap. He fell onto his side, but almost as soon as his head hit the thick pillow, a hand pushed aside the flaps and another set two worn bags on the grassy floor of the tent. It was one of the drivers of the Citadel coach. Quinn recognized him immediately. The driver's cheeks were pocked with deep acne scars, but those did not prevent him from casting a warm smile at tent number seven's sole occupant.

"Enjoy your stay, young man. Quinn, was it? I guess you're beyond ready to trade that flimsy excuse-for-a-robe for a pair of thick pants and a real man's shirt, now aren't you? Hel, the draft upward is probably freezing whatever may be pointed downward, aye?" the driver joked in a deep voice that was little more than a low rumble.

"Gods, but you're reading my mind, friend! Thanks," Quinn replied as he bounded off the cot to retrieve his belongings. "Oh, and thanks as well for the smooth ride!"

"My pleasure, son. I hope...I hope the trip back isn't too demanding on you." With that, the driver backed away from the tent flap and disappeared.

By now, Quinn was more than a little anxious to be rid of the ridiculous travel robe that the Church had furnished, but he was far more anxious to confirm that his two very special items had made the trip and made it intact. Tremors seized his hands as he struggled to grip the tiny tab of the zipper that secured the pocket on the side of his smaller bag. He all but ripped the compartment open, but breathed a sigh of divine relief when he discovered that his book and the special burlap bundle were in there, still situated just as he had packed them earlier that very morning. They had not been tampered with in the least, as far as could tell.

"Good old Arlis!" Quinn muttered as he pulled the zipper snugly to and shoved the small bag under his cot, even taking the time and effort to thread the shoulder strap through the scant springs supporting his mattress so that he would be warned should someone try to meddle with the irreplaceable bag while he was napping. Then he turned his full attention to the larger bag and rummaged through it until he located his favorite canvas pants and wool shirt...the outfit that he wore almost every other Sunaday afternoon of the year, after his stupid suit had been tossed over the back of that lone chair in his bedroom.

In no time, he had shed the ridiculous robe. With a grunt of disgust, he threw it unceremoniously into the grass beyond the foot of his cot. With any luck, he would be through with the filmy thing for good, but he had a sneaking suspicion that he would be asked to wear the blasted man-dress on the return trip. Sucking in and savoring the familiar wood smoke scent creeping forth from the weave of the fabric, he donned his favorite trousers and shirt, then pulled his boots on over his thickest pair of socks. He quickly realized that the heavy shirt was almost too warm for this strange weather, but he had packed only winter clothing. No matter, though. The nights were bound to be a little cooler. He certainly hoped as much, otherwise he would have to follow Mason's lead and go shirtless as long as the daystar was either riding high or casting shadows back to the east.

Now that Quinn felt properly dressed, he decided to have a look around the festival grounds, starting with the pavilion and the buffets…and bars. As he stepped toward the front of the tent, he almost butted heads with the tall, muscular man who was just stooping forward to enter.

"Hi, mate. Good tidings to ya!" the man offered as he stepped around Quinn and hefted his own shabby bags onto the only empty cot. The newcomer turned and silently regarded Quinn for a moment or two. The tent's low roof didn't allow this stranger to stand fully erect, but that didn't seem to bother him overmuch. He scratched his chin thoughtfully, but his hawk eyes never blinked once. His lips offered nothing resembling a smile…not exactly a smile, but a diluted and intuitive simper instead. His blue eyes betrayed a certain degree of guarded humor…humor and fierce intelligence, Quinn noted. Finally the stranger extended his hand.

"Name is Bartlitt. Just Bartlitt. I use it for my first name as well as my last…I like things simple and uncomplicated. Anyway, damn glad to make your acquaintance. You're a mighty young fucker to be picked by the Church, don't ya think? No. You see yourself as all grown up, now don't you? You don't see yourself all penned up in that box that they call Haeven. No? Well, that'll work to your benefit. Trust me on that one."

"Quinn," the younger tentmate answered simply, and he suspected right then that he and this gentleman were going to get along just splendidly. Quinn held nothing but disdain for the Church, and the Church didn't approve of swearing in the least; yet here stood his new tentmate swearing loudly and rather unapologetically mere rods from the very seat of that despicable Church. Still, the *Chosen* were to be guests of the priests for almost a week, and Quinn harbored no real desire to jeopardize either Miriam's welcome or his own…not yet, at least.

Shit and shadows! Miriam would have his hide salted and stretched over a board if he drew any attention to himself by stirring up any trouble. And she was in the adjacent tent, just a famn or two away. Bartlitt's rich voice was bound to carry at least that far. The heavy canvas might turn the gentle winds rolling in from the plains, but it let all but the faintest of whispers pass right through the weave of its coarse fabric. Even so, Quinn allowed himself the luxury of a satisfied smirk as he stepped forward to firmly grab Bartlitt's outstretched hand. He offered a hint of his own impish sneer, hoping on one neurotic level that the man would be slightly more judicious in the future. But at the same time, Quinn entertained hope that his new tentmate would keep right on being unapologetic, forthright and... and refreshingly blunt. Crude even.

"One Hel of a grip you have there, Quinn," Bartlitt exclaimed loudly as he rubbed his knuckles in mock pain, "one Hel of a grip indeed. You nearly broke my fucking knuckles. Just be sure you keep your hands off my nucking fuckles. You don't possess the equipment or the credentials to juggle those special jewels!" the older man hooted as he shot a wink Quinn's way. "There are no men allowed at that club, you see? Only ladies with exceptional abilities, low standards, and mediocre expectations!"

Quinn missed the joke, but not entirely so. He would need time to process his roomie's words, but Bartlitt's tone as well as his crafty wink inferred a context of unabashed debauchery. Quinn winced and ducked as if he was dodging a diving bee. *So much for any expectations of quiet and tactful language. Was Miriam listening...?*

"So tell me, young fella...bring me up to speed. What are you in for?"

"Excuse me, sir? I'm not exactly sure—"

"Ah, let's have none of that *sir* bullshit, Quinn," Bartlitt interrupted. "Don't go wishing years on me that I haven't earned yet. I haven't earned your respect either, for that matter, so let's just curtail the *sir* crap until I've lived up to a few more of your standards." Bartlitt sobered in an instant and leaned in toward Quinn before continuing. "And you have plenty of those, now don't you lad? Standards, I mean. Not many others have made the cut, I'm guessing. Very few have made it through your rigorous audition process, am I right? So tell me...what are you in for?"

"Yes sir...no sir...sorry. Excuse me *Bartlitt*, but I have no idea what in blazes you just asked me?" Quinn asked as he casually took a seat on the edge of his own cot. Fidgeting, he absently retied one of his boot strings that had already worked its way loose. His stomach was growling, but his stomach and the festival grounds could certainly wait a bit longer. Bartlitt was already proving to be more entertaining than anything else he had witnessed during his hike across the field, save perhaps for the magnificent view of the towers of Tarchannen Eid.

"You know," Bartlitt prompted, one hand whirling in the air as if the younger man was missing the obvious, "what are you in for? They obviously sentenced you for something. Were you caught mugging a widow...molesting a horse...raping a nun...pissing in the face of...?"

To be sure, Quinn's mind had conjured its share of vivid imagery in its day, but this Bartlitt was already crossing the finish line of a race that Quinn had not even begun to run. He blushed and prayed to gods that he didn't even believe in that his bunkmate would shut his mouth, and soon. Either his prayers were instantly answered or Bartlitt had run out of twisted inspiration. Both options seemed equally impossible. Quinn ran his fingers through his hair and shrugged as he tried to figure out what exactly his new bunkie was trying to ask.

"Neither—none—but just so you know, I'd more likely commit the first offense than the latter two—three." He had lost count and decided that it was probably for the best. "I like widows. I like horses too, but I don't like them *that* much! You make it sound more like we are sharing a prison cell than a tent at Festival."

"Ah, there. Now we have the matter by the ball sack! Is there that much of a difference, really?" Bartlitt shot back as he dug through his pack, looking for his pipe and tobac. Quinn was intrigued, but he was too confused to provide an answer to his tentmate's question, one that might have been purely rhetorical as far as he could tell. Suddenly, he found himself wishing that he had helped Tollis polish off that decanter of bourbon on the trip in. He could already tell that this would be a most memorable week, even if he never bothered to leave his tent.

Just then, Quinn thought that he caught a fleeting glimpse of a slender serpentine tail disappearing beneath the rear wall of the tent.

He jerked his boots off the ground, and his eyes remained trained to that spot as he patiently waited for any other signs of the slithering tail's owner. Could there be snakes crawling about in the fields surrounding Tarchannen Eid? Surely not.

"Are there any snakes in these parts, Bartlitt?" Quinn asked, his eyes still riveted to the grass slapping against the rear wall of their tent. "Are there any crawling about this time of year? Do you know?"

"None on this side of the wall, pal. If you ask me...and you did...the only serpents slithering about abide *within* the city walls. Bastards all!"

The tall stranger, having found his smoking rig, packed a bowl of the moist leaves that he carried in a worn leather pouch with a design stamped, or perhaps burned, onto its front. Though he only saw it for a moment, Quinn thought that he could pick out a faint outline of a goblet of some sort...perhaps a chalice? Bartlitt stared directly into Quinn's eyes as he stowed the pouch and slid the familiar pipe into his mouth. He lit it with a short firestick that he deftly struck on one of the tent's stitched seams. He maintained his dissecting gaze and blew a thick ring of the mellow-smelling smoke toward the roof of the tent before he saw fit to speak again.

"Do you mind if I smoke, by the way?" he asked as he counted the blankets on his cot. He nodded in silent approval as his count reached four. "Glad they didn't put a fucking fifth one on here. I would have yanked it off, even if it meant freezing my wrinkled sack off at night," he mumbled around the stem of the pipe that was clenched between his teeth. "Five of everything else, though...fuck me running!"

"No, sir. It actually smells pretty good," Quinn had to admit, though his eyes were beginning to water from the cloud's subtle sting. Truth be told, the smoke's cherry aroma all but beckoned his memory back to the plush couch in Obadiah's house, for even the parson lit a pipe occasionally –one packed with a very similar blend. Inhaling the aromatic smoke spilling forth from Bartlitt's lips was every bit as comforting as curling up for a nap on a stormy afternoon, with thunder rolling across the restless skies. "Seems as though you waited a bit late to ask me if I minded, I might add."

"You can drop the *sir* horseshit, Quinn. I already told you that. It makes you sound younger than you are and it makes me feel older than I am. If I have to say it a third time, I'll have to assume that either I have a speech impediment, or you have a learning disability. And honestly, I've talked my ass out of enough cracks to rule out the first option."

"That much, I don't doubt," Quinn muttered. Bartlitt only cast a wink of acknowledgment to his new tentmate as he took another long drag from his pipe.

"Very good. Anyway, you really don't see it yet, do you son? You still think that your precious Church is there like some kind of protective big brother, some guardian warding you from the unconverted world's directive to spread its taint of corruption and wretchedness." Another smoke ring was sent flying. "I'm afraid fate has planned for you some rather unpleasant surprises. When you encounter them, lad…when you find yourself pierced by the lance of your own crimson-stained legacy, just remember that ol' Bartlitt was the one who warned you first. I hate to say it, but there is pain headed your way, my friend. Don't play the part of the fool. It's bad enough to lay wounded; it is way worse to lay wounded *and* stupid!"

Quinn could feel all the blood leaving his face at the mere mention of his special legacy…his *crimson-stained legacy*. Other than Obadiah and perhaps a few of those serpents in the Church's service, no living soul should possess any knowledge of his rather distinct ancestry. He simply did not know how else to respond, so he went on the offensive.

"First of all," Quinn started in a low but forceful whisper, "you're mistaken in just assuming that I am one of the mindless sheep that the Church herds around with its empty promises and gilded hooks, because I am not. I assure you that I am not! Secondly, no one addresses me as *son* except for my dad, and he happens to be deceased—but don't you dare bother offering me any phony condolences or platitudes. I'd rather you just piss in my wine and blame it on a bad cork. And finally, if you hold such disdain for the Way, then why in Haeven's name did you agree to make the pilgrimage to Tarchannen Eid? I have to wonder why you were *Chosen* in the first place, for that matter," Quinn finished as evenly as he could manage, though his temper was beginning to flare.

In all honesty, he felt more than a little hypocritical even posing that last question, for he could not dispute his tentmate's sentiments regarding their hosts. Quinn had certainly never harbored any abiding respect for the Church, but there was something about the man's forthright manner...his bluntness...that immediately struck the younger of the two *Chosen* as abrasive. Abrasive, but not quite condescending. Abrasive, but strangely refreshing. Damn, but this Bartlitt character was a walking, smoking contradiction.

By now, twin streams of white smoke were issuing from Bartlitt's nostrils. He was exhaling through his nose because his mouth was far too occupied warping into a congratulatory smirk. Quinn realized then that he was being goaded by a master of the craft. Bartlitt leaned back against his bags and loosed a jackal's laugh as a thick fog of pipe smoke escaped through a pair of chapped and bleeding lips; there would be no ring this time, just a swirling miasma of white haze.

"Now that, son—I'm sorry—now that, *lad*, is an excellent question, indeed. One that I suppose I cannot answer right away. Why was I *Chosen*? It most probably was not for the example I set with my religious convictions, as you have likely gathered already. No, I think it was because they want something of me...though they have already taken so goddamn much." The stranger's mood sobered visibly as his thoughts scattered before the powerful winds of reverie. "And that tosses us in the bottom of the same skinny canoe, now doesn't it my new friend? We are both here, yet our presence has little to do with our devotion to the Way, and we both harbor...oh, let us call it *resentment*...because the Church took something precious from us. Or maybe someone, hmm?"

A static image of his father's wasted face morphed within the pale haze of smoke. Quinn suddenly felt cornered. His new tentmate already knew more about him than any stranger should have. Bartlitt's knowing looks and thinly veiled references were more than enough to put the young buck from Eldr-shok on guard. Master Tabor laced his fingers together and took a deep breath. He focused on transforming his own face into an unreadable mask. He thought to turn the tables by stoically scrutinizing the man from Eldr-burze for a moment, but he found that his traitorous fingers were wont to twiddle and his forehead bled beads of sweat as the uncomfortable pause dragged on. Bartlitt's weathered face remained devoid of any conspicuous expression; he sat on his cot like a tanned statue and returned Quinn's gaze without saying a word. He was clearly better prepared to win the staring game.

Quinn swallowed, though that simple act proved to be quite a chore as he tried to weather the scrutiny of this man possessing the affect of a hungry falcon. He felt like frail prey that was being hypnotized and paralyzed by the eyes of this new, wily predator. Of course, he was close enough to the tent flaps to make a bolt for safety, but he would probably not get very far. His trusty old dagger was tucked behind his belt as always, but he instinctively knew that he would be no match for this older man in any fight that counted. Much of the tan skin covering Bartlitt's hands and face was marked with a hodgepodge of pale scars. Most were thin as strands of hair and hardly noticeable, but one especially nasty wound demarcated the hairline above his left eye with a ragged pink ridge. He had seen his share of fights, this one; and he had survived them all, as his presence in this tent substantiated. The tension inside the canvas shell escalated as the silence dragged on. At last, Bartlitt slapped his own knee and hopped to his feet, causing his tentmate to flinch like a sleeping dog awakened by a clap of thunder.

"But enough of my ramblings, comrade. What say we venture from this stuffy tent and see just what our gracious hosts have prepared for us to eat? They owe us a stuffed gut and an ale buzz. They owe us *at least* that much. I'm hungry enough to beat a buzzard off of a dead deer."

"Now that's the first thing you've said so far that I fully understand, though I'd likely stop short of feasting on a rotten carcass," Quinn quipped. He exhaled and allowed himself to relax once it became obvious that his tentmate wasn't going to kill him...at least not at the moment.

Bartlitt threw his head back and loosed a raucous laugh at his new friend's jibe. He placed his arm around Quinn's shoulders as they stepped out of the tent and into the fresh air. Of course, the air in the tent had been fresh as well until Bartlitt decided to light his pipe. Quinn took a deep breath when he was outside. He was glad to be away from the thick haze of cherry-scented smoke that now filled their canvas quarters. It might have smelled good for a few seconds and it might have been just fine for sniffing and sampling, but it wasn't made for breathing over any length of time.

"Yes sir, my good lad, I think that you and I will get along jus splendidly," Bartlitt rumbled after he cleared his throat and launched a viscous stream of spittle into the tall grass beside the neighboring tent. Miriam's tent.

Quinn nodded, but he was going to reserve judgment on that matter for just a while longer. In truth, he sensed that he and Bartlitt were destined to become fast friends...if breathing his tentmate's pungent pipe smoke didn't kill him first.

♦♦♦

Not even on the most festive of Quinn's nineteen Yule's Eves had he ever witnessed a spread such as the one that burdened the long tables beneath the Church's celebration pavilion this night. Eight tables in all there were, each of them laden with tray after tray of roasted piglet, prime rib, potatoes, fruits, cheeses, sausages, and pastries of every description. Bartlitt hesitated not one second before grabbing one of the pewter plates and squeezing his way into the nearest line. Quinn, shrugging resignedly, snatched a plate off the stack and followed suit. The two men, not bothered one bit by the twin trails of gravy and rich sauces they had splattered across the wooden pavilion floor, seated themselves at one of the vacant tables to enjoy the first food they had come near since they broke fast just after dawn that very morning. Initially, neither man said a word as they dove into and devoured the delicious fare.

"Be right back," Bartlitt muttered through a large bolus of medium rare prime rib as he stepped over his bench to make another pass at the buffet. He returned in no time toting yet another brimming plate. This one he made disappear almost as fast as the first. Then he abruptly leaned back against the closest post and launched one of the noisiest belches Quinn ever had the displeasure of witnessing.

All conversations fell silent momentarily as the pilgrims occupying the neighboring tables shot disapproving glances at the older of the two men from tent seven. Bartlitt paid them no mind whatsoever as he crossed his legs and proceeded to pick his teeth with the corner of his fingernail. He spat bits of freed meat into the air, not giving a solitary damn about where they might happen to land; this rebel was thoroughly unconcerned with the snobbish displeasure painted across the faces of the other revelers. They were—without exception—a pack of snooty shits. They were all beneath his notice. And Quinn caught himself basking in the rush of vicarious abandon...until he realized that there was a price to be paid for such liberation. Judging by all the scowls that shifted to him, he quickly recognized that this same jury had deemed him guilty by mere association. He felt the searing heat of embarrassment rush to his face;

he was compensating for his tentmate's apathy by blushing enough for both of them. The youngest *Chosen* from Eldr-shok pretended to casually wipe his mouth with the cloth napkin, but he made a point to cover as much of his red face as possible — and for as long as possible.

"You've got to give our beloved Church one thing, my friend: they know how to feed their congregation," Bartlitt complimented as he continued to pick his teeth, but he was now using the pointed end of his steak knife. Then he freed another loud belch, and Quinn wondered that the rogue didn't rupture something in his throat. "They can certainly fill a plate with goodies…even though they may not do much else for the good of their blind followers," the rascal from Eldr-burze tacked on, and he took no measures to keep his voice down. Bartlitt had broadcast his criticism far too loudly for Quinn's comfort. Or for anyone else's.

Again, the other revelers within earshot turned their discommending gazes toward Quinn's fractious tentmate, and once again all of the lad's blood rushed to his stubbly cheeks. With his eyes clamped shut to diminish at least some of the embarrassment he was feeling, Quinn grabbed his goblet with both hands and drained it of its contents. The amber liquid burned a broad path as it surged down his throat.

"There you go, that's a good lad," Bartlitt taunted as he leaned close enough to give Quinn a congratulatory slap on his back. "What you'll be needing is a refill, and quick." Before Quinn's throat could recover enough to voice any objection, the tall man leapt from his seat yet again and sped off toward the drink table to fetch two more goblets of the stout ale.

Two hours and several mugs of brew later, the intoxicated duo heard the chiming of the gathering bell, summoning one and all to congregate around the raised stage to the left of the pavilion. Quinn and his first legitimate drinking buddy staggered between the tables, bumping into more than one or two of the other merrymakers. As they stumbled by the dessert table, Quinn popped a few mint leaves into his mouth and followed Bartlitt to a spot well away from the front of the gathering. Wobbling on legs that threatened to fail him at any minute, Quinn stood within the deepening shadows of the overhang, watching the other pilgrims stroll in from the surrounding grounds. When all had apparently gathered, a bloated little man dressed in the white robes of the Church labored up the steps to stand apprehensively upon the elevated stage. He gripped the edges of the podium as if they were the gunwales of a doomed boat.

"My good people," he began in what resembled a thin wheeze more than the voice of a vicar, "I welcome you to the Citadel of Tarchannen Eid... *your* Citadel, yes." All those present clapped somewhat politely, if not altogether enthusiastically. All except for Bartlitt, Quinn noted. His tentmate suddenly looked anything but inebriated. He stood stock-still, shoulders back, eyes alert and studying his surroundings like a vigilant bird of prey. Suddenly shed was the celebratory mask he had worn for the last couple of hours. His mien was now sober...unreservedly stern...as he surveyed the festival grounds and the sallow priest up on the platform. He held his hands behind his back while all the others applauded fragments of empty rhetoric.

"We certainly hope you find the fare to your liking," the squat priest-thing continued. "I must admit that I have already enjoyed more than my share," he added, rubbing his round belly for emphasis. Quinn harbored little doubt regarding this pathetic toad's last statement. It was obvious to all present that the corpulent cleric's most recent and most rigorous exercise probably involved climbing the steep steps leading up to the stage that he now occupied. His opening joke—such as it was—sounded far too rehearsed and no one in the crowd laughed...not genuinely, to be sure. The sorry bastard's attempt at humor was met with just a smattering of courteous giggles that was quickly eclipsed by the steady hiss of the late afternoon breeze. Clearing his throat to diminish his own discomfort, the wheezing priest abandoned his doomed comedy career and moved on to some of the frivolous business that justified his position.

"Yes, well...I would ask you all to pay attention to the schedule that has been posted just beside the main serving table. We have quite a week planned for you, yes. The gathering bell, as you have probably surmised, will signal the beginning of each new event—morning services, vespers, or what-have-you. For now, go and enjoy good food and drink. We are planning evening vespers in a couple of hours. If any of you have any questions or, may the gods of the Way forbid, any problems, please track down Master Mason over there," he said, signaling to the foot of the steps leading up to the platform. The young man who had escorted the visitors to their tents held up his hand. Quinn noted that he had finally decided to don a shirt now that the daystar was making itself scarce, hiding its shining face behind the mountains to the west.

"He is here, as are we all, to make sure that you have a pleasurable stay. So long for now, my good people; I'll see you back here in just a little while," the plump man wheezed as he turned to gracelessly waddle down the steep staircase. On the second step from the bottom, the toad planted his foot wrong and rolled his ankle. Quinn heard an audible snap that gave him the urge to vomit. The bloated little priest fell to the grass and began to shriek in pain as his anxious assistants hurried to his side. At last, they managed to improvise a litter and rush the histrionic cleric toward the city's east gate.

Bartlitt turned to his younger tentmate with a mischievous grin painted across his sun-browned face. The watchful bird of prey had taken flight, and the hooligan had returned.

"Did you hear that? Not the rupture of ligaments…the other part, I mean. Two hours, lad; that's time enough for an ale or five, I'm thinking. Probably more!"

"Not for me, thank you. It's off to the tent with me. The ground around here spins a little too much for my comfort."

"Ah, lad, you have to learn how to pace your intake. You also have to learn to choose the drink that suits you. Remember this one point: a drink is like a woman. It may not be with you for very long, but it can make you either very miserable or very satisfied for a short while…and then you piss her off and she's gone!" Bartlitt hooted and slapped Quinn on his shoulder as if they had been chums for years and not just for a couple of hours. "You might want to go with something lighter than that meal-in-a-mug that we were downing earlier. Have you ever tried a good amber ale? I noticed a keg of Smiling Corpse right next to the dirty syrup that we've been chugging. You simply have to try that one; it'll put fur on your sack without putting blisters on your knees!" Another slap to the shoulder.

"Later. I'll give it a go later. But for the time being, I have to repair to the tent, otherwise we might have to repair the tent." Quinn smirked at his own joke as he stumbled over a taut guy-rope, but he caught himself before he went down. And repair to the tent he did, collapsing heavily on his cot and covering his eyes with one of the feather pillows that the Church had provided. In no time, he had fallen into the deepest of slumbers. The insipid chorus of voices sus tained by the other revelers soon faded into the utter silence of dreams. Most of those dreams were silent…however, a few obligatory snippets were punctuated by Catherine Brinna's moans of pleasure as she lay beneath him, grunting her acceptance of what he was oh so willing to deliver.

♦♦♦

Catherine's warm lips were still brushing against his cheek when the sudden clamor of the gathering bell yanked Quinn out of his slumber. He pulled the pillow from across his eyes to discover that the tent was now filled with leaden shadows; it was almost dark outside. As he struggled to sit up on the edge of his cot, he surveyed the dim interior of the tent, fully expecting to see Bartlitt passed out on his own bunk. Such was not the case, for the man's shabby bags lay right where they had been tossed some hours ago. Quinn rose and stretched his cramping muscles before stepping out into the cool evening air, though it was not quite cool enough to warrant the thick shirt that he wore. Unfortunately, he had packed none that were any lighter.

Drops of sweat rolled down his ribs, which only added to the discomfort from his latest hangover, though it certainly wasn't his first. If Mason could race shirtless around the grounds all day, then Quinn figured that he could damn well unbutton his own shirt at least halfway down and let some of the cool meadow breeze sneak under the scratchy wool fabric. Now for the next order of business…he was off to the pavilion to fetch a tall goblet of cold water. His mouth was drier than a boll of cotton in a summer drought, and the stale taste of stout ale still lingered on his tongue like a coat of sticky lacquer. A sheen of sweat had developed on his forehead and was threatening to run down into his eyes. He raised his right wrist to wipe the droplets from his brow. Just then, a slender hand grabbed his arm just above the wrist, causing him to start and his heart to skip a beat or two.

"Where have you been, dear heart? I've been looking for you," Miriam inquired as she looped her willowy arm through his.

"Just taking a nap," he replied flatly. He feared that nausea might become an awkwardly incontestable issue if he chanced running his mouth any more. Already, he had an uncomfortable feeling in his chest that teased the back of his throat with the promise of spilled bile. Still, he forced himself to smile and march forth, his mother close by his side and clinging to his clammy arm.

"Do you feel okay, hon? You look a bit pale," she observed. Her tone was motherly enough, but a playful grin teased the corners of her mouth.

"Mmm fine," he muttered, fighting back the sudden urge to paint the tall grass with the stale remnants of all the ale he had ingested earlier that afternoon. All of a sudden, he found himself plagued with weak knees and a case of tunnel vision to boot.

"Good! Glad to hear it, dear heart. By the way, I had a chance to meet your new friend Bartlitt this afternoon. He's quite a character, I have to say. I just hope you don't pick up any of his bad habits, dear. He drinks a little too much for my liking. I know we're at Festival and all, but...why, it was only middle of the afternoon and the man already reeked of ale," she sang as she shifted the thick bundle she was carrying under her other arm. "I don't think he's the type to let his ale grow warm. Gosh, it smells bad enough when it's cold...just imagine how it must taste when it's warm!"

Quinn used his free hand to mop away the new flood of sweat that had broken out on his forehead. The two stepped over some of the taut tent ropes, and continued toward the gathering area in silence. At least Quinn walked in silence, for his throat could not handle two tasks at once.

"I tell you, he was seated clear across the table from me, and I could still smell the spirits boiling off of him like the waves of decay that surround a cow's carcass," she continued, apparently unwilling to let the matter drop just yet. Quinn chanced a quick look down and noted that Miriam was toting a folded blanket. He kept his head bowed as he focused on the grass at his feet. He didn't dare look into his mother's eyes at this point, because he knew exactly what he would find—he would see that *I know exactly what you have been doing* expression that she was so fond of using when he had done something to earn her disapproval. If she could smell the ale on Bartlitt from across the table, Quinn could only imagine how obvious his own stench must be at the moment, as they walked side by side and arm in arm.

"What's that for?" he mumbled nodding at the blanket, hoping to change the subject. The wave of nausea was subsiding, thankfully. But he was still craving a tall goblet of cool water...or two...or seven.

"Why, to sit on of course," she declared. "I don't plan on spending an hour in vespers with brown grass poking me in my rear end. You're welcome to share it with me, you know. That is, unless you and Bartlitt have some other pressing plans...?"

*She knows*, Quinn thought. *Of course she does. She can smell it on me.* "No, I think I will leave Mr. Bartlitt to his own designs for the rest of the evening, thank you." His answer was enough to appease Miriam, apparently, for she patted him lovingly on his arm and nudged his shoulder with her own. Sadly, the playful prod was nearly forceful enough to knock him through the wall of the tent that they were currently passing, but he managed to right himself and return to Miriam's side without losing face. Mother and son strolled on toward the field in front of the stage and found a suitable place on the thick grass to spread their blanket. Hoping to wash away at least part of the foul taste lingering on his tongue, Quinn excused himself and stepped over to the pavilion where he treated himself to several frosty mugs of cold water. Just for good measure, he dampened a napkin and dabbed his forehead with the cool cloth.

"Oh yeah," he whispered to himself as he felt the dark specter of discomfort retreating a few steps, "that's just what the healer ordered." He poured himself two goblets of cool water, one for each hand. When he returned to where Miriam was seated, he discovered that most of the other *Chosen* had already picked their places and were settling in for the service.

Of course, Quinn did not expect vespers to be led by the puffy little shirtlifter who had welcomed them earlier that afternoon. At that moment, the little toad of a priest was undoubtedly lying in a fluffy bed behind those majestic city walls. By now, he was loopy on opitol extract, his ankle was splinted, and his team of effeminate little supplicants were hovering around him like hummingbirds at a hollyhock blossom. Quinn imagined them zipping to and fro, fetching the winded and wounded charlatan goblet after goblet of rich red wine. They were likely hand feeding him from a platter of cheese cubes and peeled grapes, all the while dabbing his pink and puffy forehead with damp cloths to palliate at least a measure of his over-played discomfort.

Quinn chugged one goblet of the divinely cool water...then downed the other. Not even his bitch of a hangover could quell his cynicism. Its nauseating grip could not forestall his reflexive need to roll his eyes when he pictured the worthless, wheezing little cur lying back on his velvety cushions, feigning misery while he watched with lustful eyes his shirtless boy toys race around his quarters. Quinn pressed the cool pewter against his brow and shook his head in dread. The breathless bastard's substitute would likely be of similar build; he would likely possess even less charisma…as impossible as that seemed.

"Put fucking Ament behind the podium," Quinn murmured to himself as he threw back the last few drops of water in his second goblet. "Might as well. A droopy, taciturn dimwit could likely whip these sheep into a spiritual frenzy quicker than that wheezing pillow biter with limp wrists and weak ankles."

"What was that, hon?" Miriam asked in a reverent whisper as she leaned toward her son.

"Oh. Nothing. I was just admiring the sky."

♦♦♦

Soon after the wheezing priest's substitute finally arrived, Quinn realized how far off the mark he had been with his earlier assumption. A much taller, much more physically fit man mounted the steps and sprinted up them, taking two at a time. A cool breeze brushed across the clearing the very moment this new cleric turned to face those gathered before him…those nestled below him in the cropped brown grass. This one's head was covered with thick, dark hair sprinkled with specks of gray. His eyes were piercing…they were the eyes of a falcon, intelligent and alert…vigilant. The new priest's smile was warmer than a wool blanket, and it was far more genuine than that of the bloated little toad that had presided over the *Chosen's* gallingly pointless orientation.

"Good evening, my new friends! I am Father Eric. Welcome to Tarchannen Eid! Why don't we start by giving thanks to the gods for this opportunity to…"

The sojourners from the Five Cities, Quinn included, immediately fell under this new man's enticing spell. His voice was so strong and clear, like the chime of a heavy chapel bell cleaving through the still morning air. It stirred the night breeze and compelled their spirits Woven through his message was a gritty call to arms, but his musica voice remained every bit as soothing as the burble of a brook's clea water around a stubborn stone. This enigmatic man's words spewec forth from the womb of inspiration; none were punctuated with an

CHARLES R. WADE

trace of his colleague's annoying, asthmatic wheeze.

Without a doubt, this one was cut from a different fabric than the wounded toad, Father Sigmund, and so many of the other collared ones. Eric was in command of his elocution; he was in command of his audience. He was simply in command! And even through the jaded lens of Quinn's cynicism, he could find no real fault in this new man's eloquent address...he was able to ignore the white collar and tune out the context of the message. After doing so, he found himself thoroughly mesmerized by this new priest's charisma and by the way in which the words just seemed to spill forth from his soul.

It was all so natural. Nothing was forced; nothing sounded the least bit rehearsed. There were no melodramatic pauses in his seamless delivery, nor was there a single exaggerated gesticulation. His benevolent but unwavering gaze—his magnetism and his authoritative tone—offered more than sufficient punctuation to his words. Eric was a wordsmith; he was a man born to weave spells with speech.

Even though Quinn was far more inclined to listen to this new priest than to the other purveyors of the Way, he quickly recognized that Eric's message was—in essence—just a more poetic version of the one that Sigmund had delivered earlier this very morning back in Eldr-shok. Soon after he arrived at that realization, the wistful ghosts that so frequently chaperoned Quinn's thoughts began to beckon him, and his mind wasted no time drifting up and away from the gathering. It soared upward to float along the gentle currents that pushed the scattered collection of billowy clouds across the sky of late evening.

Father Eric's impressive magnetism notwithstanding, Quinn's distrust waxed as he stared up at the darkening skies. There were just too many inexplicable mysteries to consider. For one thing, he pondered the puzzle involving this anomalous weather. Eldr-shok—he was quite sure—still hosted a link or more of snow on its roofs and sidewalks. Its citizens were likely racing from one doorway to the next in order to elude the bite of bitter cold. Hopefully, his dear Catherine was at home in front of a warm fire and not tromping through the thick drifts. Eldr-shok was in the firm grip of Earlywinter, yet here, not four leagues to the west, he was comfortable wearing only his favorite wool shirt. Hel, he was still a tad too warm despite the early evening air.

*Could the temperate weather also be a product of Valenesti's un-*

*intentional conjuring?* Quinn asked himself silently. *Could his ancestor have possibly intended that the winds provide comfort for those who would one day inhabit this precious city that was to become his legacy?* As he brushed his bangs back from his face, his keen but curious eyes were drawn beyond the high stone walls to the gilded spires that rose toward the Haevens...golden blooms perched atop snow-white stems that remained stark against the deepening indigo of the evening sky. *Such beauty. Such flawlessness*, he thought to himself. *Surely, the hands of imbecilic humans had played no role in fashioning this template of unalloyed perfection. What prodigious magic had noble Valenesti unleashed that chaotic evening? What dark but marvelous well had he tapped into on that night of his death...that night of his rebirth? What arcane squall of devilment could have possibly carved and crafted these glorious structures from the desperate whims of a dying lunatic? Gods! What formidable forces must have been trapped within that mottled staff...forces pent up for decades as their varnished vessel lay on its cold altar beneath Hadig-vie. What powerful magic must have been involved that could coax Tarchannen Eid and its magnificent wooded moat from the barren Plains of Rayll...from cold earth and dormant sage grass!*

"Let's go get some supper, hon. What do you say?" Miriam suggested as she used her elbow to gently nudge her son out of his musings. Quinn flinched at her touch and felt a new wave of sweat breaking out on his brow. As he looked around, he found that the service had already drawn to a close, for the others were already gathering their blankets and milling about. Most were filing toward the buffet tables. Master Tabor and his mother followed suit, shaking several stray blades of grass from their blanket before folding it up and heading toward the pavilion. Cooks and caterers, all clad in white, busied themselves tending the long buffet tables. Zipping around like bees tending a hive, they smiled and nodded at all the comments and compliments offered by the twenty-four gracious guests of the Church.

Quinn discovered that he was beyond famished, despite the large meal he had consumed just a few hours ago when he shared a table with Bartlitt. And despite his recent plague of nausea. Once again he filed along with the others. Once again, he allowed the servers to pile mounds of steaming food on his pewter plate.

He ate more than his fill this night, though he did not venture anywhere near the ale table. Mother and son enjoyed a relaxing meal together as the cool but welcome breeze continued to drift through the festival grounds. Quinn stifled a belch and contemplated making a trip through the dessert line. No sooner had he rejected the notion than the captivating music began off to their left. The Church had commissioned a string quartet to provide dinner music for the gathered revelers, adding to the air of festivity beneath the pavilion on this first unseasonably warm, yet pleasantly cool, night at Tarchannen Eid.

Neither of them saw Bartlitt that evening. *Just as well*, Quinn thought. There would be plenty of time later to hang out with the enigmatic man from Eldr-burze. For now, he was perfectly satisfied to sit beneath the flickering stars with his mother and listen to the stirring compositions being played by the four performers…four performers who were clearly recipients of some special gift granted either by providence, or by a congress of all the nameless and faceless gods that Quinn had grown to deny.

Around mid of night, Quinn returned to his tent. He was bloated, but otherwise quite content, and more than just a little tired. The dull headache that had plagued him earlier had mercifully dissipated after he put some decent food in his belly and some fresh evening air in his lungs. He heard the grunting and snoring before he even pushed his tent flaps aside. Not overly surprised by the sight that greeted him, he found Bartlitt passed out on the far bunk, atop the covers.

The man from Eldr-burze had not even bothered to move his bulky luggage before falling unconscious across his cot. The rogue was snoring like a hibernating bear and he looked to be fully clothed, though it was hard to tell in these inky shadows. Releasing a resigned sigh, Quinn shrugged and walked over to pull a blanket over his drunken tentmate. It wouldn't kill him to do a good deed, after all. Quinn even went to the trouble of rolling Bartlitt off the bags; he set them down on the ground but none too carefully. He returned to his own cot and sat on its edge, readying to pull off his boots. When the snoring and grumbling fell quiet, Quinn said a silent prayer of thanks to whatever gods might still be willing to listen to the wishes of a devout cynic.

"So what do you think so far, my friend?" Bartlitt asked suddenly, breaking the silence and causing Quinn to jump in surprise.

"I think a lot of things...sir. I *thought* you were asleep. I *think* the Church puts on one Hel of a spread. And I *think* I'll leave the ale to those with more experience and fewer brains." One empty boot dropped to the tent's grassy floor.

"Watch your language now," Bartlitt chided, "we don't want your mother to think that I've been a bad influence on you, now do we?"

"I think it might be just a little too late for that at this point, actually," Quinn shot back as his other boot fell free. "She did mention that she already had the *honor* of meeting you. And she expressed her concern over our...association. I think she'll be keeping an eye on you—on the both of us—this week, actually."

Bartlitt only chuckled as he flipped onto his left side. "Well, let's hope that she doesn't watch me too closely. I've found that most of my endeavors only get more complicated when there are witnesses about. That's why I try not to leave many behind. Witnesses, that is."

"For some odd reason, I feel compelled to ask you to clarify that last statement," Quinn demanded, suddenly wondering if his own mother had just been threatened somehow.

"Oh, it's nothing lad. Will you relax? Damn, but you're a jumpy one! I just have a history of dragging folks into trouble when they know too much about my affairs. That's all that I meant."

"Somehow I don't doubt that one bit," Quinn whispered as he fell back on his cot. "You seem suddenly lucid for a man who was draped over his own luggage just a minute ago, I might add."

Bartlitt only chuckled in response as he turned up on his right side so that he was now facing away from Quinn. "Ah, yes. Let's just say that I recover quickly from whiskey, wounds, and...worse. Anyway, I suppose that it's only fair that she keep an eye on *me* for a change."

Quinn bristled. In the blink of a moment, he was propped up on his elbows and his eyes squinted in an effort to pick details out of the darkness. All he could make out was the silhouette of his tentmate lying atop his bunk.

"What the fuck are you talking about? You had better explain that last one, *friend*. You've been watching her since we arrived haven't you?"

No response.

"Haven't you?" Quinn repeated in a barely suppressed shout. Still, his last query elicited only another low chuckle from the othe side of the tent.

"Longer than that, lad," Bartlitt whispered at last, but he whispered those words into his pillow.

"What was that? I didn't hear you. Speak up!"

"Nothing, boy. I was just praying that you would stop asking questions so that I could get some sleep. That's all. I've had enough ale today to drop five sailors, so don't go expecting me to make a lot of sense in the moments right before I drop off. I don't mean you or your mother any harm. You have my word on that. Now, hush! Hush and go to sleep, will you?"

With the daystar now hours beyond the western horizon, the sky had assumed the dark shade of a widow's dress. The air had suddenly turned considerably cooler, and Quinn was anxious to make himself warm for the first time since the bell had awakened him from his afternoon nap. He crawled beneath the four thick blankets and nestled in. "Where were you tonight, anyway?" Quinn asked, though he was not at all sure that he wanted to hear the full story. His gut was full and just on the other side of the tent's canvas wall he could hear the evening breeze hissing through the knee-high sage blades. Sleep was beckoning him ever so insistently, and the prospect of conversation had rapidly lost all appeal. Even so, Quinn repeated his inquiry, this time in a barely audible whisper.

But thankfully, the only answer to his question was steady but subdued snoring.

♦♦♦

For Quinn, the next few days at Festival were spent much like that first afternoon—eating more than necessary, drinking more than he ever thought possible, napping whenever an opportunity presented itself, and attending the myriad services that the Church had scheduled for its guests. Those he attended just to appease Miriam. At no time did he attend one while sober, however; Quinn discovered early on that he resented the frivolous services far less after he had downed a few flagons of hop-laden brew.

Their hosts did arrange an abbreviated tour through the grand city one afternoon toward midweek, but Quinn and Bartlitt had started the day—yet again—with beer for breakfast. Quinn remembered very little of the tour through the maze of towers other than being jostled from side to side as the open coach rocked rhythmically along the cobblestones of the city's broad streets. He finally began to sober up, but not until after the *Chosen* had been led through the extensive library…their last destination before returning to the festival grounds.

That evening, just as they had the previous three evenings, Quinn and his tentmate took full advantage of the assortment of brews that their hosts had assembled for them. There were so many varieties, and each possessed its own distinctive flavor profile. Even the nomenclature was overwhelming: amber, pale, stout, hops, barley, malt…Quinn entertained no real desire to learn another language but, luckily, Bartlitt taught his younger charge everything he needed to know about beer in one succinct bit of advice.

"Don't waste your time with any beer you can't see through, lad. The heavier shit is for chewing, not for drinking. If you want to drink, draw yourself a mug of either amber or red. If you want to eat, go through the goddamned food line!"

It proved to be sound advice, Quinn discovered after sufficient experimentation. When it was time to drink, he knew which keg to run to. His favorite turned out to be a pale amber hauled in from the Smiling Corpse brewery in Eldr-ro. When it was time to eat, however, it didn't really matter which line he chose. Though he would not have thought it possible, the fare became even more flavorful and diverse than it had been that Sunaday afternoon when everyone first arrived. And it was always available to the *Chosen*, regardless of the hour.

One especially windy night, Quinn and Bartlitt, having recovered at least partially from a particularly zealous round of drinking, reported to the pavilion in what they judged to be the wee hours of morning. They found that they were welcomed by that same familiar buffet, beckoning them with every color found in nature and aromatic wisps of steam rising lazily from the contents of the deep metal pans. Much to their surprise, they found that a few of the others had chosen to share with them a late repast, though whether these individuals were early risers or tireless revelers, neither man could say; however, they both suspected the former. The two occupants of tent seven had discovered early on that the other participants were more than a little…hidebound.

Quinn had, as a matter of course, been introduced to all the *Chosen* from the other four cities during his stay; but he found that he had very little in common with any of them. None of the others showed any real interest in conversing on any subject that did not di rectly relate to the Church or its precious Way. He noticed very early in the week that the other *Chosen* were—according to his own admittedly cynical standards—largely incapable of original thought. Following every rhetorical question he asked, and in response to any simple observation he made, the other *Chosen* would reply by quoting straight from the Book of the Way or by offering some shallow platitude that might just as well have been written on one of the Church's weekly bulletins. Their stares were vacuous and blank; their exaggerated smiles were as permanent as any tattoo, and every bit as insincere as a promise from a drunken sailor. They were exaggerated to the point of being outright...spooky.

It seemed that the Church had picked the five most zealous individuals from each of the cities of Eldr. Except, of course, for himself and the ever-insolent Bartlitt. Tollis and Ament—Quinn's standoffish compatriots from Eldr-shok—perhaps didn't neatly fit the profile of zealot either, but those two cranks were in a category all their own, and essentially disappeared from sight for most of the week. Quinn caught a glimpse of them now and then at evening vespers, though they both appeared to be every bit as miserable as usual.

Occasionally he would spot Ament shuffling along a buffet table, but the gaunt man was rarely carrying more food than was necessary to just stain the center of his plate. Not surprisingly, Tollis made frequent trips to the drink tables, but he showed no interest whatsoever in the assortment of ales. The dour little man answered the beckons of the bourbons and stronger spirits. He would usually pour himself several rounds of amber liquor, balance them on a tray, and then the sour recluse would retreat to his tent, to the fields, or to gods knew where. Aside from those limited encounters, Quinn noted that the two freaks from Eldr-shok were conspicuously absent the rest of the time.

Quinn's cheeky tentmate was his soul's sole salvation during the sentence he found himself serving beneath the intimidating shadows of Tarchannen Eid. For better or worse, Quinn grew fonder of the inscrutable man from Eldr-burze with each passing day. He spent much of his leisure time sampling ale and listening to Bartlitt's rambling tirades about how the Church had, to say the least, been less than ruthful with its ardent followers. In cascades of bold words delivered in tones that were anything but restrained, the scarred brigand lectured Quinn on how the new Church was spearheaded by a cabal of corrupt priests who had secretly allied themselves with the very demons that the Way disparaged.

When their discussions eventually turned to lighter subjects, the enigmatic older man tutored his new charge in matters that were central to taking those vital and distinctive steps into manhood. Quinn's face burned and turned red as a spring rose whenever his new mentor shared with him some innovative and utterly delectable technique for pleasuring his dear Catherine upon his return to Eldr-shok, but that discomfiture quickly gave way to a fiery eagerness to test those techniques...in the field.

Only the gods knew how many times he had rehearsed different positions and tactics in his daydreams, and his imagination and instincts had provided a few templates that were tantalizing enough to stall his heartbeat. Quinn knew how to make the broad strokes, but broad strokes did not art make. Bartlitt taught his willing pupil how to employ nuance, shading, and feathering to create masterpieces from unsophisticated silhouettes...masterpieces that the girl of his dreams would absolutely treasure.

"Hel, lad," Bartlitt yelled one evening before taking a long swig of ale—thankfully, when he continued, he did so at a more discreet volume. "If it's true art you're lookin' to create, just have a go at this one," the rogue from Eldr-burze chuckled as he set his mug on the table. Then he used his tongue and two fingers to demonstrate on his imaginary lady-friend yet another technique. Just the visual prompted Quinn to polish off the rest of his own mug and hold the cool pewter against his forehead to steady his senses before he dared return to the kegs for a quick refill of Smiling Corpse. Perhaps if his liver was asked to work harder, his imagination could take a break. Such was his reasoning, at least.

"Now that...that'll be art that your girl will want to frame, hang on her wall, and then walk by and admire every day of her sweet life! Shit, you spring that one on her and she'll follow you around like a hungry pup. Believe me, her knees will stay so far apart, they'll wind up sending postcards to each other."

Quinn decided that he dearly needed another refill, especially when the toad-like little priest who had led their orientation Sunaday afternoon approached the adjacent table. Just as Quinn figured, the man's lower leg was now wrapped in a thick plaster cast and the rotund bastard relied on a pair of wooden crutches in order to get around. His pubescent assistant placed a tray of grub on the table and leapt behind the bench to help the pathetic priest get settled; then the acolyte retreated a few paces into the dimly-lit grass and stood by like a trained dog awaiting its master's next command.

The fat little vicar was seated uncomfortably close to the table that Quinn and Bartlitt shared. He would be able to easily overhear every word of every exchange unless Bartlitt decided to whisper, and Quinn wasn't sure that his new friend was even capable of doing so. No, the little toad-priest had taken a seat close enough to inadvertently qualify himself as another student of Bartlitt's University of Debauchery.

When Bartlitt paused to polish off his mug, the ensuing silence allowed Quinn to hear the priest wheezing and grunting as the fat man devoured one of the dozen or so pastries stacked on his plate. There was no meat; there were no vegetables...just fluffy donuts, rolls, and fruit tarts smothered in rich white icing. And they were being gobbled down by a man who already sounded like he was being smothered by a pillow, no less.

Damn all this...panting! Quinn found the unhealthy cacophony a bit much to contend with, especially when an empty mug sat before him, so he took advantage of the break in his class to rush over to the keg and fill himself two mugs. Two mugs sounded like a good idea. He might as well save himself an inevitable trip back, after all.

During Quinn's brief absence, his teacher had managed to recall yet another gift that lovely Catherine might appreciate...but only if it was adequately prefaced, executed properly and presented on just the right occasion. This demonstration, however, required a tongue and three fingers instead of just two. With half a cinnamon roll still hanging out of his mouth, the wheezing priest clumsily seized his crutches and signaled for his assistant to come and fetch the plate of sweets. He struggled to rise from his seat, and once he did he was huffing even more loudly from exertion. The wheezing gale ceased only once the offended cleric moved to the far corner of the pavilion, far and away from the two men who had been assigned tent seven.

"Boy, that'll make her toes curl and get her primed for the pearl!" Bartlitt hooted as he reached across the table to slap his younger companion on the shoulder. "You get my meaning, don't you, lad?"

Quinn, in fact, did not get the full meaning, but even so he felt like scalding water had just been poured on both of his cheeks. As intriguing as the visual might seem at present, this last particular little stunt that Bartlitt had described was one that Catherine's dear old dad certainly wouldn't approve of…wherever he was. Nor would the city constable, more than likely. *Aunt Turdnugget* would undoubtedly drop dead of a coronary if she walked into the room while that type of…*union*…was taking place. Catherine herself might even draw the line on that one. But if she did not—holy snakes and shadows!

In matters of more immediate import, Quinn…under Bartlitt's shrewd tutelage…learned how to more effectively pace his ale intake, allowing him to imbibe for longer periods of time without having to return to their tent for lengthy stints of recuperation.

"One goblet of water for every mug of ale, lad. Remember that rule and you'll never have to watch the sour contents of your stomach wick their way into the dust, and your head will never feel too big for your helmet the following day." Bartlitt repeated that point at least once an hour, but after much experimentation Quinn had to admit that the advice was quite sound. Cool, perfect water had indeed become his second best friend, buffering the less desirable effects of the potent ale and allowing him to pretty much match his friend, round for round.

That is until the fifth night of the festival, when Bartlitt quite impressively demonstrated what might well have been the limits of his drinking skills. On this particular night—Thursiday eve by Quinn's reckoning—he and Bartlitt stayed up even later than usual, sharing flagon upon flagon drawn from the kegs of the potent ale. Most of the other *Chosen* had repaired to their respective tents to rest up for the next day's excesses. Truth be told, Quinn was aching to follow their example, for the hour had grown late and the ale was at last beginning to take its toll. By now, Quinn had lost any and all desire to keep up with his buddy's insane pace, mainly because the old Bartlitt had taken his leave. The stern bird of prey had returned. The lad's friend had faded away at some point during the night, and a sulky stranger had crept in to take his place across the table…a stranger that was not only intense, but downright indignant.

# 5)

This fellow sitting across from Quinn was not the same Bartlitt that he had befriended that first breezy evening of Festival. In the matter of less than an hour, those once-friendly eyes had lost all vestiges of their characteristic, mischievous glimmer. Left in their stead were two bloodshot orbs. This new fellow's eyes reflected no hints of roguish humor whatsoever, only hollow bitterness blended into a potion already constituted from remorse and malice. Fathomless pools of cobalt surrounded by a tight network of red capillaries, those weary eyes betrayed a contradictory mix of cagy cunning and... wanton recklessness. Shielded by all the weaving shadows cast by the pavilion's oil lanterns, they were now every bit as grim as a November graveyard. Beads of sweat trickled down Quinn's chest, and he grew more sober the longer he sat staring into this familiar face that was no longer familiar.

The eyes had quite insidiously transformed into churning wells of woe, and now even Bartlitt's sly coyote grin was morphing into a malicious scowl that prompted Quinn to lean back and away from this foreigner's perverse mien. A storm was brewing in the man's soul, and it had undoubtedly been looming for some time. Its lightning was depicted by flashes of madness in those wide eyes and its volleys of thunder rolled forth in an unrepentant tirade directed at the denizens of Tarchannen Eid's higher temples.

Quinn wished that there was some way to cut his friend off and escort him back to the tent so that sleep could salve whatever weeping wounds Bartlitt sported but would not let scab over. However, he was now genuinely afraid of incurring his comrade's wrath. For the first time since the afternoon they met, he feared for his own safety, especially considering his tentmate's recent and eerily abrupt transition from amicable tutor to adversarial rebel. While Quinn sat across the table from his mentor in all things disobedient, the buzz generously furnished by the Smiling Corpse Brewery began to dissipate, and its wake birthed towering waves of drowsiness. Bartlitt continued to pour mug after mug of ale down his gullet, and the more he consumed the more boisterous his rant became. His hosts for the week were once again the targets of this tirade…the hosts who resided just behind the bleached stone walls of Tarchannen Eid.

"They'd sooner bed down with the demons that they profess to battle than give up a thimble full of the control they have attained in central Eldimorah by wainbrashing, I mean brainwashing all the… sheep? Isn't that what you called them once, son? Sheep, lambs, goats, pigs — it matters not, for they are all doomed to eventual slaughter, now aren't they?" he slurred as Quinn cast about uncomfortably to make sure no one else could overhear their conversation, for Bartlitt was taking less care than ever to suppress his invective.

"Interesting. You remember my referencing the Church's witless sheep, but you seem to have forgotten that I asked you to never refer to me as *son*," Quinn muttered. He didn't want to goad this capricious being who had suddenly assumed possession of his tentmate's body, but there were still a few points on which he simply refused to compromise.

"Ah, you're so right. My apologies," the man nodded before tossing back another gulp. For a splinter of a second, the old Bartlitt had returned, but the good-natured rascal was promptly ushered back to his cell by his sinister double. "Anyway, they stock a potent and insidious poison in their arsenal, and a measure of that venom has already been released. It spreads throughout all of Eldimorah with every passing week. It spreads all too quickly, Quinn. Just as every beat of a man's heart spreads the viper's venom to different parts of his body, every day that passes…every day that we prod into our past using the leverage of denial…helps push this Church's poison outward. Very soon, lad, it will fall to men like you and me to stop the spread of this sickness."

Bartlitt paused to take another swig, and he came near to choking as he tried to swallow while he shook his head in self-admonition over his blatant misstatement. "What am I saying? I'll be a naked pig if that day hasn't already arrived — already passed, in fact. We must be up for the task, you and I. And others of like mind. I have my own secrets to guard, as do you, lad." The man from Eldr-burze pointed back over his shoulder with one clumsy thumb, indicating the massive walls of Tarchannen Eid and the towers beyond. "You know o course that all of...this...was crafted by the conjuring of Morana Goll, by the staff that he himself designed. It was initially nothing more than a simple stick that he sanded and lacquered to a perfect sheen. Even then, though, it was really nothing more than a simple stick. But then...then he infused it with his own tortured visions of paradise. He chose to bathe it with his own black semen and varnish yet another of his creations with the liquid whims of Hel."

Quinn nodded and took a token sip from his flagon. The ale was flat and it had already begun to grow tepid. "I have...heard as much, yes." Despite his growing fatigue, he tensed and felt his heart rate speed up.

"Yes. Yes, of course you have," Bartlitt called out in condescending tones as he leaned back and away from the table; he smirked at Quinn like a drunken uncle who had just accused his favorite nephew of farting at the dinner table. "You know that much at the very least, and I suspect that you have already forgotten more regarding the birth of Tarchannen Eid than most others will ever know. You know that Morana Goll fashioned another artifact infused with its own unique... *essence*, shall we call it?"

Quinn gripped the edge of the table and his thigh muscles tensed. Given the amount of ale still clouding his reflexes, he very much doubted that he retained complete control of his legs' actions. Even so, he convinced himself that he was fully capable of bolting, should the situation demand it. Suspicion's sharp scythe had just cleaved neatly through the gauze of his alcoholic haze, severing the illusions of trust and friendship that he had allowed to cloud his judgment regarding this persuasive bastard from Eldr-shok's sister city. Quinn felt like a flinching rabbit who had just this moment sensed the invisible snare tightening around its leg. Before he knew it, his ass was off the bench and he was standing in a half crouch; he was ready to make a dash for it, though he had no idea where he might run. There were no more safe places, it seemed.

"Will you please sit down, dammit? This isn't a trap. Not a trap of my making, at least. Believe it or not—and like it or not—I am your ally in all that is to come. Traps abound, to be sure, and all of them were set by these collar-wielding shits." Bartlitt paused to take another drink from his mug, after which he stretched the muscles in his shoulders and took a deep breath. As he exhaled, he leaned forward and rested his elbows on the table. When he continued, his voice was lower; deliberate, and a good bit more calm. Quinn caught another comforting glimpse of the old Bartlitt struggling to shine through the viscous film glazing those blue but bloodshot eyes.

"I know that your father fell victim to one of those traps, Quinn. Roughly ten years past, was it not? A month or so before Yule?"

"How the shit did you know that?" Quinn demanded with a hiss as he now fought the urge to reach across the table and seize Bartlitt by the wrinkled lapels of his jacket, as unwise as that act would probably prove to be. Up to this point, Quinn had simply accepted his tentmate as a rare and welcome ally, one that shared a degree of his skepticism and more than a few of his own unpopular ideals where the Church was concerned. From day one, he had sensed that the inscrutable pilgrim from the northernmost city of Eldr was burdened by a surfeit of secrets, but Bartlitt had just disclosed that one of those secrets directly involved Tomas Tabor. Until tonight, the week at Tarchannen Eid had epitomized little more than an extended game... a game with very few constraints...one whose only instructions involved drinking, cracking crude jokes, and enduring Bartlitt's sporadic rants against the Church and its seamless assumption of power.

That innocent game had just ended, for now Bartlitt was in effect echoing the cryptic words of the old seer back in Eldr-shok. This brigand was corroborating the contents of the cherished letters that a dying Tomas Tabor left for his heir to study some ten years after they were penned by trembling hand and sealed with melted wax. Those letters were tucked into the pages of an exclusive account of Eldimorah's convoluted history, and the uncensored book had been locked shut and taped securely inside a nondescript cardboard box. Wrapped in a layer of sackcloth and adorned with a dusty green ribbon, it had then been tucked away in Miriam's kitchen cabinets where it lay protected only by the clever veil of anonymity.

"Ah, yes. Suffice it to say that knowing things like that happens to be one component of my...business," Bartlitt answered simply, but there were nuances of empathy and maybe even apology tucked within the tones of that slurred response...a response that was likely intended to sound reassuring.

"And just what does your business *happen* to be?" Quinn fired back in a low, suspicious hiss. He asked without even attempting to mask his innate sass.

"Helping people like your father, Quinn. Helping people like *you*, in fact!" Bartlitt smirked. He studied the younger man's face without so much as blinking, and Quinn began to feel less edgy even under his tentmate's dour scrutiny, in part because some tender trace of light woven through the older man's gaze assured him that they were still indeed allies. By his own estimation, Quinn had become fairly proficient at reading faces, and the face into which he now stared was certainly not the face of an enemy, nor the face of a traitor. Yes, it was undeniably marred with weariness as well as the weathered gray rings of old worries and grim burdens; the craggy cheeks were, without a doubt, scarred and eroded by the angry floods of lament. Still, there were no shadows of betrayal lingering there in those shallow defiles. Sorrow and fatigue, yes…but no betrayal. No treachery whatsoever.

"Well, I hate to point out the obvious," Quinn muttered, "but you didn't do a very good job of helping my father. You can't exactly use him as a reference, I guess you realize? Shit, you might want to consider going into another line of work. I've got it!" Quinn snapped his fingers and forced his face to sport a smile. "Maybe an ale taster for some brewery?" As soon as the words passed his lips, he regretted having said them. Damn this ale and the blatant honesty that it tended to unleash! So far, Bartlitt had done nothing to deserve such an acerbic slam. Quinn leaned forward and ran all ten of his fingers through his hair. "Bartlitt, I'm sorry. Truly. I…"

"No need to be, lad. He and I knew that the worms from the Church were going to come after the…*item* eventually, but we had no idea that they were going to act so quickly. Around that time, I was confronted with some pressing…family matters…and your dad insisted that I go tend to them. To be quite honest, I had a rotten feeling about leaving when I did, but…" Bartlitt let his sentence trail off, and Quinn thought for a moment that he was about to witness the first tear his tentmate had shed in some time. Bartlitt indeed appeared to be waging a minor war to maintain his composure, but maintain it he did. "As it turns out, I should have stayed. I should have stayed!" Bartlitt threw back the last of his ale and slammed the empty mug down angrily on the table. His face suddenly contorted into a resentful sneer. "That's likely the biggest understatement of the decade. Damn!"

"Wait just a fucking minute! Are you telling me that you…that you knew my father? You actually knew him?!" Quinn hissed. The

Smiling Corpse had finally allowed his mind to process what his ears had just heard.

"Are you dim? How can I say it more plainly? I knew him for years, lad. I knew him as well as any, save for you and your mother, I suppose."

"I want you to think very carefully before you answer my next question, *friend*." Quinn drained the piss-warm contents of his last mug and leaned forward until his nose was less than a link from Bartlitt's. All the lad's prior qualms had abated. "Are you sure that's the story you want to stick with? My mother acts like she has never met you in her life. Truth is, she doesn't even like you, and I'm not saying that just to sound like an asshole. If at any point I actually decide to sound like an asshole, you'll know it. Believe me, you'll know it. I've kept up with my practice—ask any who know me."

Bartlitt held up a finger to silently beg Quinn's pardon while he stepped over to the ale table to refill his mug once more. When he returned, he was actually carrying two mugs, one of which he pushed across the table to his irate tentmate. The rogue threw his leg over the back of his chair as though he was saddling up for a ride through the countryside. After he settled into his seat and sampled his own fresh mug, he looked Quinn in the eye and answered the boy's previous question. Sort of.

"Yes," Bartlitt stated simply. He hesitated for a second or two before nodding approval of his own reply. Then he released one of his trademark belches.

"Yes? Whose fucking question are you answering?" Quinn stopped shaking his head just long enough to reluctantly take a sip from the latest cup of his favorite poison. "Just how drunk—?"

"Yours. Your question. You asked me if that was the story I wanted to stick with. Your mother and I never met, Quinn...not once in all the years I knew Tomas. He and I met in secret whenever we had to discuss matters concerning his...special ancestry. Early on we realized that the less she knew about those matters, the safer she would be. The safer *you* would be. Tell me, Quinn," Bartlitt paused to down another swallow, "she doesn't know about the *item* yet, now does she? I'm willing to bet any trace of trust that you might still have in me that your father found some way to pass his shining silver legacy to you without your mother knowing anything about it. Am right, lad?" Bartlitt settled back in his chair with a sly but sad, cau tious but confident, smile pasted across his lined face. "Am I?"

Quinn's lips quivered for a moment while he tried to sort through all the conflicting emotions that were assailing him.

"Just how the fuck were you ever *Chosen*, anyway?" Quinn asked with a sigh as he took an extended sip from a fresh mug that he had not ordered and that he certainly did not need. The question had been rhetorical, but Bartlitt answered anyway.

"Bribery. Nothing any more complex than that, really. That's how I arranged for us to be assigned to the same tent as well," Bartlitt added with a humorless wink. "Don't be such a greenhorn teat-baby, Quinn. If enough coin crosses the right palm under the right circumstances…"

◆◆◆

"I think I need to find my cot before long, Bartlitt. Lest my knees fail me on the way. You and I, we have a lot to talk about in the morning. I just can't make sense of all this right now, as much as I wish I could. It's just too much to absorb when I'm this schmammered. I've got so many questions…and you owe me a shitload of answers, mister," Quinn slurred as he placed his palms on the table, readying himself to rise to two feet that seemed so damned far away from his brain. All of a sudden, Bartlitt's hand shot out and grasped the younger man's forearm just below his elbow.

"Remember the things that I have told you, son — Quinn. Remember them well, for you and I may not have a tomorrow. Not together, at least. Think not of me as some rambling drunk, though I admit that I may have presented myself as such at times. The Church is not an entity to be trusted. This much we both know, now don't we?" Bartlitt's voice suddenly fell to an urgent whisper and his eyes searched the shadows for other ears. It was the first time all week he had shown any real concern over the presence of eavesdroppers. "Invadrael and his disciples maintain no alignment with any deity. They are loyal only to their lust for immortality…death and deception bolster their waxing power. Invadrael plays a game of cosmic chess, and though his proficiencies are fueled and fired by madness and little else, they are still second to only a select few…a few who pace the realms that lie beyond Eldimorah's illusory borders. Believe me in this matter, Quinn: Invadrael is a serpent. He is a master of strategy, and he has a host of intricate plans already laid out…plans involving both of us, boy…dire plans. He utilizes the demons of ebon shadow to perform deeds that the Church cannot openly condone. Not yet, at least. Not yet, but soon enough. Yes, soon enough."

Quinn had no real desire to dispute his tentmate's words and no grounds for doing so. Then again, he had been offered no substantiation, no reason, to accept them as absolute truth. Suddenly, none of that mattered. Suddenly, the beams supporting the roof of the pavilion began to spin one way while the bench on which he sat spun in another. He urgently needed to get flat, and quick. Just to humor his inebriated pal, Quinn offered a polite smile and nodded his head, fighting nausea while feigning indulgence. This only seemed to fuel Bartlitt's fervor and amplify his agitation.

"Heed me, lad! Damn it, you must! My words may one day come back to haunt you. One day soon, I fear. My mother too was given a gray cloak when she came to Festival many years ago." For a fleeting moment, Quinn fought the temptation to ask his animated friend to elaborate, but the back of his throat was pitching battle against a rising tide of bile and hops. Regrettably, he was too drunk and tired to even listen to the full account, much less absorb any of its meaning—assuming there *was* a meaning to even absorb. He did, however, make a mental note to add it to all the other topics that he and Bartlitt absolutely must cover in the morning—over breakfast— before the insidious spell of Smiling Corpse had a proper chance to sedate him out of his gourd as it had done tonight, and thoroughly so.

"I will remember, I promise. I promise, Bartlitt," Quinn offered placatingly, "but I think we've enjoyed more than our share of ale for one evening. Let's go spend some time in sleep's shadows, my friend. What say you? There will always be a tomorrow. Don't you worry about *that* part." He stepped gracelessly over the bench and trusted his heavy feet to find their way safely back to tent seven. Despite his dearest drunken hopes, he didn't hear Bartlitt's chair scoot back and away from the table. The rogue was apparently intent on staying put for a while longer.

*Very well. Let the evening breeze usher him to bed, then. But damn him for waiting so late to bring all this shit up!* Quinn shouted in silence. For almost two weeks, he had been searching for answers and he had all but convinced himself that no soul survived who could provide any of them. There was always his friend Obadiah, but the parson had never shown up at Tarchannen Eid; he had not even come to the Sunaday service to offer his best wishes to his…family. Curiosity was killing Quinn, but so were his head and his mutinous equilibrium. He knew he had to hasten to his cot, despite the unexpected but intriguing turn that last conversation had taken.

Quinn simply could not wait for Bartlitt. He was already relying on simple motor memory just to keep himself from falling to his knees. The night was clear and cool, but he found himself marching through the cloying haze of bewilderment. Suffering from a numbing lack of anything resembling clarity, he ambled forward, sleepwalking like a doomed man being led to the gallows. At last, after struggling across a grassy field that insisted on shifting in a different direction each time he planted one of his booted feet, he arrived at his tent… at least he hoped it was his tent. When his stomach churned one last time, Quinn finally had to surrender to the nausea he had been battling since his last mug of Smiling Corpse. His hands and knees sank into the deep grass on the south side of tent seven, and he threw up until he swore that he could taste his boot socks. Once that foul mission had been accomplished, he pushed aside the flaps and collapsed onto his cot, boots and all. When his mattress stopped spinning like a dried autumn leaf caught in boiling rapids, he managed to reach down and remove his boots. In no time he was fast asleep. This night, his dreams had almost commenced without him.

◆◆◆

Bartlitt sat there shaking his head while he watched his young friend stumble away from their table. When he became convinced that he at last had the table to himself, he let the aggravating tear finally run down his cheek. He promptly wiped it away with his sleeve, but damn if another one did not follow…then another.

"Oh, Quinn," he whispered in a hoarse croak. "These bastards took my mother, too. They also sentenced my special angel to…execution. And the shit-stuffers alienated me from my daughters when they were just toddlers! I never even learned their fate."

With that last bitter thought bouncing around in his head, the rogue from Eldr-burze drained his last mug and stood. There were no more tears. When he left the table, he did not stagger or sway. He strode not toward tent number seven, but toward the eastern gate of Tarchannen Eid."

"I would wish you well, Quinn my friend, but it would be a wasted wish indeed," Bartlitt rumbled as he marched through the dry

sage. With a hand every bit as steady as a steeple on a summer afternoon, he donned his deep cowl. With a whisper of a wish, he blended
into the darkest of the night's shadows.

♦♦♦

Even the whippoorwills suspended their relentless calls as the
gathering bell pealed through the night air, waking the encamped
*Chosen*, one and all. Night's silence was shattered and the tides of
heartening dreams were quickly driven away as the echoes of the
great black bell rolled across the meadows just east of Tarchannen
Eid. Despite the pounding in his head, Quinn cast his blankets aside
and hopped to the grass, not from any sense of exuberance but out of
sheer reflex. Even before he came fully awake, those same reflexes
commanded him to squint just as he had done every other morning
of Festival.

Although tent seven was a still a pit of inky shadow, he raised
one hand to shade his eyes from the imagined rays of light that were
already burrowing through the canvas's coarse weave. Each bright
beam born of expectation was already eagerly competing for the
chance to burn his bloodshot eyes and dole out the first lashes of
providential punishment. It was a sentence he had served the last few
mornings when he was forced to face another bitch of a hangover...
Smiling Corpse's undisclosed aftermath, complete with a burlap
tongue and a head that felt like a log that had just been split with a
rusty maul.

But the arrival of the daystar was obviously hours away yet, and
a pall of darkness still enveloped the festival grounds. Quinn let loose
with an especially loud expletive when he stubbed his toes on the
metal leg of his cot, then he remembered that his mother's tent was
just a few paces away. At this point it simply did not matter, he decided quickly.

So he shouted another curse, for the piercing pain had not yet
begun to subside; if anything, it was escalating. Limping to favor his
wounded digits, he fumbled his way across the earthen floor of the
tent to Bartlitt's bedside, harboring the intention of waking his tentmate, though he imagined that the earsplitting bell had done a sufficient job.

"Bartlitt, get up! Something is amiss," Quinn hissed as he
reached out to shake his tentmate's shoulder. His trembling hand
however, found nothing but his friend's packed travel bags sitting

atop a cot still neatly made. His heart lurched and he began to wonder just what his comrade had managed to get himself into, especially this close to the end of the festivities. Suddenly, soft blue light filled the tent and he heard a familiar voice…familiar but quivering—partly due to the cold, but more so out of concern for her son.

"Quinn, thank the gods you are all right!" Miriam called from the front of the tent. She held aloft one of the blue lanterns that the Church had furnished each of its guests. "Where's your friend?" she asked, but Quinn noticed no hint of sarcasm in her voice tonight.

"I…I don't know. Honestly. I left him beneath the pavilion just a little while ago. What hour is it, anyway? Have you any idea?"

"I really can't say, though I would guess that it must be three hours or so past mid of night," she offered through chattering teeth. "We had better get to the gathering area. Maybe we can learn what the cause of all this disturbance is. You're going to need your jacket, by the way…your jacket at the very least."

Quinn grabbed his jacket as well as his top blanket, which he wrapped around Miriam's shivering shoulders. At that, mother and son left the tent and hurriedly made their way to the clearing on the south side of the pavilion. There, they found the other sleepy pilgrims gathered about the platform that supported the podium and the black bell. Most were wielding their blue lanterns and the eerie cerulean light revealed that everyone's breath was coming out in lazy white swirls.

All of them, Quinn noticed, had either blankets or travel cloaks wrapped tightly about their shoulders; there was a ruthless chill permeating the air tonight, the first hint of a frost that any of the *Chosen* had witnessed since their arrival at the first of the week. He buttoned his jacket and shoved his quivering hands into the cloak's deep pockets, but he continued to scan the crowd for any sign of Bartlitt.

The apostate from Eldr-burze was nowhere to be found. Quinn saw only the sheep of the Way standing in the grass this night. Sensing that something had gone dreadfully wrong, they huddled close. They shrugged and shivered as they gathered before the stage, waiting for their shepherd to appear…but there was still no sign of any of the priests.

Poor Mason was the sole occupant of the dais, but the uncharacteristic wrinkles etched across his face told Quinn that the unseasoned Festival host dearly wished to be anywhere except where he was presently posted. Mason clearly wanted to bolt, to retreat…to back out of his own skin had that feat been at all possible. Withering before the cold flames of this pale blue inferno, he was doing his best to shield himself by recoiling into the folds of his own heavy hooded jacket. To his credit, one fitful hand still grasped the rope and he continued to man the black bell. He rang it with all the fervor of an angler who had just felt a solid strike. He yanked the rope in rhythm with the night, but he largely ignored his guests' fretful inquiries. For the time being, Quinn and the others had little choice but to stand there and remain curious as to why they had been summoned at this ungodly hour, curious to discover why they were suddenly shivering with stinging cold.

They did not have to wait very long for their answer. No more than five minutes passed before a contingent from the Citadel—Father Eric and seven guards armed with long-swords and crossbows— rode through the eastern gate and thundered toward those gathered about the bell. No sooner had they reined in their mounts than Eric hopped down and strode toward a thoroughly shaken Mason, who had seen fit to abandon the bell and race down the steps to greet his superior with an erratic salute that was never returned. Though he stood no chance of overhearing the conversation from his present location, Quinn closely watched the interaction between vicar and aide.

At one point during the exchange, Eric tensed and his fingers balled into tight fists. Mason tensed as well. His eyes squinted and he winced as if he just knew he was about to be struck, but no blow was ultimately delivered.

The two men conferred privately for a minute or two longer before Eric climbed to the fifth step and turned to address those gathered before him. Most of the pilgrims noticed that the peaceful, warm expression that the priest had worn during vespers had been replaced with one of carefully restrained fury. Quinn chanced a brief glance at his mother, assessing her reaction to the man's perceptible change of demeanor. Miriam, after catching sight of Eric's face, pulled the blanket tightly about her shoulders and leaned even closer to her son, relying on his lean frame for support more than ever before.

Eric realized that he was doing a poor job of concealing his mounting annoyance. He wrestled with his will while he painted some semblance of a calming smile across his face. Despite the toxic flood of anxiety currently coursing through his veins, he nevertheless recognized how important it was to re-establish at least a fraction of the calming charisma he had wielded over these fools during Sunaday evening's vespers. Forcing his fingers as well as his anus to unclench, the tall priest bowed his head and took a deep, steadying breath before addressing the rattled and shivering *Chosen* gathered around him.

"My good people, we apologize for alarming you so, but we just wanted to make absolutely sure that all was well out here on the Festival grounds. I assure you that all is under control. All *is* well, but it seems that our sacred library was broken into a couple of hours ago. It was ransacked and defiled by at least one lowly vandal. We don't know as of yet whether the culprits have chosen to stay inside the city walls or if they will try to make good their escape tonight. His Eminence has ordered that we place guards around the Festival grounds…just as a precaution, I assure you. We don't think our cowardly vandals pose a threat to anyone, but just to be safe we would like you to stay in your tents until the gathering bell sounds again. It would help speed our investigation if you would cooperate in this manner. I assure you that the last day or so of Festival will proceed without the slightest hitch if you will permit us just this slight delay. Yes?" Eric asked with a wolfish smile. "Yes?"

The sheep were just about to murmur their collective assent when Mason interrupted them with his piercing, pubescent voice.

"I count twenty-four, sir!" Mason called from behind Eric. The younger man was standing on the seventh step and was anxiously flipping through the wrinkled pages of his roster, squinting to make out the names and identify the faces in the scant blue light.

At this, the older man's eyes shot wide. "One short!" he exclaimed to himself, and venom dripped from both syllables of that terse whisper. Quinn did not miss it. He *could* not miss it. Who the fuck could? The sound reminded him of sharp, bloodthirsty briers dragging across the legs of his thick canvas pants.

Eric then turned once more to the crowd. "Who is not present?! Did any of you leave a tentmate behind? Is anyone still…sleeping?" he asked as he scanned his small, stunned audience…his huddled, shivering herd. Everyone was shaking their heads to the negative. All except Quinn, who stood still as a tailor's dummy. He was frozen stiff; not so much from the evening chill but from a visceral fear that surpassed basic mechanical panic. He suddenly found that his throat was dry and, try as he might, he could not make himself swallow. Damn it all! Tonight of all nights, he had ignored Bartlitt's most frequently offered advice. He had gone to bed without downing any water, but he wasn't sure that it would have helped him in the least as he stood there like a scolded puppy, pinned to the spot by Eric's authoritative glower.

"The one named Bartlitt, sir," Mason called out after checking and double-checking his trusty but dog-eared list, "he is still unaccounted for. Mr. Bartlitt from Eldr-burze."

"Ah. And just who is he paired with? With whom does he share a tent?" Eric promptly barked, though his hawk's gaze never wandered from Quinn's wide eyes.

"Master Quinn Tabor of Eldr-shok," Mason answered in a raspy cough. By now, Quinn was wishing that the ground beneath his feet would just open up and swallow him like a chicken snake gulping down a defenseless hatchling.

"Ah. Master Tabor?" Father Eric called politely but urgently. The priest made a token sweep across the crowd of pilgrims with his cunning eyes, but they quickly settled back on Quinn, whose face was now pale and bathed in sweat despite the cold night air. *He knows!* Quinn tried to swallow, but he lacked the basic coordination to do so.

With little more than a single glance, Eric intimated that he knew every last one of Quinn's secrets. Even in this dim light, the youngest of this year's *Chosen* could clearly see that the right corner of the vicar's mouth twitched as his lips fought to restrain a cocky smirk. The bushy brow hovering above the man's right eye arched just far enough to allow the diffuse blue lantern light to lend verve to the fires of crimson malice that smoldered behind the priest's cobalt irises. Crimson rage barely hidden behind a veil of cobalt blue… crimson rage bared by a flood of azure lantern light.

Quinn finally managed to swallow, but he damn near choked in the process. Still, he stepped forward and called in an embarrassingly croaky voice, "Here, sir."

Eric pivoted so that his body as well as his head faced Quinn squarely. The priest offered his new adversary both the shallowest bow and the least sincere smile the younger man had ever witnessed. "Don't be afraid, lad," he offered softly, but his words sounded colder than January winds hissing through bare briers. "We just need to know if you can tell us where Mr. Bartlitt might be. I would imagine that he isn't still asleep in your tent. Am I correct in assuming that much? Hmmm?"

"No sir—yes sir—he apparently never made it to bed last... tonight. I went to awaken him when I heard the bell toll a bit ago, but he wasn't there. He wasn't in his cot, I mean."

"When did you see him last, lad? Anything you can tell us would be a great help," Eric continued as his fingers curled into fists, then extended, then curled into fists once more. His baritone voice, a voice that had been so soothing and enchanting just a few nights ago, had now taken on a cold and uncharacteristically eager tenor, and that transition prompted Quinn's defenses to engage.

His inner voice screamed at him to raise the drawbridge and lower the portcullis. It instructed him to take any necessary measures to protect his secrets...his treasures...his soul. He got the sudden but distinct impression that he should tell his inquisitor no more than was absolutely necessary.

"We shared a flagon, actually a few flagons, of ale earlier this evening under yon pavilion," Quinn nodded toward the large structure for emphasis. "Since he has more brews behind his belt...so to speak...he outpaced me, you might say. My head began to spin; I grew tired and returned to my cot. When last I saw Bar...Mr. Bartlitt, he was still sitting at the table, and he was nursing yet another round." Quinn swallowed again. Soon after, indiscretion straddled his tongue and gripped its wagging reins.

"He isn't in some kind of trouble, is he? I don't care what you think. I know him as well as any other gathered here. He is no thief... he is certainly no vandal!" Quinn blurted out, goaded by nothing but impulse. Had the daystar been slinking across its morning domain, all those gathered about would have seen a rich scarlet blush spread across features that appeared boyish regardless of the stubble that speckled them. Damn, he couldn't believe his own boldness...his own brazenness!

Neither, it seemed, could the charismatic priest. For the second time this early morning, Father Eric's eyes shot wide, either with frank surprise or rabid anger. In this shifting blue glow, Quinn could not readily tell which. Realizing perhaps that now was not the time to resort to blunt intimidation, the priest immediately recovered and again pasted a dissembling smile across his lips.

"Of course not, lad. Of course not. We merely want to make sure that your friend is...safe. Simply put, we are concerned that one of our *Chosen* is unaccounted for while at least one ne'r-do-well remains at large." Eric paused, running a hand through his thick salt-and-pepper hair in nervous irritation, a gesture that Quinn had not seen the priest perform during any of the evening vespers. "Master Quinn, would you have any objections to our having a...look-see at your tent? Maybe we can find a clue as to Mr. Bartlitt's whereabouts so that we can find him and...protect him. Above all, we want to make sure that no harm has befallen him, I assure you."

Quinn got the distinct impression that his intelligence had just been insulted. He doubted very seriously that protection was what the Church had in mind for his affable acquaintance from Eldr-burze. Father Eric's new condescending tone was seven steps beyond *galling*. Its musical lilt might have been effective had he been talking to a ten year old boy, but Quinn was twice that age. Still, he knew that he did not dare deny this simple request, no matter how it was phrased.

"No. I guess not," the younger man finally agreed. "I mean of course not, but the accommodations are not that grand. There isn't much to see, I assure you. A couple of cots and...that's about it." Then he remembered that he was basically leading Father Eric into the tiny tent that not only housed Bartlitt's bunk and bags, but the Blade of Morana Goll...as well as the old tome that could conceivably represent the downfall of the Way and the end of the Church's dominance across Eldimorah.

*Shit! Shit twice...once in my bed and once in my boot!*

"Excellent. Lead the way, lad, if you please," the priest whispered as he stepped toward Quinn and patted him on the shoulder twice. Twice was two times too many. Even through a thick shirt and an even thicker cloak, the vicar's touch burned like the coldest kiss of winter's ire.

Eric turned away just long enough to signal for two of his guards to dismount and follow him. With Miriam following close behind and still holding her blue lantern aloft, the four men stepped through the maze of tent ropes, with an increasingly nervous Quinn in the lead. A few curious members of the herd started to follow, but Mason intervened and—assuming more authority than he had probably been officially granted—abruptly waved them all back toward the clear ing.

Quinn threw back the front flaps of his tent and stood aside to let Eric enter first. He held his breath and willed himself not to even glance at his own bunk, for less than two links now separated the heels of Father Eric's black boots from the small duffel that contained the two items for which his associates had murdered at least one person—Tomas Tabor. "Which bunk is Mr. Bartlitt's, lad? I assume it is the one still made?" the priest inquired. His middle-aged face was a ghostly blue mask of determination in the glare of the lanterns' peculiar light.

Quinn nodded. Aside from that, he could do little more than point to Bartlitt's side of the tent with one trembling finger, because what he saw there left him utterly speechless…speechless with jubilation that he had to fight very hard to contain. His new friend and mentor's bunk was vacant, still. As a matter of fact, it was noticeably more unburdened than it had been just minutes earlier, following the ringing of the gathering bell. For there was not the first trace of Bartlitt's bags and belongings, just smooth blankets pulled taught and tucked in neatly at the corners.

♦♦♦

"Sir?" one of the soldiers standing just outside the tent asked.

"What is it?" Eric snapped without even trying to disguise his annoyance. Quinn noted that the disturbed priest was now gritting his teeth.

"Requesting permission to take two of my men and make a pass around the base of the city wall. If that bastard burglar has tried to make it to the forest, we can easily spot his trail in this tall grass, especially now that it's weighed down with dew…frost. And," the soldier added as he sent a venomous glance toward Quinn, "we might even happen upon our missing *guest* in the process." Just then, the centurion's left heel landed on a patch of frozen vomit. Armor clattered in the still night air as the fighter struggled to keep his balance.

"Very well," Eric agreed, ignoring the clamor. He laced his fingers through his bangs and pulled them down over his blue eyes. Quinn could tell that the vicar's level of frustration was escalating, and quickly. "Heed me, though. Whoever you happen to hunt down and apprehend, I want them brought back alive for questioning. Alive! Do I make myself clear, sergeant? If you bring me back a dead body, then I might see fit to bury your worthless carcass in the same unmarked grave. You and the library's thief can spoon like lovers for eternity while the worms have their way with the both of you."

"Are we clear on that point?" All displeasure was suddenly gone from Eric's voice. It had been replaced by the echoes of something eerily akin to apathy. His hawk's eyes were scrutinizing every detail of the tent's interior. Eric paid special attention to the bent and broken blades of sage. He knelt, caressing and palpating the grass as if it was the hair of his lover...a lover whom he suspected of infidelity. Meanwhile, Quinn was struggling to keep his own eyes focused on anything but the bags under his own cot.

"Of course, sir," the zealous soldier replied with a measure of disappointment as he signaled for his two escorts to follow him back to their mounts. Quinn could tell that the warrior was thoroughly saddened by the prospect of a hunt that held no promise of blood being spilled at its conclusion.

"Let's go find the sorry bastard!" the sergeant growled halfheartedly to his men just before they marched out of Quinn's earshot.

"I assume that those two bags are yours, Master Tabor. Am I correct?" Eric whispered the question and turned his head only partially toward Quinn as he continued to crawl through the grass. His right hand was pointing directly at the smaller of the two bags situated beneath the younger man's cot.

"Yes sir. Of course," Quinn answered in that same pathetic, hoarse croak.

"Ah," Eric nodded as he stood. "Of course they are. You seem to have taken great care to protect the smaller one. Did you not trust Mr. Bartlitt, then?"

"I brought a few coins with me, all that I own. I don't trust anyone with...everything."

"Excellent! Most excellent! I must remember that quote, Quinn. That kind of wisdom will carry you far." With that, the cleric ducked and exited the tent. Quinn stood rooted in place for just a moment. He turned to follow Eric and the others back to the pavilion only after he checked to make sure that he had not just shit his pants.

◆◆◆

After Father Eric posted guards around the perimeter of the festival grounds, he threw a boot in one stirrup, mounted up and raced back to disappear through the eastern gate of Valenesti's bane. Bathed in the shifting blue light from all the rattled revelers' lanterns, Maso stood at the base of the podium, struggling to keep a tall stack of folded blankets from falling to the side. The guests were instructed to file past and grab an extra layer or two of cover to see them through the uncharacteristically cool night. When the stack had disappeared, the *Chosen* were at last encouraged to return to their tents where most would spread those extra blankets across their bunks and go back to sleep, though the first dim hints of dawn's gray light could already be espied on the horizon to the east.

Quinn, however, was far too wired to even ponder the possibility of falling asleep again. He lay on his back and tried to divert his frenzied thoughts by staring at the shadows slowly shifting across the tent ceiling, but it was simply not meant to be. His mind absolutely refused to follow his will's bidding. It continued working feverishly to make sense out of all that had transpired in the last few hours. Deep down, he knew the truth of matters, or at least part of the truth. Enough of the truth.

All the conversations that had taken place between the two tent-mates over the last few days, and especially the discussion they had shared just a few short hours ago, had taught Quinn one thing. The *Chosen*...a few at least...were discernibly not awarded their title due to their perceived spiritual merit. They were not granted their new and glorious station because of the exceptional depth of their faith in the Way. As for the others, most were indeed just gullible sheep, random winners in the Church's equivalent of some ridiculous yearly lottery. Shortly after meeting his new pal on that first day, Quinn had just assumed that Bartlitt's presence at Festival was some kind of anomalous slip on the Church's part—precisely the same sort of oversight that explained his own presence here. No, the Church had not picked Bartlitt because of his devotion to the Way, that much quickly became obvious. The very idea now made Quinn chuckle, especially considering the depths of sacrilege that had been explored during some of those ensuing conversations.

Less than five hours ago, Bartlitt divulged that his status of *Chosen* had been purchased like a pair of new boots. Less than five hours ago, the dissenter from Eldr-burze offered cryptic hints of testimony that supported the incredible account of Tomas Tabor's untimely passing...an account first suggested by the frightening seer and an account confirmed by letters penned by his father's own unsteady hand. Sitting there on the edge of his cot, Quinn fully accepted as indisputable fact the notion that the Church of the Way was no longer merely an annoyance—it was now his most dire enemy.

This fucking church had murdered his father. Quinn had more than sufficient reason to seek revenge against these corrupt bastards that hid behind innocuous titles such as *priest, cardinal and...and father!* By killing Tomas Tabor, the Church had also cost Bartlitt a dear friend, if the rogue's intimations were to be believed. A transgression of that magnitude certainly would provide most men with enough impetus to exact some degree of retribution, but with Bartlitt, his raw contempt for the Way and its proselytes went much deeper than mere grief over a former drinking buddy. It reached much further back than just ten or twelve years and it reached much further down than the loss of a casual friend.

Quinn sensed as much during their late night binges, when his inebriated tentmate sprayed sacrilegious statements as if they were clumps of clabbered milk that he had accidentally ingested. Bartlitt hated the Church on a raw, visceral level. He had not been simply annoyed or inconvenienced by its teachings, and his suffering far surpassed grief and regret stemming from his failed mission to protect Tomas from these vipers. No, he was bitter. *Bitter.* That was Bartlitt in a nutshell...bitter and gritty. Yet, he had agreed to come to Festival. Hel, he had gone to extraordinary measures to get here if his own story could be believed. The rascal had even resorted to bribery of some Church official, and how dangerous an endeavor could that have proven to be. But why had he even taken that chance?

Quinn knew deep in his heart that his tentmate was undoubtedly responsible for the break-in at Tarchannen Eid's precious library, though what exactly the inscrutable man had been searching for, he had no way of guessing. In retrospect, at least one part of the puzzle was becoming clearer. Quinn nodded to himself as he recalled the odd look of concentration etched into his friend's face during the tour through the library and the museum a couple days ago. It was one of the few lucid memories that he retained from that afternoon's expedition to the world behind the high walls.

Though he was quite likely the most intelligent man Quinn had ever known, Bartlitt had never impressed his young tentmate as being a necessarily scholarly man. Thief, possibly. Conman, probably. But scholar, no. Thief! Quinn shot up once more to sit on the side of his squeaky cot. Bartlitt had used the tour as an opportunity to scout his target. He was memorizing the layout of the huge library so that he could navigate it in near darkness!

*But what in Hel was he looking for?* Quinn asked himself as he smacked his palm against his forehead a few times to jar his thoughts loose. Had Bartlitt just been looking for something that he could pawn for gold, then surely he could have found easier targets back in Eldr-burze. But breaking into the library at Tarchannen Eid…? Gods! That was not only incredibly ambitious, it was downright foolish. Confound it all, the pieces just wouldn't fall together.

♦♦♦

"Why is Father Eric mad tonight? You think he…you think he mad at…me?" Ament's underused voice became even more gravelly than usual as childlike tears began to course down his weathered cheeks. The tall man perching on the edge of his bunk leaned forward and bowed his head. Both of the *Chosen's* lanterns had been extinguished, so Tollis did not actually see his tentmate's tears, but he could hear them. He could hear them and the sniveling sonata was preventing him from falling into the bourbon-induced coma that he had endeavored so heartily to achieve.

"He isn't mad at you, you dolt. The mother and boy, though… that's another matter. Damn! I explained all that to you before, though I don't know why I even bothered. They are hiding something from him. They have been keeping it from him for some time and we… he…is rapidly running out of patience. Tonight's break-in did not improve his mood, as you could tell. Now go to bed and quit spouting snot like a two-year-old boy. Act your age!"

"But he looked at me like he wanted to hurt me…like he didn't even care if I got hurt. I want to stay his friend," Ament sobbed.

"He'd rather slit your throat than look at you, you miserable fool," Tollis muttered as he turned to face the wall of their tent.

"What you just say?" Ament shouted. "You say something!"

"I didn't say anything. Father Eric is still your friend. If you want to remain friends with him, then you need to crawl beneath your blankets and get quiet until the gathering bell chimes.

Tollis heard the springs of the other cot squeaking as the tall dullard reluctantly followed his instructions.

"Mister Tollis, are you Father Eric's friend, too? Can you ask him if I am still…?"

"Go to sleep!" Tollis barked. "Go to sleep, damn you." Just before the pudgy man drifted off, he muttered, "You have no need to worry. Father Eric still considers you one of his...own."

◆◆◆

Sighing heavily, Quinn slid his right hand beneath the feather pillow and his fingers became entwined in something unfamiliar. Withdrawing his hand, he pushed himself up on his right elbow and lifted the pillow with his free arm. There beneath his pillow lay a symbolic and final gift from the secretive Bartlitt: the brown leather tobac pouch with the odd insignia of a chalice burned into it. His fingers had run through the leather drawstring, probably just as his playful tentmate had intended.

Over the last several days, Quinn had seen the pouch dozens of times. Bartlitt packed a fresh pipe after every meal, and sometimes right before he went to bed. Quinn could not imagine why his friend would choose to part with the pouch. Here was yet another mystery to ponder. The man obviously returned to the tent to retrieve his belongings, and did so while the other pilgrims were shivering down by the gathering bell; but why did he find it necessary to leave such an odd gift beneath his younger tentmate's pillow? Was it a warning of some sort, or was Bartlitt merely letting Quinn know that he was one step ahead of those who would soon be hunting him? This last explanation seemed far more plausible, given the man's propensity for showmanship.

Quinn couldn't help but grin out of one side of his mouth as he considered the implications. *Shit. Good old Bartlitt. Always good for a laugh and a flashy presentation. Or a flashy exit in this case.* Still, many maddening questions remained unanswered. Quinn wished that one of his legs possessed two knees so that he could kick himself in the sack for leaving Bartlitt at the table last night. If he had known that it would be his last opportunity to have a meaningful conversation with the stranger from Eldr-burze who claimed to have known Tomas, Quinn would have stayed awake for the full story even had it required using two wooden spoons from the buffet to prop his eyelids open.

"Damn you, Bartlitt!" Quinn cursed his missing friend's choice of tactics. "Why weren't you a little more insistent that I stick around last night? And why in Sam's steaming shit did you wait until you last night among us to disclose your secrets to me? Why not the night before, or the night before that?" Canvas though they might hav been, Quinn felt the walls of the tent closing in around him. He couldn't wait to hear the din of the gathering bell. He was itching to venture out and see if he could learn more news.

"Hel, Mason. Ring it already, will you?" Quinn muttered as he rolled over onto his back and tossed the leather pouch toward the ceiling of the tent, catching it as it fell back toward his chest. None of the ground leaves fell out because the bag's mouth was pulled into a taut pucker and its drawstrings were tied into a tight knot. Though it was now all but empty, the worn leather had nevertheless been infused with that enticing cherry aroma. Chucking the bag into the air filled the tent once more with that smell that Quinn had come to so closely associate with his friend who was currently missing in action.

"Master Quinn?" the timid voice called from just outside the tent. Quinn quickly stashed the pouch back beneath the pillow before he answered.

"Yes? Who is it?" he called out, trying to sound unfazed.

"'Tis Mason, Master Quinn. Do you suppose I could I have a word with you? Please? Please," the aide repeated, and his normally mellow voice was now noticeably troubled and unsteady.

"Certainly," Quinn extended as he stepped to the front flaps of the tent and pushed them aside to admit the aide. When he did so, he caught a glimpse of the skies, specifically the gathering of gray clouds that were spilling out of the north. It looked as though a storm was threatening…one that would indeed be cold and wet. The visitors had enjoyed clear skies and such perfect weather all week long, but today the skies were ominous, the daystar's golden gleam obscured by masses of dark, roiling gray.

"Master Quinn, the gathering bell is due to ring shortly, but…" the young aide paused and bowed his head. His hands were wringing like two mating snakes, and his eyes squinted shut even though this early morning light was too meager to reveal anything but gross shapes and shadows. He was clearly on the verge of bitter tears.

"But what, Master Mason?" Quinn asked, his curiosity thoroughly piqued. In a flash, curiosity transformed to heart-stopping concern. "Is my mother all right? Damn it, answer me!"

"Yes, yes. I'm sorry! I should have made at least that much explicit to begin with. She's fine, of course. Still, I am afraid I do have some bad news, Master Quinn. It pertains to your friend, Mr. Bartlitt."

"First off, I don't think we have established that he was ever in fact my friend. *Acquaintance* is more liking to the truth, I would say," Quinn offered, trying his best to sound unaffected. Whatever puddle of shit Bartlitt had waded into, Quinn possessed no desire to paint himself as an accomplice.

"Even so, I am afraid we can no longer count him…among the living. Father Eric just sent word that Mr. Bartlitt has apparently fallen to his death."

The gods now gripped Quinn's chest in their pitiless iron grasp, and their fingers began to close into a collective fist. The firm hand of Haeven began to clench, crushing his ribs into sharp shards of glass that tore his soul apart. Like a fish floundering on a wooden dock, he fought to draw a breath, and his knees threatened to give way. He backed away until the cold cot frame banged against the backs of his legs. After his ass finished bouncing on the paltry mattress springs, he swirled his right hand in the air, mutely urging Mason to provide more details.

"Well, it seems as though Mr. Bartlitt was the one who broke into the library, though I still find it hard to believe myself. Anyhow, Father Eric says that he stole some documents and such that were especially…meaningful to the Church. Some of our guards chased him through the streets, and he did a grand job of eluding them for a while, but they finally cornered him at the west wall. He climbed atop the battlements and kept running, but in the darkness the hapless bastard took a misstep on some frosted stone and….plunged to his death." Mason paused again, lowering his head to study the grassy floor of the tent. Quinn could tell that the assistant was genuinely upset by the news that he had seen fit to deliver personally. "I'm truly sorry, Quinn. We've ne'r had such an incident at one of our Festivals. Why, I don't think we've even had so much as a pick-pocketing so long as I've been in the Church's service."

"Mason, you say that Eric—Father Eric—sent word to you? Just now? And you are sure that it was the west wall from which my tent mate plunged?"

"That's the truth of it, Quinn. The guard just arrived and told me the news. He told me also to go on and ring the gathering bell. He said to make the announcement to all of you, but I thought I might… I thought you should maybe know first out of everyone."

"I appreciate your thoughtfulness, Mason. I really do," Quin offered as he rose, shaking the young aide's hand with a warm and hearty clasp; something prompted him to clutch the aide's sweaty hand with both of his. He seriously doubted that Mason played any significant role in this mystery, which was growing more stymieing with each passing moment.

In this grand game that had just begun to unfold, Quinn acknowledged that he would likely be relegated to the role of unwitting pawn…at first. He was destined to spend more time in the dark than a creaky floor joist. Father Eric, on the other hand, knew more of the truth. Even if he had not written the script to this play, he had certainly been granted a chance to read and study it.

"You had better go ring the gathering bell. I'll bet some of the others are getting anxious for breakfast."

"I guess you're right. I had best get along," Mason sniffed as he turned to exit the tent.

When the flaps fell to, Quinn placed a hand over his mouth to conceal his grin from all the nonexistent witnesses. Hel, he was barely able to suppress a loud cheer. The Church had absolutely no idea where that rascal Bartlitt was! Eric and his allies had fabricated that whole story…the part about Bartlitt falling to his death, at any rate. They dared not admit that someone could so easily manage to penetrate Tarchannen Eid's famed defenses and live to brag about it.

Bartlitt had been here just an hour or so ago, Quinn reminded himself. The rogue recovered his possessions and hid the empty tobac pouch beneath Quinn's pillow. Neither would have been easy tasks for a dead man. Even assuming that he had fallen from the western wall and had somehow survived, he would have been hard pressed to limp his way to the opposite side of the city, all the way around to the eastern side where the festival grounds were situated. Certainly not in an hour or so—not unless he was on horseback, and he most certainly was not. Furthermore, Mason had mentioned that the man from Eldr-burze had taken a misstep on some frosted stone. Quinn was fairly sure that the frosty conditions had not developed until the Church realized that the integrity of its defenses had been compromised.

Quinn heard a few drops of rain pecking against the tent's canvas roof, so he pulled his rain jacket from his large bag and pulled it on over his heavy shirt.

"Bartlitt, you wily bastard," Quinn addressed his absent friend, but he took care to do so in a low whisper. "You finagled your way to Tarchannen Eid, broke into the library to steal whatever was so damned important to you; then you snuck out of the city, retrieved your belongings from this very tent, and now you're off to, well, Hel only knows where." No, Bartlitt was still at large, and he would stay that way as far as Quinn was concerned. He grabbed the leather pouch and stuffed it into his pants pocket. Just then, the gathering bell began to echo across the frosted meadows. Quinn stepped out of his tent to greet this grim new morning…one heralded by gray, heavy clouds pregnant with sleet and freezing rain.

♦♦♦

Quinn found Miriam wandering about the clearing beside the bell-stand and seized her gently by the arm. "Mom, have you had any sleep since this morning's… summoning?" he asked, his concern for her shown in his own reddened eyes. She looked tired beyond tired. The gray bags under her eyes affirmed that she hadn't slept a single wink, and it was apparent to him that this single sleepless night had essentially canceled out all the rest she had enjoyed throughout the four previous days.

"No, dear. I haven't been able to close my eyes. I'm worried that…" she shook her head and looked down at the tall grass that was whipping about in the strange new wind and slapping the thick pants now covering her legs.

"Worried that *what*, Mom?" Quinn asked, crossing his arms. "Spit it out." Somewhere during this short exchange, Quinn noticed that the roles usually played by his mother and himself had reversed, which wasn't as much of a relief as he would have imagined. She usually played the inquisitor, and it was usually he that sought to withhold any information that might either embarrass or implicate him.

"Oh, it's nothing, hon, it's just that…Quinn, you aren't involved in this mess in some way, are you? I mean, I know you have a good head on your shoulders and all, but you spent an awful lot of time with that vagabond, Bartlitt. He didn't tell you anything, or talk you into doing something, or…?" she paused, shrugging. She was either wringing her hands from anxiety or rubbing them together for warmth. Quinn could not tell for sure, but he suspected the former.

"Gods! Don't worry, Mom," Quinn comforted her, placing his arm about her thin shoulders, "I don't know what our mysterious My

Bartlitt was planning, or what has become of him, I assure you. Maybe we are about to hear some news." Quinn subtly nodded his approval of his own account. He knew that he couldn't very well lie to his mother, not without her sensing the mendacity, at least. But he hadn't said one thing just now that wasn't the absolute truth. He was as mystified by the man's actions and intentions as anyone else in this camp. As to Bartlitt's fate or his whereabouts, the only thing that Quinn could assert with some authority was that his tentmate was more than likely alive than dead at the moment. That bit of information, though, Quinn was determined to keep secret. At least for the time being.

Her eyes looked no less tired than they had a minute ago. Still, Miriam smiled and nodded. The nod was followed by a heartfelt sigh of relief. Some of the deeper wrinkles around her eyes relaxed, indicating to Quinn that she seemed content with his report. "Perhaps so, my dear. Perhaps so."

Mason finished ringing the bell and stepped back, allowing another of the Church's representatives to step forward. This man was shorter than Father Eric, but he was innately more intense and far more direct. He made no pretenses, did not smile, did not nod his acknowledgment to those gathered before him. He wore the uniform of a soldier—a white surcoat with a blue willow emblazoned on the chest. He pulled a folded piece of parchment from his chest pocket and began to read the post with a disturbing lack of either sincerity or sympathy.

"The Church of the Way regrets to announce that Mr. Bartlitt from Eldr-burze was killed while eluding soldiers of the Church earlier this morning." Miriam's fingernails dug into her son's arm as she reeled from the announcement. With virtually no emotion in his voice, the soldier continued with his statement. "I have no further information for you at this time, but rest assured that a full and proper investigation is underway. The last day of Festival will proceed as planned, and we expect no further interruptions. Please enjoy the rest of your stay as best you can." At that, the officer wadded up his note and tossed it carelessly onto the podium. He skidded down the steps and hurriedly climbed atop his steed. Before anyone could voice a single question, the mounted man was speeding through the brown grass, back toward Tarchannen Eid's eastern gate.

"Dead? *Dead?* What do you make of all this, dear?" Miriam

asked as the Festival guests began to mumble excitedly to each other. "I...I don't know what to even say."

"I am sure that I do not know," Quinn replied honestly, trying hard to sound dismayed at the Church's news that was not really news to him. It would have done no harm to tell Miriam about Mason's earlier visit to his tent, but that would just provide an opening for her to ask more questions, and his mind was already far too busy trying to make his own pieces of this puzzle fit and lock together.

"Do you want some breakfast, hon? It might help you feel better."

"No thanks, Mom. I'm not really hungry, if you know what I mean," Quinn lied. He was in fact starving, but he needed to maintain his ruse just a while longer if he was to avoid any further suspicion on her part. "I'll go and sit with you while you have something, though, if that would be okay with you?"

"Of course, that would be wonderful. We haven't had much time together this past week. Can you believe that we leave tomorrow evening?" Miriam put her best efforts behind a sincere smile as she nudged her son playfully in the ribs to draw at least part of his focus away from the untimely loss of his tentmate.

"It surely has flown by," Quinn conceded as he stared out and across the fields toward the shadows draped below the surrounding forest. A sudden, inexplicable shudder ran down his spine as he surveyed the margins of the dense green growth. He swallowed and used the sleeve of his coarse jacket to mop a new sheen of sweat from his forehead. Had something just shifted within those black shadows? Quinn rubbed his tired eyes, blinked a few times and stared at the location once more. There was another flash of dark brown and then... and then there was nothing. He convinced himself that it had only been a deer, but it certainly did not move like one. Though it did not move entirely like a man either.

"Why do you suppose they are having us wait until almost dark to start toward home? The trip through those woods was unsettling enough in the middle of the day, what with the narrow road and all. I'll bet the drivers would opt for another noon journey if they had their way."

"I cannot answer that, but that is the way it has always been, I'll warrant. We should be glad for another afternoon here in these beautiful plains," Miriam smiled as she grabbed a plate and stepped int the buffet line. In the distance, thunder rolled as yet another dark bank of clouds rushed toward the vale. Two members of the kitchen staff raced to the northern side of the pavilion and hurriedly hung heavy tarps from the rafters to block the winds and rain that were rapidly approaching from that direction.

Quinn wandered over to the table that he and Bartlitt had so frequently shared. His eyes remained locked on the greens and grays that marked the inner boundary of the forest that ringed the meadows of Tarchannen Eid. He could not force himself to fake any degree of enthusiasm for the festivities any longer. The whole ordeal regarding Bartlitt's ominous disclosures and his subsequent disappearance left Quinn suffering from an abiding sense of urgency and restlessness. His old nemeses, which he thought he'd managed to leave behind at least for a few days, had succeeded in making the trip with him after all. Perhaps they had slipped into the compartment of his bag containing the blade and the tome.

Quinn peered between the corner post and the tarp, which whipped in the wind. He peered once more toward the forest's edge. He already missed his friend. Drumming his fingers on the intimately familiar table top, he relived a few of the fond memories with which he had been blessed during those magical midnight hours as Smiling Corpse ale's incomparable effects enhanced his first true taste of comradeship.

"Ah, Bartlitt. My first drinking coach," Quinn whispered through a sad smile.

No longer able to fight the temptation, he lurked over to the ale table and downed a quick mug of his preferred brew, then returned to his table where he waited for Miriam. All of a sudden, he wanted nothing more than to get back to Eldr-shok and resume normal life. But he had almost two entire days to spend on the Festival grounds before he once again boarded the grand coach that would bear him back to his home...and to Catherine. Yes, he had some subjects to run past that one. One, in particular, involved a ring that would likely be tossed back in his face. Much like Bartlitt's cryptic warnings, that was another concern for another day...or night.

At present, he was faced with the challenge of killing time. Oh well, ale did a wonderful job of making time pass quickly, he had recently discovered. Perhaps his drinking partner had vanished, but the ale table certainly had not, and Quinn pledged to himself that he would have a few flagons in Bartlitt's memory just as soon as Miriam finished her breakfast and retreated to her tent.

♦♦♦

Later in the day, in order to alleviate some of the mounting tedium, he thought to take a short hike and explore some of the countryside surrounding the Citadel; but one of the stern guards stationed at the outskirts of the festival grounds scowled at him and motioned him back toward the tents with a cocked crossbow. Quinn locked stares with the skittish young guard. One brief glimpse into the soldier's soul told him that he had nothing to fear from this whelp. This excuse-for-a-centurion was merely a frightened, pimple-faced boy dressed in a soldier's garb and armed with a man's weapon.

Quinn threw up his hands and glared at the soldier, but his attention was once again drawn to the shadows at the edge of the forest, where more brown and black shapes darted in and out of the field. He could not tell much about the beasts from this distance, for they were still at least a half a league away, but he could now discern that they were not deer. They appeared to prowl about the deepening shadows on two legs. Still, they were hunched forward so that their long arms dragged through the knee-high grass.

"What are those beasts...the ones wandering in and out of the trees?" Quinn called out to the unfriendly guard who had been posted out here to suffer the steady cold drizzle. The only response he elicited with his query was a nervous swallow and another insistent gesture indicating that Quinn should return to the area around the pavilion.

"Well screw you, too!" Quinn shouted as he spun about to return to the pavilion. "I hope they rush you and have your bloody corpse for dinner. That seems to be their plan, if you ask me."

♦♦♦

Fuming, Quinn spun about and walked back toward the base of the wall. No guards had been posted who would prevent him from wandering southward for a ways, at least. His attention was drawn toward a monument of sorts constructed from brass and white marble. As he approached the structure, he first assumed that it was a tomb of some dignitary...or perhaps a crypt for his family. But when he saw the shaft of polished wood protruding from the ground just inside the alcove—when he read the inscription on the brass plaque mounted to the column flanking the man-made grotto—he realized that he was standing near the spot where Valenesti had driven the shattered Staff of Morana Goll into the ground on the night of Tarchannen Eid's birth.

Quinn fell to his knees before the metal gate that separated the lone surviving fragment of the fabled staff from the grimy hands of thieves, vandals, and other ne'er-do-wells. As he tuned out the hiss of the approaching storm's winds, Quinn swore that he could hear the echoes of his ancestor's strangled sobs from that fateful night. He stared through the gate for at least two minutes. He drank in the sight of the staff that had ultimately defined his family's cursed legacy.

When he could take no more, he pushed himself to his feet and spun about to head back toward the pavilion. Not six paces from the mouth of the shrine, he caught sight of a nondescript patch of ground on which no grass grew. Instinctively, he knew that this was the spot where Elise's tainted remains had at last decomposed and settled back into the earth for a second time. And nature had seen fit to curse the spot for the taint that it had chosen to absorb.

◆ ◆ ◆

It took only a mouse's moment of investigative work to discover that his mother had repaired to her tent for a nap on this blustery, misty afternoon, and he intended to take advantage of this opportunity to down a few more flagons of ale…a few flagons in quick succession, in fact. As he stomped through the wet, whipping grass, he began to plan his first legitimate solo drinking binge. He planned to toast his abbreviated but nostalgic brush with Bartlitt, his glorious future with Catherine… and his approaching exodus from this goatfucking place. He would toast all three, but in no specific order of importance.

◆ ◆ ◆

The untrained hands holding the crossbow began to quake, and they refused to submit to the will of their master. He swallowed hard and tried to marshal his mettle. Those cursed winds from the north drove even more stinging droplets of drizzle against his pocked cheeks. Perhaps it was only his imagination at work, but he swore that the damned winds picked up as soon as the brash young guest he had confronted turned about and disappeared from sight.

Grunts that were not quite growls drifted toward him from the east. The mute guard looked apprehensively back over his own shoulder to study the shapes that darted from the deep shadows of the forest and into the high grass marking the perimeter of the broad meadow. Once again, the soldier swallowed nervously; this time, he said a silent prayer of protection to his own gods. He could only hope that they were listening. One of the more massive creatures racing through the haze halted in mid-sprint and stared directly into the stunned man's eyes. Even from this distance, the boy could feel the hot malice boiling off the two orange pits that were the lower demon's angled eyes, though he couldn't actually see them all that clearly. The Church soldier knew that he had just been marked, and he weighed the consequences of leaving his post to return to the safety of the city walls. Perhaps no one would notice. But if they did, he would be promptly hanged for dereliction of duty.

The wind from the north picked up yet again, and an even heavier drizzle began to fall from the ashen skies, but the droplets that ran into the guard's eyes came from beneath his helmet, not from atop it. The private decided to stay until he was relieved by the next watch...and it could not arrive soon enough. Yes, he would carry out his duty, but he took several long strides toward the encampment and further away from the teeming shadows at the outer margin of the meadow. Here, he would await the end of his shift, but he continued to glance behind him every half minute or so, and the sweat on his forehead continued to spill down into his eyes despite the cool breeze that heralded this rare storm that tumbled southward, completely ignoring Lord Invadrael's wishes.

♦♦♦

Without that feisty Bartlitt present to help Quinn pass the time, he was increasingly prone to frequent fits of soul-numbing boredom. The more entertaining moments of Festival were clearly behind him, he quickly realized, and he was now more than a little anxious to return to Eldr-shok...to Catherine. He managed to pass the last day or so at Festival by napping, conversing periodically with Miriam and her new friend, Helen, and by frequently sneaking flagons of Smiling Corpse out into the restless air. There he would stand as still as a frosted gravestone and let the field's weeds angrily slap his pant legs as he downed that magical brew whose hoppy tang triggered so many painfully sweet memories.

The hours of his last day in the Festival grounds slithered by like a copperhead weaving through dried autumn leaves. Finally, just a the daystar ducked behind the crenellated battlements of Tarchannen Eid's grand walls, the black gathering bell chimed for the last time, and the twenty-four remaining *Chosen* strolled toward the assembly area. They were in no real hurry, for the posted schedule had already advised them that they were only going to receive a few instructions regarding their departure from the Citadel and their concurrent return to the Five Cities of Eldr. A jacketed Mason stood upon the stage and continued to enthusiastically pull the bell rope until the last of his group had stepped close enough to the rostrum to hear his directions. He had to wait for the bell's resonant peal to fade before he addressed his guests.

"Well, my friends, we've had quite a week now haven't we?" he asked with a broad smile, though it lost some of its light when his eyes met Quinn's. "Although the weather did not cooperate with us the entire time, we hope that you all had a wonderful experience. I know you hate to see your Festival end, but alas, the hour has arrived when you dear revelers need to return to your tents and pack your belongings for your trip home. But I assure you that warm welcomes await you." Again, he shot a nervous glance in Quinn's direction.

There were a few token groans of disappointment from the gathered crowd, but Quinn was not responsible for any of them.

"The carriages will be here very soon, and will line up just outside the gate behind me. So if you would all be so kind as to go fetch your belongings from your tents and hasten back here, we would thoroughly appreciate it. If you are swift enough, you should even have time for an ale or a cocktail from the pavilion before you climb aboard. Our drivers will help you load your luggage, then you may all settle in for your journey through the forest…your journey home! Oh, and we do ask that you don the travel robes that you all wore on your trip here to the Citadel."

Quinn ran back to the tent that he had, until two days ago, shared with Bartlitt. Mason had made mention of two topics that were very close to his heart today…ale and leaving. An ale or four just might be possible before Miriam returned to the pavilion, for it wouldn't take long at all to retrieve his belongings. His bags had been packed for hours. Ever since morning had broken, he had become increasingly eager…more eager by the minute, in fact…to return to Eldrhok and leave this peculiar place behind.

Not bothering to fold anything, Quinn had hastily crammed his things into his two bags long before Mason even suggested doing so. More obsessive now than ever regarding his special items, he felt the compulsion to check them one last time. A quick inspection quashed at least some of his anxiety. Both the book and the blade were just as he had left them. So strong was his paranoia at this point, he was relieved and even a little surprised to find them intact, though he had been gone less than an hour. He left them in the same zippered pocket of his smaller bag, but now they shared the pocket with Bartlitt's leather tobac pouch—Quinn's only tangible souvenir from this strange week—though the fond memories of his exhausting binges and extended discussions with Bartlitt would likely stay with him longer than the pouch ever would, he decided.

As he stepped out of his tent, he saw that the others had once again donned the flimsy, blue travel robes that the Church had furnished at the first of the week. He had apparently been daydreaming earlier instead of paying close attention to Mason's instructions.

"Damn it!" Quinn chided himself as he hurriedly ducked back into the tent, though he was actually more perturbed by the thought of wearing that flimsy garment again than he was by his tendency to tune out instructions. Perching on the edge of his cot, which he thought he had left behind for good, he removed his shirt but not his pants...not this time. A mere moment later, feeling more than a little naked in the light and utterly useless robe, he exited his tent a final time and headed for the pavilion. Perhaps he could salvage enough time to guzzle a couple of flagons before Miriam finished packing.

Just to the north, he could see the five coaches lined up in single file just outside the eastern gate, and four or five of the revelers already shuffled toward them, carrying their bags or dragging them unceremoniously up the dirt roadway.

"I suppose we are no longer considered *honored guests*," Quinn muttered to himself when he noted that the Church had made no provisions this time to have the bags carried for the convenience of the *Chosen*. The drivers did, however, politely take the baggage and place it on board the carriages. Like daubers laboring to repair their nest, a dozen or so kitchen personnel had already begun to dismantle the buffet trays and tables. Thankfully though, removing the keg was not presently among the workers' priorities. Quinn grabbed a mug and promptly filled it with cold Smiling Corpse. The foamy head spilled over the pewter rim and ran down over his knuckles, but the wasn't troublesome in the least. In fact, the sensation triggered a host of fond memories. In no time, he had drained the flagon and eagerly stooped down to draw a second.

Just as he topped it off, he chanced a glimpse back toward the tents. Miriam and the other three pilgrims from Eldr-shok were walking toward the wagons, but their trajectory was going to lead them right beneath the pavilion. The four were walking together, but it was a loose-knit group with Miriam and Helen in the lead. Tollis and Ament brought up the rear, but the two men who could not be more dissimilar stumbled along opposite sides of the worn path, dragging their heavy bags through the grass that had yet to be trampled.

"No real shock there," Quinn whispered to himself as he observed the two men creeping along without saying a word to anyone. He slipped smoothly around to the end of the ale table and ducked into the gray shadows cast by the massive barrels containing the magic elixir that had made yesterday and today tolerable. As his four travel companions exited the pavilion and continued toward the coaches, Quinn drained his mug and figured that he had time for a third if he really slugged it. He did so with no real challenge and slammed his empty mug onto the nearby table that he had shared with Bartlitt so many times.

"That one was for you, buddy," he stated, but his whispered toast was barely audible over the hungry hiss of the early evening breeze. The dessert table had already been dismantled, so covering his brew-laden breath with a few mint leaves was not going to be an option this time around. But...he felt no real urge to conceal anything anymore. That line of thinking prompted him to fill yet another mug and take it with him. Quinn shouldered his bags and took off through the tall grass, one hand patting the concealed Blade of Morana Goll. That fourth mug was quickly emptied and he did not hesitate to toss the pewter vessel out into the tall grass...after he gave it a quick kiss. If anyone witnessed him littering the precious field surrounding Tarchannen Eid, then screw them!

◆◆◆

He was the last to arrive at the convoy near the city gate, but by this point he truly didn't give a solitary damn. No one had boarded the coaches as of yet. Everyone was just loitering about, politely passing the time with small talk as the drivers tied down the bags with the long leather straps. As he observed the other *Chosen,* Quinn wondered again if he was the only one out of the whole blasted group to consider it the least bit strange that Miriam and four of the others had been given light gray robes.

"Malloway, you little faggot!" Quinn muttered to himself while he was still out of earshot of the others. "Spokesperson for the group," he chirped, mimicking Malloway's heavy lisp. "Horse and shit, both!" At no time during the entire festival had the five clad in gray been given any responsibilities or duties whatsoever, nor had they been recipients of any preferential treatment as far as Quinn knew. They had spent the week eating, sleeping, and shitting just like the other twenty pilgrims.

Putting that thought aside, he strode toward the coach where his mother, Helen, Tollis, and Ament were gathered. The driver who grabbed his bags was not the same one who had brought the group here earlier in the week. He was not the friendly fellow with the acne scars and the rumbling voice. No, this new gentleman was as nervous as a virgin cow cornered by a new bull. He was clearly in a hurry to be underway. He nodded and spoke to each citizen of Eldr-shok, but the greeting was far from congenial and no more authentic than a pledge of love from some seven-copper whore. With the last of the bags finally secure, the driver opened the coach door and held it so while his five passengers boarded in single file.

As Quinn had opted to bring up the rear, he was granted a chance to notice that the man's expression flattened slightly as he helped Miriam up the coach steps. The anxious man offered his arm and nodded to her but he made a special effort not to look her in the eye. However, the driver shot her son—the new *prince* of Eldr-shok—a withering glare. Even through his ale-numbed senses, a tingle of warning slithered up the back of Quinn's neck like a cold snake; it disappeared beneath his unruly hair and spread across his scalp.

Perhaps the driver's ireful glare meant nothing. Perhaps it meant more. Thanks to the time he had taken downing his four mugs of Smiling Corpse, Quinn had been the last of the five to arrive, and there was a chance that the stern driver was displeased with his tardiness. Or maybe the antsy coachman was a staunch abstainer who disapproved of the ale that he probably smelled on Quinn's breath. In either case, Quinn just could not convince himself to give a solitary shit.

"...and fuck you, too," Quinn dearly wanted to say out loud a he mounted the first brass step and met his new driver's hostile gaze. Those last precious rounds of Smiling Corpse had left him feeling rather brazen, but speaking his mind at this point would hurt Miriam more than anyone else, he knew. Still, he felt the need to dig just a little further under the disapproving driver's skin.

"Now you be sure and keep her between the trees, Jeeves. Don't you go trying to blaze any new trails back to Eldr-shok, ya hear? Stick to the main road, will you please?" Quinn taunted, barely loud enough for the driver to hear...but hear it he did. Just for the base pleasure of watching yet another vein emerge on the dour driver's forehead, he winked and slapped the man on his shoulder as if they were old war buddies—an inclination he'd apparently picked up from Bartlitt. The vein wasted no time appearing, and Quinn wasted even less time disappearing into the cabin of the massive coach to take his seat beside Miriam.

"What's that smile for, Quinn?" Miriam asked warily as her buzzed son took his place between his mother and Helen. "I'm almost afraid to ask, but what have you been up to, aside from raiding the ale table one final time?"

At this point, Quinn was not even aware that he was wearing a smile, but he certainly wasn't shocked by the revelation. Something that he wore was managing to keep him warm, and it certainly wasn't the thin robe.

"Nothing, Mother. I was just reminding our driver to be...careful. That's all."

"You might do well to heed your own advice before offering it to others," Miriam whispered as she tried in vain to fan his breath away from her nose. "I can see that even though your friend is absent, his influence is still very much present."

"He isn't as absent as you may think," Quinn mumbled to himself, but he made no effort to prevent his rascally smile from spreading even wider as he stared down at his own laced fingers.

♦♦♦

Only after the driver was satisfied that all the bags had been secured did he walk around his rig to check it for roadworthiness. He shook each of the four wheels and tested both iron axles with his booted foot. Then he strode around his anxious team to check tack and harness. He pulled and challenged each belt, following an order that was in no way random. It was more than a prudent inspection, it was a ritual that he had performed hundreds of times during his stint of service. Upon checking the left lead horse's bridle, he found one buckle that had not been tightened enough to suit him, and he resolved the matter with a quick tug. At that, he leapt up to his position on top of the carriage and snatched the long leather reins from their tether. After wrapping a thick scarf around his face to keep his skin from freezing during the trip, he pulled his hood forward and tied it tightly in place. Then the seasoned driver nodded curtly to the greenhorn that had been assigned to ride beside him and prayed that the boy was not the talkative type. He didn't want to become too familiar with someone that he was going to have to kill even before mid of night arrived.

♦ ♦ ♦

Even through the thick panes of the carriage windows, the passengers could hear the gathering bell pealing from the other side of the pavilion. The order for the five drivers to head for their respective destinations had just been given. Quinn peered out from behind the heavy velvet curtain, and his head banged against the rear pillar of the carriage as it lurched into motion. The caravan thundered out onto the plains, maintaining the simple single-file formation for half a league or more. Then, at a signal from the driver of the lead coach, the other four left the main road and headed across the unmarked grasslands. Two of the coaches, Quinn noted, veered to the left and took off to the north of the roadway, obviously heading back to Eldr-burze and Eldr-huit. The other two peeled off to the right of the main road and lit out after the retreating daystar. Though they stood no chance of catching the retreating winter sun, these two carriages would nevertheless take the southern routes through the forest to the grand cities of Eldr-tarn and Eldr-ro.

Craning and straining to glimpse the road in front of his own carriage, Quinn leaned across Miriam's lap and pressed his left cheek against the cool pane of the coach window. There, not a hundred rods away, he could see the line of mature oaks that had stood guard around Tarchannen Eid for some six generations...six generations of _his_ family. They appeared to be ancient, but Quinn reminded himself that those mystical trees were already mature when they were born neither seedlings nor saplings had they had never been. He continued staring out the window until the team thundered into the dense forest and then there was nothing but gloom and strobing shadows. Lettin the heavy drape fall back into place, Quinn leaned his head back and took a deep breath. Festival had finally drawn to an end, and the four mugs of Smiling Corpse had eased his nerves significantly, but he still suffered a mounting sense of unease regarding this evening's journey through Valenesti's forest He could not attribute it completely to all the unanswered questions surrounding Bartlitt's mysterious disappearance, or to the driver's curious behavior just minutes earlier when he had given Miriam a hand up the coach's three steps. No, this feeling of dread was more pressing...more visceral.

A few minutes later, he peered out from behind the curtain yet again in an attempt to check their progress, not that he would have recognized any of the landmarks that whizzed past in a blur of thrashing black shadows. In truth, he just needed something interesting to watch in order to keep his mind occupied...distracted. Tollis sat directly across from him, and the fat man's puckered face certainly was not the ticket.

Quinn let his mind have the reins as he watched the ballet of dim shadows cast by two bright lanterns that hung from shiny brass brackets on either side of the drivers' seat. A mirrored cone had been ingeniously attached to the rear of each mantle so that most of the light would be gathered and cast forward to better illumine the narrow road ahead. Two more lanterns were suspended from the rear of the wagon, and it was the light from these two swaying lamps that breathed ghostly life to the otherwise lifeless forest that sped by the broad window. All four lanterns swung wildly as the coach thundered along the tight forest road. Quinn could see the tips of bare branches whip past, less than an arm's length away from the side of the carriage. That none of the branches actually touched the polished coach walls was a testament either to the driver's skill or the team's honed instincts. Probably both, he finally decided.

*It shouldn't take long at this rate*, Quinn thought. He rolled his neck and allowed himself to settle into a state of guarded relief... guarded, but not complete. Even as he sunk back into his padded seat, he caught himself nervously fingering one of the buttons on his velvety seat cushion.

Shit, he could hardly wait to climb the stairs to their cramped little apartment and collapse onto his own bed. But first, he knew that he would have to build a roaring fire in the den stove. The place was probably freezing inside. Snow was probably still covering the sidewalks. Damn! He just wanted to crawl beneath his familiar covers; surely the gods couldn't deny him that simple wish. They could only delay it, damn them all. Although he had done little more than eat, drink, and sleep all week, he was still tired beyond tired. Miriam reached over and affectionately patted his left knee...two pats and a loving squeeze. He had apparently been forgiven for his earlier detour that carried him past the ale table. She knew him well enough to tell when he was feeling fidgety. She had seen it often enough during Church services, after all. And after all...he was her son.

Suddenly, all five passengers were rocked toward the front of the coach as it skidded to a rough and rapid halt. The *Chosen* could all hear dozens upon dozens of naked branches scraping and scratching along the varnished outer panels of their carriage.

"Well, I guess that's it; we're home now, yes? Excellent!" Mr. Tollis rasped as he set his drink on the side table with a trembling hand. The sound of ice cubes tinkling against glass dominated the cabin that had otherwise surrendered to silence. The toad licked some of the spilled liquor from his knuckles and then dabbed his nose with a lacy handkerchief. With a whistling wheeze, the rotund man leaned forward as if to retrieve his small bag of personals from beneath the bench he shared with the mute Ament. That solitary, simple gesture was so exaggerated and so energetic...so damned atypical. A seasoned stage actor might have employed such a flamboyant technique for the benefit of the patrons seated in the upper mezzanine of a much larger venue, but for an audience of four seated in the relatively tight confines of a carriage...?

Tollis was doing his best to come across as blithe. That, in and of itself, only served to hoist the red flags of alarm even higher. The pudgy little bastard's contrived *performance* was eerily out of character. His words spilled from the hemorrhaging womb of melodrama as if he was indeed some upstart actor auditioning for a coveted part in a play. He had been given one chance with one line, but he had over-rehearsed and had no hope of delivering it with even a hint of plausibility.

Quinn's eyes narrowed; his guard went up right away. He knew for a fact that there were no trees whatsoever in the courtyard behind the Church of Eldr-shok; he remembered only an open park paved with flagstones. He studied Tollis's bloated mug. He knew better than to search for answers in that wrinkled pink phizog. He was looking only for further confirmation that the taint of treachery was on the prowl tonight, hunting for unprepared victims.

In that single awkward moment, Tollis's face turned the color of a wilting rose petal as his eyes frantically scanned the faces of the three seated across from him. Sweat broke out on the fat bastard's forehead. Something was wrong. Quinn shuddered, and another tingle of warning raced up the back of his neck. The labored intonations in this pig's raspy voice so closely resembled the wheeze with which that useless little priest had addressed the *Chosen* on their first afternoon at Tarchannen Eid, the pathetically plump cocksucker who had lacked even the fundamental coordination required to descend a set of stairs without tearing the ligaments in his ankle.

The heavy coach shifted slightly as the driver hopped down from his perch. The round door opened without so much as a squeak of complaint from its brass hinges, and Quinn's earlier suspicions were confirmed. He could immediately tell that they had yet to make it back to the relative safety of Eldr-shok. A blast of bitterly cold wind rushed into the cabin through the oval portal, and through this egg-shaped aperture, Quinn saw a network of bare and swaying tree limbs faintly illuminated by the first of tonight's quarter moons and by the meager glow bleeding from the coach's four running lanterns.

The driver stepped hastily aside and rushed back into the blackness. Through his seat cushion, Quinn could feel the coach shift as the driver climbed back up to his station. Another man, tall and slender, now stood just outside the carriage door...his facial features remained hidden and his slim frame was silhouetted by the waltzing forest shadows. As he took a step forward and leaned into the compartment's sphere of light, at least two of the five passengers gasped in surprise.

"Father Eric!" Ament exclaimed like some lost child who had just picked his favorite uncle out of a crowd of strangers...some toddler running to the door on a winter evening to greet his daddy with a hug. There was more exhilaration, more unconditional devotion spun through those two words than Quinn had ever heard this depressed scarecrow of a man express. And that jubilant cry could not have been more discordant, especially when considering its source—the mouth of this sad and starving simpleton.

"My good people," the slender priest offered in greeting, "please do not be alarmed, for all is well, I assure you. Yes," the vicar repeated in a suppressed snicker, "all is certainly well, just as the god who rule our destiny promised."

Quinn immediately disbelieved every word uttered by this wily surrogate, the man who resembled in almost every way the charismatic Father Eric who had led all the evening vespers at Festival... in *almost* every way. But the swirling madness that resided behind this stranger's stare was not the least bit comforting. There was no peace to be found there—only chaos. Only the pounding storm without the calm. This new glare he sported was fevered and eerily reckless...a singular fire now burned behind those eyes, and its ferocious flames were threatening to melt the delicate chains of restraint.

The roar and crackle of those flames silently shouted *lunacy*. Even the more severe incarnation of Eric that had interrogated Quinn on the night of Bartlitt's disappearance had maintained a semblance of self-control, though that feat had unquestionably required considerable effort. That manifestation of Eric maintained a steady hand on the helm of his emotions, even when he could not completely control the circumstances unfolding around him. The Eric who had searched Quinn's tent that night had possessed cunning and keen intelligence. That night, a different kind of fire burned in those piercing eyes... eyes bathed in the lanterns' blue light. That fire was controlled and contained, even though it was fueled primarily by guile and displeasure.

"Yes, this is indeed a glorious night! Though it unfolds beneath the light of a waning moon, it is nevertheless spawned from the warm womb of divinity, do not doubt. Do not doubt it, my friends! Our gods occupy their gilded thrones in Haeven as they always have...as they always will. And tonight they have dispatched me to recruit one of their precious *Chosen* for a lifetime of service to the Church...a lifetime of service to the Way." Father Eric fought to keep his already manic smile from turning utterly wolfish as his gaze settled on Miriam.

The growing knot in Quinn's throat now threatened to block his breathing altogether. He had heard the rumors ever since he was a mere child, rumors of Festival attendees being recruited for a lifetime of *glorious* service to the Church. Their families back in the Five Cities enjoyed enhanced social status and the Church reportedly compensated those same families in other ways...primarily monetary— but those recruited ultimately never returned from Tarchannen Eid.

Quinn could suddenly hear his own heartbeat swishing in his

ears. It so closely resembled the rhythmic whisk of a straw broom on flagstone. The tempo only sped up as his mind raced like some rat scurrying to escape rising floodwaters. The travel robes! Their colors were more significant than he had ever imagined. However, at least four others had been aware of the distinction. Father Eric knew the meaning of the gray, obviously. Even as it plunged into confusion's spinning chasm, Quinn's spiraling mind flashed back to the driver's reluctance to look Miriam in the face when she boarded the coach not two hours past. And Bartlitt—he as much as warned Quinn that he and his mother were soon to be separated by the wicked designs of Eric and his brethren! And then, of course, there was the effeminate Malloway...

"No, you can't!" Quinn cried out, not giving a nugget of desiccated shit whether or not the Church's erratic vicar would be offended by the affront. "You can't take her. I won't allow it! I depend on her and she depends on me, damn it! I am all that she has...she is all that I have! I...love her..."

For a splinter of a second, Father Eric's enraptured face hardened, and the other passengers became suddenly convinced that the boy had bought himself a stern rebuke with his outburst. No one moved except for Mr. Tollis, who cautiously leaned forward to retrieve his drink. He polished it off quietly, except for the subdued chime of the melting ice cubes dinging against the side of the glass, for his hand was trembling more than ever. He and Helen exchanged uneasy glances.

Eric, meanwhile, was quivering with effort spent attempting to contain the churning wrath that he was so sorely tempted to unleash on his target, this defiant upstart who had yet to see his twentieth winter. The vicar's right hand twitched like a wounded dove flopping in the grass.

In the very next instant though, either the power of the priest's will or the whims of his nefarious gods intervened, for the flames of insane fury were suddenly extinguished, just as if some drowsy deity had pinched a flaming wick to snuff a candle...or extinguish a star. The Father Eric from vespers—the first priest other than Obadiah to ever make a positive impression on Quinn—returned. He reappeared emerging from the seas of swirling madness. He was suddenly standing there before the five from Eldr-shok with the evening wind's invisible fingers combing through his hair. Any remnants of tension were gently eclipsed by billowy clouds of calmness as Eric casually leaned forward and rested his palms on the sill of the coach's door.

"Of course you love her, Quinn. And she loves you. That abiding love is what makes her so special, not just to you but to her Church as well, don't you see? Quinn you are of age now, and you will want for nothing, I assure you. This is a great opportunity…a great honor for her. Of all the citizens in the Five Cities, only five are *Chosen* each year to serve their Church. And you can always visit. So be at peace, son." Thinking the matter closed, Father Eric turned back to Miriam.

"Miss Miriam, if you please," he summoned her, offering his hand. It was now as steady as a boulder shrugging off the savage surf. Everyone in the coach held their breath when Miriam wavered. She loved her Church, but now it was asking her to sacrifice the life she shared with her dearest. It was asking her to place upon the altar of sacrifice the next few precious years that she would otherwise spend alongside her beloved son…her son, the only gift that chance had allowed her to retain and the only love that had not been washed away by the tides of time. She hesitated for a moment longer. But after bathing in the swell of Eric's mesmerizing gaze for just a few seconds, she exhaled in a long and submissive sigh. Her chin fell, her shoulders rolled forward, and she became all but limp in Quinn's protective embrace. Her leg muscles tensed; Miriam moved to rise from her seat.

"No!" Quinn spat, his voice a harsh and hostile whisper. "And never call me *son*!"

"Quinn," Miriam choked, but her voice sounded so detached. It was not entirely her own. To Quinn, she sounded as though she was half asleep. Perhaps more than just half. "I have to go, hon. The Church wills it. I have been…*Chosen*."

"You have been *fooled*!" Quinn shot back angrily, but the anger was not directed at Miriam. Not intimidated in the least by this collared bastard crouching just outside the coach, Quinn stepped between his mother and the incensed vicar. Father Eric's expression had once again become a canvas for the darker shades of Hel and the hand hanging at his side twitched nervously, as if he was using the last remnants of his waning restraint to keep himself from drawing a blade and striking down this insubordinate and bothersome upstart. For several tense moments, no one in the coach spoke. The only noise came from the wind weaving among the bare branches that hovered over the roadway. No one moved. No one even dared to breathe. At long last, Miriam stood up behind Quinn and placed her hands gently on his strong shoulders...strong but trembling with rage and disbelief.

"It's going to be fine, hon," she whispered soothingly. "I'll write you, and I am sure that we can visit each other. Father Eric just promised as much. You heard him, didn't you? Yes?"

Quinn and the vicar still had their eyes locked. When Miriam mentioned the notion of visitation, some glimmer in the priest's scheming eyes told Quinn that he would never see his mother again...at least not on this plane. Miriam stepped between the two men but her intervention did little to de-escalate the standoff. She wrapped her slender arms around her son's neck and hugged him tightly. He felt a couple of her hot tears running down the collar of his shirt. Quinn did not want to back down from his stance, but he at last had to close his eyes against the flood of acidic rain spilling down his own cheeks.

"I love you, hon, and don't you worry. The Church will take good care of us both. If you need anything, just look up Obadiah. We'll always have him, now won't we? He is so special and he means so much to both of us, doesn't he?" It was not the voice of Miriam that now spoke, but the green rationalization of a twelve-year-old girl. The inflections...the lack of presence...made Quinn's mind reel and his stomach churn.

She reluctantly broke the embrace and looked deep into her son's red and watering eyes. "I'll be fine, hon. You will hear from me soon, I promise." A light kiss on his cheek would serve as her final goodbye. Without another word, Miriam turned and accepted Father Eric's outstretched hand. Gathering her gray robe like the lady she had always been, she stepped down out of the carriage and disappeared into the thirsty shadows. Father Eric turned back to the remaining four occupants of the coach. His eyes were now black pits that even the bright lights from the coach's lamps could not penetrate.

"Goodbyes are always difficult, are they not? It will be much easier if you do not watch her go," he said flatly. Quinn wasn't sure if the advice was intended for him specifically or for the group as a whole, for the priest's eyes were now hidden completely behind their shroud of unnatural shadow. "You will be underway shortly. Kee the curtains drawn for now and for the remainder of the trip. Do not worry about Lady Miriam. Her *Choosing* is cause for celebration, after all…not sorrow. No. No sorrow. Save your tears for those who have yet to accept the Way." Eric chuckled and bowed his head for a few seconds. Then all mirth disappeared and his black gaze settled on Quinn.

"Do not…do *not* look outside of the coach until you get back to Eldr-shok! Such is my wish. Such is the will of the Church, and to defy our will in this matter will be considered sacrilege and will be treated…most harshly. I know that I can count on your compliance, my dear friends. Good evening to you all, and may the gods bless." The door slammed shut and Quinn was left alone. There were three others with him but he was alone, nevertheless. More alone than ever before.

"Did you hear him, lad?" Mr. Tollis asked in a tone that could not have been any more dispassionate, and the liquor had once again begun to affect his speech. The bloated clown acted as though Quinn had no reason to be upset whatsoever. "*Lady* Miriam. That is her title now. I guess that would make you young *Lord* Quinn. Yes?" The irksome man chuckled awkwardly as he tried to mitigate some of the mordant emotion lingering in the compartment. Under other circumstances, Quinn would have found irony in that attempt because Tollis was typically the nexus of tension and not placation. The irony was lost on him tonight, though. Tonight he was focused on the pain elicited by his most recent wound, one that was not only fresh but profound—deeper than a winter freeze.

He disregarded the wheezing fool's drunken platitudes. He was not for hearing any of it. Before long, Tollis's prattling and Ament's sniveling were both drowned out by a buzzing that sounded like angry hornets patrolling the air around their pale gray nest. Something dark stirred in Quinn's chest and for a moment he imagined that he could feel a serpent crawling up his arm. His latent *gift* from the seer no longer lay dormant.

"Go fuck yourself, Tollis!" Quinn hissed as he returned to his seat and reached for the heavy drapes. He hoped to peer through them and catch at least one last glimpse of his mother being escorted away from him and the sweet life they shared. He held the obese little man's stare until Tollis raised the glass to his quivering lips. The little rodent of a man retreated into himself and turned his eyes, if not his full attention, to one of the chunks of ice floating in the tawny bourbon.

"Didn't you hear Father Eric, Quinn?" Helen placed her hand gently on his arm and patted it like she was trying to get a colicky baby to fall asleep. "We are not to look out the windows, lest we lose our standing with the Church. You don't want to chance being excommunicated, now do you? Of course you don't. Think of the price, Quinn. Miriam told me what a good boy you are. Though I tried, I could hardly get her to talk about anything else all week." She continued to squeeze his hand and pat his arm as though those simple gestures could miraculously set right all that had just gone wrong. As though a gushing wound could be sealed simply by a soft stroke and a kind word. Sweat rolled down his brow as he looked into this woman's face, but he saw only two vacuous eyes pasted above a smile that was painted and not carved. That painting still told a story, however...one that Quinn suddenly had no trouble reading.

Condescension. Subservience. Quinn had had enough of both! Casting this bitch's hand away as if it was a rose whose hidden thorns had just drawn blood, Quinn reached out and grabbed a handful of the velvety fabric that covered the window. His knuckles were white with determination, but not with restraint of any flavor.

"The *price*?! I paid the *price* the moment that door closed, you bitch. To Hel with your Church!" he hissed, eliciting even more looks of uncomfortable dismay from the other three in the coach...even Ament. Quite hastily, they all scooted across the sticky velour cushions, recoiling from him as if his words of blasphemous fire had just painted him as a target for the black lightning of the gods. "Come to think of it, Helen, why don't you go...pleasure yourself? Life is short, after all. Get comfort any way you can, woman. You can light a few candles and read all about the Way as you finger yourself right through Haeven's fabled gates. Use as many fingers as it takes to get the job done! Just try not to breathe any of the dust that comes flying off the rim of that sour pit that you've been protecting ever since daddy stole into your room in the middle of the night. How old were you then, Helen? Thirteen? Twelve? You've been carrying your scars ever since then. You've been hiding them for years, now haven't you...my *child*?"

Tears that might as well have been blood ran freely down the lady's cheeks and a kiss of repressed terror now stirred in her dir

eyes, which—until just a second ago—could just as well have belonged to some lifeless porcelain doll. Her lips quivered as bitter tears
disappeared into the narrow black gap between them. As the gusts
outside the coach began to wail, Helen began to sob in silence. She
seemed so tempted to join in their desperate song. In this moment,
she looked as if she was facing a band of muggers in one of the
shadow-cloaked alleyways in the southern sections of Eldr-shok. She
cringed. Her hands were shaking. She withdrew as though the young
man sitting beside her had somehow discovered and then divulged
her darkest secret—and he had. One that she had carried for near to
thirty years.

Quinn took guiltless pleasure in witnessing the visceral reaction
that his words had elicited. A dark well, a pit leading down to his
own inner Hel and one that he had kept concealed by sheer force of
will and resolve, had just opened up; and all of his suppressed anger
came gushing out through that jagged orifice. All of that imprudent
ire had but one goal: to scorch the skin and sear the soul of anyone
standing close enough to witness its fierce eruption. An image of the
old seer's cackling face was superimposed over all that his eyes now
beheld. The serpent's coils tightened, slowing his heart's beat to
match the rhythm of the wind. Sweet rage blinded him to every color
except for two. From the very moment the carriage door had
slammed to, he found that he could only see shades of red and black.
Red and black, the colors of blood and oblivion, respectively.

Helen was probably the first lady in many years that Miriam
would have dared to even claim as a friend. Aside from her hollow-
ness and her blind acceptance of Eric's stipulations, she had done
nothing to earn such a vitriolic attack. She had done nothing and said
very little to deserve the cruel words with which Quinn had just assailed her. But as of tonight, innocence was no longer a legitimate
defense. As of tonight, the voice of justice would be the ominous
song of shattered suppression.

A brutal beast named Cruelty had suddenly emerged and assumed the throne of Quinn's pathetic little inner kingdom...one
whose vague borders were penciled by the hand of old phobias and
inhibitions. But abdicating that throne and relinquishing all of its inherent accountability to Cruelty's significantly firmer influence was
cathartic. Hel, simple catharsis fit so neatly within the shade offered
by this new shelter of surrender. The sense of forfeit transcended the

deepest levels of liberation. This new freedom was rapturous. It surpassed orgasmic release. He felt like a ship's captain, giggling as he let go of the wheel just as the rocky shore hove into view. Cruelty chose all of Quinn's words for him now, and Cruelty directed all of his actions.

No, *deserve* was certainly no longer a consideration, for according to Cruelty's relaxed criteria, proximity was every bit as condemnatory as a trembling hand holding a blade coated in fresh blood. There were no innocents in this grim play that Cruelty choreographed. Cruelty phrased his spiteful attack on Helen, and the boy known as Quinn played no part in the venomous offensive aside from watching it from a distance. He served only as a conduit. He was an observer, and nothing more. He had been a spectator that leapt and cheered as King Cruelty crushed the opposition with some of the strongest weapons in his most impressive arsenal—humiliation, disrespect, exposure of forgotten scars...

Helen had been silenced, at least temporarily. And now it was time for Quinn to play spectator yet again. But this time, he himself would be the target of his new King's malice. This time, he would be the central character in a play directed by his heartless new King, the Lord of Suffering to which he had so recently capitulated. It was now Quinn's turn to spin into the vacuum of Cruelty's insatiable hunger.

As he pulled the heavy curtain aside, he could see Father Eric standing in a shallow clearing at the southern edge of the road. The priest's back was turned to the carriage and the folds of his long black robe were twisting in the agitated evening breeze. The vicar's left arm was holding a bright torch aloft, and by its orange light Quinn could see his mother kneeling just within the shadows of the dense trees. Her head was bowed and her shoulders were rolled forward. She looked as though she might fall face first into the leaves if a sufficient gust prodded her from behind.

Eric's right hand was tracing sigils in the cool night air, and the fingers were surrounded by a bright indigo halo whose light so closely resembled the color of the lanterns back at Festival.

Initially, Quinn could not hear very much through the thick pane of glass. He could only make out the mellow murmur of a voice that remained even and controlled. During vespers on that first night in Tarchannen Eid, Quinn discovered that Eric's voice projected, an effortlessly so. Like finely fletched arrows, its tones had a way of shearing through the threads of natural silence. And now, fed by mounting fervor, that same steady voice began to lift well above the new wind's incessant hiss. But he was not addressing Miriam; he was not speaking. He was chanting. The vicar was singing a verse from some song that was unnatural and revoltingly dissonant…one that made even the forest nervous. As Eric's discordant hymn continued to crescendo, Quinn could make out enough syllables to determine that the priest was repeating the same phrase over and again. At first, he thought it was just part of some absurd initiation ritual…another frivolous ceremony.

*Tarchannen Eid a Necros Homenel sus sacrificiun.* The last word hung in the air and resonated even through the carriage's substantial panes. Then its veiled implications suddenly registered in Quinn's reeling mind. Sacrificiun? *Sacrifice?* His twitching lips played with the foreign word as cold terror began to seize him and choke off his air. All at once, the front of the coach jerked to the side, and the four pilgrims inside could hear the six huge horses whinnying in terror. Tollis and the others sat stone still like the confused and worthless sheep they were. All their eyes and knuckles were white, but they still seemed more concerned by Quinn's defiance of Eric's direct orders than anything that might be happening outside.

Near to panic, Quinn squinted and cupped his hands about his eyes as he attempted to peer further out into the shadows. He could sense as much as see the forms cautiously stepping forth to stand just behind Miriam. Once again, the coach lunged forward as the team tried to bolt away from this new and unnatural threat. Father Eric discontinued his strange chant and held his right hand aloft, his forefinger pointing toward the restless sky.

A thin ring of blue flame sprang to life, encircling the spot where Miriam continued to kneel…her head remained bowed and her eyes were still closed. By the glow of that anomalous light, Quinn could clearly identify the true nature of the twisted forms standing so very close to his mother. They were of the same variety that had darted in and out of the forest during the last two days of festival. Blunt, black noses once again parsed the shifting air, but from this damnable new vantage point he could now discern that their coarse fur coat was in fact matted with feces and filth. In that single and most sour of moments, Quinn recalled the look of authentic fear on the young guard's face, the one who had driven him back toward the tents and the pavilion on that dismal, overcast morning when storms marched toward the untouchable city birthed by Valenesti's penitence. There were demons dwelling within the forests of Tarchannen Eid! Demons! And the pubescent guard had known it full well. So had the nervous coach driver, for that matter.

Eric's head tilted to the left as he gave a quiet command, and Miriam shrugged the robe off her shoulders so that her breasts and back were exposed. Rows of sharp, yellow teeth flashed in the torchlight as the six demons nodded and smiled wickedly at each other. They smiled their approval and then began to leer with undisguised lust at Miriam's pristine white back. Hungry, cruel eyes of depthless ebony then turned expectantly to Father Eric, who continued to stand there as still as a granite sculpture. Only the tail of his long cloak moved. It whipped about, propelled by the agitated breath of these winter winds.

Quinn's soul shuddered with the need to do something, but he found that he could not move a solitary muscle...Hel, he could barely blink. Alas, he had already been betrayed by his new master, Cruelty. His master turned a deaf ear to Quinn's impassioned pleas for the ability to break through the brittle glass windows and somehow... intervene. Cruelty decided instead to damn his newest servant to paralysis. Cruelty cradled this boy's head in its rigid arms and forced the lad to witness every second of the soul-scalding shock that was to come. Cruelty required him to sit on the velvety cushions and watch the horror unfold. When all was said and done, Cruelty was merely another primitive beast that had to feed in order to survive. This beast subsisted on the harvest of suffering, and as long as its voracious appetite was being sated, it showed no allegiance whatsoever.

Six pairs of stygian eyes began to glow an intense orange. Hunching forward, the demons tensed. They crouched lower to the ground and their coarse, greasy hackles shot skyward in malevolent anticipation as the priest's right hand slowly began to descend. When at last his arm hung limply at his side, the blue ring flared. Then it died. Quinn thought he heard a loud clap of thunder. The devils fell upon Miriam, rending her precious flesh with vicious strokes of their long nails and effortlessly snapping even her thick thigh bones in their vice-like jaws.

She had little opportunity and certainly no means to defend her self against her slavering Hel-spawned attackers. What disturbed Quinn the most, however, was that she made no move to resist the attack. She did not so much as flinch when the first dire wound—a vicious slash to the back of her neck—was delivered. Wearing only a blank stare and a cold painted frown, she just knelt there in the clearing until the jaws and claws of her slayers dragged her down into final darkness.

Shredded remnants of Miriam's gray travel cloak quickly turned black with spilt blood, then the frayed rags were ripped away altogether, leaving just a mound of twisted limbs and reddish pink organs that steamed in the cold night air. Some of the airborne droplets innocently caught by the stout winter wind's influence flew toward the coach and tainted the translucent windows with a fine pink mist.

Quinn's throat clamped shut. He was petrified with disbelief, too traumatized to move…too shocked to swallow. Some of the droplets converged and began to run down the windowpane in grim rivulets. They descended in a faltering march that eerily matched the broken pace of the tears rolling down his cheeks. He observed those pink streams meandering toward the window's slick sill; he followed them with his eyes. He watched them with the same degree of detachment with which he might have watched the spray of a heavy spring shower making its petty attempts to penetrate the panes of his bedroom window back in Eldr-shok. How many times had he watched the rain roll down his window while he listened to all those familiar, comforting sounds Miriam made as she busied herself in her cramped little kitchen? The rattle of pans being impatiently tossed onto the countertops…

Alas, those spring afternoons were now memories that could never again be duplicated. The daemons summoned from the depths of the forest surrounding Tarchannen Eid had closed that sweet chapter with gnashing fang and slashing nail. From Quinn's vantage point, it was clear that the beasts had instinctively done their best to do their worst. They had taken his world from him in the glimmer of a moment…in an orgy of shattered bone and ruined flesh.

But then the demons began to feast, and Quinn's attention was pulled past the gruesome glass and back to that scene of appalling carnage. The grimy beasts occasionally snapped at each other as if they were hungry dogs fighting over the meatiest morsels salvaged from their most recent kill. Soon, the matted tufts of hair on their pointed chins were painted red. Or maybe they were painted black. Blood and oblivion were distinguished from one another by a very narrow benchmark on this macabre, malevolent stage.

Quinn heard only sick silence. He was not the least bit aware of his own screams until Eric abruptly spun about on his heels. The vicar glared at the horrified and newly orphaned boy with eyes every bit as black and malicious as those of the foul demons that he had just summoned...beasts which he had just placated with torrents of Miriam's precious lifeblood. The drivers, whether following Eric's silent orders or acting to save their own skins, released the brakes and let the terrified team finally have the reins. As the carriage shot forward, a stunned Quinn held the vicar's piercing gaze until the grisly scene disappeared from sight, though it would never fade from memory.

Without a doubt, he had just been doomed to carry one grim image with him for the remainder of his days. Perhaps he could never purge his memory, but he could at the very least purge the contents of his squirming stomach. Stricken with grief and thoroughly devastated by the atrocity he had just witnessed, Quinn spun around and vomited in the floor of the carriage. He heaved until he could hear the fabric of his will being shredded by the strain of revulsion and mourning. The remnants of those few precious mugs of Smiling Corpse as well as tidbits from his last lunch from Festival spread out and across the coarse nap that carpeted the bottom of the coach.

His three useless companions made no immediate move to comfort him. The other *Chosen* merely lifted their feet and propped them on their stools so that the warm vomitus would not get on their sandals. The others from Eldr-shok, not having dared witness the grotesque sacrificial ceremony, could not even begin to empathize with Quinn, though they were slightly mystified and wholly disgusted by the defiant lad's sudden fit of nausea. They all assumed that it was of divine origin. It was likely a means of retribution for his stubborn unwillingness to accept the will of the Church—punishment for sedition.

At this point, Quinn could not speak, much less explain. Truth be told, he felt no need to even try and make them understand. He had no real desire to say anything to these blind sheep. He vomited, cried, and then vomited some more. Helen, following some inexplicable intuition that assured her that the earlier verbal attack levele against her was not phrased by the real Quinn, pulled a lacy white handkerchief from her handbag and handed it to him. She presented it with two fingers pinching its corner. He accepted it and dabbed the recently disgorged goo from his trembling chin. Between the lingering heaves, he managed to nod his acknowledgment of her kindness. Tollis was still thoroughly repulsed, and the balding bastard quickly moved his sandaled feet even further back until his toes rode the rear edge of the short footstool that had been provided for him. One hand cradled his glass, while the other was busy fanning the air near his face.

Ament quickly followed suit, but it seemed as though the thin man was just mimicking the actions of his chubby little counterpart. Streams of acrid puke snaked across the floor of the rocking coach, but Quinn simply did not care. He absently dabbed the corners of his mouth with the kerchief, but the tiny cloth was far too thin and satiny to handle its most recent assignment, and it was now soaked through. It was saturated. Quinn no longer used it to mop away the mess created by his retching. The dripping rag offered him comfort just because he now had something to squeeze.

Finally, he mustered the strength to push himself back onto the bench beside Helen. She reached out and started to pat his arm, but after recalling the outcome of her last attempt to comfort him, she withdrew her hands and placed them reverently in her lap. The coach continued to rock and bounce like a jagged stone rolling down a steep hillside. Quinn turned his head and spat on the curtain. He spat on it again. Finally, he tossed the useless kerchief aside and busied himself wiping his face clean with the sleeve of the Church's blue robe. The minutes dragged by, but none of the four passengers spoke…not at first.

"I think you worry far too much, Quinn," Helen offered finally, and he was appalled yet again by her insistence to use that guileless, patronizing tone with him. Especially after the savagery he had just witnessed being committed against his own mother.

"You don't see…you didn't see what just took place. He…they killed her! While I…we…sat in here like…"

"Killed her? Father Eric, you mean?!" Helen asked incredulously. "Oh, I don't think he would do something like that. Surely not! Why ever would he?" The lady had seen forty years or more come and go, yet this night she sounded like a six-year-old girl.

"Father Eric would kill nobody," Ament called out in a hoarse voice. "He kind to me and he talks to the gods!"

"They killed her, I tell you! If you pathetic cowards had even bothered to glance out the window, you would have seen them...tear her apart!" The youngest of the four remaining *Chosen* from Eldrshok swallowed hard and wiped sweat from his forehead as he battled yet another wave of nausea.

"Now Quinn, we have to trust Father Eric. Whatever he decided to do with Miriam, it was for the best. You know that by now, don't you? Of course you do," she answered her own question on his behalf, and she did so in that little girl's voice. "He is...who he is. He knows how she can best serve the Way, after all," Helen finished and nodded her satisfaction at her own conviction. Then she ever so casually looked down to pick at a bothersome cuticle.

"...for...the...best?" Quinn repeated the three words of Helen's response that disturbed him the most. "So, you don't doubt that she was actually killed? That possibility, that notion, doesn't bother you in the least?" The fire that already burned in his chest was stoked until it burned even higher. Cruelty was once again allowing Quinn to play the part of doom's cold harbinger.

"Actually, we figured that it might come to this, boy." It was now Tollis who spoke, but he was no longer slurring his speech, though he had dumped yet another glass of amber spirits down his gullet.

"We?" Quinn asked simply. Though shock and suspicion colored his careening thoughts, his voice somehow remained flat...cold. By now, it was hoarse from the harsh waves of acid and bile, but its inflections were still every bit as ambiguous as a raven's call. His muscles tensed, but he did not grant them permission to move...yet. However, he stayed every bit as ready to spring as a coiled and provoked cottonmouth. Ever since his violent bout of retching, his arms had remained crossed over his stomach to comfort the residual cramping.

His right hand was tucked beneath the flimsy Church robe and was resting on the pommel of his trusty old dagger. Prompted in part by Bartlitt's ominous warning, and in part by his desire not to freeze off certain dangling body parts, Quinn had decided to wear his thick pants on the return trip. Before exiting his tent that last time, he had cleverly rolled the hems of his britches up far enough so that the rob would conceal his ruse. His belt never left his pants and his sheath never left his belt.

"Yes, *we*," Tollis replied as he reached into the pocket of his robe. Quinn wrapped his fingers around the pommel of his dagger and prepared to leap across the cabin and strike first. However, the fat man drew no blade. Still, the item that Tollis *did* produce from his pocket elicited far more disbelief from Quinn than any steel weapon could possibly have. The pudgy little cur reverently laid the collar of a priest over his robed knee and patted it flat. He patted it as though it was a weak and frightened kitten.

"Interesting. And what about him?" Quinn asked in a low, menacing whisper as he nodded toward Ament, but his tempestuous eyes never left Tollis's.

"He's no priest, boy. Are you daft? He's merely…a prop. He's simple, if you haven't been able to tell already. His ship is afloat, but there is no one manning the wheelhouse. Oh, but he absolutely worships Father Eric; he'd do anything for that man. He'd keep any of Eric's secrets and carry them to what will undoubtedly be a discreet, unmarked grave. It was that blind devotion that made Ament perfect for this little…job."

"Job?" Quinn repeated while a disbelieving smirk played at the corner of his lips. Those chapped lips twitched and his head shook from side to side as he began to chuckle. "My mother was just shredded to pieces by the very demons from which your worthless cunt of a church swears to protect its *children*, and you dare describe your role in all this as a…a job?"

"You're a blasphemous little prick, boy," Tollis wheezed, and poured himself another drink. He took a long sip of his bourbon to steady his own rattled nerves. The fresh ice cubes again clinked against the glass, partly due to the rough ride, but mostly because his fat little hand was shaking with rage. Ever since the day he had taken his oath, the Church had been his sworn bride. Largely because no real woman would have him, the Church was the only wife he would ever know, and this orphaned piss-ant had just insulted her in the crassest fashion imaginable. Tollis's face rapidly turned red and twisted into a scowl; it now looked like some deformed beet. Quinn's last little remark had driven a spike clear through the priest's thick skin and his cloistered sensibilities. Cruelty came fully awake from its brief nap, drawn from its slumber by the familiar aroma of impending conflict...the distinctive scent of inevitable revenge...the scent of malevolence.

Though it seemed to have lifted at least temporarily while Quinn was vomiting and convulsing on the floor of the coach, the veil that filtered out every color except for crimson and black descended yet again, and this time its descent was even more swift. This time, its descent was accompanied by the lonely peal of a bell, an eerie knell that only Quinn could hear. There were no echoes. Its toll was so solitary...so fucking final. His blade was now halfway out of its worn sheath, but his nerves were astonishingly calm. He could feel the fire in his soul, yet there wasn't the first hint of a tremor in his hand; and his breathing was every bit as steady as the thundering gallop of the team that was towing the wain back to the western gate of Eldr-shok.

"Perhaps it's time you learned a lesson in respect for your superiors, boy," Tollis added with a demented grin and took another sip from his glass. "The last lesson apparently did not...take."

"Ah. And am I to assume that you will be the one to teach me that lesson personally, you fat little sack of cow shit? And did you imply that you considered yourself my *superior*?" Quinn cackled as he extended his leg to flick the cloth collar off of Tollis's knee. He knew that a priest's collar was never supposed to touch the floor, not even the floor of a coach. The fact that it happened to land in one of the puddles of Quinn's vomit added yet another poetic twist. "Why, you're just another worm...another maggot that crawled out of that reeking, diseased cunt that you call the Church of the Way!"

Tollis leaned forward, choking on his liquor. A mask of horror daubed with flecks of deepest anguish crossed the plump priest's face when he caught sight of his cherished collar wicking up ale...ale regurgitated from the mouth of an apostate no less. In a panic, Tollis hurriedly leaned down to retrieve his precious collar from the pool of filth, but Quinn's booted foot came up so forcefully it quite effectively crushed the cartilage in the deceitful priest's nose. Dropping his glass in the process, Tollis instantly brought both hands up to his ruined face and rocked back and forth in pain. He tried to cry out but he could not even draw a breath. Blood dripped from his chin and stained the front of his pale blue robe. Pain now demanded all his focus. His collar lay temporarily forgotten amid the stale discharge

◆◆◆

Cruelty was now nestled comfortably on its newest throne—it

favorite variety of throne, in fact—from which black, insistent will could so effortlessly assume sovereignty over the whims of some pathetic virgin soul. This sculpted stone seat may have well been pristine white at one time, but that detail mattered not a whit once the shadows of fate spilled down like ebony rain. The beast shuddered at first but soon settled in, drawing comfort from the hard, cold granite. It stretched its leathery wings wide while curved talons dripping with sizzling spittle drew lazy circles around this demon's gray, erect nipples. From the depths of its cavernous shroud, its dim void of a face launched choruses of laughter in disparate voices that, of course, only Quinn could hear.

That inharmonious laughter was prompted by nothing very complex…just simple, sick anticipation and imagined joy over the sheer capacity for chaos that this magical night possessed. Cruelty. Its efforts had so often been thwarted by pesky little factors like conscience and neuroticism, but this new boy was not limited by those silly constraints. Not anymore.

This one was so very much like his kinsman Valenesti in that respect. Cruelty remembered each of his favorite pets, and vividly so. Ah, dear old Valenesti, a deep well of violent potential that had come very close to falling stagnant. A deep well that roiled and erupted as soon as fate added a drop or two of mourning, its most bitter catalyst and certainly its most potent. Yes, Cruelty had waited decades for another such as Valenesti, but that exhausting wait was evidently and thankfully over. Cruelty had needs like any other…being. But those needs had not been met in some time. Cruelty had been deprived of any satisfactory outlet for its ire. It lacked a willing vessel, a suitable conduit for its insatiable bloodlust, but those needs were finally going to be met by this boy…this lad beset by a perfect storm of sudden bereavement, deferred hostility, and the blind lust for vengeance.

♦♦♦

"Now Quinn Tabor, just hush. You settle down right this minute!" Helen demanded, trying her best to sound authoritative, but her denigrating tone could not have intimidated even the shyest toddler in town. "You know that your mother certainly would not approve of—"

"Shut your cock-warming mouth, you annoying bitch!" Quinn growled, though he never took his eyes off of Tollis. "I know the Church doesn't grant priesthood to women so what's your story, slut?

Are you one of Eric's concubines, perhaps? Maybe there aren't as many cobwebs on that crotch of yours as I had first thought."

"Of course not! Don't be ridiculous, Quinn. Eric simply asked me on behalf of our Church to befriend Miriam. Your mother..." Helen looked at her lap and shook her head like she was about to reprimand a neighbor's child for breaking her favorite vase. "Your mother was apparently naughty enough to try and hide a secret or two from our dear Church. Eric and the other priests are looking for some item that is most holy, and she had the audacity to hide it from them. I tried my very best, Quinn. I really did. Don't you dare fault *me*! Though I employed every tactic I knew to try, I wasn't able to get anything out of her the entire week."

Quinn was being pulled beneath the churning waters of reason by the undertow of words that he was struggling to process, and those words were phrased in sickeningly childlike tones that left him unsure whether the person sitting beside him was four years old or... forty. But ultimately, that distinction mattered not. Guilt was guilt, no matter the age of the transgressor. His fingers tightened around the hilt of his dagger.

"I reported as much to Eric just before we left earlier this evening, and he was not the least bit happy, let me tell you. No. No he most certainly was not." Helen giggled for only a second, then she fell silent and pursed her lips into an inane pout. The carriage hit a deep rut and all four of its occupants were nearly thrown from their seats. As soon as Helen recovered from the jolt and righted herself, she laced her fingers and surrendered her visage to a mask of feigned sorrow and hollow regret. "Oh Quinn, Miriam was so nice...so very nice. She was such a good friend to me. I do wish that Eric hadn't seen fit to send her off to Haeven so quickly...but she defied him. She defied him!" Helen sniffed back an imaginary tear and began to wag her finger at Quinn as if she was trying to drive home some moral lesson. "She misbehaved, young man. She misbehaved and left him little choice—"

Helen never got to finish her sentence, for Quinn's right arm swung outward in a wide sweeping arc and drove his worn dagger completely through her throat and neck. The blade's progress didn't halt until its spear-point tip was buried deep below the varnished surface of the rich cherry paneling. Helen's stunned eyes shot wide and rolled toward the Haevens that Quinn somehow knew she woul never be granted the chance to otherwise see. She convulsed a time or two as her head lolled to the side. Crimson gushed from the deadly wound in waves that grew less forceful with every pulse of her dying heart, and Quinn discovered his own Haeven in that torrent of warm, slick blood cascading down the dagger's hilt and over his white knuckles. All the while, he held Tollis's gaze. At first, the younger man's eyes were flat and wholly unreadable, but they quickly narrowed into slits through which the ravenous fires of Hel bled.

That tense silence persisted as the coach careened around the bends of the rutted forest road. The three remaining passengers braced themselves against the turbulence while their vehicle swayed, swerved and bounced like a scrap of litter being ushered down some alleyway, tossed about by a stout autumn breeze. The hush dragged on until Ament the Simple started bawling and, like the terrified child that he essentially was, pulled his legs up until both bony knees rested against his chest. With twin streams of watery snot running from his nostrils, the dim man curled up and huddled against the glossy sidewall of the carriage.

This lanky wreck was well beyond the point of being merely confused. He was terrified by the brutality he had just witnessed, and his only means of coping with this maelstrom of mayhem consisted of crying and shielding his eyes from further acts of mercilessness with his quaking left hand. His right hand, meanwhile, was balled into a partial fist, its thumb extended and Ament's chapped lips working it like a litter's runt sucking its mother's dry teat.

"Seems you were wrong about him," Quinn addressed Tollis, and nodded toward the gangly dullard who was cowering in the corner. He chose not to elaborate for a moment or two, for he was busy cranking his stuck dagger back and forth in an attempt to dislodge its wedged tip from the dense paneling's solid, stubborn grip. "You were *partially* wrong, at least. There seems to be someone in the wheelhouse after all...a wittle baby!" Quinn stuck out his bottom lip in a mock pout. "A tot that can't even see over the sills of the bridge's windows. And he certainly can't make sense of all the dark waters churning just beyond the bow. That ship has no real captain, now does it...*priest*? No," Quinn answered his own rhetorical question, "it's a slow vessel indeed, but it is nevertheless speeding toward a rocky shore, and your worthless fraternity of pillow biters would rather see that craft smash into the boulders than make it into port. It is a doomed ship…one of many. There are no lighthouses dotting that coast. No bright beams will converge to lead her home, now will they…priest? And yet you bastards have the gall to promise us light."

The knife's point pried free from the paneling just then and Helen's limp body began to fall forward. During the corpse's graceless descent, he was able to yank his blade from her neck, and the extraction produced the same sick sound as a dog choking on a sharp bone. Even as her limp knees and elbows crunched into the thick carpeting, the right side of her face bounced and then came to rest against the side of the hot iron stove. Above the rumble of road noise, all three surviving passengers heard the unsettling sizzle of frying meat. And in less than a gnat's instant, the air in the coach was filled with the sickening, sulfurous odor of singed hair, making even the simple act of drawing a shallow breath a true chore.

In this foreign spectrum limited to shades of ebony and crimson, the acrid smoke swirling upward from Helen's shriveling hair spawned its own gray aura of malice…one that, by sheer contrast, intensified the scarlet glow of impending conflict. Even though he was wrinkling his nose in mock disgust, Quinn was battling to suppress a wicked giggle. Finally, he allowed a sneer to twist his lips as he placed the sole of his boot against dead Helen's face and unceremoniously shoved her head back toward the wall. Both of her vacant eyes were still focused on that point between her brows. Her mouth was agape and her mandible was pulled back in an exaggerated overbite. She became lodged between the stove and the wall…coils of sulfurous smoke continued to pour from her shriveling mane. Quinn stood and balanced himself on his left leg. One stout stomp and her charred face finally slid down the rear of the stove and bounced roughly against the floor. His last kick was accompanied by a distinctly sick crunch that indicated he had broken not just one, but two noses this night. "I may have flattened her pretty little nose, but she is likely beyond the point of caring. Damn, but she's going to find i more difficult than ever to find a man now," Quinn quipped as he as sessed the slaughtered and singed corpse. "That is, unless the bastard has very low standards."

Both shoulders shook in silent laughter as he returned to his sea and started to clean the bloodied blade of his knife with the hem c his pale blue robe. He hesitated and cocked his head to the side. hideous smile consumed his lips as he cut his eyes toward the squ priest seated across from him.

"Guess there is no need to clean this off just yet, now is there... Father Tollis?" Quinn teased, taking care to enunciate every syllable. He leaned forward until his elbows rested casually on his knees. Tollis looked into the emotionless pits that were at one time the eyes of a cynical but basically benevolent boy. In the span of a quarter of an hour, they had made the shocking transition into pitiless black voids—the eyes of a reaper. The fat priest recoiled in dread. For the first time in his life, he tasted his own blood and he feared that even more of it would be spilled this night. A grunt escaped his lips that might well have been a whine...a plea for mercy. Since he was still using the fingers of both hands to apply pressure to his broken and bleeding nose, Tollis had to rely on his chubby legs to put distance between himself and the leering face of his demise. He retreated as far as the velvet cushions would allow. His instincts told him to flee, but there was simply nowhere to go.

"I think you mentioned something about teaching me a lesson? Yes? Well as it turns out, there has been a change of plans, my pudgy little chump. This night, I will lead the class. This night, the lesson is yours to be learned, and I think you'll make a fine student. Oh yes, you will. For tonight, I think that the topic of my class shall be...suffering."

♦♦♦

That ancient beast named Cruelty screamed its mad laughter from the black dais on which it sat temporarily enthroned. There were no longer any dark corners in Quinn's throne room...no dingy little nooks where unsavory secrets like lust and rage could be safely tucked away and obscured by convenient shadows. There were no more shadows, for there was no more light. The entire chamber was now black and cold, like obsidian in winter. Cruelty slouched in this twenty-year-old throne, crossing its legs and balancing its newly inherited crown casually on its knee.

King Cruelty settled in with a gratified sigh. None would challenge his reign for some time, for he had established dominion over a realm surrounded by walls that were high and hearty. Cruelty peered over to where a dazzling window used to be. The cursed daystar had disappeared...hopefully forever. The darkness was absolute, but darkness was the only light that the beast had ever needed. There were no longer any vivid white rays pouring in through the window…no sunlight bathing the kingdom spread beyond.

Meadows once golden had been transformed into treacherous, rocky terrain, a bleak landscape where a ballet of black shadows stirred beneath restless skies that were darker still. All light had been eclipsed by a grieving boy's lust for absolute revenge. Black melded with crimson on yet another stage as Cruelty raised the warm goblet to its raven-shaded lips. The beast toasted this dark night's developments with a chalice of fresh blood and then continued to laugh in a low rumble as the world outside grew even blacker.

◆◆◆

The driver was no longer even bothering to watch the road. Truth be told, his eyes had been squinted shut ever since he had seen the hunched daemons step from out of the shadows. Though he valiantly managed to keep them somewhat in check during the grisly sacrifice, he was every bit as relieved as his horses to flee from the tainted clearing and race toward the perceived safety of the city gates. Just as soon as Eric gave the signal to be gone, the driver opted to just let his seasoned team have the reins. After all, they had traveled the road dozens of times over, by light of moon as well as daystar. By now he trusted their honed instincts far more than he trusted his own failing sight…or his rattled judgment for that matter.

His team was still whinnying in panic, and the cold air rushing past his numb ears generated its own characteristic hiss. But above this combined din, he imagined now and then that he could hear an anguished wail, the howl of a housecat being skinned alive…piercing screams originating from just beneath his seat…from inside the passenger compartment. Feathery flakes of falling snow stung his face as he cracked his whip above the heads of his team once more, though they needed no more prodding to make haste. Just ahead, glimmering through the webbed canopy of bare branches, he could make out the bright blue lamps that crowned the massive gate posts

"Boy? Boy! Ring that fucking bell like your life depends on it because it likely does at this point!" he shouted to his green assistant seated beside him on the slick bench. The teen, paralyzed by shock from all that he had just witnessed, was using both his rigid hands to latch onto the flimsy leather seatbelt. For this callow child, the slender leather strap represented a lifeline for his innocence as well as his physical well-being. True enough, if not for the leather strap drawn over their laps, the two coachmen would have likely been pitched off their perch and into the shadows lining the road long ago. The driver's inexperienced assistant was wide-eyed and paralyzed with fear. His boss whipped the boy's nearest thigh with the loose ends of the leather reins to get his attention and repeated the order, this time screaming over the thunder of hooves and the piercing squeak of the coach's metal suspension. His trainee, frightened well beyond the point of arguing, grabbed the bell rope and damn near wore the clapper to a tiny bead before they reached the heavy iron gates.

The guards manning those gates heard the frantic signal and hurried to pull the portal open to admit the speeding wagon. Once he heard the forest gates slam securely shut behind him, the driver planted his heels against the brass rail and leaned back against the reins with all his weight. The discomfort produced by bridle and bit at long last trumped the horses' fear spawned by the ravenous beasts that they had left behind, but just barely so. Six pairs of wide equine eyes scanned the courtyard for any sign of the foul demons that had stepped out of the shadows just a few minutes earlier. Six pairs of black and moist nostrils sprayed frenzied blasts of steam into the frigid night air. The driver set the brake even before the coach skidded to a halt just past the sanctuary's rear door.

◆◆◆

"Two lives before the month is out. Seems as though the crazy old bat knew what she was talking about after all," Quinn chuckled to himself as he shook his head more out of madness and curious satisfaction than disbelief. For the last couple of leagues, Quinn rode in isolated silence and endeavored to clean the blood from the old dagger that had served him so well this night, though it would take quite a lot more effort to wash the crimson stains from his skin and matted hair. The interior of the Citadel coach would require a good bit of attention before it could be used again, Quinn observed as he let slip the contented chuckle of a man bereft of sanity.

"A funeral coach!" Quinn screamed as he slapped his knee. "Perfect! How much more fucking fitting could it be? Place my bets now, will you? That's the future of service I'm predicting for this lovely little carriage. Though I'm afraid it might take a whole herd of recently sodomized acolytes, a crate of thirsty sponges, and a barrel or two of strong bleach to get this craft in ship shape again. Don't you agree, Mister Ament?" Quinn asked the huddled man seated across from him.

Ament was also covered in blood, and he was still curled into a tight ball, shivering like a dog left outside on a harsh winter night. Of course, Quinn didn't expect much of an answer from the dim-witted man. A response probably would not have been forthcoming even under normal circumstances, and tonight's circumstances had been anything but normal. No, gentle Mr. Ament would be especially reluctant to offer his input after tonight, and even if he wished to do so, he would find it even more challenging than ever...now that his tongue and eyes had been removed by Quinn's sharp dagger. They had been removed without any real malice on the younger man's part. It had not been a hack job, by any means. On the contrary, Quinn congratulated himself on performing the impromptu operation with such surgical precision, even though his patient had not exactly held still during the grim proceedings.

Even so, at least Ament's life had been spared; he had fared far better than either Helen or Tollis. Helen had very nearly been decapitated by Quinn's killing blow, and of course the right side of her head was seared black like a well-done steak.

And then there was Tollis. Poor old Father Tollis. Yes, that one would be a bit tougher to explain to those who claimed authority. Quinn regarded the awful mess on the floor and realized that he had very little recollection of the pudgy priest's mutilation and dismemberment...unfortunately. He felt cheated by those gaps in his memory. He lusted for an uninterrupted parade of divinely revolting images. He wanted to remember every whimper...every squirm. Somehow, with King Cruelty whispering such precise instructions in his ear, Quinn had acted mechanically and was unable to commit many of those grim procedures to memory. He recalled only a few flashes of the truly inspired brutality that had been channeled through his soul...his hands...his dagger.

He did recall enough detail to appreciate the fact that his new King had taken great care to assure that an appropriate amount of suffering preceded the inevitable desecration of the corpulent body. Quinn remembered Tollis's high-pitched pleas for mercy, especially during those first few delicious cuts, but the squeamish priest passed out shortly after the apostate dangled the traitorous cleric's severed manhood before his wide and disbelieving eyes. Quinn recognized that he experienced no real gratification beyond that point. After th

pathetic priest faded out, every slice and every malicious incision became acts of simple butchery with absolutely no sense of emotional
victory.

Once the rapture of release faded, Cruelty had whispered into
Quinn's ear yet again, reinforcing what the youngster had already as-
certained: there was little pleasure to be gained in carving the meat
when there was no accompanying bleat.

♦♦♦

Suddenly, the coach decelerated and Tollis's limbless and head-
less torso slid across the slick floor to thump against the base of the
bench on which Quinn perched. The carriage came to a complete stop
and once again it shifted slightly as the drivers hopped to the ground.
This time, however, when the door swung open there were no
branches hovering about, and there were damned few shadows…at
least there were none that shifted and danced under the influence of
the winter winds.

City lights did their best to illumine the southern courtyard of
the Church of Eldr-shok. It looked so different in this light than it
had on that bright afternoon less than a week past. With his left hand
curled into a tight fist and his right one gripping the slimy pommel
of his dagger, Quinn sprang out of the carriage, beyond eager to confront the first bastard who wore a Church uniform. He had plenty of
targets from which to choose, as it turned out. At least a dozen soldiers, fully armed, surrounded the incensed rebel…the most recent
victim of mourning's stinging lash. Five of the warriors leveled their
crossbows at him and the others held long swords at the ready.

For the most part, they endeavored to meet and maintain his
gaze, but Quinn noticed that they all kept glancing down at his robe.
He chanced a quick look downward to see what kept drawing their
attention. Except for a few patches of blue, the garment provided him
by the Church was almost black under this faint light. But he knew
its true color.

"Ah, that," Quinn nodded to the soldiers surrounding him.
'Looks almost like a red robe with a few blue stains on it and not the
everse, but I fear that such is not the case. No. Not hardly. Not
onight!"

"Where are the others?" the group's sergeant demanded, and his
teely eyes were fixed on Quinn's blood-splattered face—the glaring
ien of a madman. The seasoned sergeant no longer allowed himself

to be distracted by the stained robe.

"Oh, they're in there. Don't worry. I guarded them well. Didn't let them out of my sight for one moment. You see, I take my duties as *Chosen* quite seriously," Quinn replied, and nodded toward the open coach door. His absurd smile grew ever wider when he saw grim realization dawn on the sergeant's face.

"Check in the coach!" the sergeant commanded no one in particular. Logic demanded that the duty should fall to the soldier standing closest to the carriage. A skittish private barely past his eighteenth year kept his crossbow leveled at Quinn as he backed toward the round door and peered inside. One quick glimpse and his feet got tangled up in each other as he attempted to retreat from the horrible scene inside the coach. The private slipped on the slick snow. He fell to the ice-cloaked cobblestones and began to wretch, staining the downy white of winter with dark bile.

"Back on your feet, Jameson! Green bastard. You're a soldier of the Church now, damn it all! On your feet, I say!" the sergeant commanded, although his voice was now conveying almost as much trepidation as authority.

"Are there any survivors, Jameson?" the sergeant demanded after he allowed himself a few seconds to steady his voice.

"Don't think so...sir," the young private finally replied after pushing himself back to his feet. His haunted eyes were still pinned to the door of the Citadel coach, and the poor soldier's knees were quaking like those of a newborn colt.

"You don't *think* so? You're a soldier, Jameson! I expect your answer to be either *no sir* or *yes sir*. Am I making myself clear?!" the sergeant barked.

"Y-Yes sir," Jameson replied weakly and wiped the corner of his mouth. Still trembling and still holding his crossbow at the ready, the private took two tentative steps toward the coach. Just then, Ament's tall frame stumbled into the doorway of the coach and the dullard raised his long, lanky arms toward the sky.

"Fawah Ewic!" the mentally challenged man yelled, trying to summon the priest who had always been his hero and savior. Ament' shoulders shook as he sobbed like a small child who had been separated from his mother at market. He sobbed, but no tears flowed down those cheeks, just a few rivulets of fresh blood that continue to seep from the empty eye sockets. "Fawah Ewic!" he tried t

scream again, but he managed only to paint his chin red with yet another torrent of blood from his other recent wound…blood from the
pink stump that was all that remained of his tongue.

Unnerved to begin with, Jameson became so startled he slipped
on the icy stone and fell flat on his ass. The private looked up at the
eyeless giant towering over him, a distraught giant with fresh blood
pouring down his chin and bellowing nonsense. Out of reflex more
than volition, the unseasoned private pulled the trigger of his crossbow. Despite his panicked state, his aim proved to be quite deadly.
The bolt's vertical trajectory carried it to the soft pocket of flesh just
behind the tall man's chin and right between his jaws. Its momentum
pushed it through the roof of his mouth and into his midbrain. The
barbed tip of the bolt just barely managed to exit the lanky man's
skull, and a small tab of bloody scalp flipped back like a deep pink
book cover.

"That would be a *no sir, sergeant sir*," Quinn quipped as he offered an informal salute with his left hand, for his right one still held
the dagger. "No survivors now. That is, thanks to your brave private.
Trained him yourself, did you?" He turned his head to the side so
that he could call over his shoulder, but he kept staring into the
sergeant's wide eyes.

"Congratulations, Private Jameson! You just bagged your first
*Chosen*! You never forget your first, now let me tell ya." Quinn felt
the cold polished bit in his mouth and King Cruelty held the reins
this night. He found madness liberating, and he also discovered that
he had a real knack for it—at least a real knack for surrendering to
its rousing caprices.

"And what of the other two? I'm guessing that you dispatched
them. Am I correct, punk?" the sergeant inquired through clenched
teeth. He already knew the answer to his own question. Quinn only
heard the first part of the query, however. Red rage might have left
him less prudent but certainly no less keen.

"What did you say? The other *two*? You knew that only four of
us would be returning didn't you, you bastard?" Quinn's eyes narrowed and he saw the sergeant begin to steadily apply pressure to the
trigger of his own crossbow.

"Master Tabor!" came the call from the shadows of the Church's
southern vestibule. Another uniformed man coolly descended the five
steps leading down to the courtyard. Without any sort of weapon in

hand, this newcomer was bold enough to step within the ring of his own soldiers and stand just a couple of paces from his blood-covered prisoner. This fellow was also a soldier, but it was clear that he outranked the sergeant who still had his crossbow trained on Quinn's chest.

"Master Tabor." The new spokesman for the group once more acknowledged Quinn, and his voice was astoundingly calm, considering he had just waded into such a maelstrom of tension. The soldier was roughly Quinn's height, but the man was far stouter...and a good bit older. Beneath the strange streetlamps that surrounded the courtyard, his hair shone more pale blue than black. "We need you to accompany us, please."

"Oh, am I to be fed to those bastards too?!" Quinn asked, not the least bit intimidated by his new escort. His brown eyes were still wide and wild with his first taste of madness; and they were rimmed with red due to recently shed tears of mourning. Silence reigned for a moment. The breaths of at least a dozen men rolled out in puffs of bluish mist as he crouched and studied the face of the man standing directly before him. Quinn's chest was heaving and his fingers were rigid. He was ready for a fight even though he was clearly outnumbered. He had no qualms about dying tonight, not as long as he could drag a few more souls into the abyss with him, especially souls belonging to soldiers of the Church. The sergeant with the crossbow would be his first target, then he would just have to improvise. "Are they still hungry, you think? You fucking—"

"I have no idea what you are talking about, lad," the man said softly. Something in his voice, or perhaps the perplexed expression on his face, immediately convinced Quinn that he was telling the truth. But truth really didn't matter anymore. *Truth* and *deserve* were very similar in that both were trumped by *proximity*. "We were just ordered to take you inside for the time being. An emissary from Tarchannen Eid is on his way to meet with you. That is all that I have been told. Now," he stepped aside, gesturing Quinn toward the side door, "if you would please surrender your weapon and follow me."

"My blade stays with me," Quinn growled, and his tone made it obvious that he was not willing to negotiate the point. "If that does not suit you, then give the order and let your bowmen cut me down where I stand. I am a lone boy, essentially naked and freezing. I am armed with nothing but a short dagger, and I am surrounded by dozen of your *elite* soldiers. If you feel threatened by that, then please—give the order. Otherwise, I will sheathe it and follow you in where the air just has to be a little warmer. I've shed more than my share of blood this evening," Quinn lied. His bloodlust was far from being slaked, and his cunning leer apparently betrayed as much, for the graying officer's eyes narrowed. Squinted against the snow though they were, they nevertheless mirrored conflicting emotions regarding his new ward's predicament. Quinn assessed his captor's eyes. They were battlefields on which pity wrestled with unspoken respect. They were twin arenas in which distrust clashed with its longstanding nemeses: empathy and endorsement. Quinn witnessed the officer's emotional guard dropping and decided to take advantage of the opening. The bloodied apostate allowed his shoulders to roll forward, feigning fatigue and coating his words with its frost.

"What I suffer from at present is freezing cold. That and a lack of answers. I just lost my mother and all I ask is to hold onto the blade that was a gift from her. What say you?"

"Very well. Sheathe your blade and follow me," the officer conceded after only a second or two of hesitation.

"Sir, he…!" the crossbow-wielding sergeant started to protest.

"Hush, Kettner!" the officer hissed through teeth that had just now begun to chatter from the cold. "I agree with the lad on one point, at least. If you and your men don't feel up to the task of escorting a lone young man armed with only a dagger, then I think I will have to consider reassigning you. It's already crossed my mind a time or two lately, so I suggest that you button your mouth shut. Understood?"

No answer.

"If you would indulge me in a single, simple request…?" Quinn asked, battling back an insane giggle. He was trying to sound as diffident as he could manage. He was willing to play any role if doing so would keep his smaller duffel close by.

"I suppose. Assuming, of course, that your request *is* indeed simple."

"Could I please have my bags off the coach? We are standing in snow, and still I'm wearing this thin thing that couldn't turn a rat's fart."

"Ah. Certainly." The officer barely hesitated before responding. He curtly signaled for the sergeant to fetch the bags and bring them inside. "Now, I ask once more that you follow me inside, lest both of us freeze."

As he had promised, Quinn sheathed his knife and even placed his hands behind his back in a gesture of acquiescence. King Cruelty retreated a few paces and some of the suppressed—some of the few calmer aspects of the old Quinn—were allowed to re-emerge at that point, largely because this older soldier had by virtue of deeds as well as words separated himself from the other uniformed vermin under his command. The last surviving *Chosen* from Eldr-shok harbored virtually no desire to cause any harm to this particular man. Besides, he was determined to stick around until some of his burning questions were addressed. On this, the blackest of all his nights so far, Quinn vowed both to himself and to his new King not to leave this blasted building until he had achieved some degree of satisfaction. Tonight, he would die for even a small slice of serenity. Tonight, he would strive for restitution even though it was probably nestled deep in the coals of blue fire.

By whatever means, satisfaction would be his. King Cruelty hinted to him through a chorus of cold, veiled whispers that rapture was nigh, and its advent would be more reliant on eviscerations than explanations. Doing his best to suppress a nefarious grin, Quinn fell in behind the older man and headed for the Church's southern door. He took long determined strides and kept his shoulders rolled back. He once again held his head high. He marched like a guest and not a prisoner, though the other soldiers from the courtyard joined file behind him. His armed escort steered him through a maze of hallways and down two sets of stone stairs; and as Quinn descended the last few steps, he could see that a long corridor stretched into the shadows. Eight torches set in iron sconces lit the hallway for the first seventy cubits or so, and he could see that heavy wooden doors lined either side of the passage. It looked like a stockade. The hair on the back of his neck stood on end, but he was determined to see this through, whatever the outcome may be.

The older officer led him to the fifth door on the left and ushered him into the small room, unfurnished save for a crude table and two chairs. One torch hung by the door. Another was perched in a sconce on the wall opposite the door, and the burning pitch filled the room with a thin haze of stinging smoke. Just below that second torch, cot anchored to the wall with iron hinges and chains had been raised to allow for more room in the tiny cell.

"A prison cell. Damn you, I should have known! Emissary from Tarchannen Eid my hairy ass!" Quinn snarled and his hand reached for the pommel of his dagger.

"You are partially correct, Quinn. It was at one time a prison cell, but it is no longer used for that purpose. The door does still lock, but there is a key that fits that lock." The officer fished about in his pants pocket for a moment. "This one, in fact," he stated as he clicked the metal key onto the top of the table and slid it toward Quinn. "Try it in the lock if you like, then put it in your pocket for safe keeping. I entertain no plans to make you a prisoner."

"I appreciate the gesture, but I am a long way from trusting any of you, just so you know. You say that I am not to be a prisoner. I guess that only leaves execution then, now doesn't it?" Quinn asked simply.

"I really don't think that execution is in the cards either, my young friend. Have a seat, if you please," the soldier instructed, indicating the chair that faced away from the room's lone door. Quinn remained suspicious, but he also remained far too perturbed to even argue, so he plopped down heavily in the chair that was offered him.

"Can I get you anything? Some cool water perhaps? We may be in for a bit of a wait, after all. Do you need anything?"

"I *need* an explanation. Other than that, I need nothing that you can likely provide, I am sure," Quinn snapped as he began to drum his fingers on the rough table top. The older man only shrugged at the angry reply and pulled the other chair away from the table. He plopped down, crossed his legs casually and started cleaning his fingernails with the point of his own dagger. The silence dragged on for almost a quarter of an hour. Neither man cared to initiate a conversation, for neither man had anything to say. Not yet.

"I've changed my mind," Quinn said finally.

"Oh? About what?" the soldier asked, not remembering exactly what the younger man might be referring to.

"I thought of something you could get me, if you don't mind. Could you send someone to check on my bags that your sergeant was supposed to bring. I am anxious to be rid of this ridiculous rag that your fucking waste of a church provided," Quinn added, tugging at the front of the soiled, flimsy travel robe. He was anxious to shed it, yet at the same time, he was proud of the crimson dye that had obscured all but a patch or two of the feminine blue. "My own clothes are more to my liking." Aside from feeling chilled, Quinn felt naked and vulnerable in the gauzy robe. His main concern, of course, was assuring the safety of his blade and book. The soldier's expression never changed; he just stared at Quinn for a moment, not saying a word or acknowledging the request in any way. As the captain continued to sit there like a marble statue, Quinn began to wonder if the man had even heard him.

"He *has* taken his time, now hasn't he, Quinn?" The captain admitted with an emphatic nod, and he was clearly agitated that his orders had not been followed to the letter. "Brayers!" the man shouted suddenly, startling the Hel out of Quinn. Sword in hand, one of the soldiers burst through the door and skidded to a halt just behind Quinn's chair.

"Sir? Is something wrong? This one causing you trouble?" the flustered soldier asked, and the knuckles of his sword hand were already turning white.

"Not at all, Brayers. But go see if you can find Sergeant Kettner and tell him to get his ass down here. Remind him that he received direct orders to bring this lad's bags down. If he does not have those bags in hand, you may then inform him that he is now *Private* Kettner and that he will henceforth answer to *Sergeant* Brayers. If you cannot find him, fetch the lad's bags from the coach and I will demote him personally when he finally chooses to show up. Run along now... Sergeant."

With the prospect of promotion dangling just before his nose, the delighted soldier spun about and rushed out of the cramped little room, eager to deliver his message. The heavy door slammed shut, and the two men remaining in the old cell continued to stare at each other in silence.

♦♦♦

Just after Kettner grabbed the lad's bags off the back of the coach, he took a few moments to rummage through them. He found only one prize, but what a price it would fetch! He zipped the pocket shut and finally surrendered to his own sick curiosity, his insistent impulses to discover just exactly what had turned Private Jameson into such a heaving, quivering mess. As the sergeant's boots crunched through the fresh snow, he paused just long enough to take a peek at the nightmarish interior of the carriage. The thin pile carpet was sat urated with the red rain of recent slaughter.

As for the rest of the cabin...the paneled walls, the velvet curtains, the once-opulent cushions...it had all been painted with a fresh coat of congealing crimson. Even now, blood ran like spilled wine. The red syrup of spent life still sluggishly dripped from the curtain hems. And like islands rising from a placid sea of steaming scarlet, three mutilated bodies lay sprawled on the floor of the coach. Ament's vacant sockets told their own grim tale, their shadowy pits a testament to pitiless butchery. The other two pairs of glazed eyes stared at some distant and private horizon...one beyond which their emancipated spirits had recently fled.

Like confused and hungry puppies nuzzling the body of their dead mother, the wispy traces of three departed spirits still sniffed about as they too tried to make sense of the carnage that tainted the inside the carriage. Before finally retreating to a warmer realm beyond the cold and final veil, they screamed to Kettner. They cautioned him that some foul demon now directed the heretical young *Chosen*'s deeds. They warned him that a wicked and ravenous beast had orchestrated this frenzied feast. The guard swallowed hard against a fierce wave of bile and backed away from the door of the coach.

His boots lost traction on the patch of snow that had been packed into a sheet of ice when Jameson fell on his ass. Kettner danced and skidded, but he did not fall. Some of the bile escaped and burned the back of his throat. He recognized that, on at least one very recent occasion, Hel itself had assumed the helm of Quinn's will and the insistent whispers of madness had inspired him to express the depths of his callous wrath.

♦♦♦

After a few more minutes of quiet, the graying commander spoke yet again.

"That *ridiculous rag*, as you put it, happens to be a garment of your Church. Perhaps you should refer to it with a bit more respect. Hmm?" The captain's tone was not condescending in the least. It was more fatherly than threatening and, despite the storm of emotions with which Quinn was wrestling, it was difficult for the renegade to direct his ire at this calm, kind officer.

"It is my Church no longer," Quinn declared without any hesitation. "It never was, truth be told. If your Church offers light, then

I am sworn to the dark."

The door burst open behind Quinn and he instinctively grabbed the hilt of his dagger once again. Kettner stumbled into the room lugging Quinn's two bags by their shoulder straps.

"My apologies for the delay, Captain. With all of tonight's excitement, my stomach…I have been indisposed for a bit. I met Brayers on the steps and he conveyed your message to me. Sir, I ask that you reconsider…"

"Quinn Tabor, I think that you have already met *Private* Kettner. Private, I worry about the integrity of the wall behind me. Why don't you do your best to hold it up, and do so quietly, if you please?"

Kettner blushed, his face turning the color of Redscape wine. But he obediently backed against the wall. Had his eyes been daggers, his captain would now be gasping for breath in a pool of his own blood. Suddenly, Kettner's gaze shifted to Quinn's face and the private's scowl was almost immediately replaced with a mischievous grin. The recently demoted soldier playfully pulled aside his jerkin. Tucked behind the crooked private's belt was a sheath and protruding from that sheath was the silver pommel of a familiar blade—set with a brilliant lavender stone.

𝓙

"**𝒩**ice blade," Kettner mouthed in silence, just to tease the brash little ass who had dared to humiliate him in front of his own troops earlier in the evening…the prick who had essentially been responsible for his recent demotion.

But then King Cruelty leaned forward on his throne and peered vicariously through Quinn's squinted eyes. They bore into the corrupt soldier's soul. Kettner's confident smirk vanished; his features blanched. They blanched, for he had just moments ago surveyed graphic evidence of this prisoner's propensity for mercilessness and an especially nefarious flavor of heartless malice evoked by the primal lust for reprisal.

*You worthless load-guzzling son of a whore! You weren't shitting like you claimed, now were you? Now were you?! No, you were going through my bags, pilfering whatever you thought you could either use or sell,* Quinn screamed in impotent silence as he continued to stare into Kettner's terrified eyes, and the soldier promptly shrank as far back as the stout stone wall would allow. The thief's composure rapidly began to wither, and for a moment Quinn actually thought that Kettner might even step forward and offer the purloined blade back to him.

It would not have mattered, though. Not at this point. Quinn planned to dispatch this bastard of a private, and he would do so well before the daystar arrived for its next pass through Eldimorah's blustery skies. He was already savoring the coppery taste of the aggrieved soldier's blood on his lips, which were already caked with the blood of three other steadfast servants of the Church.

And judging by the panicked expression painted across the newly demoted sergeant's face, Kettner could clearly sense that he had finally managed to push his luck just a link too far. The beads of sweat on his brow betrayed his mounting dread. His instincts whispered to him that that his clock was winding down.

Quinn stood up abruptly, shoving his chair back across the floor with a screech; the orphan sneered when he saw Kettner flinch and raise his hands to defend himself from an imagined attack. The captain of the guard crossed his arms and leaned back in his chair, but didn't appear to be the least bit startled...or concerned.

"Do you mind if I change now?" Quinn asked the senior officer, his satisfied stare never straying from Kettner's sweaty and twitching mug. The private's bearing had, during a single instant of intimidating scrutiny, made the drastic transition from one of devious triumph to that of a rodent cornered by a hungry cat.

"Of course not. That was the point all along. Help yourself, lad," the captain agreed with a wave of his hand, but Quinn had in fact already begun to rummage through his bags. He swiftly passed a hand over the outer pocket of his smaller bag, and was surprised but utterly thrilled to discover that his precious book at least had been left in its place.

"Not much of a reader are you now, *Private* Kettner?" Quinn whispered as he pulled a damp towel from the compartment where he had stuffed all his dirty clothes. After he sensed the thief tense and struggle to phrase a reply, the last surviving Tabor of Eldr-shok proceeded to scrub at least the first few layers of dried blood from his face and hands.

"What was that, lad? I didn't catch what you said there," the seated officer asked.

"Nothing. Would you kindly ask Private Kettner to turn his back, please? I've looked into his eyes a few times now, and I am not at all convinced that he prefers women. If I had to guess, I would say that he favors sausage over bacon," Quinn jibed, and watched yet another flood of embarrassment and rage wash over the younger soldier's features. The seated captain appeared to be battling back a smirk of his own; he coughed, but made no comment. Quinn hadn't really expected him to, but the crimson-stained apostate nevertheless relaxed a bit when he realized that he had chanced across one possible ally conditional or not.

This graying soldier had spent more than two decades in service to the Church, longer than Quinn had even been a citizen of Eldr shok. In matters where blades might be drawn and then wielded to spill blood in defense of the Church's worthless flag, this enigmatic captain might never be his true ally. Still, the fellow at least possesse a sense of humor and he was evidently sympathetic to Quinn's efforts to further humiliate Kettner. Quinn and this captain might have little else in common, but they both found some degree of joy in flinging stones at a common foe—the perspiring pig of a soldier who even now stood pasted against the rear wall of this smoky little cell.

Quinn sighed with relief as he fastened the last button of his thick wool shirt. And he fought the urge to cheer when he pulled his boots on over his winter socks. In no time, the bloody robe had been shed and tossed into the corner where it would remain. He was done with it…for now and forever.

"Now that's more like it!" Quinn exclaimed as he returned to the table. He slouched down in his seat and stared into the captain's eyes. Satisfied for the moment, he bit the corner off a fingernail and spat it back toward the cell door. "There's no substitute for high boots, thick pants, and a long shirt, don't you agree, Captain?"

"I suppose not, but…" the captain began, then paused to clear his throat. "Lad," the older officer continued as he leaned forward. His elbows settled on the rickety table. "I do not pretend to know what happened on your way back from Festival this night. I am not really a soldier, you see. I am more of a mannequin who wears a soldier's uniform, just like the loser standing behind me who would sooner stab me in the back than pick his nose. And the gods only know that I've seen him do *that* enough times."

"Oh yes. I'll just bet you have," Quinn interjected, and watched the full blush return to the private's face once more. A dark scowl contorted features that portrayed more rage than shame. Poor Kettner was being shown all types of disrespect this snowy night, and he was clearly growing tired of it. But his new rank required him to stand at attention and swallow the shredded scraps of his pride.

"Yes, well," the captain continued, "over the years, I have learned to acknowledge my role and to accept it. I accept it for what it is. I have made concessions, to be sure; I have compromised who I know myself to be. Like toy soldiers, my men and I stroll around the Church grounds, parading about each day and waving at you townsfolk from our posts. It is a boring life, do not doubt, but in return for playing my part in this meaningless charade, the Church has done a fine job of taking care of me and…mine."

"You have a point, do you? If so, what is it?" Quinn demanded bluntly.

"My point, lad, is this: in my twenty-two years of service as a guard here, I have never before been ordered to detain one of the *Chosen* upon their return from Tarchannen Eid. You are the first and only. That, in and of itself, tells me that you stirred up some considerable shit. The...ahem...*mess* that you left in the Citadel coach does little to validate your credibility, I must say. Or your sanity for that matter, though you seem calm enough at the moment. At any rate, whatever trouble you have caused..."

"Whoa! Wait just a goddamned minute, now. You're suggesting that I have caused trouble?! *I* have caused trouble?!" Quinn could hardly believe his ears, and he fought to keep his voice from cracking with frustration. He leaned forward and rested his elbows on the table as well. "Let me share a few things with you, if you are for hearing them. After all, it appears we have the time." Quinn took a breath and rubbed his eyes with his palms before he continued.

"In just the last two days, a spokesman for your precious Church lied to the entire gathering of *Chosen* regarding the disappearance and demise of one of our own. Beyond that, he summoned a band of daemons most foul. He called them from the very shadows of Tarchannen Eid's forest, and then he...surrendered my mother to those same damned daemons. She was sacrificed! Do you hear me? The bloodthirsty beasts slinked forward and performed some demented dance of death before ripping her to shreds as I sat there helpless. I just stared out the coach window while Eric and—"

"Eric?!" the officer shouted. His elbows came off the table, and his eyes came alive. In them, Quinn recognized the fiery light of bitterness and suppressed vengeance. "Father Eric? You are telling me that he is responsible for...?"

"...for all that has ruined me this night! Yes! It was all Eric's doing, damn you all! Damn you all!" Quinn screamed. He blushed but out of fury, not embarrassment. His face turned deep red and his palms were suddenly pressed flat on the table. His head was throbbing and his mouth was drier than brittle grass in a summer drought. He could not continue this inane dialogue any longer—he was overcome by the sudden lust for more spilt blood. King Cruelty whispered in his ear and the dark one was once again demanding retribution.

Quinn glanced about the confines of the cell and weighed his alternatives. Though he bore little conviction to do so, he could effortlessly cut the older man's throat in the blink of a moment. Then he could pounce on Kettner before the thieving prick even knew what hit him. After delivering a few quick stab wounds, Quinn could retrieve the Blade of Morana Goll from Kettner's twitching body and…

"Ferrell. Ferrell, by the way," the older soldier offered calmly.

"Wh-what?" Quinn asked as he shook his head, confused by the sudden interruption in his violent strategizing.

"My name, lad. It's Ferrell. I don't think I ever properly introduced myself, now that I think about it. And, by the way, I will say that I don't necessarily doubt anything you just told me. I am just a pawn in the Church's service as I have already mentioned, but I have seen my share of strange goings-on. Only the gods know that Eric has…exacted *tolls* from my own family in the past. To be quite honest, I bear nothing but bitterness toward the man, but I am nevertheless sworn to defend and at least feign respect for the office he holds.

"So, what you are saying…" Quinn began as he leaned forward even further.

"So, what I am saying is that you should bear in mind that a senior emissary from Tarchannen Eid is on his way to see you, and my advice to you is to water down your attitude just a bit. You are obviously angry with the Church, and possibly for good reason. I do not know; I wear the foolish uniform of a soldier, not the robe of a judge. But insolence on your part is only going to make matters worse for you. That much I do know. It will not serve your purpose, no matter how noble it may be. Is any of this getting through to you, lad?"

Quinn leaned back in his chair and raked his hair back with the fingers of his right hand. He rubbed his aching temples a moment before answering Ferrell.

"A senior representative? Who exactly is being sent, do you know?" Quinn asked insistently, and despite how hoarse his voice had become, he could still taste the urgency laced through his own words. Suddenly he felt the cold coils of apprehension constricting him and damming the flow of air into his burning chest.

"No. No, I don't. But why should that even matter?" Ferrell shrugged.

"It doesn't, I suppose," Quinn relaxed, but only a bit. "I just assumed that, as Captain of the local Guard, maybe you would be the one to deliver any lectures or dole out any punishment that might be forthcoming. Not that a lecture from anyone wearing the uniform of our damned Church is going to change my mind or my plans one bit. Not at this point."

"Ah, lad, there is that insolence again," Ferrell managed to smile slightly, but on his face there was painted a fresh trace of friendly concern. It was the face of a frustrated father who could foresee a painful lesson in his son's future but was unable to convince the boy to take the one simple step that would allow him to avert all those costly consequences. "Just be sure you don't mention any of what I said earlier, if you please. I ask it simply as a favor, though you surely owe me none. Alas, I may have disclosed a measure too much to you. I grow tired; I'm getting old. But age and apathy have taught me to trust what is in my gut, and I sense that you and I are not destined to become enemies, Quinn. I have been wrong before, though. The gods only know how wrong..." Ferrell trailed off, and he might have been struggling to sniff back a tear.

"Do you mind if I have a smoke, Master Tabor?" the officer asked as he pulled a pipe and pouch from his shirt pocket. His voice was even, but barely so.

"I'm guessing that you really don't give a flying shit about my wishes on the matter, but go ahead. It can't smell any worse than the smoke boiling off these torches.          "No, I guess not. Not very aromatic are they?" the captain asked rhetorically, nodding toward the crackling brands as he packed and lit his worn pipe.

Quinn was amazed at how quickly the pipe smoke penetrated the heavy air in the old cell. He was astounded by how effortlessly the cherry-tinged smoke summoned so many fond images from his recent past. Gods, how he wished that Bartlitt was seated beside him right now!

At this point, Ferrell settled back in the creaking chair and enjoyed a period of his own musings. "Only three more years do I have left before I can retire and settle down with my sweet Alicia. Now *that* will be a day of celebration, I can promise you. My aim is to draw my hard-earned pension from the Church and watch my two girls grow into fine young ladies. I do have to admit, though, that hate to see the uniform that I have tried to wear with honor turned over to the likes of Private Kettner back here. Drown me in dung if I'm wrong, but this new generation of *soldier* knows nothing of honor."

"Yes. So I have noticed," Quinn muttered and shot Kettner another glare that promised retribution...reckoning.

Suddenly, Quinn heard commotion out in the corridor. Ferrell emptied his pipe and sat upright, his focus returning to the present. Behind Quinn, the thick cell door swung open ponderously on its rusted hinges, but he did not get up or even turn around to acknowledge the arrival of the newcomers. Gods forbid, that might be construed as an act of respect, or fear even. And Quinn now felt neither; he was not the least bit threatened by the arrival of any higher-ranking Church officials. Truth be known, he was looking forward to expressing his enmity to someone with more authority than a lowly, seemingly decent, captain of the local guard.

However, Ferrell was visibly unnerved by the identity of this newcomer. His relaxed features instantly morphed into a dichotomous mask of intimidation and loathing. Until just a second ago, the aging guard had given the impression of being virtually unflappable. Now though, the captain shot to attention, knocking his rickety chair over in the process.

"Sir!? Sir, I did not expect you to come…personally!" Ferrell blurted out in the broken voice of a pubescent boy. "Can I get you anyth…?"

"No. Thank you, but no," came the level reply, and the eerily familiar voice made Quinn's heart stop…then race. "We will take it from here, Captain. You may take your leave if you wish, or you can stay. If you and your sergeant choose to stay, then why don't the two of you go stand behind our *special guest*. That will give everyone a little more room to…breathe."

Ferrell could not get to the other side of the smoke-filled room quickly enough. He practically tripped over his own feet as he hastened to his new post just beside the ancient cell's door. Kettner also hastily scooted along the wall until he stood directly behind Quinn's chair. As he mopped a new wave of sweat from his own brow, the guard noted that both the chair and its occupant remained steady as stone.

"Private," Quinn corrected. Even though he couldn't see the face of his mother's slayer just yet, he imagined that Eric looked just a little bit puzzled. "In the interest of accuracy, although he still wears the stripes of a sergeant, he has just this very evening been busted to the rank of private. He has been naughty, you see? Turns out he's nothing more than a lowly thief."

Eric said nothing in response, but Quinn could sense Kettner quivering with rage as the disgraced soldier was beset by yet another surge of humiliation. And that was quite sufficient. It satisfied both Quinn and his new king, at least for the time being.

"Well, Master Tabor, it looks as though we find ourselves in quite a predicament," Father Eric announced melodramatically as he stepped around the table, righting the chair that, until a few moments ago, had been occupied by Captain Ferrell. The vicar nimbly threw a leg over the chair's back, took a seat, and eyed Quinn like a hawk preparing to descend on a field mouse. Phantoms hatched in the shadows of malicious humor played at the corners of the priest's cold eyes and twitching mouth.

Two stern soldiers raced to assume their posts, standing at rigid attention behind Eric's chair, and Quinn could tell from their hardened expressions and by the gisarmes they carried that they were clearly not members of Ferrell's division. Father Eric casually removed his black leather gloves and slapped them onto the rugged table top once, then yet again. The spindles of the old chair squeaked as the priest leaned back. He crossed his legs and ran his fingers through his wild, wind-tousled hair.

"Quite a dilemma, indeed, lad. What do you propose we do about it?"

♦♦♦

The lone survivor of Eldr-shok's *Chosen* leaned back in his own chair, mirroring and mocking his newest nemesis. He glared at Eric, but his lips wore a sadistic smile painted by King Cruelty's steady, eager hand. They did not twitch...not once.

"What do I propose, you ask? I propose that you go fuck yourself...Eric!" Quinn sang. The priest's expression did not change in the least, but Quinn noted that the two soldiers flanking the senior cleric tensed, although they continued to stare straight ahead, just as their strict training demanded. "How's that for a plan...Eric? You like? Hmm?"

Still, the vicar did not move, aside from blinking once or twice. He did not even appear to be struggling to phrase a response. At last the older man lowered his eyes and calmly studied the stained nail of his right forefinger. Father Eric understood rage. He understood it more than most. He understood it well enough to realize that the quickest way to stoke its flames was to show a reaction to it, and he had taken part in enough interrogations by this point to know that this Quinn Tabor certainly fell into a special category. From a tactical standpoint, sheer intimidation would be wasted on this one. If the subject's initial combative tendencies were allowed a chance to mellow, the odds of collecting useful information without resorting to less subtle methods would likely be increased.

"Excellent. Anything else?" Eric asked simply, and Quinn detected no tinge of irritation in the fickle priest's tone.

"You can start by telling me why you killed my mother, you worthless son of a bitch!" Quinn spat. He wanted an answer to that lone question before he unleashed his fury on this murderous bastard of a priest. No explanation offered by the cleric would save him from serving his due sentence in Hel, but Quinn simply had to hear Eric's motivations for performing the foul ceremony that had taken dear Miriam into the beyond, away from her son and the happy life that they were meant to share for at least a few more years.

Much like this wintry night's sky, Quinn's heart had grown black as pitch in just a few hours' time. Like his heart, the night was shining in darkness. He knew that hearing the vicar admitting his guilt would only add fuel to the same fires of cruelty that had so viciously ushered Helen and Tollis to the fiery foyer of Hel. His appetite for vengeance was whetted with every beat of his broken heart, every crackle of the torches that chased back the cell's cowering shadows.

Had he chosen to follow the compulsions of the "old Quinn," he would have likely just lunged across the table in the hopes of landing at least one lucky lick before the other guards rushed forward to beat him into oblivion. Alas, that version of Quinn was no more, for his craven spirit had been slain as well by the hunched daemons lurking beside the road to Tarchannen Eid. The transformed Quinn that had risen like a phoenix from the smoldering ashes of grief and rage was more of a strategist. He was more calculating and far more wily than his pathetic predecessor. This new incarnation preferred to taunt and goad his victims before the real dance commenced...before he adeptly side-stepped their most reliable defenses and began to maim them, stifling their cries. That would occur only after his voracious appetite for suffering had been sated. No, Eric was not the only rival with a strategy in mind for tonight's interrogation. This little encounter was, without a doubt, destined to become a real pissing contest. And Quinn was confident that he would emerge as victor, for the rage of all seven Hels now compelled him.

"So why did you do it, Eric the Queer? Did you hate your own mother? Was that it? Was she a whore, and was your father just another of her nameless clients that paid her a couple of coppers in return for receiving his diseased seed?"

Eric's crooked smile wilted even further and his eyes rapidly transformed into the same solid black pools that Quinn had beheld only a couple of hours before, as the carriage sped away from that damnable scene of stomach-turning carnage. Had rationality still gripped the reins that steered his thoughts, Quinn's smug confidence would have likely ebbed. Perhaps he would have even made an attempt to apologize, for the brassy youngster was suddenly convinced that he was going to die before he was granted a chance to draw his next breath. But rationality had become a fickle beast of late, and the idea of dying did not bother him—certainly not as much as it likely would have earlier that same day. After all, he was born to die, and if he was destined to die tonight, then he figured that it would do no harm to get in another few verbal licks.

"Is that why you have little boys brought to your chambers in the wee—?"

Everything went black. When Quinn's senses returned somewhat, he felt the table's rough surface abrading his cheek. He had been the recipient of a stunning blow to the back of his head. Eventually, he managed to push himself upright only to collapse against the slatted chair back. Eric's dark eyes stayed fixed on Quinn's as he spoke, though he now spoke through gritted teeth and his ire was clearly directed toward another.

"Private Kettner, although I certainly appreciate your frustration at witnessing such insolence, I ask that you not interfere in such a way ever again or I will have you demoted, yet again, from lowly private to eviscerated corpse. Do you understand me? Do not speak. A simple nod will suffice."

Apparently, Kettner nodded.

"Bring me the bowl," Eric ordered the soldier just behind him and to his left. The obedient warrior's heels snapped together. He nodded and hurried from the room.

The vicar's black eyes never left Quinn's. Rage prompted him to skip right to those less subtle interrogation techniques. He still fully intended to leave with the information…the item…he was sent to acquire, but he wanted to see this barking young dog suffer, and suffer profoundly.

Father Eric continued to glare at Quinn while he reached into his mud-spattered vestment and retrieved a short, slender dagger. The handle was bone white and dozens of emerald green gemstones were embedded in its milky matrix. One depthless peridot stone mounted close to the crossguard was much larger than the rest, though it shared the tinier stones' deep emerald color. The priest quite deliberately placed the blade near the center of the table, well within Quinn's reach. Eric smirked and tilted his head to the side as he laced his fingers together and rested his hands in his lap.

"So. You mean to kill me too, then?" Quinn inquired rather objectively. He was dispassionate because he was not at all surprised by the sentence handed down for his gruesome crimes. He was objective because he no longer cared whether he lived or died, but he was determined to leave Eric with some kind of souvenir, even if it was nothing more than a crushed testicle provided by the toe of his weathered boot.

"No lad, I am not here to kill you, though that was certainly *my* recommendation. You see, little man, I cannot think of one good reason to keep you alive." The vicar paused for effect before continuing. "However, my Lord sees fit to show mercy in this matter, though he is far from pleased with your actions or your attitude, I assure you."

"Ah. And who exactly is your *Lord?*" Quinn spat, rubbing the back of his head. When he examined his fingers, he discovered that Kettner's blow had drawn blood…it had opened a small but ragged rent in his scalp.

"Don't play stupid with me, Quinn! You are a fool, but you are not stupid. I'm referring to Lord Invadrael, of course," Eric answered reverently. His head tipped back and the black voids that now served as his eyes turned toward the skies that lay concealed by several layers of cement floors and ceilings. Even the lone soldier standing to the right of the vicar came to full attention at the mere mention of his true master's name.

"Ah," Quinn nodded. "Ah, yes. Invadrael. Lord of Stained Windows." The heretic broke out in a fit of insane giggling that only managed to confuse the others in the room. They couldn't possibly understand his reference, therefore they were not offended by it, but his tone suggested that the allusion was not exactly intended as a compliment. Before long, Quinn sobered and he glared at his inquisitor once again. Gray lines of grief made the young *Chosen's* face look suddenly old, but the raw hatred in his eyes was hot enough to melt glass...especially stained glass. "So, did my mother die on his order...or yours?"

"Your mother was invited to pass beyond the veil because that is simply the way it has been ever since Lord Herodimae took The Name. Think of it as a rebirth and not a death, if it gives you more comfort.

"It does not!" Quinn barked. "And how dare you say that she was *invited?* She was butchered!"

Eric rolled his eyes. He also rolled one wrist dismissively.

"At any rate, her special contribution has served the Church in ways you cannot even begin to fathom. That being said, I will add that—had she been willing to divulge information regarding the whereabouts of a certain article—it is possible that she could have been spared. But alas, she was...noncompliant. Now, enough of this bullshit, you brash upstart! I will tolerate no more such questions from the likes of you, *Master* Tabor. My time is far too precious." Father Eric saw Quinn eyeing the dagger hungrily.

"Ah, now. Yes. There is a look that is hard to misread. Love is a razor and so is hatred, Quinn," the wily priest purred. "You're walking that silver line right now, I am guessing. You wish to strike me down with the blade, do you? You want me dead more than anything. I can see it in your eyes. You want to butcher me and splash my blood on your face as if it was perfect water issuing from some warm spring. I know you."

"Go ahead, then!" Eric shouted. "Add yet another savage attack to your growing list of sins, you misguided young fool!"

Everyone in the room, Quinn included, flinched as the vicar's palm slammed down on the table. The blade did not so much as budge.

"Go ahead, you worthless little heretical bastard! Here is my throat; do your worst! Do your worst you miserable...orphan!" Eric screamed the challenge to his prisoner. He even leaned toward Quinn and lifted his chin to expose his own throat.

Needing no more prodding than that, Quinn leaped forward and grabbed the colorful hilt, fully intending to slash that throat and then plunge the slender blade into Eric's chest at least once for each year that his father had been gone. However, no sooner had his determine fingers closed about the handle than he fell to the floor like some drunk diving off a barstool. He never lost consciousness, but his body was wracked by fierce convulsions. He tasted blood as he bit through his tongue, and he felt warmth coursing down his thighs as his bladder emptied. When the seizure finally ended, he still lay there for a while, drooling and gasping for air that just would not fill his lungs rapidly enough. His right cheek rested on the cool, dirty stone of the cell's floor, and he was quite content to remain there for as long as he was allowed.

Though he could not yet lift his head, he did hear the cell door swing open on its old hinges, and his eyes followed a pair of booted feet as they walked past. The other soldier had obviously returned from Eric's errand. For only a moment, Quinn felt just like he had four years prior, when he had succumbed to the winter taint, the epidemic that swept through Eldr-shok. His face was sweating and he felt the sudden need to vomit, but the wave of nausea and fever passed quickly.

At last, his limbs began to respond to his commands once again. He managed to push himself to his knees, and then to his feet. It took a moment or two to regain his equilibrium, but once he did he wobbled back over to his chair. An iron bowl filled with glowing coals now sat on the table just beside the strange blade whose enchantment had just dropped him like some pitiful, dying deer. A skinny metal rod rose vertically from the center of the coals. Just beyond the rim of the tarnished bowl, Eric's satisfied smirk glimmered in the orange glow from the coals.

"What…what manner of blade is that?" Quinn wheezed as he brushed the sheen of sweat from his forehead with one unsteady hand. "Surely…surely it must be demon wrought."

"Oh, you do not know the half of it, boy," the vicar hissed menacingly, "though you are doomed to learn at least a few more of its unpleasant secrets very soon." Then, as quick as a pair of hungry snakes attacking two field mice, Father Eric's hands shot out. One grabbed Quinn's right wrist and the other snatched the jeweled handle of the dagger. Still addled by the effects of the fit he had just experienced, Quinn's reflexes abandoned him. He could not even begin to draw back in time.

The bereaved *Chosen* could only watch in something akin to detached dismay as Eric maliciously drove the curved blade of the dagger through the back of his wiry hand and into the wooden tabletop. The tip of the blade cleaved through Quinn's flesh, but it miraculously missed bone altogether. Its descent did not end until its bloodless point protruded through the bottom side of the table. The blade's crossguard was now only half a link from the back of his hand. Quinn immediately noticed that some force more clandestine than simple alarm now kept him rooted to his chair. Dozens of unseen hands held his arms and legs static. The covetous wraiths who now claimed him as their prisoner were intent on keeping him frozen in place, their firm grips not allowing him to move even a fraction of a link in any direction.

"Time for another brief lesson in history, you little bastard. This lovely little knife, as you might already suspect, is a very special blade. Yes. It is yet another relic retrieved from the dark vaults of fate...the same fate that has apparently forsaken you...and poor Tomas. Just like the blade that you stubbornly insist on hiding from us, this one was indeed conceived by Morana Goll's unbounded imagination, and was forged in the fires of Hel when he was just an apprentice. He was a very talented apprentice, don't you agree? Yes?" Eric giggled spitefully and mopped a rivulet of drool from the corner of his mouth with his sleeve.

"Irony abounds does it not, *Master* Tabor? The fact that you cannot respond to me does quite effectively answer my rhetorical little question. Ah, well. At any rate, to your credit you did correctly deduce this blade's origins. It was indeed demon wrought. Morana Goll was after all a demon, or did you not know that?" The vicar leaned in even closer, shifting his stance until his eyes were in line with Quinn's unresponsive stare.

"Something in your frozen gaze tells me that you did not. No matter, I am not here to teach history to the likes of you. Lord Invadrael loaned me this blade from his private collection. He thought that it might make my task much easier."

The vicar stood casually and leaned across the table, his palms now perhaps half a link from Quinn's paralyzed fingers. "What's that?" Eric turned his head and placed his ear close to Quinn's mouth. "Oh. What exactly is my task, you ask?" Eric mocked, knowing full well that Quinn was unable to speak, unable to move.

If he could have broken the strange paralysis spell for just half a second, Quinn would have struck like a snake and ripped Eric's ea off with his teeth, but the power of the spell was absolute. It allowed him to breathe, but just barely enough to remain conscious. Quinn could not even muster the will to force his eyes to blink, though they were dry and stinging from the smoke boiling off the tiny room's twin torches.

"My task, Master Tabor, is actually twofold. You have demonstrated unequivocally that your continued presence in the cities of Eldr will serve no purpose aside from remaining an enduring nuisance to my Church. Tonight, I am going to give you a very special little souvenir that will mark you quite unambiguously as the outcast and the impenitent heretic that you are." Eric pulled on his gloves and lifted the metal rod from the coals. This was not just a metal rod, it was a branding iron, Quinn realized. But no part of his body was capable of responding to the panic that he began to feel...nothing except for his racing heart.

"No follower of the Way, no citizen in any of the Five Cities will accept you as anything more than just that, once they see your sign. And see it they will, have no doubt. As you know, five is the sacred number of the Way." Eric turned the red brand so that Quinn could clearly see the symbol used to represent the number five in some of the older texts in Tomas's library.

"When both wings of the angel are lifted toward Haeven, this symbol stands for victory. But when those same wings are inverted, they represent defeat...misery. When turned upside down, this single letter becomes the mark of the heretic. From this day forth, you will be a man without a home, without friends. I suppose it would be silly to point out that you are already without family, would it not? Yes, I think you are fully aware of that fact." Eric cackled for the express purpose of tormenting his immobile captive. The shifting whims of madness sobered his mood in less than a second, though.

"Heed my words, young fool: you will leave the city tonight. You will flee it, and you will do so with your tail tucked between your legs like some scolded cur. Should you demonstrate enough poor judgment to return to any of the cities of Eldr, know that your life will be forfeit, and swiftly so...ruthlessly so. You brought this on yourself, you bothersome brat! None of this is my doing, even though I may be the one wielding the brand." Eric slowly turned the iron halfway around and began to ease it toward Quinn's forehead. Then he froze and cut his eyes toward the door.

"What's wrong, Captain Ferrell? Why ever would you choose to leave us now? Don't tell me you have lost your stomach for justice all of a sudden?"

"I most certainly have not. But this isn't justice!"

"It is according to Lord Invadrael," Eric fired back. His tone was confident to the point of being condescending. Obviously, he considered the matter settled.

"Then *he* is mistaken. You both are! Feel free to tell him that I said as much, should you survive this night," Ferrell replied flatly, and turned to exit the room.

"That sounds very much like a threat, Captain. Should I take it as such?"

"No, Father Eric. No threat at all. Let's just call it a hunch, shall we? I think your vaunted luck might finally be running out," Ferrell tacked on as he cast a whimsical glance at the back of Quinn's bloodied head.

"Strange. Though we've had our differences in the past, you never struck me as an insubordinate coward, Captain," Eric sang. His venomous song sprang forth from the mouth of madness.

"Glad to hear that," the captain muttered facetiously. "But for the record, you have always struck me as a demented loon. You may share that with your goat-banging master, as well, the next time you find yourself curled at his feet like the obedient pup that you are!" Ferrell shot back. "I'm sure that it shan't be long." He slammed the cell door behind him before his startled superior even had a chance to retort.

Though he was not able to shift his gaze, Quinn could still sense the fires of malice flare in Father Eric's dark eyes. The priest forced himself to draw in a deep breath as he buried the iron beneath the coals once more to reheat it while he contemplated a fitting reprimand for Ferrell's defiance. The soldier who had fetched the bow stepped forward and brought the dying coals back to a red glow with a miniature hand bellows.

"Another blasphemous bastard! Damn, what is it about this night? Hmm? Shall we blame it on the moons? Well, I'll just have to make a note to *correct* the good captain later...and I know just how to do it, too. Oh, yes." The vicar began to giggle like an eager toddler opening a yule present.

"He has two beautiful young daughters, but of course you a

ready knew that, I suspect. Am I right? He probably told you as much while you were awaiting my arrival, did he not? That is his tendency, after all. He trusts. That is his main fault, and it will be his downfall. Yes, I will bet you anything he will be more willing to show due respect to Lord Invadrael and myself once he sees just how severely a hot branding iron can mar those two pretty faces. Given enough time and driven by sufficient inspiration, I can turn his two perfect little porcelain dolls into unrecognizable...ogresses. How very tasty."

"Gods! To be sure, I'll have to concentrate. I'll have to battle to contain the syrup of my seed while I mutilate them and transform their pristine white skin into twin patchworks of perfect scars. Just imagine it Quinn...imagine the thrill I will get from nuzzling their perky breasts while I mold my two newest masterpieces. While I twist perfection into just so much melted candle wax! And their screams—their wails—will serve as a deliciously sweet bonus. That scene makes your loins ache just a little as well, does it not? Be honest now, Quinn. Be honest...my son. You can confess anything to me, remember? It will go no further than this room. After all, I am a priest."

"Ah, but I'm getting distracted by my next endeavor before this one has even been completed. Now, where were we, Master Tabor? Ah, yes..." Eric pulled the newly heated iron from the bowl and leaned in without any further warning. After spending only a second to take proper aim, he pressed the red hot metal against the center of Quinn's forehead.

♦♦♦

Quinn felt immediate and mind-shattering pain, but he had been robbed of any means by which to express his misery. He could not scream, flinch, or so much as discharge a single tear. The unmistakable sizzle and smell of frying flesh elicited the vision of Helen's dead face pressed against the side of the iron stove, but that afforded him a strange sense of...comfort. That memory kindled what remained of his dwindling faith...his belief in nothing. It made the intensity of his own physical pain abate. The burning agony subsided and then it disappeared altogether, like a candle extinguished by a stout draft. He remembered the warmth of that traitorous bitch's slick blood flooding across his knuckles. Now, paralyzed though he was, his loins swelled as he relived the sweet taste of vengeance and the rapture of unleashed cruelty.

In that rapturous and red hot moment, he knew with absolute certainty that the finger of scorn would soon point directly at his nemesis. The priest's conceited smile would soon wane. Eric, damn his smug face, would soon share Tollis's fate. This charismatic vicar was destined to be introduced to a whole new level of suffering, which he would experience at Quinn's own firm and unflinching hand. As the paralyzed *Chosen* focused on the wispy but precious promises offered by that image, the pain arcing across his forehead diminished. The fresh brand became the focal point of cool comfort akin to the veil of peace that descended after a bout of enthusiastic weeping...the distinctive and incredibly soothing afterglow of tears.

The heretic marshaled his resolve and managed to suck in a deep breath, though it was drawn through pursed lips and clenched teeth. His eyes shrugged off the stout chains that had bound his stare ever since the blade was driven through his hand. They broke free from Morana Goll's shackles and shifted to meet Eric's wild, wandering gaze. And the fields of black that now enveloped the erratic priest's eyes grew wider still. The cleric recoiled in measured shock. The vicar blinked, he flinched, thereby surrendering any advantage afforded him by the illusion of composure.

"You smile, heretic?! The power of the blade does not allow it!"

Quinn could see Eric's features, but all of his attention was focused on the featureless face of vengeance. Though it was sheltered within the shadows of the reaper's wrinkled cowl, it was now his sole source of comfort and salvation. His only other source had been brutally slain shortly after the daystar fell behind the battlements of Tarchannen Eid. The promise of reprisal filled him with peace; it allowed him to shrug off at least the tightest of Morana Goll's shackles and it somehow nullified a small part of the strange knife's inherent magic. He had to concentrate to make his lips form the words, and those two words still came out in a harsh, broken whisper. Barely audible, they were just loud enough to register with Father Eric—just loud enough to convey Quinn's principal sentiment.

"Fuck you."

Father Eric's lips contorted like a sheep shank tied in coarse cord. The knot drew ever tighter as disbelief and rage tugged on opposite ends of that taut rope. Like ten startled snakes darting through tall grass, his fingers ran through his unruly locks. He carelessly knocked his chair over as he hurried around the end of the table. Er stepped behind Quinn's chair and leaned close. His trembling lips brushed the boy's left ear as he launched another volley of hissed taunts.

"Very soon, boy, you will pray for your own death. You will walk Eldimorah searching for a means to your own demise. We gave you a choice…a chance! It could have been so different. That's the true pity of this whole blasted situation. You could have enjoyed a decent if unremarkable life as a ward of the Church. But when you chose to defy me and ignore my direct orders…when you chose to peek around that curtain, you sealed your fate. You slaughtered Helen, an innocent *Chosen*. And then you saw fit to viciously butcher one of my brethren, no less…another who wears the collar!"

"…wore the collar," Quinn corrected in that same hoarse croak, "and she was not innocent. She lost her innocence to her father."

"Enjoy your wretched life, Quinn Tabor. Enjoy wandering across Eldimorah with grief as your only guide and loneliness as your only friend. Now I must move on to more pressing matters." Eric's voice dropped to a whisper so that only Quinn could hear his words, but prominent blue veins spread across the vicar's forehead like indigo lightning.

"Your bitch of a mother would not voluntarily disclose the whereabouts of the blade, so I fed her to my pets. I plan on employing a slightly different tactic with you. It might well leave your brains a bit scrambled, but that is a gamble that I am more than happy to take. I am going back to Tarchannen Eid with the Blade of Morana Goll, and if I happen to leave behind a quivering, blubbering idiot that the fools of Eldr-shok used to recognize as Quinn Tabor, then all the better. It will be quite the legacy for your rotting corpse of a father and that dismembered harlot, Miriam." Eric snatched a handful of Quinn's hair and violently yanked the lad's head back. The priest leaned forward and his whisper sounded like the hiss of a cornered serpent. "I'll bet that all sorts of beasts are, at this very moment, dragging her shattered and rattling bones along the chilly forest floor… dragging them back to their dens so they can show their newly acquired treasures to their hungry brood."

Eric released his prisoner's hair with a vicious jerk. The cleric pulled a leather pouch from one of his vestment pockets and carefully covered all of his fingertips with its white, powdery contents. He uttered a few indecipherable syllables and his hands began to glow with amber light. The wicked priest's fingers splayed across the face of his captive and his thumbs pressed firmly into the back of the lad's head. Eric's lightly calloused forefingers were caressing the teary surfaces of Quinn's open eyes, but Quinn discovered that he could not even blink against the burn, so strong was the spell of the blade that had been driven through his hand...especially now that it had been augmented by Eric's own twisted hex. In his mind, Quinn was screaming. But his body remained as still as December stone.

Panic sprouted forth in its dark blooms, and Quinn willed his muscles to resist as the vicar began a slow chant. He was held fast. While Eric's incantation intensified in both pitch and intensity, Quinn could feel a malevolent tingle singeing the skin where the vicar's fingers pressed. The sniffing hounds summoned by that spell burrowed far below skin and scalp, digging and delving ever deeper into the petrified heretic's psyche, probing the shadowy corners of his mind previously relegated to concealing forgotten feelings and distant memories. Had Quinn not been utterly paralyzed by those steely invisible hands, he most surely would have loosed a piercing scream as the combined spells wrapped wicked tendrils around the pillars of his essence...tendrils that strangled his soul like waves of hungry ivy climbing over a weathered stone door.

♦♦♦

Eric, damn his soul, had won tonight's contest after all. Knowing beyond knowing that death or something far worse than death was upon him, Quinn retreated. He just let go. He abandoned this futile struggle against fate and embraced the burgeoning blackness like a beggar might clench some ragged blanket on a frosty night, a weakly woven shield clutched with clammy hands while the dreamer beneath wrestled with restless visions. Dragging his bruised soul behind him, Quinn marched right through the doors flanking this theater of dreary dreams and took his seat near the front row.

The house lights began to dim. On this weathered new stage shallow shadows reigned at first. Initially, they sprouted and spread like another benign bank of gray clouds. Before long, though, a howling rent appeared in the Heavens. From the depths of that rift, a pitch black curtain descended beyond which all hope lay in eclipse. But then a beam of moonlight dug its way through the clouds, and it illuminated the center of the stage. The novel little play began, using that ebony veil as a backdrop for its opening scene—a tragic scene during which retaliation was augured to prevail.

In Quinn's grim and freshly limned dreamscape, the performance opened with Eric standing over Miriam's lifeless and mangled
body. The priest was laughing maniacally, yielding to the unreserved
lust he harbored for the devilry that the ancient blade possessed.
Rivulets of drool slithered from the corners of the cleric's mouth as
he turned the Blade of Morana Goll over and over in his hands. He
admired its workmanship, certainly, but the flames of yearning that
danced behind his wild eyes were clearly fueled by the insistent
promises. The illusions of power.

Near the toe of Eric's left boot rested Miriam's severed head.
Tiny streams of her lifeblood seeped from her neck and the darkening
discharge saturated the leaves of the forest floor. Though it was pale
and lifeless, her face appeared to be so goddamned content. Her eyes
were closed just as if she was taking a peaceful afternoon nap; then
those eyes shot open and Quinn was suddenly singed by the fires of
anguish. His own eyes burned with tears that held no meaning to anyone but him. He was allowed one last lingering glimpse before saying
goodbye, then there was a flash of lavender light and the image was
no more. Blackness returned.

◆◆◆

Once more, his nostrils were being stung by the cloying smoke
of the cell's twin torches. As before, he felt foreign hands holding
him, but now there were only two, and these were clearly not hands
fashioned by magic. He could feel human fingers digging into his
muscles and bruising his skin. He could feel them gripping his shoulders and shaking him awake, back from the blissful state of non-being
that had delivered him from the horror of...

Quinn jerked awake and found that he was once more the pilot
of his own body, though his nerves were certainly jumbled. His arms
and legs continued to quake with terror's residual tremors. The re-
uctant Church guard who had been ordered to awaken Quinn backed
away hastily, and undisguised fear lingered near the margins of his
wide eyes.

"It is done," Eric rasped. The vicar leaned against the table, re-
ying on his right arm to support the weight of his upper body. He
was in obvious pain, and he too was fighting to catch his breath.
Quinn couldn't help but wonder why the entire left side of the priest's
ace was abraded and swollen. It had already started to turn a bluish-

green. Clearly, something significant had just transpired in this tiny cell. Eric had been dealt a direct blow by the hand of fate and the blood-caked *Chosen* had missed it. Damn! Quinn missed it because he was wandering through the hospitable realms of unconsciousness. He missed it while he was being subjected to that macabre scene... while he was staring into Miriam's glazed eyes one last time...while he was witnessing the first scene of a play for which no happy ending could be written. All members of that cast were doomed. They were walking toward the sound of their own screaming.

Quinn was almost fully awake now, but he was still too weak to do much besides tremble and stare at his right hand. There was no blood, no evidence whatsoever of a recent wound. There was only the hint of a white scar where the knife imbued with the power to paralyze had been driven through his flesh.

"Your hand is fine, brat. Your worries, however, are far from over," the vicar continued ominously, but his threats weren't issued with quite the same degree of conviction that Quinn had grown used to over the last few hours. "I know not how you managed to resist me, boy," Father Eric panted, "though I suspect that you have met Madeline. I can smell her influence on you, and the protection spell resembles some of her...previous work."

"Wh-who the shit is Madeline?" Quinn panted. "I don't know anyone by that name."

"No, I don't suppose you would, since she has not used that moniker in decades. She poses as a crazy old seer here in the city. Actually, she is demon born, or hadn't you already guessed as much? Madeline has quite a distinctive lineage, like yourself. That meddling hag is a direct descendent of Morana Goll, no less. Come to think of it, that might explain how you managed to resist the blade's spell though all you could do was move your eyes and whisper—"

"*Fuck you*," Quinn finished for the priest. "Ah, yes. I remember that part. The sentiment remains, by the way." Although he was as wobbly as a newborn calf, he could not forego another chance to needle this murderous, bruised bastard.

"Yes. Yes, I do believe it was something like that." Eric glared at his prisoner. His face twisted into a grimace as his left arm twitched at his side. "But no matter. Magic has its place, to be sure. However I have learned over the years that the oldest motivations continue to be the most fruitful, especially in *situations* such as this. Take the de sire to protect a dear friend from harm, for instance. You're quite close to my colleague, Brother Obadiah, are you not?"

Quinn did not respond with words, but his muscles tensed and his eyes shot wide. His reflexes betrayed him on this occasion, and Eric swooped in like a hawk falling on a young rabbit.

"Yes, I heard as much back before the list of this year's *Chosen* was even posted. And I saw as much when I was rummaging around in your mind just now. Well, down to business. It would be a horrible tragedy if he suffered a fate similar to your dear mother's, now would it not?"

Although no blood whatsoever had been drawn during the recent ceremony, Eric wiped the blade reverently on the hem of his tunic and returned it to its sheath. Only then did Quinn notice that Eric's left arm hung essentially useless at his side.

"After this damn night, nobody who wears that foolish collar is any friend of mine. Do with him what you will. As far as I know, Obadiah helped arrange tonight's slaughter. Fuck him! Does that answer your question, Eric the Queer? No? Well, let me ask you one now. It looks as though you took some kind of lick while I was out cold. Could it be that I owe this Madeline a debt of gratitude? Did her little safeguard fling you against the wall like the dickless ragdoll that you are? I'm guessing that's the case. Your face is even uglier than usual, and I'm afraid that with your left arm out of commission, you won't be able to hold the younger acolytes still while you administer…"

Eric leaned across the table and—using his right arm—struck Quinn's face hard enough to knock him out of his chair. Kettner picked him up off the floor and roughly threw him back into his seat.

"Well, at least we know that your right arm still works, now don't we?" Quinn wisecracked as he spat blood onto the table. "You don't happen to have a mirror on you, do you? I think my lip might wind up with a scar from that punch."

At hearing his insolent prisoner's last remark, Eric's trembling lips quickly relaxed. In fact, the corners of those parched lips shot toward the ceiling as if they were caught in the currents of the black whirlpools that the priest's eyes had become.

"As a matter of fact, Quinn, I do have one. I think you'll find that your split lip will not be the first feature to which everyone's attention will be drawn, however." Chuckling like a sailor flirting with a whore, Eric reached into the deep pocket of his robe with his right arm and held the mirror in front of Quinn's face. The priest-slayer studied the brand on his forehead. It was indeed the letter V, inverted so that it ironically resembled an arrow pointing toward the floor of Haeven. There would be no ambiguity. He was now clearly marked as a heretic, just as Eric had indicated right before pressing the gleaming metal into his flesh. The ragged scar very effectively covered the territory between his eyebrows and his hairline.

"So, how do you like your new look, you young fool? Rest assured that I can do much worse, and I will turn you into a quivering monument to deformity unless you give me what I want, boy," Eric demanded. "Turn it over to me, or so help me, I will systematically remove every piece of flesh from your body until only your soul remains! And then, I will tear it apart for sport."

"Kind of like what happened to your *dear* colleague, Brother Tollis? Yes, I seem to remember hearing something about that. By the way, is this little badge on my forehead just a mark of heresy, or is it also a tribute to your mother's spread legs? I know you told me before exactly what it was supposed to symbolize, but you know, so much has happened since then..."

Again, Quinn became the recipient of a punch that knocked him out of his seat, and once more Kettner lifted him and tossed him back into his chair.

Eric returned to his seat across the table from Quinn and crossed his legs. "I cannot tell you how anxious I am to use this blade once more, Mr. Tabor...just once more. That should do the job. I think I shall bring my next victim to this very room. Yes, that would be so poetic. But there will be no need for Private Kettner's presence, nor will I require my two escorts for this next endeavor. I would prefer it to be a very private session. I want that encounter to be far more *intimate*." Eric tilted his head back and his black eyes seemed to stare into space for a few seconds, but then he sat up suddenly and snapped his fingers.

"Maybe not entirely private. Actually, I think I shall invite you to witness it, Quinn. Excellent! Oh, what a fun game that will be. Of course, you will be gagged and bound to a heavy chair over in the corner, but you can watch me create what might well prove to be my masterpiece. A shrine to my special brand of handiwork." Then Eric leaned back in his chair and feigned contemplation by tapping h chin with the forefinger of his right hand.

"The logistics might be a bitch, however. Of course, I'll have to send for my tools back in Tarchannen Eid…my blades, gouges, and probes. Oh, and by all means I must remember to request my other branding irons. After all, an artist is nothing without his brushes."

"Why," Eric paused to laugh and slap his knee in evil glee, "I'll bet my soul that you'll damn near chew through your leather gag just so you can tell me everything I want to know. Then you'll beg me for a chance to tell me about all the matters about which I couldn't give less of a shit. Yes, logistics can be a bitch, but so can blind devotion and that spiritual taint that you call love." The vicar's visage grew suddenly more grim and menacing as he eased out of his chair to stand in a half-crouch. He leaned toward his prisoner. His left arm still hung useless at his side, but the white knuckles of his right fist ground against the rough tabletop as he glowered down at the brazen, newly scarred bastard. "You can stay cold inside and conceal your conscience behind a thick curtain as long as your true heart is shielded…as long as it's not about love."

In that moment, Quinn was allowed a much closer look at the cold malice boiling in the cleric's obsidian eyes.

"You think you've lost your heart and your integrity tonight, boy? I assure you that you haven't. Not yet. I know just where to find them, you little shit. I'm willing to bet that both will return just as soon as you are forced to look into her lovely eyes as I defile and mutilate her while she is held stone still by this same blade. Ah, fair Catherine…I can already smell her heady musk. Does it bother you that I can already smell what you have never even sampled? Not only can I smell what has been denied you, I can actually taste its blessed tang on my lips!"

Quinn's head hung low, but not out of despair. He stared at some point near his own lap, but he shook his head and chuckled as the echoes of Eric's last words faded into silence. The torches continued to spit and crackle.

"Oh, I doubt that very much, Eric the Queer. You see, a woman's musk is quite different from that of an altar boy. I personally don't think you'd know what to do with a crotch that didn't have a shrivled stub and a bald bag hanging from it." That remark earned Quinn his third and by far most ferocious punch he had received this night. Fettner was prepared this time, and the bitter guard managed to catch the boy well before he toppled out of his chair. Quinn was slow to come around this time, so Eric threw a cup of cool water into his prisoner's bloodied face to jar the heretic back to the present.

"Very well, *Father* Eric. Clearly, we can go on like this all night, but I'd prefer not to," Quinn sputtered. His left eye was already swelling shut. "I'm still unclear as to what it is exactly that you are looking for. I'm sure you've already searched me and my bags over there. You're trying to get something from me that I either do not possess, or perhaps it's something that I possess but don't recognize as being all that special."

"Don't you dare toy with me, heretic! You know damn well what I am searching for. I seek the blade that was to be your legacy, you young fool! A silver blade with a silver pommel, and there is a lavender stone set just…"

"Oh, that!" Quinn rolled his eyes to the ceiling and nodded a time or two while blood continued to trickle from both corners of his mouth. "Oh, that! Hel, priest, you should've just said so when you first arrived and I could have saved myself a closed eye and a couple of loose teeth. I could have also saved you a broken shoulder and a bruised cheek, for that matter. You still haven't completely explained that one to me, by the way. I sure hope I was responsible for it in some small way. I would hate to think that Madeline gets all the credit. But I digress. Hel, I know right where the blade is; I've known its whereabouts all along, so don't you worry. During my recent little visit to your grand city, I initially hid the blade in Mason's rear cavity, but I knew that was not a long-term solution. I figured if I left it there you would certainly find it eventually…probably sooner than later, yes?"

Eric's face twisted into a mask of black rage. The priest drew his hand back to deliver yet another punch, but Quinn's next statement obviated it, though the rector's arm remain cocked and ready to deliver what would surely be a jaw-breaking blow.

"Why, it was stolen from me just this very evening, if you must know—and you apparently must. Gods, *Father* Eric…you really mustn't allow yourself to get so worked up over such small things! Quinn grinned and spat a pinkish stream over his right shoulder t purge some of the blood that the minister's last blow had drawn "Anyway, it was stolen, but it certainly hasn't gone very far. Not very far at all, in fact."

Though Quinn couldn't see the private's face from where he sat, he could easily hear Kettner swallow, and the fucker swallowed damned hard. It sounded like a rat snake choking down a newly hatched robin. The panicked thief's breathing became more rapid, scratchier. Not even the cell's pair of sputtering torches stood a chance of drowning out the larcenous soldier's nervous rattle. Quinn knew the crooked guard probably planned on pawning the blade in the city, and likely for a tidy sum. Kettner was a simple man driven by simple greed. He had no idea just how valuable the knife was, and he certainly could not have imagined the lengths to which the Church would go to retrieve it.

"It's in a very safe place, you'll be glad to know. A place where at least no woman would dare go. Matter of fact, it has been parked right under your ball-sniffing nose all evening. It's tucked ever so snugly behind Private Kettner's belt back here, even as we speak. Seems as though you should have branded him and not me. Score another point for Eric the Queer's infallible judgment!" Quinn managed to announce before he leaned back in his chair and surrendered to an unsuppressed wave of mad laughter.

"Damn the gods, I'll kill you, you smug little bastard!" Kettner yelled as he stepped forward and drew the stolen blade from its place of concealment. In the blink of a sparrow's eye, the sergeant-turned-private drove the stolen Blade of Morana Goll into Quinn's chest, not just once, but twice. The first blow punctured the right lung; the second went straight through the boy's heart.

♦♦♦

The point of the blade that was to have been his legacy slithered between his ribs, piercing the center of his heart. Quinn's disconcerting laughter abruptly ceased with a wet gasp. For the second time in a single night he became the unwitting victim of a blade that had been crafted and then cursed by the demonic armorer, Morana Goll. This time, though, the injury had been sustained by his heart, not just his hand. This time, he was to be the traitorous reaper's target and not its tool. He felt his pulse fading like the daystar at dusk. Time slowed to an oppressive crawl. Sure that he could hear the cold call of the grave, he granted his heavy lids permission to close...forever.

However, the same gods who had orchestrated his apparent demise had at least seen fit to grant him one dying wish. As consolation for all the injustices recently visited upon him, Quinn was allowed a fleeting but precious glimpse of his own Haeven. For the briefest of instants, he was allowed to behold a true masterpiece of panic painted across Eric's dark features. There was no sound, at least none that Quinn could hear. The vicar was releasing a prolonged scream that seemed to be a single word...*No!*

Eager to shed the shackles of sorrow, Quinn surrendered to the mounting darkness. He bowed in front of the reaper before even realizing that the wounds he had just sustained were not mortal ones. He had no way of knowing that Kettner's assault would unleash forces, the might of which Eldimorah had not witnessed in over two centuries—not since the birth of Tarchannen Eid. The torchlight started receding and his vision grew blurry. Still, he instinctively knew that he was not dying. Far from it. His old world began to fade to black, but then it erupted anew...this time in a brilliant lavender inferno.

The priest launched himself out of his chair and lunged desperately for the handle of the knife that he had been sent to retrieve for his lord and liege, a blade that was indisputably the most special one ever to emerge from the forges of Morana Goll. But from Quinn's new perspective, Eric was moving no more rapidly than a slug trying to climb a brick step. Then a new and exquisite pain registered that reduced Quinn's already reeling senses to ruin's rust...to a child's whisper lost in harsh tornadic winds. He unleashed a wail of his own, and he sustained it not with the breath from his lone intact lung, but with his soul-consuming desire to exact revenge and impale his enemies on serrated spikes. His only thought involved sorrow. His reason for being was to inflict suffering.

Whether his eyes were open or closed he simply could not tell, for now he could see no shapes whatsoever, just a featureless field of blinding lavender light. The radiance stung his eyes but its other effects were far more profound. The lavender gleam assumed a life all its own. It was a violet serpent that wound itself around his heart— wounded but far from lifeless—and that heart was swiftly stripped of anything resembling sympathy or benevolence.

It was a serpent that kissed his soul with its sweet velvet lips. That lavender conflagration, carried by its own currents and fanned by its own flames, scorched what little remained of Quinn's unsullied spirit. In seconds, it was burned to black crust. Those seconds dragged on but he continued to scream, for he sensed that the shrie was indeed a weapon he was fated to use against his foes. And they seemed to be all around him this night. He was now manning a flesh fortress that was under siege; he was charged with repelling a tenacious army that he could not see. The scream served not only as a weapon, but as a shield to protect him against all that had gone wrong for him on this, the foulest of days.

♦♦♦

At last, Quinn willed the wailing voice to fall silent. He knew only that he was leaning forward; both his palms were pressed against the table. At first, he couldn't see anything beyond the flames of the purple inferno, so he just stood there and relied on his tactile senses to provide him with some center of focus. Ever so gradually, the firestorm abated enough to cast a few rough silhouettes. The table. The sconce on the far wall. At last, he could make out some more distinct shapes, details such as the grid work of mortar in the stout prison walls. But this new world was painted so differently than the last one that had been etched into his memory.

Earlier this very evening, malice had driven him to view the traitorous realm of Eldimorah through twin but disparate lenses—one tinted crimson, the other jet black. There had been only profiles and outlines. Red on black...black on red.

Now however, even tiny cracks in the brick became open, bleeding wounds. Cobs crawling along their wispy webs looked like hawks soaring by. The deluge of detail made his senses reel, and his heart soared on the fresh winds of nuance even though the artist rendering this strange new reality into which Quinn had been cast commanded a palette limited only to shades of lavender and gray...limited yet delightfully limitless.

Silence hung in the tiny cell like a pall. Silence and a fog of fine gray dust. The two torches still burned and the subtle crackle of burning pitch was the only noise that Quinn could hear at first, but he soon grew aware of his own raspy breathing. It was likely a result of his chest wounds and not the dense cloud of ruin that hovered in the air. It did not matter, he quickly decided. Of more immediate concern were the tiny chunks of loose mortar that were falling intermittently from the ceiling of the chamber. The old building above was shivering like a homeless urchin standing in harsh winter snow, clinging to his favorite toy and wishing for a crackling fire or even a flimsy moth-eaten quilt.

A quick scan of the room revealed to Quinn that Kettner was obviously dead, as were the two guards whom Eric had recruited to escort the vicar eastward from Tarchannen Eid. All three soldiers lay twisted and contorted as if they were rag dolls that some pitiless dog had shaken and then tossed into a corner. Quinn glanced at them just long enough to notice that their chests had been crushed—caved in like the low crowns of paupers' graves after seven days of rain. Their ribs were shattered and the ragged fragments of bone had pierced and utterly ruined the underlying lobes of lung tissue. He also observed that dark and viscous blood trickled from their ears to pool on the thirsty stone floor.

Then the relative silence was interrupted, although barely, by the shallow gasp of a dying man struggling for just one more precious breath. With all the coordination of a witless drunk, Quinn stumbled over to the far corner of the cell. There he found Father Eric's twisted body. By the malevolent but whispered whim of some miracle, the ruined man stubbornly clung to life. He was alive, but obviously he wasn't *very* alive. Like the other fallen ones, his chest had been caved in with not a single rib left intact. Most of the long bones in his arms and legs were bent at grotesque angles, turning corners where natural articulations never existed. His neck was likely broken as well, for his right cheek rested on the cold stone floor, but his wide eyes tracked Quinn's approach. His head did not—could not—move.

The vicar's eyes were no longer ebony pits. Now, they were just the wide eyes of another ordinary man…another dying man. They shed no real tears; they only bled streams of stark and eerily sterile astonishment. Perhaps some trace of fear shone through the encroaching fog of fate's breath, but absolutely no suggestion of remorse abided in these eyes that grew more dim with each second that ticked away. Quinn's instincts told him what his own eyes could not for he was still struggling to adapt to this vivid world painted in mingling hues of lavender and gray.

No, there was not the first hint of apology. Just awe and disbelief Father Eric tried to speak, but he was far beyond the point of putting thoughts to voice. This priest who had once been such an eloquent and dynamic speaker now sounded like a choking newborn. Whatever words he was attempting to phrase would just have to remain secret until his foul soul reached the molten gates of Hel.

But he was conscious…for the moment…and that was all tha

mattered to Quinn. Some measure of sweet vengeance was still within his reach. There was still some precious suffering to be harvested here. Rivulets of red blood also dripped from the dying priest's ears, and Quinn knew right away that his nemesis was likely not able to hear his words, but he was determined to make their meaning clear one way or another.

"It pleases me beyond measure to know that something that resides within me proved to be your undoing, you foul bastard," Quinn stated calmly as he kneeled down to grasp Eric's chin and turn his face toward the ceiling. The dying priest's eyes grew even wider as he gurgled and gasped in undisguised pain, and Quinn could feel his own frown morphing into a cruel smile. A steel dagger lay nearby, and its markings suggested that it had belonged to one of Eric's deceased guards. Quinn leaned forward to retrieve it from the dusty floor and bounced its pommel in his hand a time or two as he held Eric's stare. His puckish smile widened and he leaned his head to one side as he bent forward and carved a deep design into the dying priest's forehead—the mark of the heretic. The same design as the searing brand that this bastard had so cruelly inflicted just minutes earlier. Quinn pressed down on the honed blade until he could feel its sharp tip etching the front of Eric's skull.

"Now they will recognize you for what you truly are when you get to Hel...and that shan't be long, dear Father Eric. Not long at all. I *am* sorry...I am sorry that I couldn't drag your suffering out over a much, much more protracted period of time. Oh, what I would not give to prolong it? I had such plans for you. Ah, well. Time, she slips away from us all, does she not? Yes, minutes and seconds are passing us by." Quinn started to wipe the blade on the dying priest's cloak, but then he hesitated and snapped his fingers just as Eric had done moments earlier, right before he threatened to defile and maim Catherine while Quinn was forced to watch.

"Wait! I know what I *can* do for you, my friend. I can make sure you die with a smile on your face. You deserve that much, I'd say. That's the least I can do after all you've done for me." Eric gagged and gurgled. He blinked a few times in succession as his sneering slayer leaned forward to butcher both of his cheeks, slicing them back all the way to his clenched, twitching jaws. Quinn did take time then to clean the blade off on the priest's cloak. "If you don't mind, I need to borrow your gloves, old friend. I don't think you'll be needing this little prize, not where you're going. You have some rather dark trails to traipse, I suspect. As do I, thanks to your recent efforts," Quinn taunted as he pulled the right glove on and retrieved from Eric's cloak pocket the paralyzing blade crafted by Morana Goll. Then he rose to his feet and evaluated his handiwork as he tucked the steel dagger behind his belt. The cuts were jagged and not quite symmetrical, but they both angled upward and that was all Quinn was really concerned about. All of Eric's teeth, even the back molars, lay exposed by the horrid surgery.

"Now, if I am ever asked, I can say in all honesty that you died smiling from ear to ear," the apostate chuckled, holding his sides. After studying his perishing nemesis just a moment longer, Quinn's expression sobered and then turned downright grim. He placed the heel of his right boot on the priest's bloodied temple and slowly leaned forward, transferring all his weight to that foot.

"Forgive me Father, for I have sinned. You have wronged me, and now I've come undone," Quinn whispered right before his weight crushed Eric's skull like the brittle shell of a dead and decaying turtle.

♦♦♦

After scraping the heel of his boot clean on Father Eric's cloak, Quinn grabbed his two bags. Only when he tried to throw the straps over his shoulder did he realize that the Blade of Morana Goll was still lodged in his chest. Without so much as wincing, he pulled the blade free and noted with virtually no surprise that the bloodless wound closed and sealed before his eyes. Another faint white scar now stood testament to his transition. He carried yet another souvenir that would remind him of this black night, though he knew beyond all doubt that forgetting all that had just transpired would never be possible.

Still donning the gloves he had borrowed from Eric, Quinn pulled the blade of paralysis from behind his belt and dropped it into his pack. Likewise, he placed the bare and bloodless blade of his father back where it had spent the last week…in the front pocket of his smaller duffel. Kettner had obviously disposed of the scrap of burlap that had swathed the blade for more than a decade, and Quinn found that he had developed an odd sentimental tie to that old rag. After all, his dying father had wrapped it about the blade with quaking hand just a day or two before he breathed his last.

"Bastard," Quinn insulted the dead man as he kicked Kettner roughly in one of his open eyes. The former sergeant's head bounced twice and came to rest with his lifeless gaze directed at the ceiling, his mouth still open, frozen in a death scream. "It never pays to steal. How many times do I have to tell you that? Now, you try to do better in the future." Quinn shook his finger in the corpse's face and smirked. Justice was whispering in his ear and it demanded just one more gesture of disrespect, one more lesson, so Quinn cleared his throat with a loud snort and let a viscous stream of mucus drop into the thieving sergeant's gaping mouth. "Don't want ya to go and dry out on me, Private Kettner. Now quit dawdling, soldier! You're dismissed."

Enough time had been wasted in the confines of this smoky little chamber, Quinn decided. He could hear no one stirring out in the hallway, but he was not about to chance facing any Church soldiers while he was essentially unarmed. He still had the dagger that he had carried for years...the one he had used to butcher his three fellow *Chosen* earlier in the evening...and he decided to keep the dead soldier's dagger tucked behind his belt as well, partly because it was longer and in much better shape than his old one but mainly because it had been the tool he used to avenge himself and his mother on foul Father Eric.

Daggers certainly had their applications, but they would hardly suffice should he encounter any of Kettner's men while making his exodus from the dank church basement. Hurriedly, he pulled Kettner's crossbow and quiver of bolts free from beneath their deceased owner and threw the slings over his unburdened shoulder. "Gonna have to requisition this also, private," Quinn said with a wink as he pulled the former sergeant's short sword free of its sheath. After a quick inventory, he cautiously stepped through the cell door and into the dimly lit corridor.

Dust rained down from the ceiling. Broken bodies were strewn everywhere, and Quinn could immediately see that the bodies were those of Ferrell's guard. Aside from the tiny crimson streams still trickling from their ears, there was little or no blood on the men or their clothing, but most of their limbs were broken and turned at irregular angles. All of their chests were crushed just as Eric's had been. He wrestled quivers filled with crossbow bolts from two of the carcasses and slung them over his shoulder.

As he reached the foot of the stairs, Quinn had to roll one of the grotesque corpses out of the way in order to pass. Ferrell's dead, drying eyes stared blankly at some point just above Quinn's right shoulder. Thin trickles of partially congealed blood were slowly flowing from his ears and the corners of his mouth, disappearing into the margins of the captain's graying sideburns. Quinn shook his head and succumbed to a brief bout of regret. Given a choice, he would not have seen any harm come to this one. From all indications, Ferrell had been a basically good man, but fate had seen fit to dress him in the wrong uniform. And now, thanks to the whims of injustice, he lay here lifeless, sprawled amongst a dozen others who had, unlike him, given in to decadence complete.

Like Quinn, the good captain's two girls had also become orphans this cursed night. The renegade patted the captain's lapel reverently and pulled the cold eyelids down so that the weary man could finally sleep. Then he spun about and sprinted up the steps toward his freedom.

◆◆◆

The western wing of the old building continued to shudder and shake as Quinn meandered through the maze of hallways, searching for the huge door that opened out into the familiar courtyard...the courtyard in which this whole ill-fated journey had begun and ended. Burdened though he was by his two bags and his recently acquired arsenal, he ran as fast as he dared lest he speed by one of the landmarks that he had tried so frantically to mark on his mental map. He rounded a corner and ran right into, of all people, Malloway! The effeminate acolyte looked into Quinn's eyes and appeared close to fainting for a moment, but then he shook his head to dissipate his shock. Without uttering a word, he spun about and took off at a sprint

"Stop, damn you!" Quinn snarled as he dropped his bags and shouldered the crossbow. Malloway clearly had no intent to follow the command, so Quinn thought that a warning shot over his shoulder might convince him to halt. Risking just a second or two to take aim, he pulled the trigger and watched the bolt speed toward the retreating acolyte...and bury itself between two ribs just inside the boy's right shoulder blade. The force of the unexpected blow rolled Malloway forward, bringing him down in a jumble of lanky limbs and long robes. Quinn raced forward and was on him in seconds. He grabbed the exposed shaft of the bolt and began to twist it to get the acolyte full attention, but he felt warm air rush outward from the wound so he released his grip and flipped the wounded boy onto his side.

"Show me to the courtyard you little faggot, or I'll slice off your favorite plaything and toss it into the snow! Do you hear me?" Quinn could hear the fury in his own voice, but he knew that he was not just bluffing. He had proven himself capable this night of making good on even the grimmest of his threats. Apparently, Malloway sensed the sincerity as well. He held his pasty hands up in front of his eyes and began to blubber, but the effort resulted in a gasp and a gurgle that revealed to the assistant what Quinn already knew—the bolt had managed to puncture a lung. Quinn seized the acolyte's collar and roughly dragged him across the carpet to where the two duffel bags lay.

"On your feet and lead me to the courtyard door! Now, damn you!"

Wheezing with exertion as well as panic, the acolyte crawled up the wall and continued to lean against it as he stumbled along the hallway. When the two reached the very next junction, Malloway took a right and slid down the wall just beneath an oil lamp that hung adjacent to one of the outlandish paintings that Quinn had studied less than a week ago. Even in the dim light, Quinn's new vision revealed a streak of warm blood that now stained the slick paneling. Malloway was gasping for air and was obviously not going to make it much further under his own power, but not three famns away stood that familiar, massive door that led to the courtyard and the world outside.

As anxious as he was to be gone from this place, Quinn knelt down on one knee and let the shoulder straps of his bags fall to the maroon carpet.

"Look at me, boy," Quinn commanded in a harsh whisper. Malloway was conscious and somewhat alert, but his eyes remained downcast. He would not meet Quinn's gaze for anything. "Too ashamed to look me in the eyes are you? You should be!"

"Spokesperson for the group," Quinn lisped, just as he had done after leaving the ale table earlier in the day. "Isn't that what you told me that day, you ball-cupping bastard?" Still, the acolyte just sat there staring at his lap. He was focused on coaxing his lone intact lung to pump like a bellows just to keep himself alive. Without another word and without a second's hesitation, Quinn pulled the newer of his two daggers from his belt and slit the boy's throat, unleashing a startlingly copious torrent of warm lifeblood.

"Much better, in my opinion. Now you have a valid reason to be so damned pale," Quinn chuckled as he shouldered his load and marched toward the door. "Just don't blame me for that fucking haircut."

◆◆◆

Snow flurries swirled past his sweaty face, but the cold night air felt delightful on Quinn's clammy skin, and he breathed it in deeply, thankful to be out of the smoky little cell in the Church's basement... thankful to be well away from Eldr-shok's fortress of foul corruption. His legs were still wobbly and weak from Father Eric's foul spell, so he quite necessarily took an opportunity to fall to his hands and knees to catch his breath and collect his scattered thoughts. The wet, feathery snow blanketing the flagstones quickly made his bare hands go numb, but the numbness was more jarring than objectionable. More than anything, he wished that he could bury his wounded heart under that snow and achieve a similar outcome.

Light tremors continued to resonate through the streets and sidewalks, shaking the loose snow off of the streetlamps and the signs hanging over the storefronts. Quinn could feel Eldimorah's erratic new pulse even through his numb hands. Despite the late hour, some of the townsfolk were lighting lanterns and stepping out into the snow to investigate the low rumble that had disturbed their sleep. There were at least a dozen dead Church soldiers, one murdered acolyte, and the mutilated corpse of an ambassador from Tarchannen Eid in the building behind him. The Citadel coach was nowhere to be seen, but Quinn knew that yet more damning evidence resided within that vessel of varnished wood and gilded trim.

Mustering his strength, he pushed himself gracelessly to his feet and stumbled into the shadows, no longer a boy but a damaged man lost and utterly alone. Though Quinn had committed more than a dozen murders this very night, he did not consider himself a murderer. He did not consider himself a murderer, but he could not deny that one now resided within him.

Quinn saw himself merely as an avenger. After all, circumstance and subterfuge had backed him into a tight corner, and he had merely chosen slaughter as the means to make his exodus from that undesirable place. Even so, he most certainly had to acknowledge that h was no longer a mere innocent trapped in a war that he did not even know was being waged. He was now a soldier of sorts with blood on his hands and scars on his soul.

Not knowing where else to go, Quinn marched through the snow in a mental haze, determined to return to the apartment that he and Miriam had shared for the last ten years. As he turned from the buckled sidewalk to climb the stairs, he stopped and cautiously backed away, retreating once more into the darkness. Two armed figures were standing on the narrow porch just outside the doorway to the second floor dwelling. Not surprisingly, they were wearing the sickeningly familiar white and blue uniforms of Church soldiers. Quinn could only surmise that the guards had been posted to prevent him from reentering his home.

He quickly decided that they had likely been assigned their duties much earlier in the evening, perhaps just before the coach had left Tarchannen Eid, as it was highly improbable that the slaughter back at the Church had been discovered yet. Even if it had, there was no way these two could have been dispatched quickly enough to beat Quinn here. From his vantage point within the shadows, he studied the two guards and analyzed their bearing and body language. They were smoking and shivering. They were both laughing...trying not to complain, for they had doubtless learned that griping about their discomfort only amplified it.

Occasionally though, they would pace back and forth just to stay warm. Both took advantage of every opportunity to kid the other about which body part was going to freeze off first. No, these two were not on the lookout for the one responsible for the death of a dozen or so of their fellow soldiers. They were lackeys performing a duty that they considered to be pretty much pointless.

The shorter of the two paused to relieve himself on the brick wall just beside Miriam's door. Both of the oafs started chortling, and Quinn's grip on the crossbow tightened.

"Now that's downright disrespectful," Quinn whispered to himself as he contemplated offering another lesson in morals to these two new...students. For a second, the serpent coiled and made ready to strike. He pondered his odds of picking off the two guards with his crossbow. If he could take out the taller man first, he might be able to send the second bolt on its way while the pisser still had dick in hand.

But then logic stormed onto the stage and pled its case, arguing that he instantly discard that idea as any semblance of a real plan. After all, he was no marksman and had never even wielded a crossbow before tonight. True enough, his first shot with the weapon had brought down a moving target, but he had in truth intended to miss Malloway completely and have his bolt bounce off a nearby wall instead.

No, Quinn had wounds that needed to be licked before he waded into any more battles. He harbored no desire to confront any more agents of the Church this evening, so he backtracked a half a block and ducked into the alley that ran along the south side of their building. Another right turn and he stood just below his bedroom window. Quinn quickly mounted the trusty stack of crates that had allowed him to sneak in and out of his room so many times before.

In less than half a minute, he was standing in his room, drinking in all the familiar sights and smells. A week had passed, but the faint aroma of Miriam's spice bread still managed to linger in the cold air. Quinn took a deep draw of that aroma and his eyes began to burn. His fingers curled into tight fists as he fought the mounting urge to just sit on the side of his bed and weep, exactly as he had done the night he read Valenesti's tale for the first time.

Gods, but he had planned for his return home to be so different. By this hour, he was supposed to be to lugging their tattered bags up the front steps with Miriam at his side. He envisioned the two of them dragging their tired asses into the cold den as they laughed and chatted about the week they had just spent at Festival. By now, she was supposed to be chiding him about spending so much time drinking ale with that rogue, Bartlitt. Then she was supposed to fuss at him to start a fire that would warm the place to somewhere above freezing...

Now, though...now she was dead. Mutilated. Now Quinn had sent more than a dozen souls to Hel, and he had been branded as a heretical outcast. Now there was a sheen of frozen piss clinging to the brick beside the door to the only haven he had known, at least since his father's passing. He stood alone in his darkened room, not knowing exactly what to do next. He supposed the first order of business was to produce some light, so he stepped noiselessly to his bedroom door and pushed it gently to. Quinn dragged his chair across the floor and lodged its back under the doorknob just in case one of the piss-happy soldiers decided to get nosy and snoop around inside the apartment. Then, feeling his way to his nightstand, he removed the mantle of his oil lamp and lit the wick, taking care to turn it down as low as it would go without extinguishing it.

Thinking to gather more winter gear, Quinn took a step toward his closet, but froze as he glanced into the mirror hanging above his dresser. The figure that stared back at him looked familiar for the most part, but the face in the mirror possessed eyes the likes of which Quinn had never seen before...except in the stained glass window of the sanctuary...the windows that Invadrael himself had commissioned to be installed. What in blazes had the latent magic of Morana Goll done to him? Both of his eyes were fields of solid lavender, perfectly matching the color of the stones that were set in the handle of the unusual dagger his father had left him—his legacy. They even possessed the same uniform pattern of trapezoidal facets. They were beautiful almond-shaped gems, perfect specimens that immediately made him want to retch. Pupilless lavender voids, those eyes belied no emotion other than raw malice. They were violet vacuums around which swirled the flames of obsidian fires.

Only after he fought back the urge to vomit did he even take notice of the scarlet scar on his forehead, the brand that was supposed to represent an inverted rendering of the Church's sacred number and ironically resembled an arrowhead pointing toward Haeven. Eric had shown the brand to him earlier, but Quinn retained only a vague memory of that fragment of their exchange.

"Damn them!" he cursed softly as he blinked and leaned a little closer to the mirror. "Damn them for what they have done! Damn them for all they have taken! Damn this morning's dawn...the dawn of the day it all came down." He gingerly palpated the burn on his forehead. So, this was the mark that Eric had chosen, the one that would mark him as an outcast. Just by itself, the scar would have certainly served that purpose. But the violet voids were a far more profound indicator of heresy—one that his mother's slayer had clearly not foreseen. This ancillary mark had been bestowed upon Quinn strictly by chance, though some faithful fools may have preferred to call it fate. Chance had been but one factor in the complex equation describing tonight's appalling developments, however. Kettner's loathsome greed and the enigmatic conjuring of the demon armorer, Morana Goll, had been two others.

There was not a soul in any of the Five Cities that would so much as nod to him once they caught sight of his faceted lavender eyes. Ever since its inception, the Way had taught that the hue of a man's eyes revealed whether he followed a path that would lead him to Truhaeven or to blackest Hel. When the eyes were tainted...as his now most certainly were...the possessor would only be shunned if fortune was smiling. The marked one might be hanged or even burned at the stake if fortune found itself wanting for some grim entertainment. Given the toxic mix of zeal and paranoia engendered by most followers of Invadrael and the New Church, the latter was the most likely outcome for any who possessed eyes that appeared to be crafted by the clawed hands of demons.

In Quinn's case, he would not be able to deny, at least not with any real conviction, that his new eyes were indeed fashioned by one of the denizens of Hel, for he now knew that they were. He even knew the identity of the one who so adeptly integrated dark magic into his forgings. Father Eric's little souvenir of a scar notwithstanding, any follower of the way that Quinn encountered from now on would allege that he carried a plague of the spirit...a plague for which there was no cure aside from purification by fire.

*He who looks through the eyes of a devil will find serenity only in fire. Only through orange flames shall the iniquitous glimpse the gates of Truhaeven.* Quinn mouthed the verse from the Book of the Way that he had been forced to memorize when he was a child, long before he had learned to think for himself.

Of course, Quinn had also heard the legends regarding the select few who had been born with snow-white irises. They enjoyed lavish treatment from the Church, as did their parents. Born immediately into favor by virtue of nothing but their eye color, these *gifts from the gods* were promptly whisked away to the Citadel where they were treated as though they were next in line to become gods themselves. How different it would be for him now that he sported these two purple orbs where plain brown eyes used to reside. If any citizen of Eld even bothered to spit in his direction, Quinn would be amazed... amazed and relieved, he admitted to himself sadly, since he much preferred dripping spittle to the vicious lick of scorching flames.

As he fought back tears, he dumped the contents of his bags onto the floor and began to repack them with other items from his close and drawers...items better suited to battle harsh winter...better suited for travel on foot...better suited for survival in a new, hostile worl whose citizens would readily persecute him for the color of his eyes and for the unmistakable brand that now disfigured his forehead.

Standing there in his old room with the cold air pouring in through the open window, he sobbed quietly for all that had been taken from him in such a short time. Just as had been threatened, Eric and the Church had succeeded in making sure that loneliness would follow him like a tenacious shadow. There was only one person in the city that might possibly talk to him. But even that was doubtful now, since he too donned the collar and the robes of the nefarious Church. Still, Quinn had no other choice and no other plan...no other hope.

8

Driven by the harsh winter wind, the snow flurries shot across Quinn's path, flying parallel to the abandoned city streets. He took special care to keep the hood of his cloak pulled forward so that most of his face would be hidden in the deepest of its shadows. Only his cheeks were exposed to the stinging flakes, since he had taken the added precaution of wrapping a thick scarf about his head to conceal his brand and his tainted new eyes from any who might be about at this hour, though he encountered not a single soul on his way to Obadiah's apartment.

This despondent pariah who had been forced to age years in a matter of mere hours lowered his head, as much to shield his uncovered skin from the blasts of cold wind as to avoid judgmental gazes from the eyes of all the nonexistent strangers. From the lower margin of his blindfold, Quinn musingly watched his boots plow through the unpacked white powder as he hurried along that familiar and oft-traveled route to the boroughs on the southern rim of Eldr-shok.

At long last, he reached the block where Obadiah's dwelling was located. Unlike Miriam's apartment, Obadiah's abode was situated on the ground floor. Even though the benevolent parson spent weeks at a time trekking through the treacherous slopes of the Ulverkraags, he always complained about how his knees were getting too old to trudge up and down stairs every day of his life. Whenever Obadiah had been confronted with the seeming contradiction, the cleric faithfully replied, "Just because I do it at work doesn't mean I want to do it when I get home. I frequently freeze and sometimes starve during my service. I do so willingly and gladly, but not when I return home. On those occasions, I want a nice dinner in front of a warm fire. After all, that distinction is what makes home...*home*." Quinn could hear his friend repeating the phrase even now, just as if Obadiah was trudging through the snow beside him.

Quinn picked up his pace as he eyed the cleric's dwelling just across the street. He began to sprint across the lane but skidded to a halt as he caught sight of the white wreath hanging on the front door. In the cities of Eldr, a white wreath signified that someone in that household had recently shrugged off the chains of mortality and stepped beyond destiny's veil and onto the arched bridge that led to the gates of Truhaeven. There in the middle of tonight's snow-covered street, Quinn dropped to his hands and knees, wailing and sobbing in abject despair. Obadiah had always lived alone.

♦♦♦

Familiar rage that was raw and genuine washed over Quinn as his hands began to throb yet again from the wet, penetrating cold. He unclenched his fingers and withdrew them from the damnable drift of feathery snow; tears flowed as he drove his numbed hands into the deep folds of his cloak. Pushing himself erect and battling to balance himself on two unsteady legs, he grabbed his pack and stormed along the short walk leading to Obadiah's front door.

At this point, apathy was his sole guide. Not bothering to even check for the presence of Church soldiers, he felt along the narrow ledge above the entrance and deftly retrieved the key to the worn lock. In seconds, Quinn was inside the relatively warm abode and shaking off the evening snow. The distraught orphan-turned-heretic hastily dropped his duffel to the floor and began his frantic search of the tiny apartment.

"Obadiah!?" he began to wail as he entered the darkened bedroom, "Obadiah, have they…have they killed you, too? Obadiah?!" Quinn continued to call, though he instinctively knew that no answer would be forthcoming. He expected only grim silence, and that was in fact all that this night's hovering gloom offered. At last, he returned to the shadow-saturated den and plopped down on the sofa. Quinn put his head in his hands. Both of them were shaking from fatigue, grief, and rage…both were doing their best to force rationality into his head by wringing the sweat of panic out of his hair. He felt the urge to weep, but there would be no more crying this night, for all his tears had been spent, spilled, and then pressed beneath his retreating heels.

Not knowing what else to do or where else to go, Quinn yielded to fatigue's resolute tug and fell asleep in the darkness. The vapid dreams he experienced during the wee hours of morning did little to alleviate the soul-shattering pain that the previous evening had s generously bequeathed to him. He had witnessed his dear mother's slaughter at the hands of daemons most vile. He had, by all indications, lost his closest friend to the call of the grave as well. And he had been branded so that he could not even approach anyone else for aid or succor. As the air in the abandoned apartment began to nuzzle the edges of his cloak with its cold nose, he covered himself with the thick wool blanket that Obadiah always kept folded and draped over the back of the couch.

As the troubled orphan pulled that blanket and his heavy cloak tightly beneath his chin, he surrendered once more to a maelstrom of uneasy slumber. That dark night he prayed not for comfort or guidance, but simply to die in his sleep so that he could be reunited with his family. So that he would no longer feel so alone.

♦♦♦

Despite his silent but fervent prayers, he awoke in a place that was surely too cold to be either Truhaeven or Hel. He awoke on the couch in Obadiah's eerily silent apartment, and the air was so cold he could see his breath hovering above his head like misty wraiths performing a perverse victory dance. More stiff than he had ever been in his life, Quinn finally forced his sore muscles into motion. Groaning with the effort, he rose from his makeshift nest and strode over to the closet to retrieve another heavy blanket, which he promptly wrapped about his shoulders, but it would take more than a blanket to make him feel warm enough for anything even approaching comfort.

Had his late friend's home stood alone, had it been a separate house or a duplex, Quinn would not have dared build a fire, since any smoke issuing from the chimney of a dead man's dwelling would surely draw suspicion. He definitely did not want to attract any visitors, especially Church soldiers, and they would probably be the first to arrive. Given all that had transpired, Quinn surmised that the corrupt Church bastards were—more likely than not—involved in Obadiah's untimely disappearance.

Obadiah, however, lived on the ground floor of a three-story building, and Quinn knew that the three stacked homes shared a common flue. So without giving the matter another thought he hurried over to the heater and flipped open the damper. With efficiency born of repetition, Quinn rapidly transformed tinder, kindling, and a few split logs into a single spitting flame that soon intensified to a comforting blaze. He stood with his back to the heater until he found it necessary to shed one borrowed blanket. As the heat continued to chase off the chill in the den, he tossed Obadiah's other blanket onto the couch, and his own wool cloak was soon draped over it.

Quinn stepped toward the rear window of the apartment and pushed the drapes aside, but only far enough to allow a sliver of a glimpse. He peeked out just long enough to discover that the snow had continued to fall throughout the night, and a few stray flakes of feathery white still rode the determined gusts of winter wind. One glance out the frosty panes of Obadiah's kitchen window told him that the powder that had collected out on the streets and sidewalks would, by now, very nearly reach the tops of his boots.

With a few hours of fitful rest behind him, a fraction of his blinding rage had retreated. His thinking was perhaps a bit more clear, though he now, more than ever, felt as if he was adrift in a swirling sea of confusion and grief. These strange seas in which he suddenly found himself thrashing were rough...merciless. Though his body stood still behind the window, his spirit was flailing so that it would not drown beneath the incessant waves of woe. If he was indeed destined to survive, all the credit and all the blame would be attributable solely to his primordial instincts and to the bids of destiny.

He had been fighting the stormy seas for little more than twelve hours, yet he already felt too tired to continue swimming much longer. At this point, fighting for air seemed like such a foolish endeavor. Especially considering that the skies above were now every bit as dark and intimidating as the black and fathomless depths from whose turbulent ceiling his tiny legs dangled.

In this still and silent room, silent except for the reassuring crackle of the burning wood, Quinn found himself beset with fresh pangs of grief. A hot tear ran down his cheek, and then another. He started to reach up to brush them aside, but he reminded himself that the tears fell from someone else's eyes...the eyes of Morana Goll. He lowered his hand and let the tears be. They would have to follow their own course, as would he.

♦♦♦

As Quinn stood there at the kitchen counter and stared out at the empty streets, the malty scent of rye bread began to tease his nostrils and his grumbling stomach all of a sudden reminded him that he had not eaten anything since lunch the previous day...and he had spewed most of that onto the floor of the Citadel coach. He popped open the round tin sitting on the counter and discovered an unopened loaf of the dark aromatic bread and another that was missing only four slices at the most. Both were still wrapped in the brown waxed paper used by the finer bakeries of Eldr-shok.

A quick search through Obadiah's kitchen cabinets produced three unopened jars of apple butter, a large wedge of sharp cheddar cheese, a canister of dried jerky, and several jars of stewed tomatoes. He had little use for the tomatoes, but he improvised a couple of breakfast sandwiches from the other ingredients and wolfed them down, nearly choking on the dry cheese in the process. While he casually nibbled on his third sandwich, Quinn continued his inventory with an inspection of the minister's icebox. The cooler easily held enough provisions to feed a single man for a week or more. It quickly became obvious to Quinn that his friend had not planned on leaving home for any extended period of time.

The heretic shook his head. Obadiah had known that he would not be joining Miriam and Quinn at Tarchannen Eid. Likewise, he had known that he was not being sent on another mission to the settlements of the Ulverkraags any time soon. Cardinal Voss had apparently denied Obadiah's request to attend Festival, assigning him instead some bogus duty intended to keep him corralled within the walls of Eldr-shok. No, Obadiah was kept busy and distracted until the Church arranged his surreptitious removal. Whatever or whoever it was that took the benevolent cleric from this world had done so without giving him much of a warning. Quinn's suspicions blossomed as did that particular variety of black rage that had lain latent ever since his retreat from the Church's basement the previous evening.

After slamming shut the squeaking door to the icebox, Quinn rushed into the cleric's bedroom to continue his investigation. Hours ago, upon first entering the darkened apartment, he had stumbled through this very room calling his friend's name over and over in a frenzy of desperation. All that he was able to discern at the time was that Obadiah was...absent. Now, even in the sparse light of a snowy winter morning, Quinn could tell that all was terribly amiss.

Over the years, Quinn and Miriam had been guests in this house enough times to become intimately familiar with the priest's habits and preferences, all his little rituals and idiosyncrasies. Quinn knew—had known—Obadiah better than anyone else in Eldr-shok, and he'd never seen this room in such disarray. Something had transpired here over which the cleric clearly had no control. Quinn's first clue was the unmade bed.

Obadiah would sooner take off his own legs with the smooth side of a sawblade than leave his house or, gods forbid, receive guests without having made his bed. The fugitive with lavender eyes had never so much as caught a glimpse of the bed without its sheets tucked tightly in at the corners and its blankets folded neatly across the foot. The pillow shams had always been pulled tighter than pubescent pimples, their edges always drawn straighter than an archer's arrows. But now, wrinkled covers lay carelessly cast across the bed, and two of the four feather pillows lay crumpled on the floor.

Swallowing the last bite of his sandwich, Quinn took a tentative step toward the bed to look for other clues, but in the process he tripped over his biggest and most glaring clue yet. Obadiah's shoes, his only pair as far as Quinn knew, had been carelessly cast aside! The cleric would not leave his abode without shoes in any kind of weather, especially not in the middle of winter. The mystery continued to grow.

Quinn's mind raced as it sorted through all the reasonable scenarios. Of course, it was possible that the poor cleric had passed on in his sleep from natural causes. It was possible that, when he failed to report for his duties, someone from the Church had been sent to check on him. The runner might well have discovered the body and returned to the cathedral for help. When the mortician came to retrieve poor Obadiah, perhaps he and his assistants saw no need to tidy things up before they left.

Quinn scratched his chin thoughtfully as he tried to piece together the details of this, the first and most plausible scenario that would explain the wreath, the shoes, and the unmade bed. It was then that he saw the lone dark stain on the top blanket. It was a spot no larger than a copper coin, but it had the look of dark paint. Already dreading what he instinctively knew he would find, the recently branded heretic nevertheless stepped over to the bed for a closer inspection. With one trembling hand, he yanked the covers back.

A bitter amalgam of rye bread, jerky, and apple butter hammered against the back of his throat as he retreated a few steps. He had to fight valiantly to keep his breakfast down. He gasped and damn near gagged in utter revulsion when the broad patches of dried blood were revealed. Obadiah had been killed in his sleep. He had been slain brutally and with prejudice. Whatever manner of blade used during the assassination had been fairly long, for its vicious, bloody tip had managed to pierce the bottom sheet and the mattress in five different locations.

Five! Quinn continued the battle to prevent his breakfast from spewing across the room as he removed the sheets and stuffed them, along with the pair of shoes, into a canvas laundry bag that he retrieved from the top drawer of the rickety dresser...but he did not know exactly why. He watched his hands as they acted mechanically, like the hands of a stranger. His actions flowed through him; he was once more a conduit for a darker calling. There was no emotion in the act, no expression of will. He only knew that he wanted to fly the bloodstained sheets like a flag over Tarchannen Eid as it burned to the ground.

◆◆◆

Once Quinn had straightened up the mess in his meticulous friend's room...once he stacked all four pillows against the headboard and tucked the edges of the blanket snugly beneath the mattress in a fashion that he knew would better suit Obadiah's wishes, he hastened to the kitchen where he scrounged up enough food to see him through the next several days at least...a week or more if he rationed the grub sparingly. The two loaves of rye, the wedge of cheese, the jerky, and nearly a dozen spuds were hastily shoved into a canvas bag that Quinn stuffed into his already swollen duffel.

A gust of cold wind whistled past the front door, and that bleak whine prompted him to snatch Obadiah's heavy wool blanket from the couch and cram it into his pack as well. He was barely able to pull the drawstrings tight enough to even tie them into a proper knot. By now, the bag likely weighed almost as much as he did. Some of the gear might well get jettisoned beside the trail...whichever trail he decided to follow...but Quinn was determined to at least start his journey to nowhere with as much protection from the brutal elements as he could shoulder.

Out of the corner of his eye, he saw movement outside that was not at all congruent with this static winter morning. A lone shadow was shuffling past the sheer curtain covering the front window. Dropping into a crouch, Quinn waddled behind the sofa and peered over its thick, padded arm. It definitely would not do to be discovered snooping about Obadiah's abode by any of the Church's soldiers. After a cautious peek between the curtains, cool relief washed over him. He could breathe again. That shadow, Quinn quickly concluded, was being cast not by a soldier donning a white and blue tunic, but by a stooped beggar struggling along the icy sidewalk just beyond Obadiah's front fence.

The beggar was not making very rapid progress, and a closer look told Quinn just why. The poor wretch was blind, and was using a flimsy walking cane to navigate the cubit or more of snow that had fallen over the last day or so. He stumbled and slipped a time or two. Only the rickety fence fronting Obadiah's abode prevented him from falling face-first into the high drifts. This pathetic wanderer braving the frozen breath of Haeven was surrounded by a warm violet aura. Quinn did not yet entirely trust his new vision, but he maintained stanch faith in his old instincts. On this lonely and frosty morning, Quinn once again chose to play host to an unjaded heart. His wounded soul's protective crust of ice promptly melted and King Cruelty retreated into the shadows…for the time being.

His own dilemma temporarily ignored, Quinn stood upright and raced for the front door. A grown man now stood in his boots, and in that fleeting moment he felt the warm breath of contentment. He felt gratification, if only for an instant. After scanning the area for potential meddlers, he pushed the door open and whistled in a short burst to get the beggar's attention. "Good morning, friend," Quinn offered softly as he stepped to the edge of the porch so that he could keep his voice down as much as possible, "could I perhaps interest you in a hot breakfast…one served in a warm room? Does that hold any appeal?"

Unfortunately, years of hard living out on the streets had conditioned the beggar to be more than a little suspicious of any strangers who went out of their way to demonstrate generosity. For, more often than not, such gestures served only as preludes to a cavalcade of cruel pranks. He had other reasons to be suspicious this particular morning, though the boy who had just extended the invitation had no way of knowing those reasons just yet. Without so much as turning his head toward the porch, the pauper answered Quinn in even but wary tones.

"Are you sure? Do ye have it to spare, my young…friend?" the older man asked through teeth that were being willed not to chatter

"I do. And it looks like you are in need of a good warming as well. Come on in and let's see what we can do about both matters. What say you?" For a moment, there was no answer aside from the whistle of the lonely wind. Quinn released his pent up breath when he saw the beggar turn about and begin shuffling toward the door. Had he been paying closer attention, he would have noticed that the drifter adroitly reached over the gate and unfastened the latch without fumbling or feeling about in the least.

"Name is Meecham, lad." The older man held out his unwashed hand in Quinn's general direction as he neared the front door. He wore tattered remnants of two fingerless gloves that appeared to be saturated with grease and grime from months of rooting around in the city's trash barrels. "I have no way of repaying you for your hospitality. You should know as much up front."

Quinn grimaced slightly, but only slightly, as he grasped and shook the cold and filthy hand. "I expect no repayment, sir, none whatsoever. You will be doing me the favor, in fact. Not the other way around. Today of all days, it will bolster my spirits to offer succor to someone else. It might help me forget my own troubles for... for a few moments. That in itself is well worth a few eggs, some jerky, and a piece or two of toast. Let me show you where you can wash up," Quinn offered as he closed the door behind them and locked it, but not before confirming once more that no one had seen the men retreat into Obadiah's dwelling.

Before he could lead the blind man over to Obadiah's lavatory, Meecham had already poured clean water into the basin and was proceeding to scrub the grime from his hands, face, and even his oily hair. He seemed to know exactly where the basin and soap were located. He even fetched one of Obadiah's folded towels without wasting any time fumbling about. "Just take your time and I'll get you something to eat," Quinn said.

When Meecham finished scrubbing away the filth of Eldr-shok's littered alleys and ambled into the kitchen, he looked like a completely different man. After the grit and grime of the city's unforgiving streets were scoured from his face and hands, he appeared to be no different than any other dignified older man that Quinn might have encountered on the sidewalks of his home city. In fact, save for his milky, vacant stare, he reminded Quinn of Obadiah to a degree. The two men were certainly of the same build and were easily within ten years of being the same age, though Meecham was probably seven or eight laps ahead of the priest. But even aside from any physical resemblances, their mannerisms were so damned similar. Meecham—just like Obadiah—tended to pause a moment or two to consider his words before he replied to any question or query. Both men chose their words with care and deliberation, and both prefaced their replies with the same ambiguous smirks.

"Something sure smells good, lad," Meecham offered kindly. "Again, I hope I am not too much trouble."

"Trouble? That, you are not, believe me. And thank you for your compliment, but be warned...I am no chef. Salt and pepper pretty much define the extent of my seasoning skills. These plates of assorted shit just represent something I threw together. A few eggs, some jerky, and such. Still, I hope it helps. Here, have a seat," Quinn offered, pulling out one of the chairs at the small kitchen table. Meecham did so and proceeded to calmly devour every scrap of food that Quinn put in front of him, but not before bowing his head and giving thanks for his good fortune this frigid morning.

"If you don't mind my asking, Mr. Meecham, when did you last ...eat?"

"Eat? A full meal, you mean? Oh, that I can't say, lad. It has been a while though, I assure you. Aside from a scrap here and a crumb there," the pauper answered between bites. He never spoke with his mouth full. "You are a true godsend, my friend. I certainly appreciate your generosity, lad. I cannot begin to..."

"Say nothing more about it...please. In fact," Quinn snapped his fingers and leaned forward in his chair, "I have a tremendous idea. Why don't you stay here for a few days...for as long as you like, actually? I have to go away soon, and it seems wrong just locking the place up and leaving it empty while you are...in need, let us say."

Meecham said nothing at first. He nodded, but his expression did not change one bit. He just leaned forward on his elbows and continued to chew as he stared past Quinn with those blind, pearly eyes.

"Intriguing idea, I have to admit. What do you think Obadiah would have to say about that, though?" he finally asked. The question was clearly meant to catch Quinn by surprise, and it damn well had the desired effect.

After a brief tussle with his old friend *panic*, Quinn swallowed and answered Meecham's question with yet another question. "So. You know Obadiah, then?"

"Oh, yes. Yes, indeed. You may be interested in knowing that this is not the first time I have dined at this table. No, it is hardly the first time. You asked about my last actual meal, yes?" Meacham pecked the tabletop with his forefinger. "It was here, in fact. Am I to assume that you are also his friend? If you are a looter, then you are certainly a most thoughtful one, I must say."

"I am…I was his friend," Quinn answered sadly.

"Ah, yes. So you were also surprised by his sudden *illness*, no?" Meecham's eyes might have been blinded, but Quinn could still read a certain semblance of jaded humor lurking just behind those layers of pearly matrix.

"*Illness* my hairy ass. He was murdered by the Church, those butt-munching bastards!" Quinn growled menacingly, disclosing more than he perhaps should have to a man who had been a stranger up until just a few minutes ago.

"That's quite a plucky statement. Do you have any proof to that effect?" Meecham inquired, not sounding even the least bit suspicious of his young benefactor's impassioned accusations. He took a slow and careful sip from his cup of coffee.

"I have two bed sheets saturated with his blood. Obadiah's blood, I mean. Sheets punctured exactly five times by a pointed blade. I consider that proof enough."

"Damn! I suspected as much, I must admit," Meecham nodded and wiped his mouth with his cloth napkin. His opaque eyes were now rimmed with clear water.

"What do you know?!" Quinn insisted. "You have to tell me, damn it! What all has happened while I've been away at Tarchannen Eid?"

"Ah, so you must be the young *Chosen*, Quinn? Again, I thought as much."

Quinn braced his hands on the edge of the table and shook his head to clear his thoughts. Too much was happening, and too fast. Yes. Yes, I am indeed Quinn. Obadiah spoke to you of us…me?"

"That he did. Just last week, in fact. He informed me that he had been keeping himself busy investigating some of the Church's old records pertaining to the *Choosing* doctrines. Good old Obadiah was perplexed by your situation, do not doubt. From what he told me, never in all the years since Herodimae took The Name has the Church *Chosen* two from the same family in the same year. He told me that much, yes. The last time I talked to him was on another snowy evening, much like last night. I think it may have been two days before you left for Festival. Our friend had just returned from Cardinal Voss's office. Damn if that stubborn old badger wasn't determined to obtain permission to go to Tarchannen Eid. He could sense that something sinister was brewing that threatened you and your... mother. I could hear it in his voice. I could see it..."

"I think I can guess the rest of the story," Quinn growled through clenched teeth. "That bastard Voss denied his request just to keep Obadiah here in the city so that..."

"Actually, you're mistaken, lad," the blind man interrupted, wagging his finger at some invisible person seated just to Quinn's right. "Voss was nowhere to be found that day. It seems as though he succumbed to a particularly potent strain of infection. Obadiah was told that the Cardinal was ill and that it was impossible to tell just when he might return to his office to assume his duties. Our mutual friend thought it strange that an interim had already been appointed to take over for him. Knowing what we know now, it seems especially strange, does it not?" Meecham grew quiet for a few moments during which he nursed his coffee. "It was not two days later that I was passing by here and heard them taking poor Obadiah's body away."

"*Them*? Did you hear *them* say anything? Did you ask them what had happened?" Quinn asked eagerly. Suddenly, he felt faint and braced his elbows on the table's edge.

"I did not ask them anything specific, lest I draw unwanted suspicion to myself, but Adeline Reed happened by about that time, and she harbored no such compunctions. I don't know if you have had the *pleasure* to meet her. She lives two floors up. She didn't especially care for Obadiah, and she likely didn't suspect any sort of conspiracy on the Church's part. She's just a nosy old bitch. A gossipmonger. You know the type by now, lad. Don't you? At any rate, she took a tone that would've made one think that she was the damned mayor of the city, and she demanded to know just what had happened. One of the men told her that Obadiah had died and suddenly so from a terrible ailment that he contracted on one of his missions to the settlements up in the Ulverkraags."

"Seems like a lot of people close to this whole business are ge ting...*ill*," Quinn noted with obvious cynicism. He wiped his hair back from his eyes with his right hand.

"My thoughts exactly. Anyway the chap told her that it was so contagious and so virulent that they were not even going to chance a public funeral. Instead, they were taking his body directly to Red Hill Cemetery."

"Red Hill? Red Hill?!" Quinn almost overturned the wobbly table as he shot to his feet. "Obadiah served that shit-eating Church faithfully for his entire life, and they opted to reward that service by murdering him in his sleep and burying him in a forsaken old cemetery reserved for the miserable likes of outlaws and beggars." Quinn immediately regretted his last words. "Sorry, Mr. Meecham. I didn't mean..."

"Think nothing of it, lad," Meecham chuckled. "I thoroughly agree that our friend deserved far better than the treatment he got from the Church of the Way. Snooping too close to the spring-loaded trap, he was. He was apparently close to discovering something that was meant to remain undisclosed. I fear that we will never know just what he learned."

"Maybe not, damn it all, but I have to try! I owe my mother and Obadiah at least that much." Quinn had begun pacing the floor and combing his hair back with his fingers in the hopes that the combined motion would stimulate more lucid thought.

"Ah. And where do you plan to start your search for answers, if you don't mind my asking?" Meecham inquired as he followed Quinn's movements with his ears, and his ruined eyes followed along, steered by long years of habit. "I do not advise staying in the city any longer than absolutely necessary. Those of us that live on the street survive by keeping our eyes and ears open. In my case, of course, I rely more heavily on my ears," the blind man chuckled, but his mood quickly sobered. "You should know that word has already spread regarding all sorts of...excitement that took place at the Church last evening. You are being painted as quite the *troublemaker*. And by troublemaker, I mean madman as well as mass murderer." Meecham chuckled again, then paused to take a long sip of the potent coffee that Quinn had brewed.

"I will not ask if you were indeed responsible for all that chaos. Just know that I would offer only sincere congratulations if you managed to pull off even half the crimes of which you have been accused.

However, I am still curious as to what you plan to do next. I have to say that I do not envy your predicament," Meecham concluded as he nursed his aromatic coffee once again. "I do not envy it one bit."

Quinn stopped his pacing and looked at his new friend...a friend who could never return his stare, but would never judge him for the marks left on him by branding iron and blighted blade. "I know not where my path will ultimately lead me, Meecham. But I do know that it begins at Red Hill Cemetery."

Meecham, clearly impressed with the ambitious plan, whistled softly and shook his head. "You have spirit, lad. Obadiah said as much, and on more than one occasion. I can do little more than wish you luck, though I do not know what you hope to find in that forsaken place. What clues may be found in an old cemetery other than...old graves?"

"There is at least one fresh grave there, do not forget," Quinn said as he took a seat on the sofa and started to tighten the laces on his boots.

"Even so..."

"Even so," Quinn finished the blind man's sentence for him, "what evidence could possibly found in a mound of fresh dirt? Perhaps none, but I have to start somewhere. Besides, I have a ripped and bloodstained flag to fly," the determined young heretic added as he used the toe of his boot to nudge the bag containing the bloody sheets, "and I just decided where it needs to be flown."

"Curious," was all Meecham said in reply as he took another sip from his warm mug. "And just when do you plan to leave?"

"There is no time like the present, I suppose. I'm burning daylight, such as it is," Quinn responded as he retrieved another heavy shirt from his bag and pulled it on over his other layers before donning his cloak and fastening its ties.

"I guess I should be getting along too, then," Meecham said. His voice was saturated with gratitude, but it was also peppered with dread. He did not relish the thought of returning to the streets frosted by the breath of cruel winter. He set his coffee mug down and pushed his chair away from the table.

"Where do you live?" Quinn asked, but he already knew the poor man's plight.

"Out there," Meecham waved in the general direction of the front window. "Wherever I can find a place out of the wind."

"It's freezing out there, in case you haven't noticed." Quinn could not believe that anyone could survive out on the streets in this kind of weather, especially a man of Meecham's advanced age.

"Oh, I have noticed, believe me. But, I do not have a home. It is hard for a blind man to make a living, lad. Seems we are not needed for much. We make excellent targets for pranks, but that's about it; and alas, that gig does not pay very well. No."

"Well, you have a home now," Quinn said. "Stay here as long as you like. There is plenty of food stocked to last you a week or maybe two, and these rooms will be a lot warmer than the streets. There is enough split wood by the stove to keep it burning…"

"You are kind to offer, lad. But…," the blind beggar was slowly shaking his head.

"But what?!" Quinn demanded. He ran his fingers through his hair as he contemplated his breakfast guest's reluctance to stay in a warm home, especially when faced with only one alternative—a miserable, downright deadly alternative, at that.

"I do not know that it is yours to offer, if you catch my meaning," Meecham reminded Quinn of the obvious, though his tone let his host know that he was truly touched by the considerate gesture.

"No, it is not mine," Quinn conceded without any hesitation. "The true owner, your friend and mine, has been betrayed and slain. Do you really think that Obadiah would prefer his home to sit vacant while his friend, a friend who has shared his table, is out on the street shivering to death in biting winds and thigh-deep snow?" Quinn was beyond determined to see the pauper stay on, at least for a day or two. "If you do, then I have to doubt that you knew him as well as you claim to have."

"I can't find a flaw in your logic there, lad. I thank you. But what if the Church soldiers return?" Meecham asked pragmatically as he wiped his white eyes with his tan napkin.

"I don't see why they would return. Obadiah is gone, and there isn't anything here worth stealing, for the gods' sake. My guess is that you won't be disturbed for quite some time, if ever at all. If they give you any guff, just tell them the truth, or most of it at least. Tell them that he was your dear friend and that you've been a guest here many times. Tell them that he would have it no other way, and you can say that part with honest conviction, for you and I both know it to be true. Hel, even if they return tomorrow and see fit to throw you out, you will have avoided spending at least one night out in the snow. You might want to close the blinds so that no one sees you moving around in here, and I wouldn't risk lighting any lamps or…"

"Lad, my need for light left me decades ago. My eyes need a lamp's flame about as much as your soul needs another dark burden to bear. Do not worry about me. Will you come back when you get through with your business at Red Hill?"

"No, Meecham. I cannot return to Eldr-shok ever again, I am afraid." Quinn wrapped his cloak about his shoulders and stepped over to shake the blind man's hand in fond farewell. "The closet and drawers are filled with warm garments that will likely fit like they were tailored for you. If and when you decide to move on, take whatever will make your time on the street a little more comfortable. Here is the key to the front door." Quinn pressed the key into Meecham's hand and closed the blind man's fingers around it. "Keep it on you, so that you can always return for a night or two if you find it necessary."

"May the gods watch over you, lad," Meecham whispered. Two pearly eyes that had registered no light in some years were now on the verge of leaking tears springing from the wells of genuine gratitude. His lips quivered as if he was still standing in the snow.

"They've done a piss poor job of it so far, I have to tell you," Quinn mumbled as he tied the scarf around his forehead to cover his brand and his brow. Then, without saying another word, Quinn grabbed his bags and stepped into the cold morning air, taking care to avoid facing the few hearty souls who were milling about the snow-covered streets. He pulled his hood forward over his eyes and headed for Eldr-shok's eastern gate.

♦♦♦

It didn't take long for Quinn to realize that he was being followed. There weren't many people out in this weather, yet someone was marching just ten paces or so behind him and they had done so for almost two blocks. Thankfully, his tail consisted of only one person. He only heard one pair of boots crunching in the snow. With any luck, he could dispatch the hunter if he caught the bastard off guard, but it would not be the least bit prudent to do so out here on a public sidewalk. His fingers seized the pommel of his new steel dagger and he spotted an alleyway just ahead and to his left, no more than half block away.

His plan was to lunge sideways into the alley and turn to face his stalker. When the hunter turned the corner, he would be facing Quinn's knife, already drawn and at the ready. If the apostate could manage to dispatch his stalker quietly and hide the body behind some crates, he might still be able to make it to the gate undetected. He could hear his own heartbeat swishing louder as he watched the dark mouth of the alleyway drawing closer. All panic retreated and was readily replaced with the anticipation of spilt blood. Quinn wanted to gut whatever Church vermin was hunting him this snowy morning. He wanted to hold a mass of writhing entrails before his quarry's face and read the shock in the bastard's dying eyes. The one following him matched his pace evenly up until the very second that Quinn's leg muscles tensed to execute his planned move.

"Sport? Is that you?" the whisper came from just behind him, and he froze. "It *is* you, isn't it?" The snow crunched as she drew closer.

"Don't come any closer, Catherine." Quinn came near to choking on those words, the last words he thought he would ever hear himself speaking. "I don't want you to see me like this. Besides, you don't need to be seen talking to me. Not now…especially not now."

"Fine. So duck into that blasted alley like you were planning to do anyway. Silly goose. Then no one will see us."

Quinn hesitated, but only for a second or two. He stepped into the deepest shadows that were available, but he kept his back turned toward the person that he most wanted to be facing right now.

"What's wrong? Why don't you turn around and look at me?"

That voice suddenly and painfully reminded him that the Church had cost him yet another dear love, and this latest toll that he was being asked to pay would leave him a hopelessly broken man; he was sure of it. He could only answer her inquiry with a question of his own.

"Are you going to turn me in to them, Catherine?"

"Turn you…? If you keep asking me crazy bullshit like that, I might actually start believing the stories those Church fools are feeding everyone else this morning. Quinn, why would you think that I'd ever do such a thing?" Catherine was bright enough to keep her voice down to a whisper, but Quinn noticed that she could communicate her irritation quite effectively without raising her voice. Just like Miriam.

"I-I'm sorry, Catherine. So damned much has happened, I'm suspicious of everyone right now—especially now. You of course realize that I have to leave Eldr-shok." His voice was beginning to break, and he silently cursed a tear that managed to escape from the canthus of his new left eye…a pool of swirling lavender. He cursed that tiny river even though he had no intention of showing it to the one surviving person that he truly loved.

Less than an hour ago as he tightened his boot laces in Obadiah's apartment, he reminded himself that the Church had taken from him every last thing that mattered and that his forced exodus from Eldr-shok would represent a bitter ceremony…an unofficial but poignant observance of solitude. It would be a dark wedding in which he reluctantly but resolutely took that cold bitch *exile* as his wife. She would be mute and cold at first, but he entertained the hope that, given enough time, exile would grow into something more: liberation. Liberation that would allow him to celebrate isolation, renounce precious companionship and relish the night's consistent but dispassionate embrace.

Until just a minute ago, he warmed himself with dreams of this damned city erupting into flames as he stepped into the trees outside the high wall. In his vision, those hungry flames had stroked and soothed the beast named vengeance…the beast that had chosen a lavender-eyed outcast to be its transitory avatar. Those flames were supposed to have been cleansing flames, washing away a city inhabited only with mindless sheep and murderous agents of a Church inundated with corruption.

But then he had heard the one voice that could set his soul on fire with a completely different kind of flame. He succumbed and stopped willing the stubborn tear away. At this point, he was beyond feeling shame over any tears that his tainted eyes might choose to shed, for he had certainly earned the right to cry. Quinn leaned forward with his palms braced against the cold brick wall and began to sob, reluctantly surrendering to the prospect of Catherine retreating from the alleyway so that she could hurry along her life's path and hopefully find herself another man—one that was not scarred and marred. One that was not so prone to crying.

Instead, he felt her hands on his shoulders. He heard her sniff back a tear of her own. That sweet sound paired with her tender touch led him to sob even harder.

"So...are you going to turn around now and give me a hug and a kiss, or am I going to have to slither between you and that fucking wall? Because I will, you know," she purred, but her voice was laced more with fretfulness than flirtation. "I'm frightened, Quinn. I need a look at that handsome face, sweetie. I need to see it one more time before you go do...whatever it is you have to do."

"You don't understand. I am not who I was. They have...*maimed* me. You would not recognize me, Catherine. I would prefer that you remember me as I was the last time you saw me, just before I left for..." he could not finish his thought.

"I wouldn't recognize you, huh? Mister, need I remind you that I recognized you from behind, and that was with you wearing an ankle-length cloak and shouldering a pack that my sister and I could both probably fit into?"

"Can't argue with your logic on that one," Quinn had to concede, sniffing back what he hoped would be the last of his tears, at least the last tears he would shed during this distinctive encounter. "I didn't know you had a sister," he offered in a half-chuckle.

"I do, but I'm thinking that that detail isn't so important right now, is it?"

"I suppose not. But my face is...a different matter, altogether."

Her hands moved down his shoulders and she wrapped her arms around his torso. Now she was hugging him from behind, and her cheek was resting on his right shoulder. Spawned from that single intimate gesture, waves of genuine and unconditional love rolled toward the rocky shore that his heart had recently become. Beset by those seas, he had to hold his breath lest those embarrassing sobs begin anew.

"Quinn darling, I understand that you have to leave for a while to try and straighten this mess out. I don't know when you'll return, but I know that you eventually will. You must. You should know something, and I say it only because I hope it gives you comfort on your journey and not more pain. We have both been looking forward to a special night," she paused, and her embrace grew tighter. "In truth, I've been longing for a lifetime of nights like that one. I don't want just a night with you, champ. I want a life with you," she finished, but barely so, for her own voice was beginning to fail before the potent flood of emotion. He could feel her sobbing now, but she recovered after a while and withdrew just a step. Her hands gripped the back of his cloak and her voice was damned insistent now.

"Damn you, you turn around and kiss me right now, Quinn Tabor! If you do not, then we will both remember this day, but we will remember it with black regret; and regret can be a foul poison, my love. It can strangle your soul. It can kill you, and it can keep killing you after you have convinced yourself that you are already dead. Your heart needs to be warm out on this new trail that you think you must follow. It needs at least one warm memory to cling to if you are to survive this mess. I may be young, but I'm old enough to know that much. Besides, you need a taste of what's going to be waiting for you when you return for me…and you damned well better!"

"My face isn't what you…" Quinn started to protest, though his soul was screaming in defiance of his blind stubbornness. Catherine spun him around, pulled his hood back and pressed her lips against his. He was cast into the depths of rapture as their tongues wrestled. He wrapped his cloak about her and pulled her against him. Their lips and their souls remained locked for a few protracted seconds that whispered hints of forever. Her perfume wove its usual spell, and in that fragrance, he found the breath of Truhaeven.

At last they separated and she looked up at him. There was awe and wonder reflected in her angelic tear-rimmed eyes…but not the first trace of fear. There was no revulsion. Quinn was reminded of the puckish look she shot him after she had taunted him last Sunaday morning down at the front of the sanctuary.

"Now *those…those* are some sexy eyes, love!" she said with a sniff and a half-sob. "I look forward to seeing those jewels looking up at me at some point, if you catch my drift. You be sure and hang onto those, you hear? Remember—you better come back for me when all this silly business is finished. If I have to hunt you down I'm gonna make you my slave for a long, long time and you'll have to work extremely hard for your promotion."

"I think I'm already your slave. I have been for some time, but you already knew that, I'm guessing. So, what promotion could lowly *slave* ever hope for…?" Quinn asked, already comfortable with any answer that his goddess might give.

"Why, promotion to *husband*, silly goose." She gave him one last tight hug and playfully swatted his rear end with her palm.

"There is so much about you I'm going to miss," Quinn asserted as he stared into those emerald eyes.

"Oh? Such as...?" she purred.

"Your perfume, for one thing. I was planning on giving you a bottle of it when I got back from that cursed Citadel. I was planning on a lot of things, though."

Catherine leaned in to give him a peck on his cheek. As she did, she pressed a small bottle into his gloved hand. "So, now you owe me *two* bottles, don't you? Then she pushed herself away and wiped her wet cheeks with the sleeve of her coat. She disappeared around the corner, but not before sending him another of her playful winks.

Quinn stood in the dark alleyway, more confused than ever. He was shaking with the cold of winter and with the warmth of promise. He pulled the hood back over his head and turned left on the snow-covered sidewalk to make his way to the city's eastern gate. He suddenly felt invincible. Ironically, that feeling of invincibility was derived from the notion that he was already a slave. He was most certainly a slave, and his mistress was an emerald-eyed angel named Catherine.

◆◆◆

Luckily, the guards at the city's eastern entrance felt little inclination to delve into anyone's business that cold morning. Quinn found their complacency difficult to explain, but he was thankful for it. Despite the warnings that they had undoubtedly received from the Church regarding the branded heretic that was still at large, they just waved through the cloaked and hooded figure from the comfort of their heated gatehouse. This gate was certainly used less frequently than the other three, since it led out into the wilds. The Church likely assumed that their prey would try to make his escape through either the northern or southern gates as he fled to one of the other cities of Eldr.

Quinn breathed a sigh of relief. Just then, a wagon drawn by two horses rattled around the curve and approached the gate from the east, so Quinn ducked his head and stepped to the far right side of the road to keep from getting trampled. After he put thirty or so paces behind him, he chanced a glance back over his shoulder and saw that one of the guards had actually stepped out of his shack and was questioning the two men on board. Quinn thanked his luck—such as it was—that the soldiers were more concerned with the affairs of those entering the city than those exiting.

He stayed with the eastern route until he could no longer see the low city walls of Eldr-shok, then he turned north and stepped into the labyrinth of snow-crowned evergreens. With a rhythmic crunch, the thick undisturbed snow protested under his boots as he stomped his way through the tight maze of tall cedars. Every one of their boughs was laden and drooping with the weight of last night's silent contribution...one made from serene winter skies.

Quinn remembered venturing to the dreaded Red Hill once back in his earlier years. He and two of his school chums had sneaked out of the city one summer day and hiked along the faded trail that led to the desolate place. *A forgotten garden sewn with sterile seeds*, Obadiah had called it once during one of the many impromptu history lectures he had given Quinn. When the council of Eldr-shok commissioned the construction of the city walls almost two centuries ago, crews had been brought in from the distant port cities. Hundreds of swarthy men, slaves belonging to the rich contractors, had made the journey to the northeast to toil away at erecting the stone bulwark surrounding Eldr-shok and the other four cities of Eldr.

Due to the inherent hazards associated with masonry on such a large scale, scores of the slaves died during the endeavors, shedding blood on stone and losing their lives beneath it. To make matters even worse, they were not at all acclimated to the harsh northern winters, and their pitiless owners neglected to furnish them with adequate shelter and clothing. Obviously far more pragmatic than compassionate, the foremen chose a remote spot well away from the city in which to bury the dead laborers so as to preserve the sensitivities of those who would benefit from the protection offered by the massive walls...barriers erected with mortar, sweat and blood.

The eastern slope of Red Hill served that grim purpose well. Obadiah had once explained that, back in those years, the bare mountain jutted up from the grassy plains. Only a few of the now-ubiquitous evergreens had dotted the plains then. In the evenings, the diving daystar cast beams of red brilliance on the western slopes of the sage grass knoll. The effect was striking, and it provided a beautiful sight from the higher vantage points inside the city walls. That is, if the observer could somehow forget how fate had treated all the poor individuals whose final resting places dotted the far slopes.

Quinn remembered that excursion so vividly. His tongue reminded him of the salty tang of his own summer sweat rolling of his brow as he stood outside the fence, marveling at the field of fallen slaves. He remembered how the steely hand of injustice had wrung his heart when he surveyed all those sunken graves, most of which remained unmarked.

In the years that followed, the city used the cemetery to bury the occasional thug whose luck—or lack of it—had led him to the gallows, but even that practice had ended when Herodimae mandated that the Church handle punishment in all matters criminal. Considering all he had witnessed over the last two days, Quinn shivered when he considered those implications, and wondered just exactly what distasteful means such punishment might involve. As far as he was concerned, the gallows would provide a far more desirable end than being fed to the ravenous denizens of Eldr Forest.

He hiked for the rest of the morning, taking a break only once to take a swig from his waterskin and to get his bearings. The drifts were even deeper out here than they were in the city, and each step he took required the same effort as swinging his leg over a low fence. Quinn was careful to pace himself so that he would not soak his first layer of clothing with sweat, for he knew that it would then just wick precious warmth away from his skin.

Getting lost in this tangle of dense evergreens would definitely not take much effort, he decided. Especially now, with the daystar veiled behind banks of gray winter clouds that flew low enough to brush the tallest of the trees as the wispy ships slid across the grim sky. His throat remained dry, even after he downed another quick gulp of cold water. Quinn was beginning to question his innate sense of direction. The afternoon was now growing older and the seed of doubt had begun to sprout from a bed of fine frozen powder. But then the ground began to steadily rise beneath his feet, and he knew that he had reached the base of the infamous Red Hill. Pulling his cloak even more tightly about his neck to block out the breeze, he changed his course to bear right so that he would be following the base of the mount around to what he judged to be its eastern side.

Through a complex maze of bent cedars and brier-laced scrub, Quinn tromped and stumbled. Had he been attempting to make a stealthy approach, he surely would have failed miserably, for this determined traveler pushed forward stubbornly, snapping scores of snaking vines and breaking dozens of brittle limbs. As he blazed a trail where none had existed before, his advance created such a racket he wondered if the noise might awaken even the residents of Red

Hill from their eternal slumber. At the moment he did not much care if it did, for he was a servant of fear no longer. On this overcast and wintry afternoon, he was a slave to two masters, and two masters only—the momentum of will and the drive of obsession.

Finally, the barrier of thick undergrowth and warped cedars began to thin and Quinn found himself at last standing in a broad clearing that stretched up the side of the hill to his left. Jutting up from the thick drifts of snow were the pointed metal pickets of the battered fence surrounding Red Hill Cemetery. As he stood there on the white slopes, he noticed that the hiss of the cool breeze had all but ceased, and the ensuing silence was staggering…disturbing. His raspy panting disrupted that perfect silence, and he could sense the surrounding woods frowning their disapproval of his rhythmic wheeze. To the green guardians of this forgotten cemetery, the labored breath of a living man registered as only another disrespectful disturbance that mocked their vigilant watch…an affront to the souls who lay quietly at rest within the rusted arena where ghosts danced.

It did not take very long, however, for his robust lungs to recover from the deficit they had incurred during his final push through the dense undergrowth, and he soon granted the guardians' request for their coveted silence. He took another long drag from his waterskin and surveyed the lonely, windswept hillside. From all appearances, no one had been here in a long, long time, though he realized that the thick mantle of snow could have easily concealed any signs of recent passage. After Quinn capped and stowed his waterskin, he took a single step toward the cemetery then froze in place when a loud clatter disrupted the fragile winter silence that he had just seconds ago resolved to preserve.

His heart lurched in his chest as he looked this way and that searching frantically for the origin of the racket. The surrounding forest was utterly quiet once again. He stood there for several minutes waiting for his heart to slow to its normal pace and checking with a quick pat to make sure that he had not just pissed himself. Just as he lifted his left foot to take one more step toward the graveyard, another damned metallic bang harshly interrupted the stillness and made him flinch like a startled stag. This time, however, he was able to discern the source of the odd clamor: the cemetery gate was swinging freely on its rusted hinges. The shifting breeze was, quite at random, sending the frosty gate in a short arc and forcing it to slam against its r ined and rusted latch.

Relieved to discover that he was still alone on the snowy slope, Quinn resumed his short trek up the hillside. When he reached the noisy portal, he paused just long enough to scan what lay beyond. He blinked away a stray flake that struck his left eye. Though the script was thoroughly eroded and erased, worn smooth by decades of wind and pelting rain, a few weathered stone markers poked above the white, reaching toward the gloomy skies that would forever and ever remain out of their reach.

Just as he remembered, only a select few of the unfortunates buried here had earned even a rudimentary monument. There were no elaborate headstones or sculptures like the hundreds that filled Eldr-shok Memorial Gardens, which were arrayed in neat little grids and surrounded by a painstakingly manicured carpet of grass. No, the few stones that peeked above the thick snow that now blanketed Red Hill were modest to the point of being pointless. No artisan had been recruited to prepare these markers; that much was obvious to Quinn. A few names and dates had been hastily carved into slabs of unpolished stone. Even so, at least someone had made an effort to mark those few. But the rest of Red Hill Cemetery was a desultory field of unmarked graves, a tangled mass of bare vines and briers. Many of the older graves had sunk into the earth over the years, as evidenced by the shallow, oblong depressions in the overlying snow.

When Quinn stepped through the gap in the fence, he reached behind and secured the gate by bending its latch back into a more functional contour. His nerves were already on edge just from being in this playground of forgotten spirits, and he did not care to have the noisy gate clanging to every few minutes. No new snow was falling, though the swirling late afternoon breezes nudged loose flakes from the encumbered tree limbs that stretched overhead. The winds tossed those flakes about, giving the illusion that the gray clouds racing across the sky were continuing to send even more of their powdery burden to dust the burial ground that was already shrouded in a delicate white mantle...one that shone pale pink through the prisms fashioned by Morana Goll's imagination.

Quinn waded to the center of the bleak graveyard and turned slowly around, scanning the eerie surroundings with his watering, lavender eyes. Unfortunately, he had no idea what he was actually looking for, and even if he had, the thick snow would have made the search difficult, to say the least.

Disgusted and more than a little discouraged, Quinn brushed the snow from one of the wider markers and sat down, shrugging off his pack and dropping his other bags in the snow. Dejected, he crossed his arms and hung his head, staring at the toes of his boots as though the answers to all of his problems might somehow be burned into their worn leather. Perhaps he had wasted his time in coming here, after all. Perhaps he should have just stayed at Obadiah's apartment with Meecham for a day or two—at least long enough for the snow to melt and for a better plan to take form.

From the looks of things, no one besides himself had ventured to this forsaken place in many years. The men removing Obadiah's body from the apartment could have very well made up the story about bringing the remains to Red Hill just to satisfy Adeline Reed's pesky curiosity. According to Meecham, that old busybody had a propensity for sticking her nose everywhere it did not belong, so maybe they were just having a laugh at her expense. Maybe they were hoping that she would come out here to see for herself and freeze to death in so doing. Whatever the case, Quinn was beginning to believe that he had embarked on a fool's errand...a freezing fool at that. He had hiked almost two leagues into the woodlands, plodding through knee-high drifts of snow just to find an old cemetery that no one had visited in ages.

To make matters even more interesting, the daylight was rapidly fading. He could not very well go back to Eldr-shok, and he surely did not want to spend the night anywhere close to Red Hill. Shaking his head, he cleared his throat and spat the green stream into snow which quickly yielded to its slimy warmth. If he had just offended any ghost by spitting on his or her grave, then he would just have to suffer the consequences. After all, what could a specter do to him that had not already been done? What could a vengeful spirit take from him that had not already been taken? He knew where he did not want to be, but he had no idea where he needed to go. Damn it all!

Just then, a crow left its perch in the trees on the north side of the graveyard and circled the cemetery's only living visitor once or twice, cawing coarsely as it rode the cold breeze. Distracted from his woes temporarily, Quinn watched the old rook as it landed on a snow covered mound several rods away, near the northwestern corner of the cemetery. He watched the excited bird hop about on the moun for almost a full minute before his troubled mind finally grasped the incongruity. There were no other such mounds anywhere else in the graveyard. There were sunken graves aplenty...but no other mounds! Pushing himself to his feet, he sprinted over the uneven ground, tripping on the treacherous vines and briers, falling hard to his knees at least twice. The crow observed the flailing figure rushing toward him, then calmly spread its dark wings and took flight, retreating back into the thick conifers just beyond the rusty fence.

Quinn skidded to a halt a few paces away from the mound, taking a moment to assess his new discovery. The little area of raised earth was five or six cubits long and perhaps half as wide. Although no stone was present, it was evident that the mound marked a recently closed grave. Quinn leaned over the low fence and grabbed a bushy cedar limb, breaking it off flush with the tree's slick trunk. He then used his makeshift broom to sweep away the loose snow, casting rigorous strokes fueled by desperation. He swept like some spasmodic madman until the prickly needles at last revealed red earth. There could be no doubting it; though the red clay was frozen and hard, the telltale mix of smooth clots and porous soil offered testimony that shovels had broken this ground and only recently so.

♦♦♦

Cold winter winds whispered promises of isolation into his ears, and for the first time he heard their message. A fresh wave of grief washed over Quinn, and he cast the cedar bough toward one of the nearby drifts. On an intellectual level, he had known from the moment he saw the white wreath on Obadiah's door that his friend had passed beyond. His discovery of the bloody sheets drove home the grim realization that there would be no more fake punches to the gut and no more clandestine winks to accentuate any spontaneous words of wisdom.

Kneeling here beside his best friend's actual grave, Quinn's sorrow made the sudden and jarring transition from conceptual to tangible. Rationalization retreated into the shadows of harsh awareness. Burning tears welled up in the corners of his violet eyes as he fell forward onto the frosty mound, and after angrily casting his pair of warm gloves aside, Quinn loosed a scream of primal despair. It was his first of the afternoon, though it would not be his last. The gloves were soon accompanied by the scarf that he had used to conceal the raw brand on his forehead during his exodus from Eldr-shok.

Slender fingers, raw and chapped, plunged into the frozen red clay like ten metal picks. A few brittle nails were chipped and brutally shorn from their beds, but pain meant little to a man who had so abruptly found himself caught in the pitiless grip of Hel's furor. The pain was hot, yet the cold was numbing. Some might have found comfort in that odd balance; some might have found a hint of solace in the irony, but not Quinn...not now. Gods, not now! Balance was just another illusion spun by the cruel gods. Ultimately, it was just another agent that reduced susceptible spirits to the flaking rust of ruin. Another evil drug to make them lose their minds.

Bitter cold and numbness...a dichotomy that in the matter of less than a day's time had begun to define a pattern. It was a pattern that, if allowed to persist, might well become his new life's theme. Bitter cold and numbness...twin shadows rising from the horizon toward which he was being so deliberately ushered. They loomed on his horizon and waved him back with insistent warnings, but his spirit was too crippled to even notice. There was simply no other direction to follow. If only those forces possessed the power to numb his deeper pain, then he would embrace their plagued promises and surrender to oblivion. He would use his bloodied fingers to dig himself a grave here among the briers of Red Hill, crawl into the peaceful pit, and pull the frozen dirt in after him.

Suicide had crossed Quinn's mind more than once this day, and on each of those occasions he wondered if the stern ghost of Valenesti was whispering in his ear, urging him to end his chapter now, before desperation led him down pathways that were darker still. Maybe surrendering to the grave's frigid embrace was indeed the antidote to the loneliness that he was just beginning to experience. Quinn had only been able to count two people among his true friends throughout his years—his mother and the cleric. Now, both were dead, killed by the very Church they had always endeavored to serve.

"Why did they have to kill you, too, Obadiah?!" Quinn screamed into the winter air, not giving a damn about any ghosts he might disturb with his tormented outburst. Tears ran into his mouth like rain though they tasted quite like service wine. "I need you here with me, I need someone here with me!"

Quinn bowed his head and began to sob in earnest. His fingers worked the frozen clay like ten bloodied spades even as his aching heart fought its own battle against the prospects of loneliness. H vision, still defined by that odd spectrum of lavender and gray, became blurred by the flood of tears washing over the facets of his jeweled eyes. All detail retreated. All the pieces of this latest picture scattered like a startled covey of quail. Only gray silhouettes remained. Without warning, even the boldest of those silhouettes disappeared in a flash of lavender light. He was blinded once again, just as he had been right after the blade of Morana Goll was thrust into his chest. His eyes were now ruined, as was his heart.

That same heart that was on the verge of breaking nearly quit beating altogether when a single cold hand burst out of the frozen ground and firmly latched hold of his wrist. Anguish quickly gave way to blind panic, and Quinn reflexively threw all his weight backward as he attempted to pull away from the ghastly grip. The steel grip, however, did not yield. Quinn's efforts to escape the unbidden clutch only managed to pull the grave's occupant free of his earthen prison.

"O...Obadiah?" The blinding flare of lavender light faded quickly; still, Quinn's mind refused to accept the implausible afterimage, for surely it was a phantasm molded by madness, grief and erratic afternoon shadows. This figure crouching just in front of him resembled his old friend in many ways, right down to the cleric's familiar vestment. But this newcomer was so thin, so pale. Whereas Obadiah's hair had been jet black sprinkled with gray, this creature sported hair every bit as white as the snow that had until recently covered its grave.

"Who is there? Who are you?!?" the reanimated corpse coughed, its voice hoarse with disuse. The resurrected man somewhat resembling Obadiah was futilely attempting to wipe frozen red clay from his eyes with palms that were equally filthy.

Quinn was incapable of answering the corpse's questions with anything aside from another question. "How is this possible? You are...were...are...dead!" Quinn leaned forward timorously and draped one of his scarves over the corpse's left hand. "Try that," he managed to whisper.

"I certainly feel like I was dead," Obadiah managed to say before coughing up a handful of rich, brown mud. The vile bolus tumbled from his bottom lip and fell down the front of his already filthy shirt. He finally wiped enough clay from his face to open his eyes. He cast about before his gaze settled on Quinn's shocked face. "What has happened, lad? Who are...we?"

"It's me, Quinn. Beyond that, I-I don't really know where to begin, Obadiah. You are Obadiah, aren't you?" Quinn was giggling like an infant being teased with a new rattle, but it did not register with the renegade that he might quickly be losing his grip on reality, for he had so little recollection of anything that was ever real.

"Obadiah...Obadiah...," the newcomer tried the name a few times in that hoarse whisper then threw up another lump of moist mud. "Yes, that does seem to fit. But, how did I come to this place? How did we get here? Where *is* here? Red Hill, is it not?"

Quinn could only nod, but he couldn't force himself to stop tittering. The gray light was fading fast, and he wanted to be well away from the cemetery before night fell. Not because he felt unsafe, but because he felt un-sane. With his new lavender and gray vision, he could see that he was surrounded by a host of wispy apparitions... the spirits of those long dead who were stoically standing guard beside their sunken, unmarked graves...unmarked and forgotten by all except for the lingering and lonely souls of their occupants. Those phantoms hovered in solemn silence. Quinn could not see any of their faces, for they were merely faint orbs of roiling, milky gray. Even so, he could sense that they were fully aware of his presence in this, their last refuge from a world gone astray. He could sense that they were regarding him in passive tranquility, not with the first hint of malice but with...sympathy. Perhaps even pity?

"We have a lot to sort out, but let us be away from this dire place. I want to gather some wood for a fire while I have enough light," Quinn suggested softly after his fit of chuckling passed. Obadiah nodded in agreement, and he seemed quite content to follow his young rescuer out of the cemetery.

"Wait here a minute, though. I have to get something from my bags," Quinn called over his shoulder as he ran back to the gravestone from which he had first seen the crow. When he realized that the old raven was dancing atop a new mound, he left all his gear behind. Obadiah watched his old friend—his young rescuer—with something approaching curiosity as Quinn pulled a bloodied sheet from the canvas bag and fastened two of its corners to the trunk of a bare maple sapling that had, perhaps three seasons past, set root near the head of Obadiah's now-vacant grave. Quinn reached to the bottom of the canvas bag and pulled forth the pair of shoes that only fate's whispe had prompted him to pack. With a flick of his wrist, he tossed them to the snow at the pale cleric's bare feet.

"Now we can go," Quinn said, as much to himself as to Obadiah. The two turned about and, with Quinn in the lead, walked down the slope and toward the pitted, rusty gate. As Quinn pulled the gate firmly to, Obadiah looked back up the hill to the spot where the ghastly, mottled flag flapped in the evening earlywinter breeze.

"Kind of a strange sight, isn't it?" Obadiah observed.

"It has been a strange week," Quinn replied flatly, though he fought the urge to giggle at his own understatement. "A strange week, indeed," he repeated in a whisper as he listened to his recently resurrected friend cough up another batch of moist clay.

♦♦♦

As the men pulled the metal gate shut, the old crow launched from his perch and disappeared into the darkening northern skies. His mission here had been accomplished, but surviving to witness the next dawn would be his sole reward for accomplishing his latest assigned task. There would be no rest. He was already being summoned by his master, that insistent voice that continued to trump even his innate and ever so keen instincts. The puppet wielding black wings would fly through the night until he reached his master's lair. Tired though he was, the raven rose above the swaying cedars, battling the winds and low clouds as it flew to the west. For now, its only obligation was to return to Tarchannen Eid. Before long, however, it would be sent afield with another order to follow. There would be plenty of other tasks that demanded his attention...plenty of other traps to set.

♦♦♦

"Are you sure you don't want something to eat?" Quinn asked as he chewed some cheese and jerky. "You haven't eaten in at least four days by my count."

"Yes, well...you don't tend to get too hungry when you're dead, I'm discovering," came the sarcastic response. Obadiah sat across the crackling fire from Quinn, staring into the lad's strange new eyes. Once in a while, the revived cleric would succumb to one of his coughing fits that wracked his lanky frame and produce more of the brown, muddy discharge.

"I wish you would quit joking about it that way," Quinn snapped.

"I was not joking, Quinn. I have been dead, and now I am not.

What would you have me say?"

"People do not just come back from the dead, Obadiah. As a cleric, surely you are aware of that. Maybe you were just drugged. That might be an explanation for…," Quinn postulated with a wave of his hand as he took another bite off his stick of jerky.

"That is what I tried to tell myself while we were collecting firewood earlier. True, the last thing I remember prior to your arrival was going to bed Wednesday evening. It is possible that I was drugged and carried to Red Hill, but that does not explain the blood all over my sheets. It does not explain my sallow skin or my thin frame. It does not explain…these," Obadiah lifted his shirt to reveal five perfect puncture wounds that bled no more—three in his chest and two in his pale abdomen. Any one of those could have been fatal, but no one could have survived the effects of their combined damage. "I was dead Quinn. Dead until you arrived and resurrected me, that is."

"I did no such thing, and I wish you would quit saying shit like that! How in Hel could I manage to accomplish a feat like that? Answer me that, Obadiah! Do you not remember me? I'm Quinn. Just Quinn!"

Still tinged with remnants of vomited mud, two pale lips twisted back into a smile that was essentially cheerless. "Tell me then, *Just Quinn*…have you seen your own eyes lately?" The question stung Quinn worse than the cold wind ever could, but he knew that Obadiah had not posed it to be hurtful.

"Yes, damn you!" he hissed before lowering his head and holding a palm forward in apology. "I'm sorry. Of course I have," the younger man answered softly and stared into the dancing fire. "I got my first glance at them in the mirror of my bedroom back…home. Back home." Quinn held his breath and leaned away from the fire as the wind pushed smoke into his face. "After I killed one of your fellow priests, a queer acolyte, and about a dozen Church soldiers, I decided to drop by the old place and check on things. You know, just to make sure that all was still neat and tidy," he finished through clenched teeth. Then his jaws relaxed and he allowed a chuckle to escape.

"If I am to help you figure out just what kind of turd tornado we've managed to find ourselves flying around in, I have to know the whole story, Quinn. It's nearly impossible to find a solution when—"

"—when you haven't even identified what the problem is," Quinn finished the pale man's sentence. "I know, I know. You've told me that at least a thousand times over the years."

"Yes, I guess maybe I have," Obadiah smirked as fond memories began to pop up like green chutes in a spring garden. "So this makes a thousand and one, I suppose. Still, I don't think the advice has ever been more pertinent than it is this very night." The cleric hacked up a pellet of mud and spat it out into the snow. "Don't you think?"

Not for the first time since leaving Festival, Quinn wished that he had a few mugs of Smiling Corpse in front of him. Perhaps six or seven rounds of his favorite ale would allow him to recount his tale without having to relive all the pain. Out of nowhere, an absurd thought struck him, and he had no choice but to chuckle at the irony.

"Fuck me...I have a Smiling Corpse in front of me, after all! One way or another, we always manifest our deepest desires, now don't we?" he tittered to himself.

"Lad, you've already lost me." The parson sitting across from the fire pulled his knees to his chest. White hair whipped about as he shook his head.

"Nothing. Private joke." Quinn resituated his packs and leaned back against them. After he rolled his neck and took a deep breath of the cold night air, he offered Obadiah a full account of the days leading up to that terrible night. He had to pause a moment before he described the return journey, but he told his resurrected friend every detail that he could remember, starting with Miriam's sadistic murder and ending with his harried exodus from the sanctuary. He disclosed every detail regarding the deaths of the other three *Chosen*, his arrest, and his subsequent interrogation in the cramped little cell. He described the jeweled daggers and the uncanny roles they played as the events of that unforgettable evening unfolded.

"Damn!" Obadiah was clearly struggling to process all that he had just heard. "Damn! That's all I can say, lad."

"Are you familiar with the spell, Obadiah? Is there a way to reverse it? Tell me that there is." The dejected tone in Quinn's voice revealed that he already suspected the answer. No optimism abided in his pathetic plea. None whatsoever.

"There is so much to ponder...so much has happened," Obadiah closed his eyes and pressed his hands against his pallid forehead.

"Yeah, I hadn't really noticed," Quinn shot back as he wrapped up the scrap of jerky and tucked it back into his pack.

"First things first, Quinn. Just bear with me. I *have* been dead for a few days, remember? Brandings have been performed before, though not for many decades, and even then, such severe sentences were issued only when the transgressions were *most* extreme. You say that this priest held you fast with another blade that he drove through your hand? I have to say that no such feat is recorded anywhere in Church history. Who exactly performed that spell?"

"Eric, damn his name," Quinn hissed as he pulled the blade from his smaller bag, unwrapped it and tossed it with gloved hand into the snow at Obadiah's bare feet. "He claimed that it was also a product of Morana Goll's conjuring."

Obadiah leaned forward and studied the blade as best he could by the fire's dancing light, but he did not seem the least bit tempted to touch it, much less lift it from the snow for further inspection.

"I met him, Quinn. Just a couple of years ago, in fact. However, the Father Eric that I remember was not nearly as charismatic as the man you describe, nor was he even remotely capable of performing a spell of that magnitude. Hel, I can feel this blade's power from where I sit, and it only makes me want to scoot even further away. No. It's hard to imagine that a man like Eric could change that much in such a short span of time—unless, of course, he has gained considerable favor with Invadrael through some means of negotiation. I suppose we must assume that he has done as much." It was now Obadiah's turn to stare into the dancing flames for a minute or two of potent introspection.

As the silence dragged on, Quinn grew restless and tossed another dried branch onto the fire. It crackled and spat, and that song was a symphony in the winter silence. When the resurrected cleric spoke again, his words jarred Quinn out of a tantalizing reverie involving the lingering kiss that he and Catherine had shared in a cold alleyway just prior to his hasty departure from Eldr-shok.

"You say that this Sergeant Kettner…"

"Private Kettner," Quinn corrected, milking as much selfish enjoyment as he possibly could from the crooked guard's sudden and utterly humiliating demotion.

"Yes, yes. Whatever," Obadiah waved away the insignificant detail as if it was a wisp of smoke burning his eyes. "You say that the Private Kettner was the one who drove the other blade into you chest, the one that your father bequeathed to you. Am I correct? Eric had nothing to do with the application of this other spell? The one that appeared to have granted you your…gift?"

"Gift?! Are you mad? I killed and crushed a dozen men with some devilish scream that I barely even remember releasing. I now sport eyes that are better suited for some oversized fucking housefly, and well, have you seen yourself lately? You are just a shadowy reflection of the old Obadiah—the true Obadiah. You are a gaunt and pale corpse with white hair and a repulsive tendency to hack up foul wads of mud. You do not eat, you do not seem to feel the cold, and you smell like last week's catch gone bad. And yet you think that I have utilized a *gift* to make you so?!"

"Well, thank you for the kind words, Quinn," Obadiah responded sarcastically, and his tired smile defused much of his rescuer's escalating ire. Quinn could not maintain his anger any longer. Despite the many ways in which this newcomer differed from the old Obadiah, at least the priest's sense of humor had survived a brutal murder and the subsequent yet brief stint in the grave. For the first time since he had shared that last flagon of ale with Bartlitt, Quinn had a reason to laugh, and it felt wonderfully invigorating. As he laughed, the most caustic components of his ire were cast into the frigid breeze.

♦♦♦

Even Obadiah smiled at his own odd predicament. He sensed as well as Quinn did that many aspects of his old self remained buried at Red Hill, but a few of the fonder memories and most of the familiar feelings had remained intact through the grand transitions. With each passing minute, he found that he could think more clearly, as if he had just awakened from a long nap and only needed more time to get oriented. More time and more silence. And without a doubt, this new body was far tougher and far more resilient than the soft one on which he used to rely during his travels through the brutal Ulverkraags. After a while, the laughter around the spitting fire died and the lingering smiles faded back into the shadows of solemnity. Neither man spoke for a minute or two.

♦♦♦

"Lad?" the parson finally broke the relative silence. His voice was meek to the point of being apologetic, but his eyes were ablaze with rapacious curiosity. "Just how did you do it? What was going through your mind when you…when I came back?"

"Desperation," Quinn answered simply and without any trace of hesitation. The heretic shrugged and spat into the fire. "Desperation and little else. I envisioned myself finding a grave of my own, not liberating someone else from theirs. I had pretty much decided that I wanted to die rather than live on in loneliness."

"Do you think you could repeat the feat? If desperation was taken out of the picture, do you think you could find inspiration from some other quarter?" Obadiah reached forward to throw another stick onto the fire. The crust of snow that caked the wood sizzled and spat as it hit the red coals.

"I don't think so. Even if I had reason to try. Right now, I cannot think why I would ever…"

"What about Miriam?" Obadiah interrupted without even looking up from the bed of coals, and the prospect caught Quinn completely by surprise. At no time since the cleric's extraordinary arrival had Quinn even considered the possibility of bringing his mother back. He had thought the odd incident at Red Hill a one-time, utterly unexplainable occurrence—a single anomaly. But Obadiah had stirred within his inconsolable young comrade's imagination a sudden rush of strange new alternatives. Miriam…liberated from the grave to live out her natural life with her son as it was meant to be.

"You're forgetting that she was never granted a proper…grave. She was slaughtered. There were so many…parts," Quinn's throat clamped shut with raw pain. He rolled his head and blinked tears from his lavender eyes.

"I know, lad. But my new body hardly resembles Obadiah's… corpse. You pointed out as much not five minutes ago. I'm wondering if your abilities really require an intact body in order to summon one's essence from the grave's cold grip. We don't know the limits of Morana Goll's spell, now do we?"

"Shit, you might be onto something there, my undead friend," Quinn replied, and slapped his own thigh. He was smiling across the flames at Obadiah, but it was the smile of a jackal captured in a frame of dancing flames. "I've been at a loss until this minute. I've been longing for a meaningful plan, and fuck me running if you did not just give me one. At first light, we can hike around the south side of the city wall and head into the Eldr Forest. We should make the margin of the cursed wood by nightfall tomorrow." Quinn was truly growing excited with the plan, so much so that he grabbed a stick from nearby and began to sketch a rough map of Tarchannen Eid and the Five Cities in the snow.

"I see some flaws in your plan, lad. But I cannot offer a better one just now." Obadiah leaned over and spat out another deposit of thick mud out into the snow.

"What flaws?" Quinn scoffed. He seemed almost offended. "And why is it *my* plan all of a sudden? Weren't you the one who just suggested that—?"

"Yes, yes. I just think that you might want to think this through a bit more. Perhaps you should be prepared for a few possible...disappointments. Even if we—you—manage to revive your dear mom, your *ability*, as remarkable as it is, is not without its drawbacks. You admitted as much yourself. Remember, you pointed out earlier that I am not exactly who I was a week ago. All I am saying is that perhaps you should not count on Miriam coming back just as you remembered her."

"You are, of course, right. Even so, I am willing to take *that* chance in order to give her *any* chance." Quinn paused and took a quick swallow from his waterskin. He stared out into the darkness that was waging war against the margins of the fire's light. "Does that make me selfish, Obadiah?"

"Far from it, by my reckoning. Far from it," Obadiah answered, sounding a bit like a proud father.

"It is settled then. Tomorrow we head south and make for the cursed road that leads from Eldr-shok's western gate to Tarchannen Eid. I do have one concern, though. We seem to be a bit...defenseless against what we are likely to face. The daemons that took my mother, even one of them alone, would be more than a match for either of us even on our best of days. Of course, I have the two blades of Morana Goll, both of which will stay tucked safely inside this bag, I assure you. Aside from those, all I have are my two daggers and Private Ketner's crossbow, along with two or three dozen bolts. And you..." Quinn trailed off, too considerate to state the obvious.

"Don't worry about me, lad. You see, clerics of the Church enjoy a certain degree of *protection* from the denizens of Eldr Forest. At least, I was told as much. Bear in mind that I have made the trip to Tarchannen Eid probably less than six times over the years. You must believe me, lad—at no time did I even suspect that daemons roamed the foul wood. Hel, for all I knew back then, a rabid badger was the most vicious critter that crawled through that forest."

"Back then, your assumption was probably correct. Something tells me that the daemons were not invited into the forest until Invadrael assumed leadership of the Church. If Herodimae still had The Name, then your rabid badger might well be the worst of our worries. At any rate, we now know that there are far more brutal beasts, do we not?" Quinn offered as he endeavored without success to prevent the events of that damned evening from playing over in his head yet again.

"That we do," Obadiah agreed, gingerly fingering the wounds in his torso as the fire before him crackled and spat.

♦ ♦ ♦

Though no more fresh snow fell that night, the winds picked up considerably in the wee hours as Quinn huddled close to the sputtering fire. His new companion—his old friend—tended the fire vigilantly and kept the orange beast breathing, even though Obadiah seemed completely unaffected by the cold winds. Quinn, however, did not enjoy the same degree of immunity. The temperature plummeted, and not even his thick bedroll and cloak combined could insulate him sufficiently from the determined chill. When morning finally broke, Quinn hurriedly packed his things and they set off to the southwest. He had a plan, such as it was, and he was determined to see it through. Obadiah did not possess nearly the same degree of determination, but still he followed closely on Quinn's heels, much like an obedient dog that blindly trusted its master to choose the right path.

Well before midmorning the two reached the road that, had they chosen to follow it westward, would have led them directly back to the gate of Eldr-shok. Neither man, however, entertained any desire to return to the city that had been their home for so many years. The frown now painted across fate's face indicated that such a return might never again occur. After pausing beside the route long enough to ensure that they would encounter no other travelers, revenant and cleric scurried across the worn roadbed and quickly disappeared into the tall grass and scrub on the southern side of the thoroughfare. Quinn and his undead companion took care to stay just out of sight of any guards that might be peering out from the ramparts of the high city wall. Their journey around the eastern and then the southern perimeter of Eldr-shok took several hours, since they had to conten with both an indirect, un-blazed route and a grueling hike through the knee-deep snow.

An hour or so before nightfall, Obadiah and Quinn reached the irregular and indistinct edge of Eldr Forest, a forbidding barrier fortified by rippling oaks and veiled in vines and black shadows.

"We will need to make camp here for the night," Obadiah directed as he made for a dense cedar thicket that stood several hundred paces from the forest proper.

"Camp? Are you daft? We can put another quarter league or so behind us before it gets too dark to march on," Quinn argued as he planted his fists on his hips.

"Now Quinn," Obadiah replied calmly, "you've got to think, lad. Think! It is already too dark to travel in yon forest. There is precious little difference between night and day in there, believe me. At any rate, night falls early among those trees, and it is a different kind of night. It confines and smothers. Even if its denizens were somehow held at bay, you still would not want to spend the night beneath that canopy. And since I know of precious little that would keep them at bay…" Obadiah trailed off, lowering and shaking his head. "Quinn, those foul daemons you saw the night your mother died continue to stalk Eldr Forest, and it is likely that they do so along with scores upon scores of their abhorrent kin."

"So what? Do they not hunt during the day as well?" Quinn asked simply, anxious to get on with the business he had committed to last night as he and Obadiah perched beside their first fire.

"That they do, I suppose," Obadiah nodded, pausing to spit out a crumb of mud. "But personally, I would much rather face them when the shadows are not quite so deep and ravenous. My position— my former position, that is—as a cleric of the Church affords me a certain latitude with the denizens, as I mentioned last night. At least, I hope I still enjoy a degree of it. I want there to be enough ambient light for them to at least catch a glimpse of my collar."

"I thought you said that you did not know about the demons, yet you keep mentioning this protection offered you by your collar. Don't you think you might be contradicting yourself just a tad? You knew about the dwellers in the forest even back then, didn't you?" Quinn asked. His tone was heavy with raw suspicion. He even backed away from Obadiah a step.

"Wait just a damned minute! Before you make the mistake of

accusing me of something inexcusable, let me first explain a couple of things. You see, lad, I was just one of many lesser clerics in the Church. In the greater scheme of things, I suppose our duties were a bit ordinary, but we performed them with pride nonetheless—back when we held the erroneous assumption that our Church was a force for the good, anyway." Obadiah paused, trying to shake the sudden pangs of regret for precious years spent obliviously serving the likes of Invadrael.

"Our duties, on a few occasions, required us to make the journey through that forest to Tarchannen Eid. We did not know the nature of the threat that lurked in the gloom. We were told that the woods had been infused with a magical defense, a sentience called forth by noble Valenesti when he thrust his staff into the ground decades before. It was also explained to all the Church's initiates that ordained servants of the Way were as one with the guardian of the forest."

"Trusting fools, every last one of us," Obadiah spat. I doubt that any of my brethren ever suspected that the wood was home to daemons summoned to do Invadrael's rotten bidding. And I do not know at what point he invited them to dwell within. We can probably assume that certain changes began to occur as Herodimae's health withered and his understudy's lust for power began to burgeon. In all likelihood, the demonic infestation of Tarchannen Eid's forest reached its peak shortly after the passing of The Name. Gods! I can only hope that Herodimae did not condone their presence."

"And you are counting on your old link with the Church to protect you...to protect us...when we go in there tomorrow?" Quinn asked doubtfully as he nodded toward the wall of black shadows. "You are counting on protection that was promised you by liars, and protection that was never really tested? You are counting on protection that was promised you by the very snakes that had you murdered in your sleep?"

"Alas, that is all I have to count on, Quinn. I have no other weapon. Though I am not the one in danger, if you stop to think about it."

"I guess not," Quinn agreed. He was well aware of what Obadiah was saying. After all, to what degree could even a daemon harm someone who was already dead? The two had not been granted ample opportunity today to discuss the matter very explicitly. Their exhausting march through the briers and deep snow had kept them a bit to winded for a philosophical discussion regarding the finer points of reanimation. Those matters would have to wait and be explored around a warm fire that would push back against the tide of night's shadows.

Before daylight failed them altogether, the gaunt cleric ventured close enough to Eldr Forest to gather several armloads of wood for the fire that would offer them some protection against the freezing night air. Quinn made for the copse of cedar and found a suitable spot for their second camp. He had yet to thaw out from last night, and his standards for tonight's campsite were far more rigid. Keeping those standards foremost in his mind, he scouted an ideal site in minutes. Deep within the thicket, he found a modest clearing surrounded by a tall, dense ring of mature cedars and sage grass. The impenetrable wall of boughs and blades turned away all but the most aggressive gusts of winter wind.

As soon as Obadiah located the younger man and deposited his first heap of tinder, Quinn fished through the haul and found a log almost as big around as his own upper leg. Using his hatchet, he deftly split the wood and then used one of the flat sides to shove the snow to the edges of the clearing. He did not conclude his excavation until a large patch of bare ground had been exposed at the center of their shelter. The knee-high wall of snow offered them an added measure of protection against the icy nighttime winds that would surely come hunting for them from across the Plains of Rayll.

"Damn! Are you planning on building a fire or a cabin?" Quinn joked as Obadiah returned with his seventh armload of firewood.

"Tonight, I think I would vote for both," Obadiah answered quickly.

"The cold did not seem to bother you last night," the younger traveler observed playfully before uncorking his waterskin and taking a long drink.

"No, it wasn't the cold that was such a nuisance. Your chattering teeth, on the other hand, just about drove me up the fucking wall."

Quinn coughed and nearly choked to death. He slapped the cork back into the mouth of its container while water ran from his nostrils. Finally, he cleared his airway enough to speak, though his voice was strained. He could not hide an impish smile.

"Excuse me? What did you just say? I thought profanity was a sin, after all."

"I'm not sure about sin anymore, Quinn. When I was dead, I saw no sign of either Haeven or Hel. I realize that I might well have spent most of my life serving an illusion."

"It's better to serve one than to chase one...I suppose," was all that Quinn could offer. His smile faded when he heard the exasperation woven through the cleric's words.

"I suppose," Obadiah echoed in a low whisper, clearly unmoved by the sentiment. Quinn could feel his associate's waxing remorse from across the clearing. His friend was feeling hollow because the paradigm around which the parson had shaped his life was now crumbling to piles of fine dust. The branded one thought it best to change the topic to something lighter.

"So you are saying that it is basically in your best interest to keep me warm and comfortable?" Quinn was determined to take advantage of every opportunity to rib his old friend, though this new Obadiah physically had little in common with the aging and pudgy priest. The apostate again found himself thankful that his friend's wit, at least, had not been lost during the incredible cycle of death and resurrection.

"In this instance, I suppose that is so. But don't get used to me waiting on you hand and foot. If it is a slave that you want, I'll be glad to drag your spoiled ass back to Red Hill so you can shop around for one. There are plenty of those about." Quinn had no immediate reply. He was still uncomfortable with references to his anomalous feat that had allowed this new incarnation of Obadiah to crawl out of his cold grave.

The parson coughed up another lump of clay as he secretly congratulated himself for besting Quinn in their latest round of verbal jousting, but those congratulations were a bit premature.

"Suits me," Quinn finally said with a shrug. "I just hope the next one is a mute...a mute that doesn't smell like a mule's ass. Write that down on my shopping list so I won't forget what I went after."

"Go to Hel," Obadiah croaked, but he was wearing a tired smirk.

"Seems kind of odd hearing that from some asshole wearing priest's collar," Quinn shot back. "I thought you fuckers were supposed to show us the *Way* so we could steer clear of Hel." Quinn knelt near the center of the clearing and started preparing the tinder for the fire that he was desperately going to need this cold night.

"I can't help but notice that you aren't quite as bothered by pr fanity either…not as much as the Quinn that I once knew," Obadiah observed. Although he tried to make his statement seem like a casual comment, he immediately realized that it had sounded conspicuously…priest-like.

"Oh, I was never bothered by it in the least, Obadiah," Quinn admitted with a decadent chuckle. "I just didn't use it very often around you and my mom because you two *did* seem bothered by it. Besides, that *old* Quinn died the same night my mother did. If something as arbitrary as a spoken word is a sin, then I am already bound for Hel's basement, for I have committed far worse transgressions in the last couple of days."

Quinn's eyes narrowed, but through those slits poured rays of lavender radiance. His voice dropped to a sinister purr. "And Obadiah, my dear old friend, I might as well tell you that I plan on leaving a long trail of carrion behind me as I travel along this path that your precious Church has set me on. Before I arrive in Hel, I'm going to unleash it, just as I did in the coach that night. I have to tell you, priest—maiming your colleague, Mr. Tollis, was very cathartic. Very cathartic, indeed. My only regret is that he passed out so soon. He missed most of the fun, the little rascal."

Obadiah had ventured to the grave and beyond, but no part of that whole experience chilled him the way that those last few sentences had. They had come from Quinn's mouth, but not from Quinn…not the one he had always known. For a moment, the parson wished that he had spent more time studying the history of Morana Goll's arcane artistry. In the next moment, he decided that he was better off having ignored it.

◆◆◆

Just as the last remnants of gray light faded, Quinn struck his flint a few times, sending a shower of sparks to settle on the nest of downy tinder that he had prepared by shredding cedar bark into fine threads. Spark gave birth to smoke and then to flame. The two companions drank in the warmth, even though Obadiah still seemed perfectly content to wander about with a single layer of clothing, despite the biting winds. Quinn munched casually on some of the jerky and cheese, but the parson, for the second night in a row, refused Quinn's insistent offers of food.

The sky overhead rapidly darkened and the icy winds hissed through the cedar boughs surrounding them, but Quinn coped by wrapping himself within the thick cloak and scooting closer to the blaze. Toward mid of night, he rose to stretch his cramping legs.

"I'm going out to check the skies," he called over his shoulder to where Obadiah sat as still as a statue. The resurrected parson was staring into the flames as though their dance was revealing to him the elusive secrets of Truhaeven...and perhaps they were, Quinn decided. Those secrets were just as likely to be found in the hypnotic dance of perfect flames as in some book penned by foolish men who were far less perfect.

He received no acknowledgment from the mesmerized cleric as he stepped away from the fire and into darkness, but it did not really matter. In truth, he badly needed to relieve himself. But he also wanted to see what the weather was promising...or threatening. Only a few sparse clouds were creeping to the south and east. Two of Eldimorah's moons were staring down from their lonely winter thrones and flooding the plains with the frozen light of night. Bereft of the protection offered by the dense conifers, Quinn came near to freezing before he finished his business. The stout winds drove the frigid cold right into his bones.

His eyes began to water as he stood there melting a patch of snow at his feet. At first, he thought that he was seeing things as he peered eastward toward the edge of Eldr Forest. He saw movement just outside the ring of deepest shadows...movement that was not synchronous with the gusts of wind that twisted the branches of the mighty oaks. Quinn followed the inky shapes as they ambled almost gracefully along the very edge of the plains. He strained to make out some details but the cold drew tears from his eyes and he was only allowed to see blurred silhouettes. Fastening his trousers, he blinked and squinted once more; this time his heart almost stopped. Four pairs of fierce orange eyes stared back at him maliciously. He could feel waves of their unrestrained hatred even at this distance.

Although they were several hundred paces away, Quinn found that he was all but paralyzed by their venomous gazes. Even now both his hands were numb with cold. Still, he patted himself clumsily searching for his hunting blade, but knowing all too well that it would offer little or no protection against these foes should they decide to attack him. Quinn realized then that he had left his laughable little weapon with his other gear anyway. He slowly started to back away not daring to chance sudden movement and not capable of breaking the magnetic summons of their collective gaze. Not until he felt a hand settle on his tense shoulder.

"Goddammit!!" he screamed. Flinching and flailing like a farmer who had disturbed a hornet's nest, Quinn spun about to find the pale cleric standing still as stone.

"It seems as though we have an escort," Obadiah stated simply, trying not to sound worried. He was most unsuccessful. The parson sidled past his startled associate and took a few steps out into the deeper snow...a few steps closer to the dark shapes prowling about. Quinn could see that the orange eyes followed the parson suspiciously as he halted in the ankle-deep powder.

"*Almdek Te Hoi*," Obadiah said the words forcefully, but barely loud enough for even Quinn to hear them. Surely, there was no way that the dark intruders could hear the phrase. "*Almdek Te Hoi*," he repeated, though not a bit louder than before. The words of power floated along on the wind until they reached the perimeter of Eldr Forest and the dark shapes that patrolled its shadows. Recognizing the arcane order to desist, the ebony demons turned about and retreated, though ever so reluctantly, into the forest deep. Quinn finally took a breath and leaned over to rest his hands on his knees.

"What were those?" he wheezed, nodding back toward the west.

"Don't ask questions when you already know the answers," Obadiah replied evenly, and then disappeared back into the dense cedars. Quinn chanced a final glance at the edge of the woods and then followed his peculiar partner back to the clearing where the welcome bright flames still danced.

♦♦♦

Well before the first hint of dawn arrived, Obadiah awakened Quinn by shaking his shoulders gently. Quinn sat up immediately, and had there actually been pupils to dilate and sclera to lay exposed, panic would have been evident in his eyes. Yes, panic may well have been apparent in those orbs had they not resembled faceted violet stones.

"Are they back?" he whispered as he latched onto Obadiah's forearms. He had not slept well, and he found that he could not entirely blame the cold for his restlessness this time. His dreams had been tainted with brief glimpses of those orange, penetrating eyes that followed him as he struggled through the snow on his way to Karchannen Eid.

"No. We are alone so far," Obadiah answered softly. "I just want us to get an early start. We need to be ready to enter the forest as soon as first light breaks. Get your gear together and eat something. You likely will not get another chance until we get back here tonight."

"What?! You plan to come back to this place?"

"I do," Obadiah answered without any hesitation. "It will take us half a day to find the spot where she...to reach our goal. Hopefully, it will not take too long to tend to business. Even so, that leaves us barely half a day to get out of the forest before night falls. After last night, I think you know how important it is for us to be free of those woods before darkness descends."

Quinn found that he could not argue with the resurrected priest's logic. This cozy thicket would be a welcome sight after a day of racing through the damned shadows of Eldr Forest and—hopefully—evading its foul, bristly denizens. They would need a place to confer and decide what their next move should be.

"Do you think that I should just hide my things here, in the trees?" Quinn asked, motioning at the thick boughs around the campsite. "I mean, if we are coming back, they should be safe here for a day. Hel knows I can move faster among the trees if I am unencumbered. All this shit weighs as much as I do."

Tapping his chin thoughtfully, Obadiah considered Quinn's suggestion. "No, I think you should take everything with you. Plans, I think you will agree by now, have a way of changing in the blink of an eye. If we are forced to take another route out of the forest, you will be left without provisions. Let us not take that chance."

Again, Quinn found Obadiah's logic sound. He treated himself to some bread, cheese, and jam, after which he scrubbed his hands in the snow to wash away the sticky residue. When he turned back to the dying fire, Obadiah motioned for him to come closer. Quinn noticed that the parson was crumbling a black clump of ash from the fire between his white fingers.

"Hold your head still," the parson instructed as he reached down and started to draw on Quinn's forehead. The symbol was not very intricate, Quinn could tell. Obadiah had spent only four or five strokes on the design. At last, satisfied with his work, the parson nodded and wiped his hands on his tattered vestment. A futile gesture considering all the other grime clinging to Obadiah's hands and garment.

"Should I even ask?" Quinn inquired, pointing to his own fore-head.

"Just a little added protection, I hope. It disguises your *souvenir* somewhat and it will let the bastards know that you are with me," Obadiah explained.

"And what if they do not acknowledge your position in the Church any longer?"

"Then," Obadiah said with something resembling humor dancing in his once-dead eyes, "we shall both get plenty of exercise this day...so lace your boots up tightly."

Charles R. Wade lives in north Mississippi.
This is his first novel.

Made in the USA
Charleston, SC
17 April 2015